LUCAS TRENT 3
Grand Theft Magic

LUCAS TRENT 3
Grand Theft Magic

A fantasy story

Written by

Richard Blunt

ISBN 978-0-9858011-0-6 (sc)

ISBN 978-0-9858011-1-3 (hc)

ISBN 978-0-9858011-2-0 (ebk)

Library of Congress Control Number: 2012913447

Index

Prequel

It was a cold December day; the year was 2008. Within the corridors of a chemical plant near Luton, England, a teenage boy was running behind two security guards.

"I know that he is here somewhere," the boy said after running around a corner. "I saw him go that way."

"I saw him, too, but it seems that he is gone now," one of the guards said. "Damn thief. Almost like a phantom."

The guards walked around another corner, continuously looking. The boy continued down the corridor he was convinced he had seen the thief run into. He walked it up and down twice before he spotted the shadow behind a closet.

"Here he is!" he shouted.

Immediately a figure jumped out of the shadow, dressed in a black suit, looking like a modern day Ninja. He ran off through the corridor, the boy in pursuit. After having chased him through a number of hallways, they finally approached a dead end, with only office doors alongside and a small window almost two meters above ground level at the far end of the brick wall.

"Stop. You have nowhere else to go," the boy yelled.

But the thief had no intention of complying. With an impressive jump, he plunged through the half-open window out into the yard.

"Damn it, what kind of circus clown is that?" the boy cursed. But he didn't slow down and jumped through the window also, following the man in black.

"Base, Base, this is team four," the security guard that followed a few meters behind yelled into his radio. "The thief has left the building through a window. He should be on the meadow, west of the main entrance."

"Base copied," a voice said. "We will send a team immediately."

Another security team instantly raced out the front entrance to the described area. When they were halfway there they heard two gunshots and in response immediately drew their own weapons.

"Shots fired, shots fired," the second man in the team yelled into the radio.

When they finally came around the corner, they saw someone lying in the grass.

"Man down, man down. Send an ambulance," the guard yelled into his radio again.

The first guard continued on around the next corner, while the second one approached the body. It was the teenage boy, lying there unconscious, blood soaking his jacket and his jeans.

"They are gone." The second guard now also approached the boy as well, holstering his weapon.

"Hold on, boy, hold on. Help is on the way." The guard had taken the boys hand, pressing it firmly.

Only two minutes later, the ambulance arrived on scene, with three men jumping out of it immediately. The guards made a few steps back.

"Multiple gunshot wounds," the medic commented. "One in the leg, one in the lower back." He then started touching and tweaking the boy before continuing, "Patient is alive but unconscious. We need to get him to a hospital ASAP. Jimmy, get the spine board; Paul, see if you can get us a helicopter."

The other two ran off while the first one started carefully cutting through the boy's jacket. He had just started giving him fluids intravenously when Jimmy returned with the spine board.

"The bird can be here in 15 minutes at best," Paul yelled from the car.

"Too long, by that time we can have him at Luton General ourselves," the first one replied.

He and his colleague carefully moved the boy onto the board and carried him into the ambulance.

"We are heading for Luton General," he then said to one of the guards. "Please inform the boy's parents."

He then jumped in, closed the door and signaled the driver to go. Then they started supplying the boy with oxygen and giving him medication.

"He is coming around," the second man in the ambulance said.

The boy reached for him and pulled him down to his face.

"Guardian...," he said with a very weak and shaky voice.

"Yes, your parents have already been informed. They will be with you at the hospital," the medic replied, smiling at the boy. "Hold on, we are almost there."

"No." The boy weakly shook his head and pushed the oxygen mask aside. "Not parents… Guardian…." He coughed and closed his eyes in pain, tears running out of them. "Guardian…," he then continued with an even weaker voice. "IT College… Lucas… Trent… Darien… Stance… Call them… Please…" With that, he faded out again.

CHAPTER 1

Pain

About half a year earlier in Luton IT College…

"Maybe you have not noticed it yet, Mr. High, but summer break is over," a man in his late fifties said with a slightly elevated voice, looking at a young man sitting in the last row.

"Come on, Professor, it's the first week, give us a little slack to adjust," the addressed student replied. He was a muscular guy, red-blonde hair, wearing a short-sleeve t-shirt and old blue jeans.

"You can have your slack until next Monday, if you are willing to have an exam then, covering last year's topics." The teacher smiled at him.

"Oh, that's mean," another student, sitting next to the first one, said.

"You stay out of this, Mr. Tait," the professor addressed him. "You wouldn't even be here if it weren't for Mr. Trent. So either you both shut up now or we will test your knowledge on Monday. What's it gonna be?"

"I'm sorry, Professor Tatarski," Tait replied, looking down at his desk.

"That's better." The professor nodded and walked away from the desk.

As he arrived in front of the classroom he looked into the crowd and started speaking again. "Even though you still have two more years to go before we let you loose onto the market, you should still already be thinking about your future. To give you a little support with that, we will once again host a career orientation event in a little more than a week. And even though you are legally allowed to not participate in it, I would strongly urge you to be there. We will have tons of experts from various companies and public institutions. Use this chance to speak to them and get an idea of what's out there."

"Do you already know which companies will be participating this year, Sir?" a young man asked. He was 16 years old, quite tall and had dark-blonde hair.

"Yes, we already know most of them, but unfortunately, I don't know them by heart, and I don't have the list with me," the professor replied. "But if you like you can accompany me to the teachers' room afterwards. I can give you a copy."

"Thank you." The student nodded and looked down at his notes while the professor continued his talk about the importance of a career and the ways students could plan their career paths. He listened silently and scribbled down bits and pieces of what was spoken. For him there was no question about most of all this. He had been raised from his early childhood knowing that money is what makes the difference between a good life and a crappy one, and that a good career was the only thing in the economic environment of 2008 that could earn you enough money to have a good life--unless, of course, you had the luck of being born rich or winning the lottery, and he had neither. As a result of that he had, for a very long time now, known what he wanted to do, where he wanted his future to be. His presence in this school, the Luton IT College, was a result of those thoughts, as was the fact that he was among the best in that school, striving for knowledge like only very few others did. But the last 12 months had changed a lot of his confidence in his future and in the world around him. In this time he had found out the hard way that things were not as they appeared to be.

It had all started out when he had visited the pagan chatroom in Timestop bar and met the five others who were now his best and closest friends: Darien "The Professor" Stance, a year older than him, also an IT geek, and also in Luton IT College, just one class above him; Stephanie "Airmid" O'Brien, Jasmin "Psycho" Kramer, Marcus "Cougar" Gracer and Cedric "Whirlwind" Mason. Their pure interest in esotericism had brought them together back then with one simple question: Is magic something that only exists in myths and fantasy books? Or was there really a grain of truth in all the stories that they had heard and read during their childhood? And amazingly, it had not taken them all too long to figure out that there was much more than just a grain of truth in the stories. But they also had found out in this time together that with the power of magic comes great responsibility and that things are always a little more complicated than they look at first. And now that he was back in school, back in the real world, things started once again to become complicated. Life had been so easy during the three weeks in Buxton, where he and his friends were surrounded by others who shared their interests. It had been so easy to block out the cold reality during that time, the reality of school and work and the day–to-day life in Luton.

"Mr. Trent, would you like to accompany me to the teachers' room?" the professor asked him.

"Sure." Lucas nodded and stood up, following his teacher through the corridors of the college. He waited patiently outside until Mr. Tatarski came back and handed him the list.

"As I said, it's not final yet, but most of the exhibitors are already on there. It would be nice to see you there."

"You will for sure, Sir. Thank you very much," Lucas said and walked away, studying the list.

"A typical picture of Lucas Trent. Can't even stop learning while he is walking," a young man addressed Lucas with a laugh. He was quite tall and slim, wearing small, round glasses.

"Says Darien Stance, who normally never takes his nose out of his books." Lucas joined in the laugh, looking up at his friend. "And I am not learning by the way, just reading." He showed the list to Darien.

"Oh, it is career orientation time again, almost forgot about that." Darien smiled. "Any interesting companies this year?"

"Don't know what you deem interesting. There are at least two on the list that I know: JDC Inc. and Harlington Research." Lucas pointed out the two lines with mixed feelings. He liked what the companies were doing, but the fact that one person who was partial owner of both companies, a man named Marcel Jackson, seemed to be somehow involved with a group of Satanists that he and his friends had taken on not too long ago made the companies appear under a quite different light.

"Well, I'll for sure have a chat with many of them this year." Darien browsed through the list. "It's my last chance before I am out of here."

"Lucky you," Lucas said.

"Don't know how much luck that is, but I guess we will see."

Lucas just nodded silently.

"There is something else I wanted to ask you, if you don't mind me changing the topic," Darien said.

"Not at all. What is it?"

"My parents normally don't care all too much about what I do in my spare time, but ever since we came back from the camp they have been bugging me about you and the others."

"Parents." Lucas laughed. "So what do you want to do about it?"

"I don't know. That's what I wanted to ask you. What would you do?"

"Honestly can't tell you. I have somewhat the same problem. We should talk about this with the others next Monday. I am quite certain that sooner or later that topic will appear on everyone's list, except for Psycho, maybe."

Monday was their traditional meeting day. They had started this habit right at the beginning of their friendship and had stuck to it ever since. Every week they would get together at their little magical retreat, nicknamed "O'Brien Mansion" because of the fact that it belonged to Stephanie's parents. It was not much of a mansion though, only a small hut in the countryside a few miles away from Luton. Out there they deemed themselves undisturbed, which made the place a perfect training area for their various not-so-normal activities, like alchemy, rituals or pure spellcasting--in short, everything that would get them flagged as completely nuts if someone should see them, or might in fact bring them into trouble, if someone actually spotted them doing it successfully.

"Good plan." Darien nodded.

"The most obvious is sometimes still the best." Lucas smiled and patted his shoulder. "Sorry mate, have to go. Interesting lesson coming up."

"What topic?" Darien shouted, but Lucas didn't hear him.

Monday came quickly, and although Lucas had given the parents issue a lot of thought over the weekend, he was still unsure what to do. So far they had tried keeping their circle to themselves, to avoid questions they would not be able to answer easily. After all, they were a group that, besides Darien and Lucas, had nothing in common, aside from magic, but that was something they could not easily disclose to their parents. Marcus was a sports guy and as far as his parents were concerned had no interest in anything else, not even school. Cedric came from royal blood and was more or less expected to keep the same company, although his parents didn't care too much. In the end he was more or less a loner anyway, keeping "friends" only for appearances. Stephanie was a good student and had a vast interest in medicine. She would probably have had the least problem explaining strange friends, if it weren't for the fact that she was a girl and that girls that age seldom mixed with boys about the same age, at least not for friendship. And then there was Jasmin, who was quite some years older than the others. All the more amazing that the few occurrences they had to master so far went fairly well. Lucas' parents were the first to get curious about the group when he had asked for permission to go on a camping trip with them a few months back, so he invited Jasmin over for a quick meet and great. Luckily, his parents were in quite a hurry that day, so they had little time to ask too many questions. Stephanie's parents, the only others that had met parts of the group so far, were not quite so easy. Lucas had had a hard time convincing her mother of his pure motives without going into too much detail.

"Guys, we need to chat about something," Lucas started off the topic after they had assembled around a campfire. He quickly summarized it before looking around waiting for someone else to pick it up.

"The Professor is not the only one with the problem right now." Stephanie was first. "My parents are asking questions, as well, and I don't really know what to tell them."

"Me neither." Darien nodded. "And I am running out of excuses."

"So why don't you both tell them the truth?" Jasmin said.

"You are not seriously suggesting we bring them in on our secret, are you?" Lucas looked at her.

"Of course not," she laughed.

"So what, then?" Marcus asked.

"You have to listen to the details. I didn't say to tell them the whole truth," Jasmin said. "What's the problem with telling them that we all met in town at a bar? I'm aware that some of you don't go out that often, but you have to have been out enough so this is plausible. And after all... It is true..."

"True, yes," Lucas responded. "But only part of the issue. I am quite sure that my parents would not leave it at that; they would at least want to meet all of you and ask you stupid questions themselves. You should know, Psycho--you already had the pleasure."

"So let them," Jasmin said. "Why don't we just make an intro round, meet at everyone's home once, for whatever fake reason, and get it over with?"

"Why don't we bring all of them together somewhere?" Marcus suggested, looking unsure about what he had just said. "I mean, I don't know if this is such a bright idea, but if we are lucky they will maybe start doing their parent thing and stick together, leaving us out of it."

"That's a really cool idea." Lucas grinned. "What did you have in mind?"

"Nothing so far actually. I have to admit that I have not thought it through yet." Marcus thought for a little while. "The first thing that comes to my mind would be to go to a soccer game or something like that."

"That might be a little tricky." Cedric laughed. "My parents normally avoid crowds."

"Yeah, and finding an event that all parents accept is almost impossible, or at least impractical," Darien said.

"Why don't we host a picnic? We could even use the shack for it," Jasmin threw in.

"Better, but I think if we want my parents in it we need to do it at my place." Cedric shook his head. "I could have my parents invite all of yours to a barbecue, though. That might work."

"I am not so sure if meeting at that villa of yours is such a good idea. It might give a wrong impression," Marcus said.

"Well…" Lucas started after a moment of silence, "I think it will be hard enough keeping our one secret from them. Trying to mask Whirlwind's blue blood will not work for too long, no matter how we spin it, so we can come straight from the very beginning, as well. What do you think, Whirlwind? After all, you are the one who wanted to keep this from us in the beginning."

"We are long past that point, Guardian. And I agree with you, once our parents meet they will find out sooner or later anyway, so what's the point?"

"Very well then… Any objections?" Lucas looked around, but although they all seemed a little uneasy with the idea, nobody spoke up.

"So how do we go on with this then?" he asked Cedric.

"I will talk to my parents tonight and see what they think about it. Then I will text you a date."

"You will see what they think and then text a date? Shouldn't there be some convincing in between that?" Jasmin looked at him.

"My father is a count. If I tell him that you are all important friends of mine, he will not be able to resist. Showing his skills as a host is in his blood," Cedric laughed.

"And who do you want to invite? Only the parents and us? Or should we include siblings?" Marcus asked.

"Good question." Lucas nodded. It took him a moment to realize that he had no idea which of them even had siblings.

"Easy question," Cedric laughed. "In nobility it's all about family, so of course your siblings will also be invited. Unless you would prefer not to have them, in which case you should maybe forget to mention that invitation when you tell them."

The others started laughing and quickly ended the discussion. After all, they were primarily there to practice, not to chat, and they were all eager to get going.

"So who has plans for today?" Lucas asked. As usual, everyone was looking at him, waiting for his ideas, but again as usual, he didn't have any. In fact his thoughts had been racing around the parent issue so much, he hadn't even spent a second making plans for the training session.

A moment of silence followed that almost felt like it lasted forever. Finally Darien responded, "I would like to do something, but I am not even sure if it's appropriate to ask for it."

"Are you kidding?" Lucas looked at him. "What could be inappropriate in this group?"

"I could think of some things." Cedric grinned.

"I know you could," Jasmin laughed. "But the Professor is not like you."

"Spit it out," Lucas said.

"I would like to watch you create a new spell. After all, it seems that you have mastered this art by now."

"Interesting idea." Lucas smiled. "And why would you deem that inappropriate?"

"Well, after all, your magic is yours, and me poking around in it is somewhat an intrusion into your privacy," Darien said. "And on top of that, I am not really sure if this would be another of the topics that everyone has to discover on his own..."

"Well, I don't know." Lucas thought about it for a moment. "But I don't think that that's a problem. And you watching is definitely not an intrusion, at least not from where I stand."

Lucas again thought for a little while before continuing. "And what exactly do you want me to create?"

"I don't know. Nothing fancy." Darien shrugged his shoulders.

"Have you ever tried to form a shield that would reflect things instead of just stopping them? Like a mirror?" Marcus asked.

"I once tried creating something like a rubber wall, but only on a small scale so far," Lucas answered.

"Well, why not do it in full scale then?" Darien said.

"Sure." Lucas nodded. "And how do we test it?"

"Depends if you are up for a challenge." Marcus grinned at him.

"Always. What did you have in mind?"

"American football, of course." Marcus laughed. "I will tackle you."

"And I will fix you up if this goes sideways." Stephanie joined in the laughter.

"Very well then… Let's do this." Lucas jumped up.

It had been a while since he last tried this kind of spell, and it had only worked out once, with a few metal balls in his room. He thought a little about this experience and about just trying to recreate it, but in the end decided to start from scratch. He fell into deep concentration and slowly started pulling his energy together. Then he stretched his hands out, creating strings of energy in front of him and weaving them together into a tight net. His mind was focused on rubber bands while he built more and more of those strings, weaving the net tighter and tighter together.

"CONTEGO TENERUS!" he finally shouted before he relaxed and nodded in Marcus' direction.

The others watched carefully as Marcus gathered speed, running right at Lucas, shoulder first, shouting some kind of battle cry. Lucas remained completely calm, focused on his protective spell. Then Marcus finally hit the shield wall. Lucas could feel his protective spell giving way, and for a second he thought that Marcus' sheer power would overwhelm his protection, but when he saw the approach slowing down, his confidence went back to its original level. About an inch before crashing his shoulder into Lucas' chest, Marcus was stopped dead in his tracks and then without warning lifted off the ground and tossed back a few meters, as if he had been pulled back on a rope.

"Holy cow," Cedric commented as he watched Marcus slide across the lawn. He walked over and reached out to him to pull him back up. "That looked like a hell of a tackle. Are you all right, Cougar?"

"Yes, sure." Marcus laughed and dusted off his clothes. "That felt really cool."

"And it looked cool, as well." Darien walked up to them.

"So, was it what you expected to see?" Lucas joined them, together with the girls.

"It was interesting, yes." Darien nodded. "It looked as if you were weaving a net of rubber bands."

"That was exactly what I was visualizing." Lucas nodded back.

"So how did you come up with the spell, then?" Stephanie asked.

"The same way you do all the time. It was just there." Lucas said. "Although that might not be entirely true in this case. I did this spell before, so maybe I used the words before. I honestly can't tell. When I experimented with this before, I looked up some words on the Internet."

"Can you do the same thing again?" Darien asked Lucas.

"Sure. If Cougar is up for another flying lesson." Lucas smiled. "What are you looking for?"

"I want to see how your prep work changes, now that you have done the spell before." Darien looked at Marcus. "Are you up for it again?"

"Anytime, Professor." Marcus grinned. "Best practice I ever had. Guardian, maybe I should invite you to football training. You would make a hell of a buffer stop."

"Very well then, let's do it again."

They repeated the whole scenario a few more times and Darien explained every single time what the changes were and how it looked different from the other trials. Lucas then gave feedback on his impression, most of the time just confirming Darien's observations.

"So basically what you are saying is that in the beginning you need to be very specific about every detail and the more often you repeat the spell, the less thought you need to give it," Jasmin tried to sum it up.

"That's my impression, yes." Darien nodded.

"Is it enough to go into the details the first time? Or is there anything else to focus on?" Jasmin was looking at both Darien and Lucas.

"I couldn't see anything else going on, but I am the guy without spell magic so far, so I wouldn't know..." Darien said. "Guardian?"

"For me, it's all about the details. Somewhat about transforming the raw energy into what you want it to be." Lucas thought a little. "But I honestly can't tell for sure, either."

"So why don't we find out?" Cedric had turned away from the others, stretching his arm out toward the open land.

Lucas watched him eagerly but couldn't tell what was going on. He could feel that Cedric was building up energy but had no clue to what end. He tried to see what Cedric was aiming at with his hand, but there was nothing in that direction other than a few branches lying on the ground. And as Cedric had already proven his storm powers before, Lucas just couldn't think of anything new there.

"INCENDIO!" Cedric suddenly shouted.

Lucas watched closely, but nothing happened.

"What was that all about?" Marcus asked after a short while.

"Answering the question of whether detail is enough." Cedric walked back and sat down at the campfire.

"I could see the energy vortex building up around those pieces of wood, but what exactly were you trying to accomplish? Set them on fire?" Darien followed Cedric back.

"Exactly." Cedric nodded.

"But isn't fire a little out of your normal working zone?" Lucas joined them.

"That's the whole point of it." Cedric nodded again.

"Why don't you first try building a spell within your expertise, before you move out of it?" Lucas asked.

"Well, for one, because there is right now only one other spell I could think of in my area that I would like to try, and that one I don't want to toss at you, and for the other, because we wanted to know if concentration and detail is everything. Now we know."

"What would that one spell be?" Jasmin was curious.

"Something along the lines of your second one." Cedric smiled.

"So bring it on." Lucas looked at him.

"Seriously?" Cedric was unsure. "I don't want to hurt you."

"I think I can take a little pain, don't you? Especially after playing punching ball with Cougar."

"Well, if you really want to..." Cedric stood up, shaking his head. "Airmid, you better stand ready, just in case."

Stephanie nodded in reply, her face showing worry.

"Ready when you are." Lucas had taken position in front of Cedric, just like he had done before with Marcus.

He tried to relax as much as possible, so as not to block whatever Cedric was trying, but given the very mean and evil look on Cedric's face, it was very challenging. Then suddenly he started feeling a tickling in his left arm. Goosebumps formed around his forearm, the hairs standing up and shaking as if they were in the wind stream of a fan. And the more Lucas thought about the feeling, the more he got the impression that there actually was some kind of breeze forming just around his forearm. Slowly the tickling got more intense and the breeze swelled up to something that felt intense enough that it could have ripped his skin apart, but when he looked down there was nothing special to see. He was so focused on this strange feeling that he almost didn't hear Cedric cast his spell.

"CONDOLESCO," Cedric said in a loud, firm voice with a very low modulation, almost a little spooky.

And suddenly the tickling turned into pain and Lucas had the feeling that his whole arm was just about to be ripped apart. For a short moment he was so stunned that he didn't even react to it, but then the pain took hold and he broke down with a loud cry.

"Guardian!" Cedric had dropped his concentration, running towards him, the others following close behind.

Lucas was still trying to catch his breath. The pain stopped immediately as Cedric had stopped his spell, but he was still stunned by the effect.

"I'm sorry, mate, I should have been more careful." Cedric had kneeled down next to him. "Airmid, Professor, please check him out. I hope I didn't do too much damage."

"You actually didn't do any damage, Whirlwind." Darien had grabbed Lucas' arm and was examining it carefully. "At least none that I could tell. Airmid?"

Stephanie looked at the arm now, too. "What am I looking for? I have no clue what just happened."

"Yeah, what did you do to him?" Marcus asked.

"I sent two tornados into his arm, with different spin directions, basically trying rip the skin apart." Cedric looked a little contrite.

"Oh, that is mean. Even for your standards." Jasmin slapped him over the back of his head.

"What's that supposed to mean?" Cedric looked a little offended.

"I can't feel any damage either." Stephanie had let go of Lucas' arm. "But I am not really an expert on that."

"It feels all right again." Lucas had finally stood up. "So it seems whatever exactly happened, it was just temporary."

"Damn. And I thought I could do damage that way." Cedric had more thought than spoken this.

"What are you trying to do? Evolve into a battle mage?" Jasmin shook her head. "This is not a fantasy film. There are no magical battles around here."

"And the spell would not be effective if there were." Cedric was still in his thoughts.

"Well I have to contradict you, Psycho." Darien had walked up to them slowly. "There are magical battles and we have already been in at least two of those, some of us in even more. And although that spell might not be helpful to inflict damage, it is for sure helpful in stopping someone."

"And it would make for a good torture spell, too." Lucas had joined them.

"Battle and torture. Don't you boys have anything else in your heads?" Jasmin was again shaking her head.

"I'm just saying…" Lucas smiled at her.

"So what do we do now?" Cedric asked.

"We do what we came here to do I would say." Lucas smiled. "Do it again."

"You are not serious, are you?" Marcus couldn't believe it.

"Sure I am." Lucas nodded. "Whirlwind, how about we do it one more time like this and then I try to block you out?"

"Whatever you say, boss," Cedric replied.

They went through the spell again, Lucas trying hard to be prepared this time while still not blocking Cedric's work, but he just couldn't. The pain once again was so overwhelming that he just tumbled down and cried out once again.

"You are getting the hang of it." Lucas laughed in agony. "This was even worse than before."

"Did I do damage this time?" Cedric seemed majorly concerned, looking at Lucas.

"Nope." Darien shook his head after examining Lucas' forearm. "This is a very powerful torture curse, nothing more."

"Nothing more… That's a good one," Jasmin commented.

"OK, again." Lucas had jumped up. "And this time I try to block you. Are you fit enough with the spell for me to do that?"

"Sure thing." Cedric nodded and got into position. "Ready when you are."

"Bring it on." Lucas nodded.

Cedric started his spell again and as soon as Lucas could feel the tickling, he fired up his "Seperatio" charm, building a force field between them. He was confident that this should stop Cedric's attack, but to his surprise it had no effect whatsoever.

"Professor, help me a little," Lucas shouted toward Darien, without taking his eyes off Cedric.

"This is not a bolt, it's just an energy flow. It is adjusting its path to flow around obstacles. That's why your shield is useless," Darien analyzed it quickly.

Lucas nodded and dropped the spell, trying to come up with an alternative quickly, but it was already too late. Cedric had pushed his "Condolesco" spell onto him and he was once again down on the ground.

"Once again, please," Lucas addressed Cedric after the round was over and they had huddled together.

"You are not starting to enjoy this, are you?" Cedric took a few steps back.

"Not at all." Lucas shook his head. "That's why I want to find an effective defense against it."

They took position and Cedric started again. Lucas could feel that Cedric had gotten the hang of it by now, as the tickle was coming much quicker and much more intensely.

"Guardio," he whispered, focusing on his body, building a shield right on top of his skin, surrounding his entire body. And immediately the tickling stopped.

"CONDOLESCO," Lucas heard Cedric shout, but nothing happened.

"NICE ONE," Marcus complimented.

"It's amazing," Cedric laughed after he had dropped his spell. "I need all my concentration and energy to develop this spell and it takes you only two quick runs to counter it."

"Yeah, but only because I had the Professor's help." Lucas had sat down at the campfire again. "Congratulations, by the way. You created your first spell on purpose."

"Thank you." Cedric sat down too, looking a little exhausted.

"So what do we do now?" Lucas looked at the others.

"I don't know about you, but I've had enough excitement for one day," Stephanie said.

"And so have I," Marcus agreed. "My shoulder hurts a little after all."

"Do you want me to have a look at it?" Stephanie asked.

"No need to, it will be fine. But thank you." Marcus smiled at her.

"I am getting a little tired too. My magic eyes might be on by default, but it still takes a lot of concentration," Darien yawned.

"So unless you have something in mind, Psycho, I would suggest we call it a day," Lucas said.

"There was too much madness for me for one day," Jasmin laughed. "Let's stop it now before it gets even worse."

They all nodded and stood up slowly. After thoroughly putting out the campfire and cleaning up the place, they bid farewell and split up. As usual the girls separated first, Jasmin driving off in her blue Suzuki and Stephanie going cross-country on horseback. The boys rode their bicycles back to Luton together. Normally this was a ride that was full of chatter, but today they were all exhausted and were keeping to themselves.

"I will call you tomorrow with the date for the picnic." Cedric broke the silence when they approached the crossing where they had to part. "Let's hope this works out."

"Have a good night everyone." Lucas had stopped and stretched his fist out. "Brother to brother, yours to the end."

"Brother to brother, yours to the end." The others replied putting their hands on his fist. The quote was a reference to the Knights of the Round Table and had by now become traditional between them, showing the depth of their friendship and their bond.

Lucas smiled at them a last time before heading off into the twilight. It had been a great evening, but he now was looking forward to getting home.

CHAPTER 2

Doubt

When Lucas came back to school next day, he was still exhausted from the training and his thoughts were again racing around Cedric's torture spell. The longer he thought about that spell, the more it scared him. After all, this one was very dark in its making. But he also realized how important it was to have such spells around in their circle. After all, it had taken him two attempts to block it, and that was with outside help and a friendly attacker that waited for him to be ready. If he had encountered something like that in his fight against Wolfman a few months back, he would not have had two attempts... So training for it and being ready, just in case, seemed to be a good idea.

He walked into his classroom, still deep in his thoughts, and almost tripped over some cables that were laying around on the floor.

"Caution, Mr. Trent." Professor Tatarski was standing in the middle of the room.

Lucas looked up and was amazed. A group of workers was in the process of redecorating the room. Tables were moved around to form booths along the wall and tons of cables were being laid and secured to provide each booth with power and network lines.

"What are you doing with our classroom, Professor?" Lucas stepped aside to make way for the workers.

"Preparing it for the career orientation of course," Tatarski laughed. "And you have been moved to one of the lab rooms for the reminder of the week. Didn't you see the sign downstairs?"

"Must have missed that, sorry." Lucas smiled. "See you later, Professor."

Lucas walked back down to the lab rooms and picked a desk in the first row. Most of his classmates were already there, fighting for the spots in the last rows.

"Stop fighting and get seated," a man in his early thirties shouted through the room as he walked toward the teacher's desk.

"That would be NOW!" he raised his voice even further as students were still not stopping their quarrel.

It took almost a minute before everyone had a seat.

"It once again seems that we only prepare a first row so people can sit in the second one." The professor shook his head in exasperation.

Lucas had to smile as he realized that he was in fact the only one sitting in the first row at all.

"Trent." The professor addressed him.

"Yes sir?" Lucas looked up.

"How much do you know about the intricate ideas behind Polymorphism in modern programming languages?"

Lucas didn't need to think too much about this; the question was all too easy for him. He started reciting his understanding of the topic until the teacher interrupted him.

"I asked you how much you know about it, not to prove your knowledge to us. We all know that you are a geek." The professor sounded a little annoyed, but had a grin on his face.

"Sorry, Professor Cooper." Lucas stopped.

"Would you please free up the first row?"

Lucas quickly packed his things, stood up and turned around. There was not a single spot left in the rows behind, so he turned back toward the teacher and was about to ask where he should sit when Professor Cooper spoke again.

"Not back there, Trent. Out there." He pointed at the door. "Professor Tatarski asked for some volunteers to help with the prep work for Friday, and you just volunteered."

"Happily sir." Lucas nodded and walked out of the room. Professor Cooper taught object-oriented programming in his class, a topic that Lucas liked very much and was not too happy to miss. But he knew the professor well enough by now to not argue with him. He walked back toward the classrooms, spotting professor Tatarski in one of them.

"Trent? Are you lost?" The professor looked at him as he entered.

"No sir, I was asked to report to you for some volunteer work." Lucas shook his head.

"Ah, good." Tatarski smiled. "So here is what I want you to do: The guys from stand 36c will arrive shortly. Please show them the way and help them get settled in."

"36c, sir?" Lucas didn't quite know what that should be.

"Oh, sorry." The professor handed him a piece of paper with a plan on it. "36c is in your classroom." He pointed out the spot in question.

"Got it, sir." Lucas took the map and walked down to the entry hall. A lot of people were arriving there, all of them carrying some equipment. Some looked like craftsmen; others looked like business people. Lucas took another look at the map, trying to figure out who he was looking for. He had seen company names printed next to the stands, but he was unsure how to find the right guys in the crowd. When he looked at 36c, he had to sigh a little bit. "Harlington Research", the line below it read. He knew the company, but that didn't quite help as the only one he knew there was the CEO. Fortunately, he got a lucky break when he saw two guys with green sweatshirts that had "HRC" stitched on the back.

"Excuse me," he approached the two. "Are you the people from Harlington Research?"

"Yes," one of them nodded. He was in his late twenties, wearing an elegant shirt with a necktie under the sweater.

"Then follow me, please. I will guide you to your booth," Lucas said. "Can I help you carry your stuff?"

He waited for the men to shake their heads before walking off toward the classroom. He quickly showed them around, pointing out the washrooms, the booth and anything else he could think of and then hurried as they asked him to get them another multi-way power connector. When he came back, a third man had joined the group. Lucas immediately recognized the face.

"Good morning, Mr. Dexter." He bowed a little. "What a pleasant surprise to see you here."

"Good morning, young man. What could be more important than to look for the next generation of bright minds?" Dexter smiled at him. "Do I know you?"

"I'm sorry, sir. I am Lucas Trent. I am acquainted with your daughter, but I don't think we've met."

"Pleasure to meet you." Dexter shook his hand.

"So how are things at HRC?" Lucas asked.

"Always changing." Dexter smiled. "But that's how it is when you work in research."

"Is it the research, or the new owner?" Lucas was curious.

"A little bit of both, I guess." Dexter did not look too happy about the question, but was quick to get his smile back. "But we are getting along."

"That's the important thing." Lucas smiled back. "So what are the key projects you are dealing with right now?"

"You should visit us on Friday. I will give a presentation about that stuff then. But to give you a little preview: We are of course still running environmental analyses and research projects, but with a little less steam these days. Our focus now lies on alternative energy projects. But again, more on that on Friday."

"Sounds nice, looking forward to hearing the details." Lucas said. "I will leave you to it now. If you need anything, please let me know."

The others only nodded, so Lucas walked off. There were more people coming in who needed directions, and Lucas kept busy until noon escorting them around--so busy, in fact, that he didn't even notice the hours passing by.

"What are you still doing here?" Professor Tatarski snapped him out of his routine just as he dropped off another new arriver.

"What do you mean?" Lucas looked at his watch. It was already past 2 o'clock. "Oops..." he continued and looked up to the teacher, who was smiling at him.

"That's what I mean. Now off you go, enjoy your afternoon."

Lucas nodded and walked out of the school, grabbing his bike. On his way home he tried to relax and let his thoughts flow freely, which immediately brought him back to the training yesterday and his experiences with Cedric's spell. But this time it was not so much the Torture curse that grabbed his attention, but Cedric's attempt to set the branches on fire. Lucas had been sure that one spell was just like any other, and the more he thought about it, the more he was astonished that Cedric's pyro-spell had failed. More than anything, it made him curious about his own limitations. So far everything he had done was somehow within his specialty: a shield. Even the Repellum charm took the basic idea off the Seperatio shield charm, just making it move. He had thus far not tried to walk outside of that boundary. And he wasn't even sure if it would have been wise for him to go that way; after all it took him way too long to counter Cedric's spell last time, so he was far from perfect in his own expertise.

A phone call brought him out of the thoughts. It was Cedric.

"Hi Guardian," he started and immediately continued, without even giving Lucas time to reply. "I've got the green light from my father. He is preparing a barbecue at our place this week, on Sunday. Lunch will be ready at high noon, so you should arrive around 11 a.m. if possible."

"Sounds great, thanks." Lucas said. "I will talk to my parents immediately. Did you tell the others already?"

"No, you are the first one. But I will call them right away."

"Do you want help?"

"Would be highly appreciated, mate. If you don't mind, I will call the guys and leave the girls for you."

"Sure thing, Whirlwind. But please make sure to mention that this was your wish, not mine. I'm getting a little worried about my reputation lately," Lucas laughed.

"If you insist." Cedric laughed, too. "Oh, by the way, my father insists that you don't bring anything with you. He would see a gift as a sign that you think we are in need."

"Jesus." Lucas laughed again. "I'll try my best to avoid that, but you know how things are in our world… You normally bring a gift if you are invited."

"I know, I know. And I did explain this to him. Let's just hope we find a good compromise and nobody loses face."

Lucas again assured Cedric that he would try to convey the message before he hung up and called the girls. In the end they all agreed to talk again on Thursday, after they had had time to talk to their families.

Lucas jumped his parents on the same evening, eager to get it over with. His father was doing dishes in the kitchen and his mother was sitting on the couch reading a magazine when Lucas walked in.

"Mum, Dad, do you have a minute?" Lucas started.

"I feel a catastrophe coming up." His father laughed and walked into the living room, drying a plate as he went.

"Not this time, Dad." Lucas joined the laugh and waited for his mother to put away the magazine.

"You have been bugging me for a while now about those friends of mine that I went to the camp with a few months back."

"Yes, the ones that you have been hiding from us for quite some time now." His father winked.

"Not hiding, Dad." Lucas looked a little annoyed. "And after all, you already met one of them, remember?"

"Yes, I remember. We barely said 'hello' to each other when you dragged her out the house again."

"Anyway…" Lucas tried to get to the point, "you wanted to meet them, so here is your chance… Cedric's parents have invited us to a barbecue on Sunday. The whole group will be there."

"That's lovely, honey." His mother smiled. "Charlie, we have to get some wine or something to bring. Do we have a good bottle available?"

"Hold your horses, Mum," Lucas interrupted. "We were specifically asked not to bring gifts."

"But we can't just show up empty-handed, honey. That would be VERY impolite."

"Apparently showing up with a gift would be insulting. So take your pick," Lucas responded. "And I, personally, would rather be impolite than insulting."

"Why would a gift be insulting?"

"Relax, Emily, will you?" Lucas' father jumped in. "There are a lot of people around who think that way, for various reasons. Many of my clients don't like the race for the best presents, or the necessity to smile at an annoying one for pure politeness."

"Thanks Dad." Lucas was happy to have the discussion over.

"I still don't want to show up empty-handed." Lucas knew that his mother could be stubborn sometimes, but he for sure had not expected it to be over that topic.

"Maybe there is a compromise." His father walked back into the kitchen. "We are invited for barbecue, right?"

Lucas nodded in reply.

"Well, then, why don't we bring our grill-timer as a present?"

Lucas almost had to smile at the idea. The grill-timer was a device he and his father had built together a short while back, after he had almost turned a whole day's worth of food into charcoal due to his complete lack of feel for grilling. The outcome was a device that had a probe to measure the heat of the grill and combine it with the thickness of the meat to give a signal once the piece was ready for turning over or serving. It made grilling foolproof, even for him.

"Cool idea, Dad." Lucas smiled. "Although I still would not do it."

"Why is this stupid set of wires and chips a good idea, while a good bottle of wine isn't?" His mother seemed less than convinced.

"Simple, Emily: Because it's unique. It is not a gift you can buy in the shop, it's a personal item. Most people I know see something like that as a token of respect. But these are Lucas' friends, so if he wants us to go there empty-handed, that's what we should do."

"The least we should do is return the invitation at some point," Lucas' mother sighed, "if I can't convince the two of you to be polite guests."

"You can negotiate that directly with Cedric's dad if you like." Lucas was convinced that this would also be pointless, but at least it was not his problem for now.

"We are supposed to arrive at 11, by the way. I hope that fits your other plans?"

"We will make it fit." His father nodded.

"Well, that's settled, then." Lucas smiled. "Thanks." He was quite happy with the outcome and amazed at the help of his father when it came to the gift discussion. He had never before met anyone who resented presents and was quite astonished that it seemed to be common enough for his father to be acquainted with it. But then, his father did have quite a number of business contacts, so who would know if not him?

When Lucas called up the others on Thursday afternoon, he was happy to hear that all parents had accepted the invitation, including Jasmin's. Somehow he was looking forward to finally meeting all of them, although he was still a little worried about how the discussions would turn out.

Fortunately, Lucas had little time over the following days to think too much about possible problems during the big meeting of their parents, as the career orientation day was before that, getting his thoughts quickly back to his normal life. When he arrived in school on Friday morning, the whole building looked like more of a war zone than a school. Filled with twice as many people as usual, the place was clearly overcrowded. And as if that wouldn't have been enough to cause tension for most of the participants, the program also was packed to the limits. More than 40 companies had established their booths, inviting students to come and chat. Four classrooms had been cleared out for simultaneous breakout sessions, where every company would have a one hour slot to present itself to interested students.

Lucas had trouble getting his schedule together. There were a lot of companies that he was interested in and would have loved to watch their presentations, but some of those were running at the same time. Also, if he had wanted to watch all those, there would have been no time left in between to actually talk to the people at their booths. In the end, he decided to listen to seven presentations and reserve the remaining time for discussions.

The first half of the day went by just as planned. Lucas listened to two manufacturing companies first. The way those worked was fascinating to him, but not as appealing as a workplace as he had thought before. Next on his list were a bank and an insurance company. Lucas was aware that the financial sector used a lot of computers to do their work, but what the presentations showed him was far from what he had expected to see. He had never thought that this business would be so extremely complex, and so very fascinating at the same time. He decided to skip the planned chat with the industry guys and use the chat hour solely with the financial people.

After taking a short lunch break Lucas was back in the presentation room. The fascination with the financial sector was still in his mind and it almost made him walk out of the presentation before it even started, but in the end curiosity won. And his attention was back to 100% when he saw who was next to speak: It was Colin Dexter. Lucas listened with fascination as Dexter talked about Harlington Research, the company structure, the philosophy and the history, but his enthusiasm was brought to an all-time high for the day when the presentation progressed to the current projects of the lab. Lucas was fascinated by all the environmental topics that HRC was tackling at once. The projects spanned environmental impact analyses of large building projects to traffic pattern analyses. It was almost at the end of the presentation when one particular project made Lucas curious: "The future of energy" was the slide title.

"Every single one of you will for sure be aware that we are currently living on borrowed time with our energy consumption worldwide," Dexter started the topic. "Fossil fuel, which we all depend on right now, both for power and mobility, is a very limited resource, and much worse, it has a lot of side effects, like global warming."

The crowd nodded silently as Dexter continued, "A lot of ideas have been generated over the past decade to counteract those problems, but unfortunately so far none have proven to be reliable enough to really be helpful on large scale. The only 'clean' alternative, at least from a global warming perspective, currently is nuclear power, which you will all agree with me is a bad solution on a long-term scale, as well. And of course it is also dependent on a limited fuel, in this case uranium."

Dexter stopped for a moment.

"Now I am proud to tell you that Harlington Research has started its own project to tackle that problem and it looks very promising so far."

When Dexter switched to the next slide Lucas held his breath for a moment. The schematics it showed looked familiar to him, but he couldn't immediately make the connection.

"Welcome to the power of the crystal," Dexter continued with a smile on his face. "I unfortunately don't have the time to go into the details of the system, but from a very high level perspective it is pretty simple to understand: The crystal in the heart of the reactor is more or less a store of pure energy. In a very delicate procedure, we are harnessing this energy by basically breaking up the crystal. This then powers a high pressure turbine, which generates electricity. And the beauty of it is, all that remains from this process is water and salt." Dexter had already jumped to the next slide and wanted to continue when he suddenly jumped back. "I see we have a question here?"

"Yes sir, sorry for interrupting." Lucas recognized the voice. It was Darien, sitting in the last row. "This is for sure an awesome technology, but aren't you again working off a resource that is limited? In this case the crystal?"

"You don't miss much, young friend, do you?" Dexter laughed. "Yes, you are right, it is not a really final solution, but if you remember what you were taught in physics classes, you can't truly create energy, you always only convert it. And you always lose some in the process. It's called entropy."

Lucas saw Darien nodding.

"The true beauty of this crystal energy is that this crystal is more or less a converted form of seawater. And as you might know, we do have a lot of that at our disposal."

When Dexter switched back to the next slide, Lucas finally realized where he had seen this project before. About a year ago his class had visited a London-based computer science company called JDC Inc. The CEO of that company, a man named Frank Donovan, had presented that project, but had at that time told them that it was about to fail, as their partner company had gone bankrupt.

Lucas was deep in his thoughts and almost missed Mr. Dexter jumping to a slide saying "Discontinued projects". He quickly browsed through it and finally understood what Dexter had meant the other day. All the projects on the page were studies that were centered around finding root causes for environmental problems.

"I am running out of time it seems," Dexter grinned as the door opened and two other people in suits entered the room. "But if you are interested in more details, I am always happy to have a chat at our booth. And if you are interested in more details about the crystal energy project, you might very well stay in the room, as the next session is from our partner in this project."

Lucas turned around, looking at the two approaching people. He immediately recognized both of them: They were Chuck Sandler and Frank Donovan from JDC. He had not originally planned to stay for JDC, as he already knew much about them, but in light of the last presentation he decided to change his schedule. It proved to be a worthwhile investment of his time. Sandler and Donovan also shared a lot of details about the crystalline power plant, and their part was even more fascinating to Lucas, as it involved the whole IT side of the project. The rest of the presentation brought little new, though. The other projects they showed Lucas had already seen a year ago, including the now discontinued mobile mass-spectrometer.

When Lucas stepped out of the class after the presentation Darien was waiting for him in the corridor.

"Interesting presentations," he said.

"Agreed." Lucas nodded. "I had heard some of it before already, though. But at that time it looked a little different." Lucas quickly summed up his first encounter with Donovan.

"Interesting," Darien commented.

"Yeah, lucky break for JDC that Harlington took over that project."

"Or maybe a lucky manipulation..."

"I don't follow, Professor. What do you mean?"

"Wasn't it shortly after that near-breakdown of the project that Harlington Research was bought by Mr. Jackson and his mysterious companion?"

"What are you saying? That this whole thing with the Satanists was a plot to save the future of the planet with this new energy form?" Lucas looked dubious.

"Would make sense, wouldn't it?"

"But this would also mean that we..."

"... nearly destroyed the future of the project with our intervention." Darien interrupted him, nodding.

"Bold theory, mate..." Lucas looked thoughtful now.

"Yeah. And it still begs the question if the end would justify the means in this case."

"Hardly..." Lucas was still in his thoughts. "But it is clearly not that black and white anymore."

"Shall we go have a chat with Mr. Dexter? I am curious to hear more," Darien asked.

"Sure thing." Lucas nodded. "I had planned to talk to him, anyway."

The two boys walked up to the classroom. A lot of students had started besieging the booths, including the one for HRC, so they had to wait for quite a while before they finally had a chance to break through to the front. Mr. Dexter was at the booth, together with two other people from HRC. They were all pretty busy answering questions, sometimes gesticulating wildly to emphasize their points. Lucas and Darien listened in fascination for some time. When the crowd finally got lighter, they had already been there for more than an hour. Lucas imagined that the three guys would have had to be exhausted by now, but at least Mr. Dexter didn't show any sign of fatigue so far.

"Another pair of spectators," he laughed when finally turning to Lucas and Darien. "Hold on, I know both of you." Dexter seemed to think for a moment. "You are the one that asked the question during my presentation," he addressed Darien, who nodded in reply. "And you…" he looked at Lucas. "You are the friend of Jacqueline's."

"Great memory." Lucas said. "And actually, we both are friends of your daughter. This is Darien Stance," Lucas introduced him.

"Nice to meet you, Mr. Stance." Dexter shook his hand. "So what brings you to our booth?"

"Curiosity," Darien laughed.

"Well, then bring it on."

Lucas tried really hard to follow the discussion that unfolded next, but he only understood bits and pieces of what was going on. And judging by the looks on the faces of the other HRC guys, they had trouble as well. But neither Mr. Dexter nor Darien seemed to notice, or they just didn't care. they were both too deep in their discussion about entropy, energy conservation and the laws of physics and chemistry.

"You have a tremendous understanding of physics, Mr. Stance," Dexter commended Darien after he had finally stopped poking deeper into details. "And I mean this not only for a student. I know very few people that are on your level of expertise."

"Thank you, sir." Darien smiled. Dexter's opinion obviously meant a lot to him. "It is a fascinating matter, so I try hard to develop a good understanding."

"Good understanding is the understatement of the year." One of Dexter's companions laughed.

"I have to agree." Dexter laughed, too. "If you ever consider turning your back on IT, let me know. We could use somebody with your knowledge."

"Thank you, sir." Darien bowed a little. "But I highly doubt that my skill level would be high enough to be of any practical use for you."

"Humble as always," Lucas laughed.

"Too humble indeed." Dexter nodded. "And those were not just empty words, Mr. Stance. I really would like to offer you a job at Harlington Research, if you are interested in this career direction."

"I am honored, sir." Darien smiled. "But first I have to get myself through school." He thought for a moment before continuing, "But if you really mean it, I would love to take you up on your word after that."

"By all means, please do." Dexter nodded and handed Darien a business card. "Give me a call when you are ready. I will be waiting."

Darien thanked Dexter again before the two boys left the booth.

"That was truly impressive, mate." Lucas said when they were alone again.

"Thanks."

"Are you considering taking him up on that offer?"

"Sure. Wouldn't you?"

"Hell, yeah I would," Lucas laughed.

"But a lot can change in one year. Let's see what the future brings."

Lucas nodded.

"I will head home now, Guardian." Darien had looked at his watch.

"Yeah, me too," Lucas agreed. "It's been a long day."

"And we do have a tough weekend coming up," Darien grinned.

"Don't remind me." A light shiver run over Lucas' back. The closer the date approached, the more uneasy he grew.

All the more reason it seemed strange to him that his thoughts were circling more around HRC and JDC on his way home and never even touched the barbecue. But the idea that Darien had planted in his head was far more present right now. Had the Satanist circle really been a necessary means to save the crystal power project? Had they really almost ruined that project? At the time, he had been so sure that putting Wolfman out of business was a necessary move, and that it had been a very pure one, too. After all, all they had set out to do was to protect a young girl. Lucas was by now used to the fact that things always became a lot more complicated the deeper you looked into them, but the idea of having been so terribly wrong was much to take on for him. A cold shiver ran down his back again as he thought back. Could that man, that evil guy, really have been one of the good guys, after all? Could they have made a terrible mistake? And what would that mean for the group they had met in Buxton? And that strange liquid that they used? Nothing really made sense to him anymore at that point. And the worst of it all was: He was almost certain that this was still not the bottom of it all. Once again he felt very small, very much behind.

CHAPTER 3

Family

When Sunday arrived Lucas was still feeling a little uneasy because of the energy project. So uneasy, in fact, that it took him a good while to get his focus back on the upcoming barbecue.

"Honey, are you really sure that you don't want us to take a bottle of wine with us?" His mother was holding a bottle of Chardonnay when he came down to the living room.

"Yes, I am sure." Lucas was annoyed.

"Drop it, Emily, will you please?" His father was laughing. "Or Lucas might rethink taking us there in the first place. And I would really like to meet his friends."

"Thanks, Dad."

"Which reminds me..." His father looked at him. "You have not told us where we are supposed to go."

"Oh, right. It's not too far away. I guess we will be there in less than 15 minutes by car." Lucas had turned around running up the stairs. "I am sure I would find it by heart, but let me fetch the address just to be on the safe side," he yelled back down from his room.

"That still means that we have to leave shortly," his father yelled back. "It's already 10:30!"

"Yeah." Lucas was hurrying down again. "Although I don't think they would mind too much if we run a little late."

"They might not, but your mother for sure would," his father laughed.

"Good point." Lucas joined the laugh. "Let's not risk that."

During the drive over Lucas slowly started getting nervous again. Something about this meeting still had a bad feel for him, although he just couldn't pinpoint it. After all, there was little risk to it. Their parents would for sure not find out anything about their secret, and apart from that there really was nothing to worry about. The worst-case scenario was that some of them would not get along and leave early. For sure, none of them would try splitting up the group because of it, and even if they tried, it would hardly happen. He tried to relax and calm himself down as best he could, but it was not easy.

"Are you sure you've given me the right address?" his father asked as they were approaching their destination.

"Yes. Why?" Lucas moved to the middle spot of the backseat so he could look out the windshield. He had already been here, so the sight was familiar. On one side of the street there were apartment blocks with patches of lawn in front here and there. The other side was lined with a long, high wall, which surrounded the Mason estate.

"There it is." He pointed out the big gate. "Right where the GPS brought you."

The gate was impressive to look at, even though Lucas had seen it before: the double wing steel opening with the letters "RWM" on top.

"There?" His father looked at the gate. "That's the Mason estate."

"Yes, it is." Lucas nodded.

"Do you know the Masons?" Lucas' mother asked his father.

"Not personally, no. But we did business with them a while back." His father shook his head. "Do your friends' parents work for the Masons?"

"Not exactly…" Lucas felt the uneasiness again. "Could we please just get going?"

His father pulled up to the gate and a man immediately approached the car. He was in his early fifties, wearing a spotless suit and necktie. Lucas recognized him from his last visit.

"Good morning, ma'am. Good morning, sirs," he greeted the Trents, looking through the open window of the car. "May I inquire your name, please?"

"Trent," Lucas shouted, sticking his head through the middle of the car, smiling at the porter.

"Oh, hello again, sir, I did not recognize you back there." The porter smiled back at him. "Please enter, you are expected." With that he bowed and took a step back. At the same moment the doors started to swing open.

Lucas yelled his thanks and waved as his father drove through the gate slowly.

"Have you been here before?" his mother asked.

"Yes, but only once, to pick something up." Lucas replied. "Oh, you should maybe stop right here, Dad. I don't know where they would like us to park," Lucas addressed his father as they approached the main entrance.

He then took a quick look around. The villa was still amazing to look at, even though he already knew it. The big garden on the other side of the road, which normally was just lawn with some bushes and flowers, had been redecorated for the barbecue. Two large charcoal grills were standing to one side, some luxurious tables right next to them and a selection of beverages waiting ready in the background.

"Good morning, ma'am." Lucas had not realized that another man in his fifties had walked up to the car and had now opened the passenger's door, guiding his mother out. After that he quickly walked over to the driver's door, greeting his father as well. Lucas was quick to jump out by himself.

"I will have somebody park your car, if you don't mind," the butler addressed Lucas' father with a small bow. Lucas almost had to laugh, looking at that scene. His father was still so much in awe about the surroundings that he didn't even realize what was going on and just nodded silently. And before he even realized it, a younger man had approached the car, put a blanket over the driver's seat and drove off to the garage area.

"Seems we are the first to arrive," Lucas addressed his parents after looking around a bit more, giving them some time to adjust.

"Yes, sure." His father slowly came back to reality. Lucas now had to laugh, looking at both of his parents. He had never seen them so beside themselves.

"Yo, mate. Early as always." Cedric had just stepped out of the main entrance and was approaching them.

"Not bringing your timelines in jeopardy, are we?" Lucas grinned, giving Cedric a warm welcoming handshake and pat on the shoulder.

"Not at all, my friend, not at all," Cedric returned the greeting before the two boys approached Lucas' parents.

"Mum, Dad, meet Cedric." Lucas did the introductions.

"Thank you for joining us." Cedric shook their hands. "It is a pleasure to finally meet you. My parents will be here shortly. Can I offer you something to drink in the meantime?"

"The pleasure is all ours." Lucas' father smiled at Cedric. "Thank you very much for the invitation."

Cedric had walked them over to the tables and handed them their drinks.

"This is a lovely place. But you shouldn't have gone to these lengths just for a barbecue." Lucas' mother was still looking around, seemingly humbled by the scene.

"No lengths are too great for us when we expect such important guests as yourself, milady."

Lucas quickly turned around when he heard the voice from behind. Without them noticing, a couple had approached them. The woman was in her late thirties or early forties, wearing a long white dress. She looked really good for her age, with her long, dark hair and a big smile on her face. The man at her side was much older; Lucas would have estimated him in his early sixties, very tall, and walking with an elegant black cane with a silver stud on top.

"Mother, Father, may I present Mr. and Mrs. Trent, and their son Lucas." Cedric did the introductions.

"It is a pleasure to meet you." Cedric's father kissed Lucas' mother's hand before shaking his father's. "I am Robert William Mason, and this is my wife Doris. Welcome to our humble home."

"Come on, let's give them a bit of privacy," Cedric whispered to Lucas and walked off with him.

"Oh man, my parents will need a while to recover from that." Lucas laughed when they were out of hearing distance.

"Why's that?"

"Because they seriously thought that your parents worked here." Lucas was still laughing.

"And let me guess: You failed to correct that thought?" Cedric had joined in the laugh while Lucas was nodding.

"Here are the next ones." Lucas pointed toward a car that had just cleared the hedge that was blocking the view to the main gate and was now approaching.

"Let's go welcome them before my parents do." Cedric was already walking there.

Lucas followed him quickly and only saw from the corner of his eyes that a second car was pulling up now, too.

"Welcome, and thank you for joining us." Cedric was already at the first car.

Lucas took a quick look at the two adults who had climbed out first. The woman was a little younger than his mother, had slightly dark skin, and looked as if she loved eating. The man looked like the same age, and even more gave the impression that food was his main hobby. Lucas almost had to laugh when Marcus climbed out of the car last. His parents seemed to be quite the opposite of him, although on closer look, and when one blanked out the build, the resemblance was clear.

As Cedric still had his hands full showing the Gracers around, Lucas turned his attention to the second car. He quickly recognized the three people climbing out as Stephanie and her parents.

"Good morning, Mrs. O'Brien. Good morning, Mr. O'Brien. Nice to meet you again." Lucas approached them stretching out his hand, but before he had a chance to greet any of them, Stephanie had already jumped him, greeting him with an intense hug that almost threw him down.

"Jesus, Airmid, be careful. You might be a feather-weight, but I am not Cougar," Lucas laughed.

"It's nice meet you again too, Lucas." Mr. O'Brien patted his shoulder. "And please call me Stan."

Stephanie finally let go of Lucas, giving him a chance to shake her mother's hand.

"Impressive place." Stan O'Brien had started looking around. "Who do we owe the invitation to?

"That would be Cedric." Lucas pointed him out. "Or his father, to be precise. Come on, I'll introduce you."

Lucas quickly did the intro round and got himself introduced to Marcus' parents in exchange by Cedric. The parents quickly started a very lively discussion, giving the children a chance to take off and be by themselves again.

"Four down, two more to go." Cedric smiled. "And it's going pretty well so far."

"Don't celebrate too early, mate. This has only just begun," Lucas laughed.

"Here comes the next one…" Marcus pointed out a car that just approached. "And we all know who it is."

"Yes, sure." Lucas laughed. They all knew the blue Suzuki by now, and the aggressive driving style that Jasmin had had also become legendary. "Come on, let's go say hi."

"Stop complaining, or you can walk back home," Lucas heard Jasmin yell at someone in the back seat as she was climbing out.

"Relax, Psycho." Lucas gave her a quick hug. "Otherwise you will end up with a heart attack shortly."

"You drive with those three and try to relax." Jasmin seemed a little upset. "They are driving me crazy."

"Maybe you should stop driving like crazy, so they would not have a reason to drive you crazy," Marcus laughed.

By now three more people had climbed out of the Suzuki. The first person Lucas noticed was a woman in her fifties. Red hair, same build as Jasmin, same face.

"It's a pleasure to meet you, Mrs. Kramer." Lucas smiled and shook her hand. "I am Lucas Trent. Please let me introduce you to our host, Cedric Mason, and two more of our pack, Stephanie O'Brien and Marcus Gracer."

Jasmin's mother smiled and shook all their hands while Lucas was turning to Jasmin's father, who was also in his fifties, quite tall, slim and had short, grey hair. After quickly shaking his hand too, he turned his attention to the third person, a girl who seemed to be little older than Jasmin, quite a bit smaller than himself, slim like a thread and with long fire-red hair.

"May I introduce you to my sister Michelle?" Jasmin did the honors. "Her husband couldn't make it today, but one is better than none," she winked.

"Nice to meet you." Lucas shook her hand. "Shall we go join the others now?" he continued after giving her a chance to greet the others. They quickly did an intro round with the other parents before withdrawing again.

"That leaves the Professor." Cedric looked toward the entrance.

"Yeah, and it's not like him to be late." Lucas looked at his watch. It was already way past 11.

"He warned me that his parents are usually not exactly on time," Cedric laughed. "So don't worry too much."

"It's nice to meet casually again for a change." Marcus smiled and walked around in the garden a little.

"Yeah." Lucas nodded. "We have done this far too rarely over the past months."

"Yes, but keep in mind that we did spend three full weeks together not too long ago," Jasmin said. "And now that all our lives seem to be back to normal again, I am sure that we will find more time for that too."

"You are right, Psycho." Lucas smiled at her. "But it still feels like ages since we just had a casual afternoon together. The last one I remember was months ago, when we had pizza in the mall."

"Here comes the lost sheep." Marcus ended the conversation abruptly, pointing out a car that was approaching.

Cedric was already walking to greet them, so Lucas decided to stay back and just watch. And it turned out to be an interesting sight for him, because again, as with Marcus' parents before, he would not have called those. Darien's father was a muscular guy, very tall, very proper, but clearly a worker. When Lucas shook his hand, he could feel the rough skin. His mother seemed to be older than his father; her long grey hair was shining in the sun. She was good-looking for her age and also dressed very nicely, though the dress looked cheap on closer inspection.

After the introductions were finally over, the parents were eagerly chatting with each other, and even Jasmin's sister seemed to enjoy the company. It was only when one of the Masons' employees came out with a plate full of meat and sausages that the group broke up a little.

"Emma seems to love overdoing, don't you think?" Lucas addressed Cedric when he saw the amount of raw meat. He already knew the woman from his first visit here, when she also had provided them with food, so much that they had a hard time carrying all of it.

"No one is to stay hungry at our estate," Cedric laughed. "And besides… My dad is grabbing his apron, so some of the good meat will be lost forever."

The others joined in the laughter.

"Come on, Airmid, let us give our host a hand." Jasmin walked toward the grill with Stephanie.

"Oh boy, that will be fun." Cedric started following them, but keeping a little distance.

"Why?" Lucas walked with him.

"My father is only doing the cooking himself because he wants to show off. And he for sure will stop after the first round, leaving the scepter to Emma. So he certainly will not like help for that. But on the other hand, he also will not be impolite enough to push the help away, especially not when it is offered by young girls."

Lucas had to grin at Cedric's comment. And it really was fun to watch Mr. Mason trying to keep the girls away without telling them no. The boys watched the scene until the first batch of food was finished and Cedric's father called everyone to the table. And as Cedric had prophesied, Emma immediately took over the grill at that point. The afternoon went on with them eating and chatting and everybody having a good time.

"Did you notice something?" Darien whispered to Lucas about two hours later.

"What's that?" Lucas looked at him.

"We have been here for nearly three hours, and none of the parents have bothered talking to any of us so far."

"You are right." Lucas had to laugh. "It seems Cougar's idea was a full success."

"Do you think we should do anything about it?" Darien asked.

"Hell no. Just let them be."

Lucas leaned back, looking around a little bit, trying to listen in on the discussions that were going on around the table. He was just following a talk about babies, initiated by the fact that Jasmin's sister had a two year old son named Stuart, when Darien poked him in the side and indicated that he should listen to a discussion between Cedric's father and his own.

"Can you go into more details?" Mr. Trent was just asking.

"Well, as I already said, it happened in one of my factories. In a beverage plant, to be precise." Mr. Mason answered. "The storage room we have there is not exactly a Swiss bank vault, but it does have a state-of-the-art security door and a new alarm system that includes CCTV coverage. Our guard team was watching the room constantly, and we also have patrols around the premises, of course. But still, all of a sudden, about fifty crates full of soda cans were gone. Just like that."

"Fifty crates is not exactly something you can just carry away in your pocket." Mr. Trent was shaking his head in disbelief.

"Exactly. And there were no signs of forced entry; in fact, there were no signs of entry at all. The windows were closed, and of course barred, and the door's security system shows no entrance during the entire night, except for the security patrols. It is just as if the crates had magically disappeared."

"And did you have a forensic team search the place afterwards?" Mr. Trent asked.

"Yes, of course, but there were no usable traces. But we of course did not go into DNA analysis. This would be pointless, anyway--too many people are going in and out of that room every day."

"Did you hear that?" Darien whispered to Lucas.

"Yes I did." Lucas nodded.

"And are you thinking what I am thinking?"

"Unfortunately, yes."

"So what do we do?"

"I don't think that there will be much we can do about it, Professor. But we should discuss that tomorrow."

"Mr. Mason," Darien addressed Cedric's father. "When did you say this happened?"

"About a month ago," he answered. "Why? Are you planning on becoming a P.I. and looking for a good mystery?"

"I study IT, sir. And IT is all about problem solving and finding explanations for strange behavior. So I guess it is natural curiosity."

"Well, feel free to stop by if you want to try solving this one," Mr. Mason laughed. "But I guess it is not exactly a computer problem, so there might not be an exact solution here."

"I would still love to take you up on that offer, sir. But more because I would love to have a look around in a beverage factory. I never had a chance to see one in action."

"I love your enthusiasm, Mr. Stance. That's something you don't see that often anymore in young people." He was looking at Cedric.

"What's that supposed to mean?" Cedric sounded offended. "I am getting myself through school OK now, aren't I?"

"But you never showed any interest in the real world of work. At least, I have never seen you in any of our factories."

"You should not blame him too much, Robert." Lucas' father smiled at Mr. Mason. "School is hard enough, and I doubt that many students think too much about what comes afterward."

"Still, some do." Mr. Gracer jumped into the discussion. "Marcus will visit my employer later this semester with his class."

"Yeah, but only because our teacher insisted," Marcus whispered to Cedric, making Stephanie giggle quietly.

"Where do you work, Mr. Gracer?" Mr. Mason asked.

"I am a lab worker in a medium sized chemistry shop. You will most likely not know it, it's Brix & Burton. We mostly deliver base components for other manufacturing companies and do quality assurance for them as well."

"Oh, I in fact do know that company. We sometimes have them run QA assessments on our plants."

"Well, then maybe I have worked for you in the past and didn't even know it." Mr. Gracer started laughing.

The chat went on until late into the night, covering various topics, but almost always staying between the parents. Lucas and the others were happy about that, happy that nobody asked too many questions in their direction and also that their parents seemed to get along just fine. It was close to midnight when they started breaking up. Once again Lucas was amazed about the organizational skills of everyone on the Mason staff. Their cars showed up right next to them exactly when they were ready to leave. He and his parents were last, with his father still intensely discussing business topics with Mr. Mason until the very last moment.

"That was a lovely day," his mother said when they finally were on their way. "And you have really nice friends, honey."

"Interesting for you to say that." Lucas laughed. "You hardly talked to any of them. But you are right, they are all really nice and so are their families, it seems."

"We still should return the invitation at some point."

"Have you proposed that to the Masons, Emily?" his father laughed.

"Not yet, why?"

"Because I hardly think that we could give them the appropriate surroundings for that."

"Ah… Nonsense, I will talk to them. And you will see that they will agree."

"Have fun trying." His father was still laughing.

"So, honey, how did you end up with those friends? They are hardly your average buddies, are they?" Mrs. Trent switched the topic.

"And what exactly would you think my average buddies would be?" Lucas was not sure if he should feel insulted or honored by that comment.

"Well, you know, like people in your school…"

"Jesus, Mum, you seriously don't know me it seems," Lucas laughed. "The only guy in the entire IT College that is more or less on the same page with me is the Professor. And as you might have noticed, he actually is one of the group."

"So how did you end up with this group then?" His father now got curious, too.

"You maybe won't believe it, but I met them in a bar."

"And what makes them different from the people in your school?"

"Simple, Dad: They don't treat me like a geek, they treat me like a friend."

"I was under the impression that they treat you like more than a friend," his father said. "They all seem to look up to you, especially that young girl."

"Yeah, I know. And I am working hard to fix it." Lucas was amazed that his father had caught that by just watching them.

"Why would you want to fix it? It didn't really look broken to me."

"Maybe you can't understand it, Dad, but I would like all of us to be equal. And right now we are not."

"And you never will be, that's a fact of life." His father was laughing again. "Each of them has their strengths and weaknesses. And if you are really good friends you will always look up to the strengths of the others and at the same time try to counteract their weaknesses. And it should be your goal to be an inspiration for them in the areas that you shine in, so they can learn from you."

"Your father is right, honey." His mother smiled at him. "You should see it as an honor that they look up to you, not a problem."

"Yeah, maybe I should." Lucas nodded, his thoughts racing around the topic. It felt weird to hear those things from his parents, even more so as they had no idea what was really going on between him and the others.

One day later the group had assembled once again for their traditional Monday meeting. Many of them, including Lucas, looked a little exhausted after getting back home so late that last evening. They had assembled inside the shack this time, as it was very cloudy and looked as if it could rain any minute.

"That went very well yesterday." Marcus was the first to speak.

"Yeah, for you," Cedric laughed. "My father is still asking me why I never show up at one of our factories."

"Don't blame that on me." Marcus looked uneasy. "That was the Professor's doing."

"Yeah. What was that about anyway, Professor?" Cedric asked.

"Didn't you guys catch the discussion between Mr. Mason and Mr. Trent?" Darien was a little baffled, even more so when the others shook their heads. "They talked about a theft in the beverage factory."

"So?" Cedric looked questioningly at him.

Darien explained, "The crates with the cans just vanished. No signs of break-in, no signs on CCTV, the guards saw nothing, they were just--poof… gone…"

"You are not suggesting that we have magical thieves around now, are you?" Jasmin asked.

"I am not suggesting anything." Darien shook his head. "But the thought has crossed my mind."

"So what do you want to do about it?" Marcus was curious.

"Not much, as this was a month ago. But at least I would like to have a look and see if there are traces of magic anywhere around," Darien answered. "And of course, I really do want to see a beverage factory in action." He laughed.

"I would love to accompany you if you don't mind." Lucas said. "I am quite certain that there is nothing I can do to help, but I am curious about the factory, too."

"Sure thing." Darien nodded.

"And what are you planning on doing if this should really turn out to be a work of magic?" Jasmin asked.

"I honestly don't know," Darien replied. "And to be quite frank with you, I am somewhat hoping to find out that there was no magic involved after all. The thought of a magical thief gives me goosebumps."

"And the thought of my dad finding out about magical thieves gives me headaches." Cedric was uneasily sliding around on the bench.

"Well, maybe you should blow off some steam, then," Marcus laughed. "That will divert your attention elsewhere."

"Are you up for a duel?" Cedric grinned at him. "That would blow off steam."

"But it would be a little unfair, don't you think?" Marcus winked at him.

"And hurtful for sure, no matter who wins it," Stephanie laughed.

"I would be, if you like." Lucas looked at Cedric. "I mean... it might still hurt... but..."

"Challenge accepted," Cedric interrupted him. "What did you have in mind?"

"First I would love to try something new. And to do that I would need you to hit me with your 'Ventus' charm." Lucas waited for Cedric to nod before continuing. "And if we still have energy left after that, I am happy to just give it a freestyle go if you like."

"I feel a nightmare approaching fast," Jasmin laughed.

"And I think we should start selling seats and popcorn." Marcus laughed, too.

The group stepped out of the shack. The clouds were still not looking too inviting, but so far it had stayed dry at least. Lucas and Cedric took positions a few meters apart, facing each other.

"Ready when you are," Cedric said.

"Professor, would you be so kind as to watch and analyze for us?" Lucas looked at Darien, who just nodded in reply.

"Bring it on." Lucas focused on Cedric.

A few seconds of silence followed, with the two just looking at each other. Then suddenly Lucas could feel a little tickling in his chest and immediately started trying to build up his newly thought-of charm.

But he didn't even have enough time to get his thoughts straight when he heard Cedric.

"VENTUS," he cried and suddenly Lucas was tossed backward and to the ground by a gust of wind.

"Hell, that was fast," Lucas laughed when he was back up on his feet.

"Should I go slower?" Cedric asked.

"No. If my protection is to be any good, I have to be able to be quicker than you are. Let's do it again."

This time Lucas started preparing his shield charm even before he felt something from Cedric. It felt a little like cheating, but he had never done this before, so he dropped that thought quickly.

Lucas focused on Cedric and waited for the first signs of him attempting a cast. It was almost spooky but for a split-second he thought he saw Cedric's eye color change. That was when he fired up his protection, and it proved to be just in time.

"VENTUS," he heard Cedric shout.

"SPECULUS," he shouted back at the same moment. The next thing he heard was Cedric crying out in surprise when he was tossed back.

"That's what I'm talking about." Lucas laughed and went over to help Cedric back up on his feet.

"What the hell was that?" Cedric still seemed unsure what had just happened.

"Mirror shield," Lucas grinned. "You just knocked yourself down."

"That was the most amazing feat of magic I have seen so far." Darien joined them. "You completely redirected his energy stream."

"It was nice, but also very demanding," Lucas said. "It took a lot of energy and too much time to build."

"We already know that this will get better with more practice." Darien patted his shoulder. "There is one thing that I would be curious about: how this new shield charm holds up against Whirlwind's 'Condolesco' curse."

Marcus started laughing loudly. "I love the idea of Whirlwind torturing himself."

"I am not sure if that would be the result." Darien shook his head.

"One way to find out." Lucas smiled. "If you are up to it, Whirlwind."

"Are you kidding? Of course I am." Cedric grinned and got into position.

Lucas focused on Cedric and nodded as a sign that he was ready to go. The tickling that he was familiar with by now started almost instantly. Lucas realized that he had to work quickly to even stand a chance.

"SPECULUS," he shouted, just a blink of an eye before he heard Cedric's deep, spooky voice.

"CONDOLESCO."

Moments of silence and eager awaiting followed that felt like ages for everyone. Then a cry of pain ended the silence abruptly, and Lucas dropped down to the ground.

"Thought so," Darien commented dryly.

"What went wrong?" Marcus asked while pulling Lucas back up on his feet.

"Same thing that went wrong a week ago. 'Speculus' seems to be a variation of the 'Seperatio' charm. It is like a shield. Unfortunately, what you need to protect against 'Condolesco' is not a shield, it's a full body armor."

"So it seems I have to build a mirror-version of the 'Guardio' charm as well," Lucas laughed.

"Are you up for more?" Cedric asked Lucas.

"Always," Lucas laughed. "But maybe someone else has plans as well?" He looked at the others.

"If you two want to continue to show your dark sides, please do so by all means." Jasmin laughed.

"Why don't you show us a little of your dark side for a change?" Lucas grinned at her. "You have been awfully quiet lately."

"Maybe I don't have a dark side." Jasmin winked.

"Says the Psycho." Darien laughed.

"Very well, if you insist." Jasmin looked a little cranky. "Who wants to be my lab rat?"

"Who do you want?" Lucas asked.

"Well, if I have free choice... I would opt for Cougar." Jasmin smiled. "And please, Professor, have a watchful eye."

"Bring it on then." Marcus smiled, but looked a little nervous.

Darien and the others stepped back and watched.

"OK, here is what I would like you to do:" Jasmin addressed Marcus. "Just walk toward me and try to touch my arm. I will try to stop you."

"Oh, and please take it slowly for starters," she grinned.

"Very well." Marcus nodded and started slowly walking toward her.

Jasmin's look got cold; she barely moved a muscle when she hissed in a deep, demon-like voice. "PAVERE."

"Wooohhhww, that's a good one." Marcus suddenly took a step back, as if something had just appeared in front of him.

"What's happening?" Lucas asked

"Don't you see that?" Marcus replied in disbelief.

Lucas tried hard, but there was nothing there. At least nothing he could pick up. "No," he slowly responded. "I see nothing. Professor?"

"This one is really good. I saw a short flash of energy, but now I don't see anything either."

"You mean you both don't see that giant, angry bull that is standing between Psycho and me?" Marcus was still in disbelief.

"It's a mind game, Cougar. An illusion." Lucas laughed. "Good one, Psycho."

"Psycho, how do you want me to proceed? Now that I am aware of the illusion."

"The mission has not changed, Cougar. If you can get to me, do so please."

Lucas watched Marcus taking one step at a time, slowly and very cautiously. Looking closely, he could see Marcus sweating a lot, as if he either was working heavily or was under great psychological stress. But after a few painstaking minutes, he finally reached Jasmin's arm.

"Nice one," Jasmin commended and visibly dropped her concentration.

"Thank you." Marcus dropped down on the ground, breathing heavily.

"Jesus, mate, was she pushing you that hard? You look exhausted." Cedric approached Marcus and sat down next to him.

"It's not physical exhaustion, I would guess, but the effect of pure terror." Lucas patted Marcus' shoulder. "That was an impressive spell, Psycho."

"Thanks," Jasmin nodded. "But obviously not impressive enough. After all, he got through."

"Yeah, but only with the help of Guardian and the Professor." Marcus slowly stood up again. "That thing looked so real, it took me every piece of willpower to break through, even knowing that it was an illusion."

"Still, you got through…" Jasmin seemed unhappy.

"Well, sorry. Do you want to try again?"

"I would like to try something else, if you feel up to it." Jasmin nodded.

"Sure. What do you want me to do?"

"Same as before, just give me a minute to prepare."

"OK."

"What about us? Should we help again? Or stay out of it this time?" Lucas asked.

"Please help again. Cougar should have the best possible shot at this," Jasmin said and waited for them to nod before she turned to Marcus, who was standing by, waiting for her signal. Again she fell into deep concentration, but Lucas was under the impression that there was a lot less dark intention behind it this time. In fact her voice sounded almost charming when she whispered, "Capere." After that she nodded in Marcus' direction.

Lucas watched eagerly to see what would happen next. He could see that Marcus was totally relaxed this time when he started moving forward slowly. And then he suddenly stopped.

"What is that?" Marcus started holding his hands out as if he was touching along an invisible wall.

"I don't see anything," Lucas said.

"Neither do I," Darien replied.

"Are you telling me that I am bouncing into an illusion again?"

"Seems so." Darien nodded.

"OK, that we can check quickly." Marcus took two steps back and then took a tackle at the barrier. Lucas was stunned by the effect. It was just as if he had run into his 'Seperatio' charm. Marcus tried again and again, but no matter what he did, he couldn't get any further.

"Little help, Professor." Marcus finally looked at Darien.

"It is all in your mind. To me it looks as if your muscles would contract in a way to simulate a wall for you. So it all comes down to muscle control, I would guess."

"It's still no good." Marcus shook his head after trying for a while. "Psycho, all I can think of now would be to go against it with my own magic."

"Do it." Jasmin nodded. "Let's test this to the breaking point."

"Roger." Marcus nodded. He then shouted, "LEVIPES" and took a few steps back to gather momentum for a full speed leap at the barrier. Lucas watched eagerly. At first it looked as if Marcus would fall short and be stopped once again. But the sheer force of his magic in the end overwhelmed Jasmin's spell and Marcus broke free.

"Jesus, that was a challenge," Marcus laughed after walking to Jasmin.

"It seems this one works better than the other one," Jasmin laughed. "At least for you."

"What was that?" Lucas asked.

"A banning circle. I always wanted to try something like this. It's like a prison built in your mind."

"Nice one. That could come in handy at times," Lucas laughed.

"Yep, I would think so too." Jasmin joined in the laugh.

"What's next?" Marcus asked with a grin on his face.

"I would like to try that spell against your protective charms if you don't mind, Guardian," Jasmin suggested.

"Good idea." Lucas nodded.

Unfortunately they didn't have a chance to continue, as a loud thunder roared in, announcing the approach of a storm.

"I guess we have to postpone that." Lucas looked up. "We should hurry out of here, otherwise we might just be trapped for a while longer than planned."

The others nodded and quickly started packing up their things. After a quick goodbye with their traditional greeting they hurried off toward Luton. As much as Lucas would have loved trying that spell with his shields, he was happy when he arrived home without getting too wet in the process. There would be other times to finish that experiment.

CHAPTER 4

Life & Death

Months had passed by since that picnic at the Masons' place. Lucas and Darien had visited the factory but hadn't found any conclusive evidence in any direction, leaving them speculating for a while about the true nature of this theft. Unfortunately, no new hints developed, no matter where they looked, and life also got more and more hectic for them, so they soon discontinued their efforts completely.

It was on a Wednesday around noon in the middle of December. Lucas was just sitting in the classroom listening to a lesson in database engineering when an announcement over loudspeaker brought him out of his routine.

"Students Darien Stance and Lucas Trent, please report to the principal's office immediately. Darien Stance and Lucas Trent, principal's office, please."

"Anything we should be aware of, Mr. Trent?" the teacher asked.

"No, sir. At least nothing that I would be aware of right now." Lucas shook his head. "May I leave the class?"

"Sure, go." The teacher nodded.

Lucas was a bit nervous when he hastened down the corridor. This was the first time ever that he had been called into the principal's office, and he was not aware of anything he had done wrong. And what made him even more nervous was that they had called for Darien as well. Everyone in school was aware by now that he and Darien were friends, but nobody was supposed to know the connection. Halfway to the teachers' room, he saw Darien hastening along the corridor as well.

"Any idea what that is all about?" he asked him as they joined up.

"No. But being called to the principal is never a good thing." Darien shook his head.

They continued down together silently. Lucas took a deep breath before he knocked and opened the door to the principal's foyers.

"Yes?" the principal's secretary looked at them as they entered.

"Students Stance and Trent--we were asked to report here," Lucas said, still a little nervous.

"Ah yes, Principal Snyders is waiting for you. Please go right in."

Lucas took another deep breath before knocking on the principal's door.

"Enter," a voice from behind the doors said, so Lucas and Darien walked in, closing the door behind them.

The room looked intimidating. A large wooden desk stood in the middle of it, with a computer on the side and a lot of books and files distributed all over it. A big metal sign was standing right in the middle, facing the entrance door. "John Snyders Ph.D., Principal", it read. Behind the desk in a large leather chair a man in his fifties was sitting, reading through a file, when they came in.

"Students Stance and Trent, reporting as ordered, sir." Lucas almost sounded military with that statement. He was not sure if this was an appropriate way to address the principal, as he had never been here before, but he gave it his best shot.

"Please sit down, gentlemen." The principal pointed at two chairs at their end of the table, looking at them with a very strict look. Lucas tried to figure out what kind of feeling Snyders had behind this face, but couldn't. The principal waited until they were seated before continuing.

"Do you know a boy by the name of..." he started to browse through some lines scribbled on a piece of paper, which looked as if he used it whenever he needed to write something down quickly. "Ah, here it is... Marcus Gracer. Do you know him?"

"Yes, sir," Lucas responded, now completely surprised and unsure what was going on. "Is he in trouble?"

"You could say that." Mr. Snyders nodded. "Could you perhaps tell me why he explicitly asked that the two of you would be contacted even before his parents?"

"No, sir." Lucas shook his head. "I mean, we are very good friends, but I have no idea. What's wrong with him?"

"Luton General Hospital has called me, informing me that he is in a coma right now, after suffering a gunshot wound. He only awoke briefly after the incident, during his ride to the hospital, and apparently the only thing he said to the paramedics was that they should call either one of you."

"Oh my God. How did this happen?" Lucas was stunned.

"I have no idea. I told you all I know." The principal looked at both of them. "And by the looks on your faces I would suggest you get to the hospital right now and find out." Snyders stood up and walked towards the door.

"But sir, I have an exam upcoming in an hour." Darien finally found his voice.

"Stance, the exam can wait. Or even be skipped in your case. Get your priorities straight, will you?" The principal now opened the door, addressing his secretary. "Sheila, please take these two students to Luton General Hospital."

"Right away, sir," she answered.

"Go." Snyders addressed Lucas and Darien, who were still stunned from the message.

They quickly jumped up and followed the secretary to the car. It was only a ten minute drive to the hospital, but for the boys it seemed to be forever. Neither of them could think clearly right now. When they finally arrived, they both jumped out immediately and ran through the main entrance. They didn't even notice their driver shouting, "Good luck for your friend" behind them.

"Where can we find Marcus Gracer?" Lucas hastily asked the woman on the front desk.

"Who would you be?" she replied slowly and calmly.

"Lucas Trent and Darien Stance." Lucas was getting uneasy.

"Are you family?"

"No, but Marcus had the paramedics call us, that has to count for something." Lucas was so pumped with adrenaline that he felt his arms shaking.

"That's all right Maggie." A nurse had approached the front desk. "I will take them up; they are expected."

Lucas and Darien followed one step behind the nurse as she led them through the corridors of the hospital.

"Why would Cougar ask for the two of us?" Lucas asked Darien.

"I don't know. We are not really helpful here right now," Darien replied.

"Airmid," Lucas suddenly shouted and grabbed his cell phone. "Professor, call Psycho and Whirlwind."

Lucas was hectically looking through his cells address book, cursing the fact that he didn't have Stephanie on speed dial. When he finally found her number and hit the dial button, it seemed to take ages until the call finally got connected.

"Hi Guardian. Did not expect your call," Stephanie greeted him. "What's up?"

"Airmid, we need you at the hospital right away. Cougar is in trouble," Lucas almost shouted into the phone.

"What happened?" Stephanie's voice sounded uneasy.

"Don't know yet; all I do know so far is that he suffered a gunshot wound. Please get here as quickly as possible."

"I'm on my way." Stephanie said and hung up.

Lucas looked at Darien, who was still on the phone.

"Psycho is coming over," he said after hanging up. "Calling Whirlwind now."

"Thanks Professor." Lucas pocketed his cell phone and tried to calm down a little bit.

"Mr. Gracer!" Lucas hurried right toward him when he saw him walking up and down an aisle.

"Mr. Trent, I had not expected to see you here so soon." Marcus' father said in a shaky voice. Lucas could clearly tell that he was in a very bad shape, nervous, obviously in sorrow.

"What happened?" Lucas asked.

"Our company got robbed. Some crates with chemicals just disappeared. Marcus and his classmates were on the tour at the time we discovered the missing goods. And somehow he seems to have caught the thieves by surprise. That's when they shot him." His voice was shaking more and more with each word.

"Oh man... How is he?" Lucas was trying hard to sound calm, but he couldn't.

"I don't know yet. They have taken him for some tests. Nobody has told me anything so far. All I know is that he was unresponsive when they took him away."

"Steven!" Lucas nearly got run over by Marcus' mother, who had just come running down the corridor toward his father. He took a step back to give them some privacy.

"Whirlwind is on his way over as well," Darien said.

"Good." Lucas nodded.

"Have you thought this through, mate?" Darien was now whispering, pulling Lucas a few meters away, where nobody could hear them.

"What do you mean?"

"What do you suggest we do here?"

"Help Cougar, in any way we can. What else?"

"Think about this. We are in a hospital. There is NOTHING we can do here, at least not without raising a lot of suspicion."

Lucas had not thought about that yet. Marcus was too important for him, so important in fact that he was willing to risk their secret to save him.

"Let's hope we don't need to intervene," Lucas sighed and looked at Darien.

They sat down in the corridor, waiting anxiously for something to happen. Almost twenty minutes passed by. The rest of the group had arrived by then, too, before finally a doctor showed up and addressed them.

"Are you Marcus' parents?" he addressed the Gracers and waited for them to nod. "And you must be his friends, then." He waited again for Lucas and the others to nod. "I am your son's physician, Doctor Tackman. Please follow me."

The doctor led them through some more corridors before entering a room. It was a patient room with only one bed. Marcus was lying in it, a lot of monitors and machines attached to his body, as well as fluids and medication dripping from various bottles. Lucas was shocked when he first had a chance to look at the scene.

"Marcus is, as you can see, still unconscious," the doctor started after the room door closed behind them.

"Will he survive?" his mother interrupted.

"The next 48 hours are still critical, but his chances are good to make a full recovery, if no complications arise. He was hit by two bullets. One fractured his leg, the other one hit his stomach area from behind, but so far it seems no major damage was done. We still have to wait for a lot of test results, though." The doctor quickly looked around and then addressed Stephanie directly. "You are the one they call Airmid, right?" He waited for her to nod. "Would you like to look at the results yourself? I hear that you know quite a bit about medicine."

"Thank you." Stephanie nodded and took the file from the doctor. She seemed very relaxed, given the diagnosis, and was eager to see the details. Lucas watched her as she looked through it. He first thought about looking at it too, but he wouldn't have been able to understand it anyway, so he just waited. The diagnosis had him eased up too at that point, but only for a short moment. For some reason Stephanie got more and more uneasy with every piece of paper she looked at. She had walked to the very back of the room and was leaning against the wall, with her face getting as pale as the wall she was leaning on.

"What's up?" Lucas whispered after walking over.

"The diagnosis is completely wrong." Stephanie looked at Lucas, tears in her eyes. She was also only whispering so nobody else could hear them. "If I read this right, then Cougar has very little chance of survival, and even if he does, he would be crippled."

"What are you saying? That the doctor is lying?"

"Either that or someone made a terrible mistake."

"Let's ask him."

"Better wait for his parents to leave, I don't want to scare them in case I am wrong."

Lucas nodded and walked back over to the others with Stephanie.

"I hope you found the file interesting to read?" the doctor smiled at her.

"You see, Mrs. Gracer, your son is a really lucky man. Those shots could have been a lot worse. But when you have a Guardian and an Angel close by, then the goddess of healing normally is not far behind. And with such a combination, nothing can go wrong." The doctor patted Mr. Gracer's shoulder. "Please follow me now, there are some documents I need you to sign for the treatments." He then turned to Lucas. "I will leave you with your friend if that is all right."

Lucas nodded and waited for the three adults to leave the room.

"This doctor is hiding something," Jasmin said immediately after the door had closed. "He is smiling all the time, but underneath that smile he is terribly uneasy."

"I know. And we also know what he is hiding. Airmid told me before." Lucas nodded.

"Cougar is dying, isn't he?" Cedric said and Lucas nodded in reply.

"Maybe not." Darien jumped in.

"Why's that?" Cedric looked at him.

"Didn't you hear what the doctor just said?"

"He was obviously trying to calm the Gracers down with his guardian angel thing." Cedric didn't get it.

"You didn't listen." Darien looked at all of them. "Hasn't anybody caught that?"

"No. What is it?" Lucas asked, as all eyes focused on Darien.

"He didn't say guardian angel, he said a Guardian and an Angel." Darien was clearly amped up. "And the goddess of healing." With this he pointed at Stephanie.

"Do you think he knows about us?" Stephanie was shaking a little.

"About us, and obviously about Angel, too." Darien was nodding. "Why else would he have handed you that file?"

"So what do you suggest, then?" Lucas looked at him, slowly getting his energy back as well.

"I suggest we do exactly what the doctor told us to. Ensure that Cougar makes a full recovery."

"That will not be so easy." Stephanie had opened the file once again. "The bullet went through his spine and hit organs as well. Those are serious injuries."

"And we have the best healer in the world, right next to his bed now. If anybody can fix this, it's you." Lucas had laid his hand on Stephanie's shoulder.

"This will be hard to do for me." Stephanie held up an x-ray against the light. "The bullet is still in there. We need to get it out before I can do anything, and as soon as we get it out we need to fix him up or he will bleed out. And to make it worse, to do this we need to turn him over. Not something you should do with a patient that has a broken spine."

"I am all ears for other ideas, Airmid." Lucas looked at her.

"I don't have any." She again had tears in her eyes. "I just don't know if I can do this. What if I make it worse?"

"If we don't do something, he will die. What could be worse?" Cedric asked.

"Relax, Airmid." Jasmin had taken her into her arms. "You can do this."

"I don't know." Stephanie's voice was shaking. "Guardian, what shall we do?"

"Only you can make this call, Airmid. We will support you, no matter what you say." Lucas was stroking her hair.

"OK, let's give it a try." Stephanie finally nodded and walked to the bed.

"No." Lucas was standing on the other side of the bed. "No tries. We will do this. And we will do this right." He had laid his hand on Marcus' fist. "Brother to brother – yours, to the end."

The others followed his example before they all looked at Stephanie.

"First we need to turn him around, without further injuring his spine." Stephanie looked at Lucas.

"How do we do that?" Lucas asked.

As Stephanie did not respond, Darien did. "We need to pack him into a kind of corset before moving him. Can your shield charms do that?"

"One way to find out." Lucas nodded and started building up a new sort of shield. This time he visualized metal straps, all around Marcus' body.

"Good to go," he said after finishing the spell.

"Psycho, watch the tubes and cables, please," Stephanie said.

Darien, Lucas and Cedric had taken position alongside Marcus, ready to turn him.

"On the count of three." Lucas stated. "One, two, three." With that, they gave Marcus a quick pull and turned him over.

"Good." Stephanie was already working to take off the bandages from the wound.

"Oh boy, that looks bad." Cedric shivered when looking at it.

Stephanie was leaning over Marcus' body now, looking into the wound. "I can see the bullet, I just don't know how to get it out."

"Can't we use a clamp and just grab it on those indentations?" Darien suggested after having a look for himself.

"What indentations?" Stephanie looked again. "Those weren't there just a second ago. How did you do that, Professor?"

"I didn't do anything." Darien looked defensive.

"Pure luck." Lucas almost had to smile. "We have to get used to that with you, it seems."

Darien had grabbed a clamp and was offering it to Stephanie.

"One of you has to do that. I need to seal the wound as quickly as I can once the bullet is moved," she said, and when she saw Lucas reaching for the instrument she continued. "And not you either, Guardian. If he starts to bleed your shield charms are the only hope we have of stabilizing him long enough for me to react."

"Let me do it, then." Darien leaned over Marcus again and grabbed the bullet with the clamp. "Ready?" he asked Stephanie and waited for her to nod before he pulled it out with one quick motion.

The wound immediately started bleeding. Lucas was quick to cast a shield charm on top as best he could.

"I can't see anything. There is too much blood still in the wound." Stephanie looked at it.

"My shield is worked just along his body, so the blood should be on top. Can't we just suck it out with a piece of cloth?" Lucas suggested.

"I think I have an easier idea." Cedric approached, just holding a piece of cloth over the wound. "Ventus."

Lucas watched the cloth getting red. "Nice one."

"Pleasure." Cedric took the cloth off and stepped back.

"Now I can see it, but I am afraid that my overnight healing will not do the trick here." Stephanie looked extremely uneasy now.

"Relax, Airmid." Jasmin had put her hand on top of Stephanie's head. "You will come up with a solution."

Stephanie nodded and almost instantly fell into a deep trance. For about a minute she just held her hand over the wound before she finally whispered, "Balsam Medela." Then she collapsed onto the ground.

Lucas was eager to run over to her, but he was still holding his shield charm up and didn't want to lose focus, so all he could do was watch Jasmin kneel down to her.

"She says you should drop your shield now." Jasmin addressed Lucas without standing up.

Lucas nodded and complied. He sighed in relief and walked over to Stephanie, helping her back up on her feet.

"What now?" he asked.

"Now we have to wait."

Stephanie had not even finished that sentence when Marcus suddenly started crying loudly, as if someone had just stuck a pike through his whole body.

"What's wrong?" Lucas looked first at Stephanie, then at Marcus.

"I don't know." Stephanie had focused again on the wound on Marcus' back. She was just about to say something when the door burst open and the doctor came running in. Lucas tried to quickly think of some explanation he could give but the doctor was quicker.

"Don't waste time. I don't want to know what has happened, and I would most likely not understand it anyway. Just tell me if there is something I need to do."

Stephanie was still looking at the wound. "No, there is nothing you need to do, it's fine. It just takes time."

"Shall I give him something for the pain?" Tackman was looking at Stephanie now.

"No. Don't interfere." Stephanie shook her head. "Psycho, can you block the pain out somehow?"

Lucas saw Jasmin nod and walk up to Marcus' head before he took a look at the wound for himself again. What he saw there took his breath away. The whole area had started to heal from the inside out. It was as if little robots had been let loose and were stitching everything together again. Lucas estimated that at this rate the wound would have been gone completely in less than 10 minutes. Unfortunately he had no chance of watching it any longer, as Stephanie had put the bandage back on again. Marcus had stopped crying by now, too, but Lucas could not tell if it was Jasmin's intervention or if the pain had just gone away.

"What shall I tell his parents?" The doctor was still looking at Stephanie.

"That he moved and cut off the flow of pain medication. And that everything is all right again."

The doctor nodded and walked back to the door. Lucas could hear him take a deep breath before he left the room.

"That was close." Lucas looked at Stephanie.

"This whole thing was close to start with." Stephanie looked back at him. "I hope I don't have to do something like this again."

"Are you up to looking at his leg, too? Or do you want to leave this for the doctors?" Darien asked, pointing at the bandage on Marcus' right leg.

"That one should be easy." Stephanie looked at the x-rays again. "But you are right, better if I take care of it. BALSAM SOMNUS."

"What would we do without you, Airmid?" Lucas gave her a hug.

A minute of silence followed. Stephanie looked extremely exhausted, and everyone else was not sure what to say or do next. Jasmin was the one to break it.

"You know, I still don't get how this doctor knew about us." She said.

"Yeah, but we are lucky that he did. Or at least Cougar is." Cedric answered.

"Lucky this time. But if anyone can find out that easily, we might have a problem." Lucas was not so happy. "I think I should have a chat with that doctor later on. Psycho, maybe you should come along to that."

"Do you think Cougar told him?" Stephanie asked Lucas.

"No. The way this guy behaved when he ran in just before was way too prepared. He has dealt with this before." Lucas shook his head.

"Do you think he is one of us?" Jasmin asked.

"I don't think so." Darien was the one to respond, although the question was clearly directed at Lucas. "Do you remember his comment? That he didn't want to know what was going on because he wouldn't understand it anyway? Somebody told him about magic, but I highly doubt that he uses it himself."

"It's all speculation, guys. We should talk to him," Lucas said.

A loud moaning dragged their attention away from the topic. It was Marcus, who had turned around on his back again and was now looking up at them.

"Your treatment hurts like hell, Airmid," he said with an agonized grin on his face.

"Yeah, but you know the good thing about pain?" Cedric patted his shoulder. "It lets you know that you are not dead yet."

"I agree. And I am grateful beyond words for that." Marcus took Stephanie's hand and pressed it firmly.

"We should get the doctor. And your parents." Lucas suggested. "They will be happy to see you awake."

"You do that." Marcus nodded, still looking agonized and exhausted.

Darien quickly walked out to fetch the others. When he arrived back with them, the relief on their faces was clearly visible. Especially the doctor looked as if a load had just dropped from his heart.

"Come on, guys, let's give the Gracers a little space." Lucas walked toward the door. "Don't get too comfortable in there, buddy. We would like to see you outside again ASAP." He grinned at Marcus before leaving.

They walked a few meters off and sat down in some chairs that were lining the wall there.

"So what now?" Cedric looked at Lucas.

"Now we wait and see what happens," Lucas replied.

"That's it?" Cedric looked unhappy.

"What else would you like to do?" Lucas looked back at him now. "Airmid just saved Cougar's life, but we are still not out of the danger zone. Or how do you suppose we explain that a bullet wound in his spine just vanished? We have to wait and see what this doctor had in mind for that."

"That's actually not what was on my mind." Cedric had calmed down a little. "What I meant was what do we do? I mean… Somebody just shot one of my best friends. I am simply unwilling to let this stand like that."

"I tend to agree." Lucas nodded. "But one, we are not the police. And two, even if we wanted to do something, we still would have to wait for now, because as long as Cougar hasn't told us what happened, there is really nothing we can do."

"Right." Cedric nodded, but still looked unhappy.

"Why don't you all take a break? Go home, try to calm down. And let's meet again here tomorrow afternoon and visit Cougar. We will have him for ourselves then and can talk freely." Lucas suggested. "Psycho and I will stay and have a chat with the doctor."

"I don't think I can relax today, mate." Cedric was very uneasy. "But you are right, there is nothing more to do."

"Yeah, come on, Whirlwind. Let us give Airmid some company on her way home. She still looks exhausted," Darien suggested and stood up.

"Good idea." Cedric nodded. "I'll see if somebody can pick us up."

They walked away toward the main entrance of the hospital, leaving Jasmin and Lucas behind.

"You know, I am with Whirlwind for a change." Jasmin addressed Lucas. "I normally don't go for revenge, but I also don't want to leave this issue unanswered."

"Neither do I, Psycho, you should have known me long enough by now to realize that." Lucas looked down at the floor. "But running into this head on would just get us shot, too. If we want to do this right, we need to have a plan."

"You are almost certainly right." Jasmin nodded. "But I still think we have a good chance against a bunch of thieves. I mean… we can literally blow them away if we have to."

"Yeah, and Cougar can literally dodge bullets… It still didn't help him much this time though," Lucas replied without looking up.

As Jasmin did not respond to that, a few minutes of silence followed. Lucas was trying hard to remain calm and wrap his head around all the things that had been going on those past hours. He was so focused on this that he almost missed the doctor walking by him.

"Dr. Tackman!" Lucas jumped up as soon as he realized it. "Do you have a minute for us?"

"Of course." The doctor stopped and nodded. "What can I do for you?"

"Could we talk in private somewhere?" Lucas asked, noticing a lot of people walking the corridor.

"Sure." The doctor nodded again, seeming to get a little uncomfortable. "Let us step into my office."

They walked through two corridors until they reached the office. The sign on the door read "Gordon Tackman, M.D., Head of Emergency Medicine".

"What can I do for you?" The doctor sat down in his chair and offered Jasmin and Lucas two guest chairs on the opposite side of his desk.

"I don't want to waste too much of your time, so let me get right to the point," Lucas started. "We are very grateful for all you have done for our friend and we would like to understand why. Or better asked: How?"

"I thought you would know." The doctor seemed surprised.

"No… Humor us." Lucas shook his head.

"Well, we've had this sort of silent agreement now for a few years. I don't ask too many questions and as a countermove, some bad cases would just be taken care of for me."

"So how did you know about Angel? And the 'Goddess of Healing'?" Lucas inquired further.

"Well, my contact said that I should wait for a group of teenagers to come visit the patient. He said that there would be a young girl in that group, calling herself Airmid, and that I should show her everything we had. He said that it should be enough for her to see, but when I was unsure I should mention 'Angel' and 'Guardian', then she would understand for sure."

"And who exactly is that contact?" Lucas was curious.

"I told you before: Part of the agreement was that I don't ask questions, so I never did."

"Interesting." Jasmin looked at the doctor. "You cover up an almost fatal injury just because a stranger tells you to. How did that happen?"

"Look…" The doctor sighed. "All I know is that whenever those people have showed up so far, a miracle happened. I don't know how and honestly, I don't care. All I care about are the lives that get saved. I assumed so far that they were part of some government agency or something; obviously, looking at you proves me wrong with that, but in the end it doesn't make a difference. I can add another dash to the list of people that would not be alive anymore otherwise. And that does make a difference."

Lucas looked at Jasmin for a moment before standing up.

"Thank you for your time, doctor. And for your help," he said and walked to the door.

"Thank you for saving a life today," the doctor replied. "I will discharge your friend on Monday, just to keep the appearance."

Lucas nodded a thanks in reply and walked out of the room, followed by Jasmin. He had not understood this situation before, and he certainly did not understand it any better now, but there was no point in poking any further. The only one that might maybe have given him an explanation to this would have been Angel, but he was more than sure that this would never happen.

CHAPTER 5

Thieves

The next day felt like hell for Lucas. Not only was he exhausted after a rough night, but everyone in school also poked him about his disappearing yesterday. At one point, even Principal Snyders and his secretary showed up in the classroom asking for details, which was a terribly strange feeling and had everyone else in the room hold their breath for a few minutes. Lucas could not understand why everybody was so extremely interested in this and why they couldn't just leave him alone. He had never liked spectators too much, and now that he was the one they were looking at, it was even worse. When school was finally over and he could head over to the hospital again, he felt a little relief, although it hardly helped with the fatigue.

The hospital was full of people at this time of the day. Many walk-in patients were still heading for clinics, while the afternoon visitors were also already starting to pour in. Lucas thought for a moment if he should approach the front desk but then decided against it and just walked down the corridor where they had been yesterday. When he walked around the last corner, he could just see a person vanish into Marcus' room. He walked up to it without taking too much notice of the people around, knocked and entered.

"Hi there, fearless leader." Marcus grinned at him.

"Hi Cougar." Lucas smiled. The rest of the group was already in the room. Stephanie and Jasmin had pulled up chairs to Marcus' bed. Cedric was sitting on the window ledge and Darien was just taking off his coat. He obviously had been the one arriving just now.

"How long have all of you been here already?" He looked at the others.

"The girls arrived about half an hour ago. The boys have just gotten here," Marcus smiled from his bed.

"Seems now that you are injured you are becoming the ladies' man," Lucas laughed and put his coat on a hanger.

"And in contrast to you, I have no problem with that." Marcus winked at him.

"Looks as if you are feeling much better already." Lucas pulled up another chair to the bed.

"I am actually feeling all right again." Marcus moved around a little in his bed. "The doctor said that he wants to keep me until Monday, just so nobody will grow suspicious."

"Good to hear." Lucas smiled. "Now, we are all eager to hear what happened. If you are up to telling us, that is."

"Believe me, I have been as eager to telling you as you have been to hear it," Marcus said. "So... Where to start?"

The others watched him silently, waiting for him to talk.

"We were at Brix & Burton to see the real life work in a chemistry plant. You perhaps remember my father telling about that at the barbecue in summer? A study trip from my chemistry class," Marcus started. "So we were in the middle of the tour through the plant when security guards started showing up near the exits. At first I didn't think too much about it, but when I heard two of them talk about a theft in the hazardous material storage compartment and that they were unsure how somebody could get in there without appearing on CCTV, it made me curious because somehow it sounded like what had happened at the Masons' factory."

Marcus stopped for a moment to see if anybody wanted to add something to that, but as nobody did he continued.

"So I couldn't do too much at this point, but I tried to at least keep my eyes open as we were walking along. And that is when I first caught a glimpse of them."

"Of who?" Stephanie was curious.

"Patience, I am getting there," Marcus laughed. "At first it was only a shadow in a side corridor. I had to look twice because there were two guards standing right next to that area. The guy was good, though. He moved only when everybody was turning his back to him. I caught the movement in a reflection on a flask. So I walked over there, trying to look as if I was just looking around so I wouldn't scare the guy off, but when I approached the guards to alert them, he suddenly took off."

"That sounds like a pro," Cedric said.

"Yeah, and it gets better," Marcus nodded. "I alerted the guards of his presence and they rushed after him, with me following just a few steps behind, but when we came around the next corner the guy was just gone. The guards then turned around and said that we were just chasing a ghost there. I continued down anyway, as I was convinced about this. And you will not believe it, but I walked right by this guy twice before once again a reflection gave him away. He had taken cover behind a closet and almost melted into the shadow with his black suit. This guy was incredible. When he realized that I had spotted him again, he took off. I followed him down the aisles to a dead end where only office doors were at the side. I thought I had finally cornered him, but then this goon just leapt through a window. But not a standard one… One that was 2.5 meters from the floor. And only partially open when he took the jump, I might add."

"Wow…" Cedric was eagerly listening, and so were the others.

"I hesitated for a second, but I didn't want to let this guy get away, so I jumped through the window after him. Stupid move in hindsight; took me all my skills to land this jump without breaking some bones. This guy really was a pro." Marcus took a sip of water before he continued. "But it did pay off. I caught up to the guy and pushed him over, tearing off a part of his black suit. That's when he finally stopped and attacked me. And that guy was good. Even with my magical speed, I was almost unable to keep him at bay, let alone having any chance of bringing him down. So I tried to stall him until the security guys showed up, but when his two friends showed up first, I just had no chance. I was able to slow one of them down; that's when the third one shot me."

"Oh boy…" Lucas was stunned. "That's like straight from an action movie."

"Yeah, but normally the good guys win in those movies," Marcus laughed. "Anyway, at that point there was nothing more I could do. They ran around a corner and I could hear them drive away but didn't even see the car."

"Was there any magic involved by the others?" Cedric asked.

"How would I know?" Marcus shrugged his shoulders. "I didn't see anything that would have suggested it, except of course the almost magical way this guy moved."

"Did you see the faces of the guys? Could you identify them?" Lucas asked.

"Unfortunately not. They were wearing masks with their suits, a little bit like you see in Japanese Ninja movies."

"So we have nothing to go on," Lucas sighed. "We can just hope that the police will pick something up."

"Oh, I still have the piece of the suit," Marcus said. "At least I hope I do. Put it into my pocket when I jumped back up. I don't think anybody bothered taking it out." He pointed toward the dresser in the corner.

Cedric jumped off the window ledge and walked to get it.

"Jesus, mate, what do you carry around in your pockets?" he asked while searching through them. "Ah, here it is." He pulled out a piece of cloth that looked like a part of a sleeve from a black t-shirt.

"Interesting souvenir. I doubt that it will help much though." Cedric looked at it before handing it to Lucas.

"That's good quality cloth." Lucas turned it over a few times. "Strange that it would rip that easily."

"Nobody said something about easily," Marcus laughed.

"I have to agree with Whirlwind, though. It doesn't look like too much of a clue," Lucas said.

"Not at first glance, at least." Darien took the piece out of Lucas' hand. "If you don't mind, Cougar, I would like to have a detailed look at it and see if I can find something that actually helps."

"Be my guest." Marcus nodded.

"Like this spot, for example." Darien had held up the piece of cloth against the light.

"Looks like dirt." Lucas looked at it, too. "Not too much of a clue."

"Maybe, maybe not." Darien folded the piece carefully and put it in his pocket. "I will still have a look."

A minute of silence followed, with nobody knowing what to say. In the end Lucas was so uneasy at the atmosphere that he just started any topic.

"So, did the doc actually take another look at your wounds?" he asked Marcus.

"Yes, and he had me do all the x-rays and CTs and stuff again." Marcus nodded. "He told the people in radiology that the old ones had been lost because he spilled coffee over them."

"Now we know how he explained the sudden difference," Lucas laughed. "So what do the new pictures look like?"

"I actually haven't seen them. But judging from the way the doctor acted, it seems to have been a hell of a change." Marcus grinned. "All thanks to you, Airmid."

"Yeah, that was an amazing piece of work." Darien nodded. "And a new one too. Instant healing… Might come in handy sometimes."

"Handy maybe. But VERY painful." Marcus laughed.

"And that's good," Stephanie commented. "Otherwise you guys would get way too comfortable getting hurt."

"I think we should let Cougar get some rest, guys." Lucas smiled. "You should get up to 100% until Monday, so we can start looking for those guys."

"Yeah, I am eager to setting that score straight as well." Marcus nodded. "But right now I am more concerned about dying from boredom until they let me out of here."

"Which reminds me…" Darien grabbed his backpack and started searching inside. "… Ah, here it is," he finally said and pulled out a box and some cables.

"What's that?" Cedric had walked up to him.

"Shock-resistant laptop. Got it from an uncle who loves hiking and tends to take such devices with him on those trips. This was actually originally designed for the military." Darien grinned. "It's not exactly the newest model, but it has wireless Internet. And I took the liberty of installing some games on it for you." He handed it over to Marcus.

"Wow…" Marcus took it and looked at the device. "I am speechless. Thanks Professor."

"My pleasure. That should keep your brain intact until Monday."

They all wished Marcus a quick recovery, which for Lucas seemed pointless on second thought, as they all knew that he had already recovered, and left him alone with his new toy.

Lucas didn't have any more time to visit the hospital for the remainder of the week and the weekend, so when he rode his bike down to O'Brien Mansion Monday afternoon, he wasn't sure if Marcus would be able to join them for the meeting or not. All the greater was his happiness when he spotted his bike next to the shack.

"I see they let you roam freely again," Lucas grinned as he greeted Marcus inside.

"Yeah, not a moment too early." Marcus grinned back at him before focusing his attention on the fireplace again.

"I like this place much more in summer." Stephanie was standing next to Marcus, shivering.

"Patience, Airmid. I'll have the fire going in a moment, and then it will be nice and warm in here," Marcus said without looking up.

Lucas sat down on the bench on the far side of the shack. He was cold as well, but preferred not to show it too much. He hated the winter months, for the cold as well as the dark, but mostly for the fact that he couldn't be out as much as he would have liked.

"Here we go." Marcus finally jumped up.

"Much better." Stephanie smiled and stepped closer to the fire, warming her hands over it.

When the others finally arrived, the shack had already warmed up significantly. It was in fact warm enough that Lucas decided to take off his jacket.

"So… how do we go forward with those thieves?" Marcus seemed eager to get the topic going immediately after they had all sat down.

"Relax, man," Lucas laughed. "You haven't even been out of the hospital for 24 hours and are already eager to get back in?"

"I am not planning on getting back in." Marcus looked at him with a sort of mad look. "I am planning to get somebody else in, though."

"For that we first have to find them," Cedric reminded him. "And that is most likely not going to be easy."

"And even if we find them, we still need to find a way to deal with them," Lucas added. "After all, you are the fighter in the group, and even you couldn't stop them."

"But together we can, for sure," Marcus said confidently.

"Revenge is a bad motive for a fight." Jasmin shook her head.

"There are no good motives for fights, Psycho." Lucas looked at her.

"Yeah, but there are good motives to only fight those you can actually win." Jasmin seemed not at all happy about the situation.

"You don't fight the fights you can win. You fight the fights that need fighting," Lucas replied, still looking at her. "And I am afraid this will be one of those."

Jasmin sighed in reply, but slowly started nodding.

"And relax, if they are that good chances are slim that we find them in the first place." Lucas patted her shoulder.

"I am not so sure about that." Darien had been quiet so far, but was now joining the discussion.

"Why? What did you find?" Marcus asked him impatiently.

"The spot on the sleeve you tore off." Darien pulled out the piece of cloth. "It contains iron ore, as well as clay."

"So?" Marcus watched him eagerly.

"Well, there are only so many places around here where you would find those two together." Darien put the cloth in the middle of the table. "I could only come up with three that are within a reasonable distance."

"Nice one," Lucas complimented. "But 'places' are still quite large areas; how do you suppose we find them in there?"

"I have not thought that through in detail yet," Darien had to admit. "But I am certain that our resident Boy Scout will come up with something."

"Be sure I will," Marcus grinned.

"Wouldn't it be more efficient to give that clue to the police and let them handle it?" Stephanie suggested. "I mean, after all, they have helicopters, dogs and a lot of people."

"Yes, they have. But what would you, being a thief, do when suddenly helicopters started circling above your hideout?" Marcus asked.

"Most likely run," Cedric answered with a grin.

"Exactly. And then hide again, somewhere else, where nobody will look." Marcus nodded.

"So what's your plan then?" Lucas asked.

"Find those clowns, call the police once we know exactly where they are, and make sure that they stay where they are until the cavalry arrives," Marcus replied.

"OK Professor, bring it up then." Lucas nodded. "Where exactly are those three areas you were talking about?"

"Maybe I can show you." Darien said. "Cougar, did you bring my laptop?"

"Sure." Marcus jumped up to fetch his backpack, pulling Darien's computer out of it.

"Look here." Darien opened up a satellite image of the area surrounding Luton. "Here, here and somewhere around here." He pointed out the three areas.

"I know this area." Marcus pointed at one of them. "There is a lot of woodwork going on there, so if those clowns are hiding there they will hardly be undisturbed."

"So we start with the other two, then." Lucas looked at the others.

"I would start with this one." Darien pointed out the one farthest away from them. "It's a pretty small patch."

"So what do you suggest?" Lucas looked at Marcus. "It's winter, we can hardly just cycle out there and start a hike."

"That was pretty much what I would have suggested," Marcus grinned. "Although I would maybe have taken the train there instead of making the distance on bike. It is quite a long way to go, after all."

"I am not exactly fond of this plan." Jasmin looked at Marcus. "I don't like to run around in the cold for too long if I can help it."

"Neither do I," Stephanie added quickly.

"Same for me." Darien nodded.

"That would leave three of us." Marcus grinned after waiting to see if the others would bail out too.

"Are you up for that Whirlwind?" Lucas asked.

"Wouldn't miss it for the world," Cedric grinned.

"So how about next Saturday, then?" Marcus suggested. "Gives us enough time to prepare."

"Are the three of you available on Saturday? Just in case we need a rescue team?" Lucas looked at Darien and the girls.

"I am, in case you need a pickup. Can't help with more, anyway, I guess." Jasmin nodded.

"I am too, but don't know what good I will do." Darien nodded.

"Me too." Stephanie nodded. "But I hope that it's not another surprise visit at the hospital."

"Good." Lucas nodded. "So I will get the train schedules for Saturday and figure out how to get there. Cougar, will you take care of the rest?"

Marcus nodded in reply.

"That's settled then." Cedric grinned. "What do we do now?"

"Hey don't look at me," Lucas laughed when, as usual, everyone was looking in his direction. Unfortunately for him, the others seemed not to care about his comment too much.

"Since everyone is staring at me anyway, maybe you can help my curiosity out a little," Lucas finally started.

"Your curiosity? That's a new one. Normally you are the one satisfying our curiosity," Cedric laughed.

"Bring it on." Darien smiled at him and the others nodded.

"OK." Lucas looked first at Darien, then at Jasmin. "Tell me what the deal is with Airmid."

"What do you mean?" Stephanie looked surprised.

"Well, we all know you in your usual way. Always active and dedicated, but also always a little shy and insecure," Lucas started. "No offense meant," he quickly added.

"None taken." Stephanie smiled.

"But the day we faced Wolfman, you were…" Lucas thought for a moment before he continued. "Different. Focused, cool… Powerful would be a fitting term."

"Thank you." Stephanie smiled even more now.

"The thing is… I have seen this side of you again a few times over the past months, last when you worked that miracle with Cougar in the hospital. But at most of those times, Psycho was involved in it somehow." Lucas looked around. "So what's the deal?"

"I hope you don't expect me to give you an answer to that." Stephanie's smile had vanished. "I certainly am aware of this, but I have no clue what it is, other than Psycho's magic."

"Psycho's magic would explain a lot of things, but not the attitude you had with Wolfman." Lucas looked at her.

A minute of silence followed. Lucas eagerly looked from one to the other, waiting for one of them to answer. Then he caught a strange thing. Darien and Jasmin were looking at each other way too often and way too intensely for his comfort.

"Psycho? Professor? Anything you would like to share?" He addressed them.

"Do you want to tell him? Or should I?" Jasmin asked Darien.

"Be my guest." Darien made an inviting gesture.

"We also noticed the behavior during the Wolfman incident. I think we all did," Jasmin started. "At that time I didn't think too much of it either, but a while later, during the summer camp, the Professor approached me."

"You remember when Airmid brewed her first potion?" Darien jumped in. "That was the first time Psycho had brought her into this state of mind, and that's when I noticed something within her."

Darien paused for a moment to see if Jasmin would pick up again. Then he continued. "I had a chat with Psycho about this, trying to figure it out, but it took way longer to get to the bottom of this, at least as far bottom as we could go."

"Go on." Lucas was eager to hear more.

"Airmid's zodiac sign is Gemini," Darien continued. "And she seems to be a very typical case of a Gemini. You see, I always saw two very different energy patterns flowing in her body. And it turns out that those are two very different faces of her. So I approached Psycho again and discussed the theory with her, and it turns out that we pretty quickly came to the same conclusion."

"So when you did calm Airmid down in the hospital, it was not really you calming her down, but you just brought her second face to the surface?" Lucas was amazed.

"Yes, exactly." Jasmin nodded.

"Why didn't you tell me?" he asked

"And why didn't you tell ME?" Stephanie asked in a quite annoyed tone.

"Because we have been asked to keep it to ourselves as long as possible," Darien sighed.

"By whom?" Lucas was curious.

"Take an educated guess, Guardian," Jasmin said with a short laugh.

"Sometimes that woman drives me crazy." Lucas shook his head.

"Who are you talking about?" Cedric hadn't followed yet.

"Angel, of course," Lucas answered. "So what's the deal with it, then? And why can you tell us now?"

"Angel asked us to keep it under the wraps as long as possible," Darien said.

"And she explicitly asked me to not work that trick again, unless it really mattered," Jasmin added.

"So how can I make use of that second face myself, then?" Stephanie was curious.

"That, unfortunately, is something I was explicitly asked to not tell you at all, Airmid. It seems you have to find out on your own." Darien looked a little unhappy.

"Sometimes I hate that, too." Stephanie was between smiling and crying when she looked at Lucas. "But it seems that's the way we have to go."

"Don't worry, Airmid." Lucas laid his arm around her. "I don't have that order from Angel, so I will try to help you figure it out if you like."

"Thanks," she replied with a small smile.

"Maybe we can give you a chance for that right now? While doing a little alchemy?" Jasmin suggested. "We haven't done this for a long time, and you have after all fallen a little short on training time over these past months, anyway."

As everyone agreed, they used up the remainder of the afternoon and evening to try some new ideas Stephanie brought up, but with mixed success. In the end all potions had the problem that they diminished in power pretty quickly and no matter what Stephanie tried to do, this effect seemed uncontrollable. Also, no matter how hard she tried, her insecurity was always around.

"We will figure it out at some point," Darien said to her when they were packing up. "But it seems that you will need a completely different approach to this matter."

"I agree." Stephanie nodded. "And I am sure at some point we will find it together."

On his way home Lucas thought a lot about Stephanie and her two faces. He too was a Gemini, but somehow he had never felt that he had an alter ego. The further he thought, the more he came to realize that this was not true, though. The two lives he had juggled over the past year and a half proved that all too well. And there was a part within him that he rarely let out at all, not because he wouldn't know how, but rather because he didn't like that part too much. He thought back to the moment when he and Jasmin had come under attack because people mistook them for Satanists. When that guy hit Jasmin with the baseball bat, Lucas had just gone berserk. The result was a completely uncontrolled first shot of his now well known 'Repellum' charm that sent the guy crashing into a wall. In this very second he would have killed the guy if he had had the power to, and that very fact made Lucas afraid of himself right now. But the more he thought about it now the more he realized that this was also a part of him, and if he ever wanted to rise to his true potential, he would need to embrace this part as well. And that thought scared him even more.

Over the next days he had little time to think about it further, as school kept him busy and all the time he had left went into planning the trip for the weekend. When Saturday finally arrived, Lucas was eager to get going and find the thieves' hideout. He could almost feel the success coming up, but dismissed that thought quickly, as he was all too aware that chances were in fact slim they would find anything at all.

"Ready to catch some thieves?" Marcus seemed even more amped up than him when he greeted him at the train station.

"Always ready, yes, but I doubt that it will happen at first try," Lucas said.

"Positive thoughts, mate," Cedric grinned. "I can feel that we will hit the jackpot today."

"As long as it's not Jack hitting us with a pot I am good with that," Lucas laughed. "But let's try not to get ahead of ourselves, shall we?"

They hopped into the train and found themselves a seat. The train was mostly empty, so they could talk freely.

"I got us a map of the area." Marcus laid it between them.

Lucas could see that he had drawn a lot of lines and marks onto it, all over a certain area.

"And I came up with a search grid for today," Marcus continued.

He then explained the plan to Lucas and Cedric, pointing out their moving paths, as well as a few special areas that he considered to be hotspots.

"Why is your grid so much wider here than it is on the other side?" Cedric asked, pointing out the walking lines. "Do you think we would run out of time otherwise?"

"Chances are that we run out of time no matter what," Marcus laughed. "But no, those are farther apart because in this area there are a lot of small hills and open areas, so we should be able to cover a wider radius with each pass."

"Where do we start?" Lucas asked, still studying the map.

"My plan was to start at the point farthest away from the train station. It gives us more ground to cover before we actually start, but it means that we don't have the extra mile to go at the end."

"Good plan," Cedric grinned.

"Yeah. If they are in the area we will find them before lunch time." Marcus nodded.

"Looking forward to it." Cedric still grinned.

"Just let me be very clear..." Lucas looked Marcus straight in the eyes. "If we should find them, we will call police and only risk a fight if we absolutely have to."

"Yes, boss." Marcus nodded. He seemed very unhappy with the statement, but the way he had responded made it very clear to Lucas that he not only understood the plan, but in fact accepted it. Lucas was uncertain, though, if this was out of respect for him, or just because Marcus also was not very fond of the thought of getting shot again.

The boys continued discussing the details over the reminder of the train ride. A lot seemed still unclear, although Marcus had gone through quite some lengths to plan ahead as good as humanly possible.

"All set?" Lucas asked when they had gotten out of the train.

"Let's check our equipment again, just to be sure." Marcus had set his backpack down on a bench and opened it.

"OK, let's see." Lucas followed his lead, and so did Cedric. "Enough water?"

"Check," Marcus replied.

"Food."

"Check." This time Cedric nodded.

"Compass?"

"Check." Marcus pulled it out and opened it quickly.

"Cell phones?" he then asked.

"Check," both of them replied at the same time.

"What else?" Lucas could not see anything else in his backpack.

"GPS," Marcus commented and pulled the device out, waiting for it to come online.

"And check." He nodded after it did.

"Money," Cedric threw in. "At least enough on each of us to get us back home."

"Check," Lucas replied after having a quick look at his wallet.

"Check," Marcus also replied shortly after.

"Then we are all set." Lucas smiled after all of them had picked up their backpacks again. "Let's find some thieves."

CHAPTER 6

Lair

The three boys left the train station, Marcus leading them. The first part of the way they walked along a country road that was bordered by wide open fields on one side and a forest on the other. For Lucas it almost felt spooky. He knew that they had just left a train station behind that was on the edge of a village, but even though they were still quite close, there was no sign of civilization around. The road was covered with snow and ice, the set of tire tracks in it seemed hours old, and nothing moved around here, other than the trees waving in the wind. Lucas watched his surroundings carefully, but even after more than an hour of walking, nothing had changed. The only sign of other people being in the area was a smoking chimney he could see on the horizon. But at that distance he couldn't even tell if it was a house or a factory that he was seeing.

"Finally." Marcus brought Lucas out of his thoughts.

"Are we there?" Cedric seemed majorly out of breath.

"You should try getting some more exercise," Marcus laughed. "But yes, we are here. Now we head in and start looking."

"Maybe we should take a few minutes so we can all catch our breath," Lucas suggested. "We might need it, after all."

Marcus nodded, cleaned the snow from a rock and sat down. "But we shouldn't wait too long. If we cool down too much, we might catch a cold."

Lucas nodded and also sat down. After he was sure that Cedric was back on track, he nodded toward Marcus.

"Let's head on," he said.

Marcus had pulled out his compass and started leading them through the thick forest. He was so light-footed that Lucas and Cedric had trouble keeping up with him. Lucas tried to keep track of where they were going while at the same time looking around for any clues, but both seemed more or less impossible.

"Damn, that's bad." Marcus suddenly stopped and grabbed his GPS.

"What is it?" Lucas walked up to him.

"Look at this." Marcus showed Lucas the compass and then, while Lucas was watching, took a few steps back. Much to Lucas' amazement the compass needle moved a few degrees off.

"What is that?" he asked.

"Magnetic field obviously," Marcus commented. "Some of the iron in this area seems to distort the earth's natural field, which brought us off track."

"So what do we do?" Lucas looked at him.

"The obvious," Marcus laughed. "Switch to a different navigation device and get back on track." With that he put his compass in his pocket and looked at his GPS.

"Good idea." Lucas grinned. "Could have been mine."

Marcus quickly led them back to where they were supposed to be, and they continued on to the first hotspot.

"Careful now," he said and stopped. "The area ahead has fewer trees than we had so far. And we are heading up a hillside."

"So what makes this area a hotspot?" Cedric asked.

"Up on the hill there are a lot of good places to hide. And from up there you have a good look out over the surrounding area, so you see people approaching from a long distance away."

"How will we get up there without being seen by them, then?" Lucas asked.

"Carefully," Marcus laughed. "But honestly, I don't think that this will be the place."

"Why?" Lucas was curious.

"Because it has a drawback: No roads lead up there. So you would have to carry everything."

"Let's still be careful," Lucas suggested.

They slowly walked up the hillside, trying to get as much cover as possible from the trees, but Lucas was pretty sure that if somebody was up there they would have spotted them nonetheless. Much to his relief Marcus had been right, and there was nothing there. The place looked undisturbed and empty.

"Nothing here," Cedric commented.

"Yeah, and nothing in the surrounding area either," Marcus replied after having an intensive look with his binoculars.

"So let's keep moving, then," Lucas said.

Marcus nodded and headed off toward the next area, and the next after that. They had searched quite a number of places when they finally decided to stop for lunch.

"I guess this will be a nice hike, but nothing more," Cedric said after taking the final bite of his sandwich.

"Yeah, unfortunately it seems so." Marcus didn't seem too happy about this.

"Relax, Cougar. Our chances were slim to start with," Lucas reminded him and also finished up his meal.

Lucas could understand Marcus' frustration all too well, but he tried not to let this shine through. They continued walking the pattern as proposed, moving back closer to the train station the farther they got.

"We will lose daylight soon." Cedric looked up between the trees.

"Yeah." Marcus nodded. "But we only have one spot left, then we are through anyway."

They slowly walked up to the last hotspot Marcus had had on his map. It was a very dense patch of forest, with a small dirt path leading into nowhere. From looking at the map, Lucas assumed that at some earlier time this area had been worked by lumberjacks.

"Stop," Marcus suddenly whispered and jumped behind a tree.

"What is it?" Lucas and Cedric had taken cover as well.

"Something moved up ahead." Marcus was still whispering.

Lucas waited silently, watching the area Marcus had pointed out, but there was nothing there--at least nothing he could recognize. Marcus had started sneaking forward, one tree at a time. Lucas and Cedric followed him a few steps behind, trying to move in the shadows as well, as much as possible. Finally Lucas could spot the movement, as well. A person in a black suit was walking up and down a small open area not even 20 meters away. Even though this guy walked openly, he somehow managed to move from shadow to shadow, melting into the background.

"Is that guy using magic?" Cedric whispered.

"I don't know," Lucas replied as quietly as possible. "The way he moves almost looks like it, but nothing else would point to it."

"So what do we do?" Cedric asked.

"Let's wait a little while and watch," Lucas replied.

"Silence," Marcus whispered, pointing down to the open area.

Lucas once more had trouble recognizing what Marcus had seen. But then, suddenly, he saw a second guy walking up to the first one, wearing a similar black suit and also moving from shadow to shadow.

"What are you doing out here?" the second man asked the first one.

"Waiting for Carl to return with something to decent to eat. Stupid boy," the first one replied.

"Where did you send him?"

"Town… And he should have been back by now."

"Why did you send him there? All he will do is get stuck in a pub and come back drunk and without food for you."

"What would you suggest I had done?"

"Watch and learn." The second guy pulled out a knife and walked a few steps towards the denser forest.

"What is he trying to do?" Cedric asked, once again whispering.

"I don't know," Lucas replied. "I am having a hard time seeing him, not to mention understanding what he does."

For about a minute nothing happened. Then suddenly Lucas could see the knife blinking in the fading sunlight and a moment later he heard the guy laughing.

"That's what you do," he said another minute later when he came walking back out of the forest with a rabbit stuck on his knife.

"Did this guy just really hunt down a rabbit with a knife?" Cedric was amazed.

"Seems so." Lucas nodded.

The guy had handed over the knife with the rabbit on it to his companion and then both walked off.

"That was truly amazing," Marcus whispered.

"Could you do something like that?" Cedric asked him.

"Maybe, but if at all then only with the help of magic," Marcus responded. "That being said, I am not a hunter…"

"And you think this guy is?" Cedric still seemed amazed.

"I think this guy is amazing. I don't know if he is a hunter, survivor, soldier, spy or ninja, but whatever he is, he is good."

"Yeah, and he is not alone," Lucas threw in. "The way this other guy moved is almost the same. Although he seemed to have no idea how to get the rabbit."

The others nodded silently.

"What do we do now?" Marcus finally asked.

"Find out where they went, I would suggest," Lucas said.

The boys slowly sneaked up in the direction where the two thieves had left. It was easy for them to stay in the shadows of the forest and with daylight already fading they had no trouble at all staying invisible.

"Look, there." Marcus was again the first one to spot the hideout.

A few meters away from them a hut had been built into the middle of the forest. It looked old, the windows almost opaque and the wooden walls overgrown with climbing plants. Smoke was coming out of the chimney, and Lucas could spot flickering light through the milky window glass. Next to it a tent was erected, almost as tall as the hut, painted in camouflage coloring. Fitting for the winter, a net had been thrown over it, covering it in white and beige colors, almost melting it into the landscape. Lucas had seen tents like this before, but only in movies. They were normally used by armed forces for equipment storage. Between the hut and the tent Lucas could see some bundles lying on the floor but couldn't identify what they were.

"I will have a quick peek through the window," Marcus whispered.

"Be careful." Lucas nodded and watched him sneak away.

It was long two minutes for Lucas and Cedric until Marcus finally arrived back from his trip.

"Can't see anything through the milky glass." Marcus shook his head when he had ducked back into cover with them. "Only shades and shadows."

"Do you know what those are?" Cedric pointed at the bundles Lucas had recognized earlier.

"Camo-nettings I would guess," Marcus whispered. "Most likely to cover a vehicle."

"I would like to take a look into the tent too if you are OK with it," Marcus continued after a short moment of silence.

"OK." Lucas nodded.

Marcus had just stepped out of his cover and was about to run over to the tent when Lucas heard the sound of a car approaching.

"Cougar! Caution!" he yelled with a dampened voice, but Marcus obviously had heard it himself.

"Levipes," Lucas heard him say before taking a leap back into cover--and not a moment too soon, it turned out. Marcus was not even back on his feet yet when a van drove around the corner. It was painted completely white, which made it hard to spot in the snow, and the fact that it had no lights on didn't help.

"There comes Carl," Cedric whispered.

Lucas nodded and watched a guy jumping out of the van after parking it between the hut and the tent. He was wearing all black, too, and was carrying a paper bag. After the guy had vanished into the hut Marcus started his run again, only to have to do another leap back when the guy stepped back out again a few seconds later. To Lucas' consternation Carl had stopped on the doorstep and was looking in their direction. His thoughts were racing. Had the thief seen them? What would they do if he approached? Where to run to?

"What's up, Carl?" a voice asked from within the hut.

"I thought I saw something moving," the thief replied.

"Afraid of bears again?" the guy from within the hut laughed. "Shut the damn door, it's cold."

"Yes, sure." Carl nodded and closed the door.

Lucas sighed in relief as the thief walked up to the car. He watched him picking up the bundle that was sitting right next to it, unrolling it and throwing it over the van. Marcus had been right, it was a white camouflage net, identical to the one that had been thrown over the tent. And with it the car almost completely vanished into the landscape, hard to spot for anybody who didn't know what to look for.

"I am going over there now," Marcus whispered.

"No." Lucas shook his head. "You have nearly been caught twice. We should call the police now."

"Whatever you say." Marcus was clearly unhappy but stayed in cover.

Lucas quickly pulled out his cell phone, but to his annoyance there was no reception out here in the forest.

"I can't get a signal here. How about you?" Lucas asked the others.

"No." Marcus shook his head.

"Same here." Cedric shook his head, too.

"Damn," Lucas cursed. "One of us needs to get back to civilization and make that call."

"I will go." Cedric offered. "But how do I lead the police here? Where exactly are we?"

"Take this." Marcus quickly scribbled some numbers on a piece of paper.

"What's that?" Cedric asked.

"GPS coordinates. That should help you get back here. And also take my compass. The train station is due south; you should be able to find it easily."

"OK, I will try to hurry." Cedric nodded and retreated hastily.

Lucas and Marcus sat in their cover position for about five minutes after Cedric had left, watching the area with nothing happening.

"They will not come out again," Marcus suddenly whispered. "We should try to find out as much as we can until the police arrive. Just in case."

"Ok." Lucas nodded after thinking for a moment. "But I will come with you this time."

"Sure." Marcus grinned and started slowly working up his way to the hut.

"We should maybe go around there and approach from the far side of the tent. They will not be able to spot us from there," Lucas suggested.

"Good idea." Marcus nodded and changed direction accordingly.

They slowly walked up to the tent, trying to make as little noise as possible.

"I will try taking some pictures of the van." Marcus walked past the tent. "Get the license plate, and whatever else I can."

"Good idea." Lucas nodded. "But don't forget to switch off the flash."

"Thanks for the reminder," Marcus grinned.

Lucas watched him walk up to the van and between it and the tent. He could see him taking pictures of the license plate, the tires, the driver's door, a shot through the windshield and the back of the vehicle.

"I am not sure how much good those will do us." Marcus whispered after arriving back at Lucas' position. "But better to have them."

"License plate should help, if nothing else," Lucas said.

"The ID number might. The plates don't match front and rear, so they are most likely counterfeit or stolen."

"Good catch. I would not have seen that, most likely," Lucas complimented.

"Shall we look into the tent now?" Marcus suggested.

"Sure." Lucas nodded and followed Marcus sneaking to the tent entrance.

Inside there were some crates piled up in multiple piles, but most of the space was taken up by wood, water bottles and other things that looked like supplies.

"Why did he send the guy to town when they have all they need right here?" Marcus walked through the piles.

"Maybe he wanted to get something other than canned food for a change." Lucas shrugged his shoulders. "Or maybe they are storing this for later use."

"Some of the pallets are open, so I doubt it." Marcus shook his head.

"Maybe they have stolen this as well?" Lucas suggested.

"That would be hardly worth the risk don't you think? I mean… Who steals water bottles?" Marcus was still looking around.

"Good point. Let's have a look at those crates there." Lucas walked over to the piles.

"Most of those have the Brix & Burton logo stamped on the lid," Marcus said after having a look, aided by his cell phone's backlight. "So they seem to be from last week's robbery."

"Agreed." Lucas nodded. "But that would mean that they either have done this the first time, or they have already sold everything else they stole." Lucas looked around, but there were no other piles to see.

"Or maybe they have a stash somewhere, and this is just their hideout," Marcus suggested.

"Good point." Lucas nodded.

"Hey, look here." Marcus had walked up to another crate. "Those are the same crates, but they have no logo on them."

"That's strange." Lucas walked over. "And look, it's only a few that are missing the logo; the rest of the pile has it."

"Yeah, down here is another one." Marcus had looked through the entire pile. "Seems they were also taken from Brix & Burton."

"Maybe they are newer? And not yet stamped?" Lucas suggested.

"Might be." Marcus nodded. "Let's open one up and have a look."

Lucas watched Marcus pull out a pocket knife and start levering the crate open.

"Packed to the limits it seems," he said after putting the knife back into his pocket.

Lucas looked into the crate now too. It was filled with wooden flakes and some raw sawdust.

"Let's see what we have here." Marcus had started bulging through it, pulling out a flask in the end.

"What is that?" He looked at it under the light of his phone. "No label, no logo, just a plain flask."

"I've seen those before." Lucas became a little pale when he pulled out one of them himself.

"Where?" Marcus asked.

"Cypher gave me one exactly like it in Buxton," Lucas answered. "With that strange, smelling substance in it. You remember that, don't you? After all, you were there with me."

"Right." Marcus nodded and looked at the flask again too. "And the substance also looks quite similar."

"I would not go that far." Lucas laughed quietly. "Transparent, oily liquid is not that uncommon now, is it? Most likely it's just the same flask."

"I'll still take one with me." Marcus pocketed the one he was holding.

"Let's have a look into another one of those, shall we?" he then pointed out a second unmarked crate.

"Sure." Lucas nodded and started taking some pictures with his phone.

"Watch out," he suddenly whispered urgently at Marcus, but it was already too late.

Marcus had pulled the second crate over to get a better grasp on it, but with this had caused the open one to tip over and crash into the ground with a loud thud.

"Damn it," Marcus cursed and jumped back.

Lucas had a quick look. About hundred flasks had fallen out of the crate and smashed on the forest floor.

"Let's hope that this was not highly toxic." Lucas took a step back, too.

"Let's even more hope that this was not too loud," Marcus threw in.

"What was that?" Lucas heard a voice from outside the tent.

"Seems it was." Lucas immediately became alert. He also shoved the flask into his pocket and turned, facing the tent entrance.

"It came from the storage tent. Hopefully not another wolf." He heard another voice from outside.

"What now?" Lucas looked at Marcus.

"Get ready for them," Marcus replied, focusing on the tent entrance now, too.

The first guy had come running into the tent with a flashlight in his hand. When he saw Lucas and Marcus, he immediately stopped.

"Intruders!" he shouted.

"Here comes the fun part," Marcus said.

"Repellum," Lucas cast and tossed the guy back out of the tent.

A second guy looked around the corner of the entrance.

"That's the guy from the chem-plant," he then shouted.

"How did he get here? I did shoot him, didn't I?" another one asked from behind.

"Obviously you didn't. But we can change that," a third person said.

"Oh-oh," Lucas heard Marcus say and at the same moment he heard a metal clicking outside that sounded like the loading of a gun.

"Seperatio." He casted, forming a shield over the tent entrance. "We need to get out of here right away," he then said to Marcus.

"I agree." Marcus nodded and looked around.

Lucas also started looking for another way out, but there was only one entrance, and that one was blocked. The next thing he heard was shots from at least two pistols being fired right through the tent entrance, but luckily his shield held. Looking there he could see at least three guys standing outside.

"Time to go," Marcus yelled from behind.

Lucas quickly turned around and saw a hole that Marcus had cut into the tent. He nodded, quickly jumped through it and continued running off into the forest. He could hear Marcus following close behind and some more steps following behind Marcus. A quick look over his shoulder showed at least five flashlights in pursuit, motivating him to run even faster. After about five minutes he finally stopped, completely out of breath.

"I think we lost them." Marcus had stopped right next to him. He did not seem too exhausted at all.

"I think they just stopped following us." Lucas gasped for air.

"I counted at least five back there. How about you?" Marcus asked.

"Same." Lucas nodded.

"We need to get back to them," Marcus said. "We can't let them get away."

"Are you kidding me?" Lucas couldn't believe his ears. "We just barely escaped. You don't really want to face those shooting-frenzy clowns again, do you?"

"We need to stop them from getting away," Marcus protested.

"Five on two might work in summer camp, but not in a gunfight," Lucas objected. "We can head back there if you like, but we will stay in cover and not risk another run-in with those goons."

"OK, let's go." Marcus nodded.

Lucas sighed a little but then followed Marcus, who slowly and carefully made his way back toward the hut, watching every step and trying to ensure that nobody was hiding out around them. It took them more than three times longer to get back than it had taken them to run off, but in the end they finally arrived at the hut.

What they found was unexpected, though. The tent was gone; so was all that had been in it. The van was gone, too. Only the shattered crate was still lying on the floor. Lucas started looking around carefully. He could see some bullet casings on the ground and on closer inspection found the projectiles not far away from them, where the entrance of the tent had been only half an hour before. When he and Marcus approached the hut, they could see that the fire was still burning there. They were just about to push the door open when three cars pulled up behind them. Suddenly the place was brightly lit, with all cars turning their headlights on and flashing blue lights appearing on top.

"Armed police! Don't move!" Lucas heard a voice from behind and a group of people suddenly jumped out of the cars.

"Don't shoot! We are the good guys!" Marcus had raised his hands and tried to stay as still as possible.

"Those are my friends," Lucas heard Cedric yell from behind.

"Leave them! Secure the scene!" Lucas heard yet another voice. He still had not moved an inch. "It's all right boys. Come over here."

Lucas slowly turned around. A group of 12 armed police officers in heavy body armor were walking forward now slowly. Behind them he could see another one, his weapon hanging down on a sling, standing next to Cedric. He followed Marcus toward that person.

"I am Inspector Corben, SO-19," the policeman introduced himself.

"I am Marcus Gracer. This is Lucas Trent." Marcus did the intros on their side.

"What happened here?" The inspector asked.

"We tried to gather some evidence, just in case those thieves got away or managed to pull some tricks from their sleeves," Lucas answered. "But unfortunately we broke something and they heard us." Lucas pointed at the crate on the floor.

"What happened then?"

"They started shooting at us, so we made a run for it." Lucas pointed at the shell casings on the floor.

"Clear!" he could hear a man yell from behind. Obviously, they had just finished searching the hut.

"How long ago was that?" the inspector inquired further.

Lucas thought hard. "I honestly didn't look at my watch, but I think about 20 minutes or so."

"Look at your phone, mate. The picture should have the time," Marcus suggested.

"Good idea." Lucas nodded and grabbed his phone.

"Picture?" the inspector asked.

"Yeah, we took some pictures of the van and the crates in the tent," Lucas replied. "I took the last picture just a minute before that little 'oops' with the crate."

He looked through his phone's files.

"Here it is," he finally said. "Exactly 28 minutes ago."

"So you are saying that not even half an hour ago, they still had camp here?" the inspector asked again.

"Yes." Lucas nodded. "They must have worked pretty quickly."

"That is an understatement." The inspector laughed. "You were obviously dealing with professionals."

"We know," Marcus jumped in. "I met some of them already last week when they robbed Brix & Burton."

"Oh, you were the kid that got shot last week?"

"Yes." Marcus nodded.

"Then why did you come here on your own, boy?" The inspector looked unhappy. "Do you have a death wish?"

"Not exactly," Marcus grinned. "We just wanted to find them and make sure they get arrested. We really didn't think they would be here. It was more or less luck that we stumbled upon them."

"It is more or less luck that you are still alive," the inspector laughed. "Please come to us earlier next time, will you?"

"Yes, sir." Lucas nodded.

"How did you find them, anyway?" the inspector continued his inquiry. "After all, our specialists have been working on this for months, and you did it in a few days."

"Dumb luck, I would say," Lucas laughed. "One of our friends came up with the idea of this area."

Lucas quickly told the story of the torn sleeve and the metal traces.

"Impressive detective work," the inspector complimented.

"Can we take a look around now too?" Lucas asked.

"Sure, but please don't touch anything if possible." The inspector nodded.

The boys wandered off and took a look around. Lucas was the first of them to approach the hut again. He was eager to see what the thieves had left behind. The door was wide open; obviously the policemen had not bothered closing it. When he took the first peek into the room, he was amazed. The hut was small, even smaller than their shack--only one room, partly covered with a steerage and a ladder leading up to that. The thieves had not left anything, it seemed. Only from the outlines of the dust on the floor could Lucas tell that there had been five people sleeping in here, but the mattresses were gone now, together with everything else.

"Damn, those guys are good." Lucas was amazed.

"They seem to have trained for a quick escape." Marcus nodded after looking around himself. "They even took the firewood."

"Bears the question why they didn't stop to take the bullet casings and the broken crate." Lucas had stepped out again.

"I would think that they didn't have the time to pick up the shards of the broken flasks, so they left the crate. The bullet casings are a mystery to me, too." Marcus had stepped next to him.

"It's a shame that we didn't get them." Cedric had joined them.

"Yet." Marcus looked at him. "This is not over."

"For today it is I would say." Lucas looked at him. "We should get out of here."

"Agreed." Marcus nodded.

The boys walked back to the inspector, who was still standing near the cars.

"Satisfied?" he asked.

"More or less." Lucas nodded. "It's just a shame that they got away."

"Well, that's life." The inspector laughed. "The good guys don't always win, unfortunately."

"Unfortunately." Lucas nodded.

"All of you will be required to give a statement about today's events," the inspector addressed them. "Our colleagues in Luton will contact you regarding this."

"Of course." Lucas nodded.

"Oh, and they will also want to see all the pictures you took."

"I will collect them off the various phones and prepare a copy." Lucas nodded again.

"Very well then." The inspector smiled. "I have your contact details already from Mr. Mason, so if you want, you are free to go. We can, of course, also give you a ride back to Luton if you like, but then you will have to wait a little longer, until we are finished here."

Lucas quickly looked at the others before responding. "I think we will wait around, if you would be so kind to give us a lift," he then said to the Inspector. "I am not really in the mood for a train ride right now."

"Understandable." The inspector smiled.

"Area is secured, sir. No incidents," another policeman said, walking by them.

"Thank you, Constable." The inspector nodded.

Lucas and the others followed Inspector Corben to the largest car. It was a command van of sorts, with a lot of room in the back. He offered them seats inside and took one himself, next to a woman who was sitting at a computer and radio. Lucas was happy about sitting down after the events of the day, all the more as the car was properly heated.

"Area secured, no hostile contacts," the inspector said to her, watching her type some sort of protocol.

A short while later the door was opened by another policeman.

"Tracks lead down to the main access road and are untraceable thereafter, sir," the officer said. "And Forensics just arrived."

"Thank you, Sergeant." The inspector nodded before he turned to Lucas. "Seems we will be on our way shortly, boys." Then he jumped out of the van.

Lucas had made himself comfortable in the corner. He had not felt it so far, but was now starting to get really tired. After all, he was not used to so much physical activity. Cedric and Marcus were sitting on the opposite side of the van. Cedric also looked exhausted, while Marcus still seemed to be pumping with energy. Lucas again was amazed at Marcus' stamina and for the first time felt a little jealous about it. He closed his eyes and tried to relax.

A sharp breeze brought Lucas out of his daze. The inspector had opened the door just a little bit and was standing outside talking to somebody.

"The area is secured and my men have all pulled out, so the scene is yours." He spoke to someone Lucas couldn't see.

"Thank you, inspector. Please make sure that we get DNA swabs from all your people for comparison," the other person, a woman, said.

"Sure will. Including the three boys." The inspector nodded. "Do you need anything else from us, or can we head out?"

"I am good, but only the chief can call that shot," the woman replied.

Lucas could see the shadow of a third person approaching.

"Inspector Corben, SO-19," the inspector introduced himself and shook the other guys' hands.

"Detective Chief-Inspector Murphy, C.S.I.," the other one replied. "If Forensics is good with the crime scene, I don't want to keep you. Have a good night and a safe trip back."

Lucas had the strange feeling that he had heard this voice before, but he was very unsure. He tried to get a quick peek at the person, but it was too dark outside to see.

"Thank you, Chief-Inspector," Corben replied with a nod. "SO-19, move out!" he then shouted and stepped into the vehicle.

Lucas quickly dismissed the other policeman. He was happy that they were finally on their way home.

CHAPTER 7

Challenges

Two days later Lucas was back on his way to O'Brien Mansion. He had spent a quiet Sunday and used his time between school and the meeting to walk to the police station, so that they wouldn't call him at a bad time. After all, he didn't want his parents to become aware of what had just happened. It had been bad enough that Mrs. Gracer had told his mother about the shooting incident with Marcus; her finding out about the trip from Saturday might have resulted in his first detention in years. But now that he had it gotten over with, he felt better again. And he was confident that the police would find the perpetrators shortly; the license plates, vehicle ID number and the logo on the van should provide enough evidence for them. And all of those were clearly visible on the pictures he had handed over.

Arriving at the shack, Lucas was last this time. The fire was already burning and the others had settled down at the table waiting for him to show up. It was a strange mood, though, when he entered the room. The three stay-behinds seemed primarily happy that everything went more or less fine, although Jasmin seemed to be a little beaten up as far as Lucas could tell; Cedric was cheerful to no limits because they had actually found the thieves and provided evidence en masse to the police; only Marcus seemed deeply frustrated.

"Now we can finally hear the details." Darien smiled after Lucas had closed the door behind himself. And before he could even reach the chair Stephanie had jumped in his arms.

"I'm glad that you are all back safely," she said, nearly knocking him over once again.

"Back safely, but only partially successful," he replied and sat down. He then told the others in detail what had happened, stopping sometimes to let Cedric and Marcus add some comments.

"I'm impressed," Darien said. "And of course I would love to see those pictures, as well."

"I sent them to you about two hours ago," Lucas grinned. "Have fun with them."

He then turned to Marcus and Cedric. "Have you guys been with the police already, giving your statement?"

"Yeah." Cedric nodded. "Was a short one for me, though. I was, after all, not present when the action commenced."

"Me too." Marcus nodded as well. "Unfortunately, I made the mistake of telling them that I took one of the flasks."

"Why was that a mistake?" Darien asked.

"Because they made me give it to them as evidence." Marcus looked contrite. "And I really wanted to show it to you, Professor."

"I totally forgot about that." Lucas almost had to laugh.

"Why? You didn't take one, did you?" Marcus looked at him.

"Yes I did." Lucas nodded. "I had one in my hand when you threw the crate down and just pushed it in my pocket when the thieves approached us. It should still be there. I totally forgot about it."

"So where is it?" Darien was snoopy.

"In my other jeans. Hanging on a clothesline to dry," Lucas answered. "Well... Just hanging there right now, I would guess. It should be dry already. I'll bring it with next week. It's the same flask Cypher gave us at the camp, but I highly doubt that there is anything special in there. Brix & Burton just seems to have the same container manufacturer as our black friends."

"Maybe that's a way to track Cypher and his friends?" Darien suggested. "Cougar's father can for sure find the manufacturer of those."

"Worth a try." Lucas nodded.

"It's still a shame that we didn't catch those guys on Saturday." Marcus was still unhappy.

"I agree." Lucas nodded. "But we gave the police a lot of hints and clues, so they can track them down easily now."

"I would still love to be there when they get them," Marcus said. "Can't we try to track them down ourselves?"

"I think it will be hard for us to track license plates and VINs, Cougar. The only hint we have to go on is that logo on the door." Lucas tried to slow Marcus down a little. "But you could go and ask Inspector Corben if he would be so kind as to keep you in the loop. I highly doubt that he will do that, though."

"And it's not Corben that you would need," Cedric added. "SO-19 only comes in when the action is happening. You would need this other guy--what was his name again?"

"Murphy, I think. Detective Chief-Inspector." Lucas nodded in reply.

"Sounds important." Stephanie grinned. "Detective Chief-Inspector."

"You are right." Darien looked thoughtful. "Why would a DCI be involved in a simple robbery?"

"What do you mean, Professor?" Marcus asked.

"A DCI normally oversees multiple investigation teams. People at that level rarely get involved in cases themselves and even more rarely respond to a scene like the one on Saturday. Unless, of course, the case is highly complex or needs a careful hand."

"Well, Inspector Corben said that they have been searching for those guys for months, so maybe the case is way bigger than the Brix & Burton incident," Lucas suggested. "Maybe those are really the guys that had stolen the things from Whirlwind's dad as well."

"That would explain a DCI involvement." Darien nodded. "But it would be even stranger then."

"How so?" Lucas asked.

"Thieves are normally highly specialized." Darien said. "I mean, an art thief will most likely never steal a car. And from what you told us so far those guys are not highly specialized; they are top-notch pros. So why would they first steal from a soda factory and then from a chemistry plant? Where is the connection?"

"Well, first of all, those thefts were pretty similar from all we know." Lucas tried to find an answer. "Goods stolen from a storage room, with the simple pattern of stealth."

"Simple pattern." Cedric laughed.

"Simple from the idea," Lucas corrected himself. "Highly difficult to do."

"So?" Darien was not convinced.

"Maybe they are just common thieves? Maybe they are just out to sell whatever they can steal?" Lucas suggested.

"I don't believe that, sorry." Darien shook his head.

"Any why not?" Lucas asked.

"Jesus, Guardian," Darien started. "Those guys make Ethan Hunt look like an incompetent school boy. People who can do this don't just steal for fun."

"Who is Ethan Hunt?" Stephanie asked.

"You don't watch TV that often, do you?" Marcus laughed. "Ethan Hunt is an action hero. The main character of 'Mission Impossible'. And the Professor is right. Those guys make him look like a rookie in comparison."

"So what are you saying? That there is an evil plot behind this?" Lucas asked.

"I would tend to think so, yes." Darien nodded. "At least, there has to be something more behind it than pure chance. I mean… Those guys bypass highly advanced security systems, they move like Ninjas from all I have heard and they are ruthless enough to just shoot to kill, without hesitation. Come on, does this sound like a common thief to you?"

"You are right, Professor, but I still don't see the connection." Lucas nodded. "The goods they stole from the Masons were not that valuable to justify the risk and effort. I don't know what they stole from Brix & Burton, but I highly doubt that they have high value materials there, either. There must be something else behind this."

"But unfortunately, I don't think that we are the right people to find out," he quickly added. "Maybe we will read it in the news at some point."

"You are most likely right." Darien nodded. "But I will look at the pictures anyway, maybe we'll get another lucky break."

The discussion about the topic went on until late into the evening. In the end Lucas was almost glad when the meeting was over; the topic had started causing him a headache and he almost couldn't stand it anymore. He was especially frustrated that after Marcus, now Darien also seemed to be more than eager to get to the bottom of the issue, and not only Cedric but also Stephanie went along much of the time. Only Jasmin didn't get involved at all, which felt very strange to him. It was almost as if she was far away with her thoughts. Lucas decided to stay out of it as much as he could. He even took the flask to school on Tuesday to hand it to Darien, hoping that the topic would be done before next Monday's meeting and they could focus on other things again. To his delight Darien had work to do when he approached him and didn't have time to bring up the issue again, so Lucas just put the flask into his backpack and left him to it.

When he came back home from school that Tuesday his mother caught him before he even had a chance to take his schoolbag up to his room.

"Honey, is that you?" she shouted from the living room before he had even closed the door.

"Yeah, it's me, Mum," he replied, untying his shoes.

"Could you please come in here? We need to talk," she asked.

Lucas immediately got a little nervous. Had his mother found out about the Saturday incident? He quickly dropped his backpack and put his jacket on the hanger before stepping into the living room. To his surprise, his mother was sitting on the couch drinking tea with Stephanie's mother.

"Good afternoon, Mrs. O'Brien." Lucas smiled at her, although he now was even more uneasy. "I did not expect to see you here."

"Hello Lucas." Mrs. O'Brien looked a little uneasy, too. "I hope the timing is not too inconvenient?"

"Ah, nonsense, Agatha," his mother smiled. "Come, honey, please sit down."

"Sure." Lucas nodded and slowly walked over to the couch. He still had no clue what was going on, and the situation made him very uncomfortable.

"So what brings you to us?" Lucas asked after having sat down.

"It is about Stephanie," Mrs. O'Brien started. "But you will have figured as much already."

Lucas still didn't get the scene. Stephanie's mother seemed strangely nervous, which was unusual; after all, whenever he had met her before she had been very hard and focused. At the same time his mother seemed awfully cheerful, which was also strange. He just couldn't make any sense of it.

"Is something wrong with her?" Lucas asked.

"Well, no," Mrs. O'Brien almost stuttered. "I don't know how to ask you this…"

"What is it?" Lucas grew more uneasy by the second.

Mrs. O'Brien took a deep breath. "You will most likely not understand this, but I am a little worried about her right now."

"And why's that?" Lucas uneasiness changed a little toward curiosity.

"Because one of her friends from school has invited her to a Christmas party."

"And?" Lucas still didn't understand what was going on, but somehow the fact that his mother's grin was getting wider by the second suggested that she knew, and that was annoying to him right now.

"Well… she has never been to a party before," Mrs. O'Brien slowly continued. "And I feel terribly uncomfortable letting my little girl go there. But I also don't want to deny it."

"What Agatha is trying to ask you is if you would take the time to accompany her to that party." Lucas' mother couldn't hold it anymore.

"Sure thing." Lucas was still not sure what was going on. "But why me? I'm not a party person at all."

"Because I am sure that when she is with you she will be safe." Mrs. O'Brien seemed to slowly get her confidence back now that the message was delivered.

"Begging your pardon, Mrs. O'Brien, but do you expect me to be her watchdog on that evening?" Lucas asked. "Because if that's your expectation, I am not sure if I would be able to meet it."

"And why do you think that?" Finally the Mrs. O'Brien Lucas knew seemed to return.

"Well, because your daughter is old enough to make her own choices. And whatever those are, I will respect them. So I will not stop her from doing anything at that party, no matter what." Lucas also by now had his confidence back.

"I know that," she answered. "And even though I would have liked knowing that you watch over her decency as well, I am very well aware that it won't happen. All I am asking is that you watch over her safety."

"And I will happily do that of course." Lucas nodded. "If they let me into the party to begin with, that is."

"They will. I already talked to the parents of that girl."

"If you don't mind me asking, what did Stephanie say to this?" Lucas asked.

"She was not really happy. But she accepted it. Well, we didn't exactly give her much choice in the matter I have to admit…"

"OK. And when will this party be?" Lucas was not sure he liked being drawn into this, but in the end his protector-instinct kept the upper hand.

"Friday evening, week after next. It's not far from our place, so I would appreciate if you could pick her up around 6?" Mrs. O'Brien smiled. "And you can of course sleep in our guest room afterwards if you want."

"I will be there." Lucas nodded. "Anything else?"

"No, thank you, honey." His mother was still grinning.

"Then I will leave you to your tea." Lucas bowed a little, stood up and walked out.

He was happy to get up to his room, and still a little unsure of what had just happened. He was a little annoyed to be asked to be a watchdog for a girl, especially at a party, which was a place he didn't like to be to begin with. But on the other hand, he felt a little proud that Mrs. O'Brien entrusted Stephanie to him. He couldn't really explain why, but this meant a lot more to him than he had thought at first. On the other hand it put him in a strange position. After all it felt as if Stephanie had more or less been forced to accept his presence, and that was something he didn't feel comfortable with. He was just happy that there was still time until then and he would have opportunities to talk to her before that.

Early the next morning Lucas was back in school. He was almost always early, but today he was among the first to arrive there. There was a big two-hour test upcoming and he wanted to be as prepared as possible for it. So he walked straight to the lab rooms and started running through the entire subject matter of the test, trying to challenge himself with scenarios of ever-increasing complexity. It was little surprise to anyone that the real questions and tasks were by far below those, and posed very little challenge in the end. That left Lucas finished with the entire exam after less than one hour, and that was even after he had rechecked everything three times, just to be on the safe side. So he handed in the papers to the teacher and walked back to his seat to study for the upcoming lesson.

"What are you doing?" the teacher asked him as he was approaching his desk.

"Trying not to disturb anyone, Professor Cooper," Lucas replied.

"And you can do this best when you are not in here." The teacher pointed toward the door. "Get out. NOW!"

"Yes, Professor." Lucas nodded and walked out.

Out in the corridor, he was a little unsure what to do. He couldn't prepare for anything, as all his books were in his backpack, which was in the classroom. There was also no lab room available, so he couldn't work there either, and everyone else was in classes, so there was not even a chance to have a chat with somebody, even though he wouldn't have liked to chat right now, anyway. So finally Lucas decided to walk around the building a little and just wait for time to go by. When he came down to the main lobby he had to smile. The hall had been decorated for Christmas already, although that was still a few weeks out. Brushwood had been tied to the handrails in the staircases, a big Advent wreath was hanging from the ceiling with a flickering electric light simulating one burning candle on top and sticky white powder had been distributed all over it, like artificial snow. Even the bulletin board had been decorated in Christmas style, with all the announcements being printed with a frame of either emblazoned fir trees or Santa Clauses in their sleds. Very prominent in the middle of the board was one large poster, with a big letter announcement. "Invitation to the annual Christmas party on December 19th. All students wishing to attend please register at the custodian's office until December 12th."

When Lucas saw the sign his thoughts immediately jumped back to yesterday's talk with Mrs. O'Brien. And almost instantly they started to race around the whole situation again. It was still a very weird feeling for him. So far he was always pretty certain that the others liked being close to him when they were. With this party he was pretty certain that Stephanie would resent him being there, and that he didn't want, no matter what. And the more he thought about it, the more he became sure that what he really wanted was to bail out of this and just not play along with Mrs. O'Brien's wishes. Unfortunately for him this was not an easy thing to do. Not only had he agreed to it yesterday, and he was after all proud of his reliability, but there was the very real risk that her parents would just deny Stephanie the party at all if he was to do that, and that to him felt like treason against her, and was something she surely would resent, and most of all just didn't deserve. Staring out the window, he thought the situation through for a while and only frustration brought him out of those thoughts in the end. The conclusion seemed simple: There was no way for him to win in this. He only had the choice between two bad solutions and needed to figure out which one was the lesser evil, and even that was a hard thing to do. Half an hour and thousands of bad scenarios later, he was close on giving up. Stephanie's friendship meant the world to him and in his mind no matter what he did, the outcome could only be bad. Thinking about this almost made him cry right here, in the middle of the school lobby. Finally he forced himself to stop. He couldn't make a decision on his own; he needed advice in the matter. And he already was desperate, making it hard for him to think clearly. Who did he know that could help him with this? It took him another five minutes from that thought before the obvious choice popped into his mind. With a sigh of relief he grabbed his cell phone and browsed for the right number. And once again he cursed himself for not having his speed dial set up.

"Hi Guardian." The short greeting was from the other side.

"Hi Psycho." Lucas' voice was almost racing. "I am sorry to bother you, but I need your advice."

"Sure. What's up?" Jasmin asked.

"It's a bit complicated to explain that on the phone. Is there any chance we can meet somewhere and talk in person?"

"I am a little incapacitated right now," Jasmin replied. "Unless, of course, you would like to visit me in Dunstable."

"What is in Dunstable?" Lucas was surprised.

"I live there. Didn't you know that?"

"No." Lucas nearly had to laugh.

"It's quite a distance, though. Especially as you don't have a car."

"Honestly, right now I would visit you on the moon if I had to," Lucas said. "Even if I had to walk there."

"All right, I will text you the address, then. Let me know when you are here. I will be home shortly after noon."

"Thanks a lot, Psycho," Lucas said and hung up.

He took a deep breath and sighed in relief. Things would be better now. Jasmin would for sure know what to do. He started walking back up to his classroom, almost cheerful at that moment, when it occurred to him how rude he had just been. Jasmin's comment about being incapacitated was clearly a means of saying that she had other things to do as well, and now that he came to think about it, he had noticed a strange tone in her voice. She sounded cool, almost dissociated, which was not at all like Jasmin, who normally was very warmhearted and inviting in her tone. Suddenly all his joy was gone again and doubt filled his mind. Was he about to stumble into another bad situation with this? Or was it maybe about him in the end? About him invading her privacy? Should he rethink his approach leave her alone and wait for a better moment? In the end he decided to go to Dunstable nonetheless and see what would happen. He could always retreat from there if the situation went sideways, which he desperately hoped it wouldn't.

The break had begun by now and students were starting to fill up the hallways. Lucas was almost back at his classroom when a voice from behind made him stop and turn around.

"Mr. Trent! Hold on a second."

"Yes, sir." He smiled at Professor Tatarski, who was walking up to him.

"I was wondering if you were interested in competing at a contest early next year," the teacher said when he finally had reached him.

"Depends on the type of contest I guess." Lucas was a little unsure.

"It's about computers, of course." Tatarski grinned. "I would like you to meet someone; would you please accompany me?"

"Certainly, sir. But I do have a class starting in five minutes." Lucas nodded and followed him down the aisles.

"I am sure your teacher can spare you for a few minutes, don't you think?" Tatarski patted his shoulder. "What topic is on the menu?"

"Advanced software engineering, sir." Lucas was a little confused now. He was used to strange things going on around him by now, but never so far had a teacher asked him to not be in class.

"That's Professor Simmons, right?" his teacher inquired further. Lucas just nodded.

"Good, good," Tatarski said and pulled out his keys.

Lucas watched him open the door to the teachers' room and took a step to the side when he walked in.

"Are you coming?" the teacher made an inviting gesture.

"Sure." Lucas nodded. He had never been in that room before. Students were normally asked to stay outside or at best wait in the door if they were just fetching something. Slowly he walked in behind the professor and nodded greetings to the teachers he knew. Very much to his astonishment, nobody really seemed to care much about him being in here.

"Hey Mike!" Lucas heard Tatarski shout through the room, the target obviously being Professor Simmons. "I need to borrow Trent for a while. You don't mind, do you?"

"You can't do that. He's the only student in that class who understands what I am talking about," Simmons replied and suddenly half of the teachers in the room started laughing.

"Maybe you should change your teaching style then." Tatarski was laughing, too.

"Seems so." Simmons grinned before turning to Lucas. "Please don't let him scare you away from us. That would be a terrible loss for this school."

"Thank you, Professor." Lucas smiled.

"Thanks Mike." Tatarski patted Simmons' shoulder before addressing Lucas again. "Come on, boy. Let's go."

Lucas followed him into a back room, which turned out to be a meeting room of sorts. At the main table three men were sitting and hacking into their laptops. Two of them seemed to be in their late fifties; the third looked much younger. Lucas estimated him around thirty.

"Mr. Trent, allow me to introduce you to Professors Wainwright, Freeman and Seinefeld." Tatarski introduced first the two older men, then the younger one, waited for Lucas to shake their hands, and then offered him a seat.

"This is Lucas Trent." He then introduced Lucas to the others. "The smartest student we have here in Luton."

"Do you feel ready to represent Luton IT College in this contest?" Professor Wainwright asked Lucas.

"Excuse me?" Lucas felt completely overrun by this question.

"We have not come to that part yet." Tatarski laughed. "I haven't even told him yet what it is all about."

"Oh..." Wainwright smiled. "We should change that then. Graham, would you be so kind?"

"Of course, Professor." The youngest one, Professor Seinefeld, nodded.

"You see..." he turned to Lucas. "We at the universities very often get asked to consult by companies from all around the country concerning different aspects of IT projects. In the past few years this has especially been true for security-relevant topics and design questions along this line, as more and more traditionally offline companies are feeling the need to have an online presence. Lately we have been accused of being too academic with our approaches, and that we are not taking the modern developments into account. That's why we designed a competition for all IT-centric schools and training centers in the country. Every house will send one candidate to compete in a series of challenges, until only the best remains."

"And what types of challenges are those exactly?" Lucas was curious now.

"Computer wars," Seinefeld grinned. "It will basically be showdowns. All competitors in one match, which will normally be two, but sometimes more, get the same business system specification. Your job then will be to make the system foolproof, including a state-of-the-art security for it. After everyone is done, your next task is to penetrate the security of the other systems, while at the same time defending yours from getting hacked. The competitor whose system stays up and running longest wins."

"You know, that sounds extremely cool, but I am not really a security expert. So I highly doubt that I will prove to be very successful in this." Lucas really loved the idea of competing in this, but at the same time was afraid of getting stultified.

"That is why you will get some training before the event and will have two IT security students, one from Oxford and one from Cambridge, at your side during the matches to assist." Freeman jumped in.

"If I get those experts on my side, wouldn't it in the end be more of a challenge between the experts, then?"

"I think you need to explain the rules in more detail for the young man to understand the idea." Professor Wainwright smiled. "You see, Mr. Trent, the 'experts', as you call them, are also only students, so they might have some advantage over you in theory, but not in practical experience. And the rules of the match state that they must not under any circumstances touch the computers themselves."

"Additionally, they will only step in when you ask them to," Seinefeld added.

Lucas still felt unsure about this thing, but somehow became more and more eager to be part of it with every passing minute.

"So, are you interested in this?" Tatarski asked Lucas after a moment of silence.

"First of all I am curious," Lucas replied. "Why me?"

"Do you know anyone better suited for this?" Tatarski smiled at him.

"Sure… The Professor would be the perfect candidate for this." Lucas nodded.

"Only students are allowed to enter the competition, no teachers," Seinefeld said.

"The 'Professor' Mr. Trent is referring to is in fact a student," Tatarski laughed. "His name is Darien Stance. But he is in his final year and will hardly have time for this." Tatarski then addressed Lucas. "Also, Mr. Stance might be knowledgeable, but from what I experienced so far you are by far ahead of him when it comes to ingenuity."

"Your trust in my abilities honors me, Professor." Lucas bowed a little.

"Being brought into this room alone should be enough for you to know that all of us have high confidence in you, Mr. Trent. After all, there is also a lot to gain, or lose, in this," a voice said from behind. Without Lucas noticing, Principal Snyders had entered the room and was now sitting down next to him.

"What do you mean, sir?" Lucas asked.

"This whole event is sponsored by a lot of big companies," Seinefeld explained. "This of course has to cover the event itself, after all there is a lot of investment involved, but it also includes a significant award for the winners and the schools that sent them."

"You once complained about the old equipment in our lab rooms, Mr. Trent; here is your chance to get it replaced." Tatarski laughed and patted his shoulder.

"And I will for sure do my best to make that happen." Lucas grinned.

"So you are interested in competing?" Seinefeld asked.

"Interested might be an understatement," Lucas laughed. "You completely sold me."

"That's how I know you, boy," Tatarski laughed. "All in and not even asking what's in it for you in the end."

"I honestly would go for that challenge even if there was nothing in it for me." Lucas was still laughing. "But out of curiosity… What does the winner get?"

"Besides most likely a lot of job offers from our sponsors, the top three contestants will be offered full scholarships at either of the hosting universities, with free choice of primary field," Seinefeld said.

"Those universities being Oxford and Cambridge, of course," Freeman added.

At that point Lucas had to take a deep breath. So far his plans had been to take a job after finishing his education here. Having an option to study at one of the elite universities in the country had always been far out of his reach.

"Gentlemen, you have just met our representative." Principal Snyders smiled at the others.

"And I think we need to get this representative a little fresh air before he collapses." Tatarski laughed once again and stood up. "Come on, Mr. Trent, we can discuss the formalities later; you look as if you need a coffee."

Lucas nodded and bowed a little before the others and then followed his teacher out of the room.

"Congratulations, Trent. I know you will make us proud." Professor Cooper patted his shoulder as they went by his desk in the teachers' room.

"I have something for you, by the way." Professor Tatarski had stopped at a desk and taken a book out of a drawer that he was now handing to Lucas. "You can keep it; I hope it will help you prepare."

Lucas took it and quickly looked at it. "Hacking – The Art of Exploitation" was the title. He opened a random page in the middle and studied the code snippet that was shown there. At that point it became very clear to him that there was still a lot for him to learn, especially in this area. It was not particularly hard to understand the general idea of what was discussed on that page, but the amount of detail in the explanations was by far deeper than what he was used to from school.

"Thank you, Professor." Lucas closed the book again and walked out into the corridor.

"I will approach you again once we have all the paperwork together for this," Tatarski said when they were standing outside the teachers' room. "At that point most likely we will also introduce you to the trainer that Professor Seinefeld mentioned. The final details are not yet completely outlined, but be prepared to have a two hour block each week for this."

"I will, sir." Lucas nodded. "Thank you for considering me for this."

"Don't thank me," the teacher smiled. "This is entirely of your own making."

With that he walked back into the room, leaving Lucas standing there alone. Lucas sighed a little, mixed feelings flowing through his body, ranging from anxiety to pride to fear. He always knew that he was amongst the better students here, but so far that had never made a difference. This new recognition for his hard work was not easy for him to fully take in, though. After all, it came with a lot of extra work, and with a lot of responsibility on his shoulders. He was quite sure that everyone in that competition would be at least as good as he was. Most of them would most likely even by far outclass him, and still the expectation was that he would come out of this as a winner. After all, he had been chosen to represent the whole school, and he would move heaven and earth to ensure that he would come out on top in the end.

CHAPTER 8

Personalities

Over the rest of the school day Lucas used every free minute he had to browse through the book. At the beginning it was just about grasping the concepts, so he would be prepared when the contest came, but the further he looked into it the more he became fascinated with the methods that were outlined. In school they were always taught how to quickly and efficiently solve problems, mostly for business solutions, and at best how to optimize those solutions for more performance or less resource consumption. This book was way different. Every scenario showed him new ways to think about a problem outside the box. After all, as Lucas quickly came to realize, hacking was all about thinking about angles that everyone else had forgotten about. What he also came to realize pretty soon was that knowing all this would help him in the future, not only for the contest, but also for his own programs. Now that he understood those patterns, he had a far easier time protecting himself against them. And the more he thought about it the more he realized that this was not only true in IT. After all, fighting Cedric was what made him get better in his shield magic. Right now it made him wonder if it would be beneficial for him to explore his own dark side in magic, so he would start to understand the patterns there, too. It was, as with the practice of hacking, a very fine line to walk though. When he read about the exploits in the book his first thoughts always went into how to protect against them, but in some moments he caught himself thinking of how to use them as well. These thoughts were what made him a little afraid of the matter, especially when it came to magic. If in a weak moment he used this dark power, it could result in damage that he never intended to do. And in the end repairing such damage was always harder than not doing it in the first place.

The thoughts didn't leave Lucas alone, even on his way to Dunstable. He had known for a while now that at some point he would have to face his dark side, as it was after all a part of him. So far he had managed to keep the issue under wraps though, until now. He wondered for a while if it would be a good idea bringing Jasmin in on this topic as well, but then decided against it. He would have loved to get Angel's opinion on that topic, but as he had not seen her since summer camp in Buxton that was very unlikely to happen. And on top of that, he was pretty sure that talking to her would not have gotten him anywhere.

When he arrived at the apartment block that Jasmin's address had pointed him to, he had to force the topic out of his head to get back to the reason he was here in the first place. He took a few moments to focus before ringing the bell. The buzzer of the front door answered his ring almost immediately, as if Jasmin had been waiting for him. The apartment was on the third floor. Lucas debated for a moment whether he should take the elevator up, but then decided against it. Walking the stairs would give him a little more time to get his mind straightened out. As he made his way upward he could hear someone yelling on one of the top floors. For him, growing up in a house, the nearest people that could yell were the neighbors, and they were past a hedge, so they would normally not be audible for him. He had never realized how different living in an apartment would be.

Arriving at the third floor, he could still hear the man yelling. Lucas could not yet grasp what it was all about, but it didn't sound very nice. He could see a half-open door down the corridor where the voice seemed to be coming from. When he got closer he could even see the guy gesticulating wildly inside, making the scene all the more uncomfortable to be close to. Unfortunately, judging from the numbers on the doors he walked by, it seemed that he had to get past the angry guy on his way to Jasmin's apartment.

"What do you expect me to think?" Lucas heard the guy yell. "You always sweet-talk me into trusting you and then you head off somewhere without telling me anything. How can I trust you if you don't trust me?"

Lucas tried to make out what the other person in there was saying, but couldn't hear a voice at all. Whoever it was, was keeping their voice down.

"I had about enough of you, bitch." His tone got even rougher. "If you want to continue like this, you'll have to do it without me."

Lucas had gotten pretty close to the scene by now, and only then realized that the yelling guy was actually standing within Jasmin's apartment. He crosschecked the door number with the text he had gotten from her earlier, before he walked up to it.

"Screw you." The guy yelled as Lucas was just about to knock on the door. Then he stormed out of the apartment, almost running him over.

"Should I come back later?" Lucas asked a little sheepishly, looking at Jasmin. She looked as if she was on the brink of tears but quickly tried to pull herself together when she spotted Lucas standing in the door.

"No, please come on in." She shook her head. "I would have taken the opportunity to introduce you to my boyfriend, but I am somewhat unsure if I actually have a boyfriend anymore."

"What was that all about just now?" Lucas stepped in and closed the door.

"Well, that was one of Robert's typical jealousy attacks." Jasmin sighed. "But please come on in."

Lucas took off his shoes and followed Jasmin into what seemed to be the living room. It was by far smaller than what they had in his parents' house and it seemed quite overflowing with things. A couch in the corner, a desk on the wall next to it with an old computer on top, a hamster cage in another corner, next to an aquarium, and a lot of things just lying around somewhere on the floor.

"Sorry, I should have cleaned up, but I didn't have time." Jasmin sat down on a chair and offered Lucas a place on the couch.

"No problem. It's still tidy compared to my place," he said. "I hope that outburst before had nothing to do with my visit?"

"No, we hadn't even gotten to that point yet." Jasmin shook her head. "I like my privacy, for several reasons, but Robert somehow doesn't get that."

"So how is it that you are still together?" Lucas was curious.

"I honestly don't know," she replied. "He always comes back after a while and apologizes. And then it is just as if nothing had ever happened."

"Interesting."

"Yeah. Sometimes I am unsure if I am doing something to cause that." Jasmin looked at him.

"Like what?"

"Like magic." She sighed. "It's the only explanation I have for this."

"Maybe he just really likes you?" Lucas suggested.

"Did this just sound like a guy who really likes me?" Jasmin had to laugh in agony.

"It sounded like somebody who was upset," Lucas said, "which does not imply that he doesn't like you."

"Yeah, right... Then he has a serious anger management issue." Jasmin shook her head.

"Come on... Is it THAT bad?"

"Well, not bad enough to be dangerous, no," she said. "But bad enough."

"So why don't you dump him then?" Lucas asked.

"Because I do really like him." Jasmin looked at him. "And that is, unfortunately, not something that happens very often."

"And did you ever use magic on him?"

"No." Jasmin shook her head. "Not on purpose at least. But you know how it is. How can I be sure?"

"Have you thought about asking the Professor to take a look?"

"Thought about it, yes. But I am not sure what good it will do. There is so much going on between Robert and me that I am quite certain that even the Professor would have trouble telling magic from pure feelings."

Lucas sighed a little. He was not sure what else to say to her. She was the expert when it came to feelings and psychology, and even more so when it came to relationships. He felt a little outclassed right now, and completely useless and unprepared for a situation like this.

"I'm sorry, where are my manners?" Jasmin suddenly started after a moment of silence. "Can I offer you something to drink?"

"I don't want to keep you too long...," Lucas replied, but Jasmin interrupted him before he could continue.

"Ah, nonsense, you came a long way." She stood up and walked to a side door, obviously leading to the kitchen. "Are you good with tea?"

"Sure, thank you." Lucas nodded and stood up too, following her over.

The kitchen was very small and cramped with cupboards and cabinets. Compared to the living room, it did look pretty clean, though. There were no dirty dishes in the sink, no things lying around at all, other than a pot sitting on the stove.

"So what are you going to do now?" He asked.

"You mean about Robert?" she replied. "Nothing. Wait until he comes back. Or maybe doesn't come back."

"How long will you wait for him to be back?"

"As long as it takes me to find someone else I like," Jasmin laughed. "So he might have a while."

"Interesting answer." Lucas had not quite expected such a comment.

"Why? What did you expect?"

"It sounded as if you were constantly on the lookout, and him being with you was just the best thing to do until something better came along."

"I am never on the lookout." Jasmin laughed. "Which makes him the best thing for a long while, most likely."

"Still interesting. I had not figured you for the type that would have a hard time finding someone to like."

"It's not hard to find someone to like." Jasmin was looking though a cabinet, searching for cups. "It's hard to find someone to love."

"I am unfortunately not so sure that I really know the difference between those two," Lucas sighed.

"See, and that's the problem. Most people don't. And they start telling you that they love you even if they don't. And I honestly can't stand that."

"So how can you tell?" Lucas asked. "Or more importantly: How can you tell those apart that tell you?"

"Well, I am the Psycho, remember?" Jasmin grinned. "It would be bad if I couldn't."

"Maybe you can teach me one time." Lucas grinned back.

"Well, I for sure can try." Jasmin laughed. "But I'm guessing that this is not what you came here to talk about, is it?"

"No, it's not." Lucas shook his head.

He watched Jasmin pour the tea, took some sugar, and then followed her back into the living room.

"So what is uncomfortable enough for you to go through all the trouble of coming here?"

"I need your advice," Lucas started before taking a sip from his tea.

"I figured as much," Jasmin laughed. "Please go on."

"Yesterday Mrs. O'Brien approached me at home," he said. "She asked me to accompany Airmid to a Christmas party."

"Sometimes mothers can be very overprotective." Jasmin laughed again. "So what's the problem, then? Go and have fun."

"Well first of all, I don't like parties, so I will most likely not have a lot of fun there." Lucas was not really amused. "And second, I am quite sure that Airmid will not really like me being there, either."

"You should stop worrying so much," Jasmin replied.

"Easy for you to say."

"Jesus, Guardian…" Jasmin shook her head. "You know, Airmid likes you a lot, even more than you realize. So if there is any man she would like to be there with her, it would for sure be you."

"That might be, but the thing she would for sure like even more is being there alone."

"I doubt that." Jasmin had a firm look on her face now. "And even if you are right, I am still quite sure she wouldn't mind you being there."

"Why would you say that?" Lucas was curious.

"Let's start it the other way round: Why would you doubt that she would like you to be there?"

"Well, for one, if she would have liked me to be there, she could have just asked. The fact that her mother did the asking says a lot, don't you think? And for the other, how much would you have liked your big brother accompanying you to your first-ever party?"

"See, and that's where you are wrong twice." Jasmin smiled.

"How so?" Lucas was surprised.

"Well, first, I would have liked my brother to be around at that particular party. It is, after all, good to have somebody that you trust close by. Unfortunately, I don't have a brother, though, so I had to go through it alone." Jasmin grinned. "And second, you are not her big brother."

"Yeah, but I am the next best thing to that."

"I think you don't realize what you really are, Guardian." Jasmin had leaned forward, looking straight at him.

"And what would that be?"

"Something almost no girl that age has: a true friend."

"And you think that makes a difference?"

"That makes all the difference in the world. A brother always is more or less accountable to the same parents that you are. A friend is not. And I am sure Airmid knows this as well as I do. I know that you would rather shoot yourself in the foot than be her parents spy at that party, and so does she. And I am almost certain that she will be grateful for you being there." Jasmin smiled. "If you don't get in her way, that is, of course," she quickly added.

"I hope you are right," Lucas sighed. "I don't want to put our friendship in jeopardy over this."

"I am sure that I am right. But if you are uncertain, why don't you talk to her?"

"Maybe I should." Lucas nodded. "Thanks for the advice, and for your time. I'm sorry that I bothered you with this."

"Don't be." Jasmin was still smiling. "That's what friends are here for."

"Still, friends should not bother each other with their problems."

"Why not?"

Lucas had to think a little before answering that. "Because I value your wellbeing more than my own. And bothering you with whatever is something I rather would not do."

"See, Guardian, and that's where you are once again not seeing the whole picture," Jasmin laughed.

"Why's that?"

"Let me ask you this: If I told you now that my old computer had a problem and I couldn't figure it out, would you look at it for me?"

"Happily." Lucas nodded.

"And would it bother you?"

"No, not at all."

"Why?"

Lucas again had to think a little before he could come up with a reply. "Because on the one hand I like dealing with computers, so the topic itself would not bother me at all, and on the other, I value your wellbeing more than my own, so even if it was uncomfortable I would still do my best to help you, just so it doesn't bother you anymore."

"See, and the same is true the other way round as well." Jasmin patted his shoulder. "Asking me a question that comes down to human emotions is like asking you a question about computers. It's what I love to do, so it doesn't bother me at all. And valuing the other one over yourself is something we all share in our group, so even if you still haven't got that, none of us will ever let you down or feel bothered when you are in need."

"I highly appreciate that, but I still will try to keep it to a minimum." Lucas stood up. "And again thank you for your time."

"Anytime." Jasmin stood up too, accompanying Lucas to the door. "You know, you asked me before to tell you the difference between liking and loving."

"Yeah?" Lucas looked up from tying his shoes.

"The feeling you have for Airmid is love," she said. "Maybe that will help you figure out the rest."

"You are kidding, right?" Lucas laughed, in a mixture of sarcasm and disbelief.

"No I am actually not." Jasmin shook her head.

"Come on…" Lucas stood up again.

"Why do you think differently?"

"Because, at least from what I have learned so far, love also brings the desire for intimacy," Lucas said. "And I would rather bite my hand off than touch Airmid."

"And why is that?" Jasmin grinned.

"Are you kidding?" Lucas couldn't believe that question.

"No, I am asking you a very serious question." Jasmin shook her head. "Why would you not touch Airmid in that way?"

Lucas had already opened his mouth to give a quick answer, but then held his breath and started thinking. And the longer he thought, the more it became clear to him that this question was actually not easy to answer.

"Because it would feel weird…," he finally said.

"Not good enough," Jasmin replied instantly. "Give me a real reason."

Lucas had leaned against a wall and was again thinking laboriously. It took him several minutes before he could finally come up with an answer that he thought would satisfy Jasmin's question.

"Because I am sure that it is not what she would want," he said.

"Exactly," Jasmin said with a grin and clapped her hand against a closet with a loud bang.

"I don't follow…" Lucas looked at her.

"When you think about Airmid, it is primarily about what she wants, and not what you want," Jasmin explained. "And that makes the difference between love and everything else."

"But I feel the same way about all of you." Lucas was confused.

"Yes, you do." Jasmin nodded.

"But how can I love all of you?" Lucas was getting more confused by the minute.

"Why is that a problem for you?"

"Love is something between one man and one woman, isn't it?"

"Love is a feeling that one person feels for another person," Jasmin stated.

"Sorry, I didn't mean to be discriminating with that statement," Lucas jumped in.

"Not the point I was making." Jasmin shook her head. "True love in the end is about caring more about someone else than caring about yourself. This has nothing to do with what society teaches you about relationships."

"Well, then you clearly have a different definition of love than most couples have." Lucas had to laugh.

"Well, unfortunately, many relationships at some point boil down to being more about habits than being about love." Jasmin sighed. "And that's one of the main problems of our society."

"So what are you saying? That most people are never really in love? And that at the same time I am in love with five people and still don't have a girlfriend?"

"For most people love is very short-lived, at least that is my experience. And yes, that is what I am saying."

"Then I am doing something wrong," Lucas laughed.

"How do you figure that?"

"Come on, you remember the situation we had in Buxton... About me and Rachel."

"And you think that you are wrong with that? And that Whirlwind and Cougar are doing better just because they have more sex than you do?"

"I am not sure who is right and who is wrong, but I am certainly feeling as if I was missing out on something." Lucas nodded.

"Don't get me wrong with what I am about to say now." Jasmin looked at him. "I am convinced that you are again a victim of society. And the only reason you feel left behind is because somebody put that picture in your mind, no matter if that is the situation in Buxton or the way society works in general. I am convinced that if it was only for you, you would not feel unhappy about this."

"And why do you think that?"

"Because you had your chance to change it, and didn't."

"That's hardly a distinction." Lucas laughed in agony.

"Yes it is. I have never seen Whirlwind back down..."

"Jesus, please don't compare me with him. At least not when it comes to girls." Lucas had to grin now.

"I'll make you a deal." Jasmin looked serious. "You take your time and think this through. And when you are REALLY convinced that you have a problem with this, you let me know, and I will help you to fix it." She extended her hand toward him.

Lucas thought for a moment before shaking it. "Accepted," he said. "And I hope you have a solution ready, because I am quite sure that I will take you up on that."

"By all means, please do." Jasmin smiled.

"And now I will finally leave you to it. You have trouble of your own to fix." Lucas smiled. "Good luck. See you on Monday."

"Same to you. And if you need something, please don't hesitate to call."

Lucas walked out and closed the door behind him. He felt a lot better now concerning the situation with Stephanie and her Christmas party, but at the same time he felt a bit more uncomfortable with his general situation. And once again it brought his thoughts back to his dark side. Jasmin was right with the things she had said, and he was very well aware of that. What made him think about it twice was that he had the feeling that he only backed down so much more than Marcus and Cedric because he did not want to give his darker side a chance to surface. He was convinced that if he would let that alter ego out of its cage, the result would be very different. And once again this thought made him feel uncomfortable. He needed to spin it around quite a while though, before he realized that it once again came down to the same reasons: He was afraid that his darker side could cause damage that he didn't intend to do and that in the end he would not be able to live with himself knowing that he had done that. Lucas almost had to laugh when he realized that this was the first time he had found something that made him more uncomfortable than girls. And this time there was nobody to blame but himself. This was just who he was, and the feeling he had deep inside himself, so he just had to learn to live with it.

On his train ride back to Luton he started thinking through his options on how to bring his dark side out safely and immediately had to admit that it was even more of a challenge than dealing with girls. But he had done magic long enough by now to realize that holding back on who you are would only get you one direction, and that was straight into trouble. So in the end he decided to stop messing around with it and find himself a safe area to play with his evil twin and learn all about the missing part of his personality.

He had already closed the topic in his mind when a question popped up in his head: Darien and Jasmin had seen the alter ego within Stephanie and had started acting on it, as well as attracting Angel's attention to it. But were they aware of his alter ego too? Or had he managed to hide that part so well that even they hadn't noticed it yet? And this brought up another question as well: If he actually had managed to keep this from them, how would they react when they found out? Would this change anything in their relationship? This question was burning now even hotter than the others had before, so he decided to seek out Darien and ask him, at least about the first part.

Early the next morning the issue was still bothering Lucas so much that he literally had set up camp outside Darien's classroom, waiting for him to show up. It was a painstaking wait that even Professor Tatarski's book could not make any more pleasant.

"Yo, mate, are you lost?" Darien laughed as he approached.

"The only thing I maybe lost is my mind." Lucas laughed too, closed the book and jumped up from the ground.

"What are you reading?" Darien took a look at the cover.

"Professor Tatarski gave it to me. Preparation for this security contest," Lucas explained.

"So they really picked you for it?" Darien smiled. "Congratulations, mate."

"Thanks, but you would have been the better choice." Lucas patted his shoulder before a thought crossed his mind. "Hold on, how do you know about that?"

"Senior years had been informed up front and asked for opinions on the best candidates. After all, there is no time for us doing that," Darien laughed.

"Why didn't you tell me?"

"I figured that you would find out soon enough anyway." Darien grinned. "After all, the vote in my class was unanimous."

"I don't believe this." Lucas was bewildered. "How do your classmates even know me?"

"Jesus, Lucas… Everyone knows you here." Darien laughed again. "But what's on your mind? You hardly came here to brag about that now, did you?"

"Actually no." Lucas shook his head. "I need to talk to you about something else, if you can spare a few minutes for me."

"Always, mate." Darien nodded. "Let me put down my backpack. I will be right back."

Lucas waited impatiently for Darien to return. When he finally did, the two boys walked to the end of the corridor, where they would be more or less undisturbed.

"So, what's up?" Darien asked.

"I am curious," Lucas started. "Psycho and you knew about Airmid's second personality for a while now."

"Yes…" Darien was looking suspicious.

"Did you notice something similar in me?" Lucas asked. "After all, I am a Gemini, too," he quickly added.

"I am not sure if I get the question." Darien seemed evasive. "Airmid's personality was clearly visible to all of us; you have never shown such a behavior."

"Come on, Professor, stop bullshitting me." Lucas got a little impatient.

"What do you want me to say?" Darien asked.

"The truth would be a good start," Lucas answered.

"Very well." Darien nodded. "Do I see a second personality within you? Yes. Is it similar to Airmid's? No."

"I don't follow." Lucas was confused.

"Airmid is kind of special in that her second face is quite distinctive and quite broad spectrum in the things it brings with it."

"I understood that much, but what are you saying about me?" Lucas was still confused.

"Everyone has a lot of different parts to his personality, and those do reflect in the energy patterns. You are no different in that."

"You are bullshitting me again." Lucas was getting annoyed.

"Why don't you ask me a straight question so I can give you a straight answer?" Darien was getting impatient now, too.

"OK, how about this: Do you think that I have a dark side?"

"That's the question?" Darien laughed. "Hell yeah, I do."

"Really? And that doesn't bother you?" Lucas was surprised.

"Why should it?" Darien was still laughing. "Everyone has a dark side. Some are just hiding it better than others."

"So what do you know about my dark side then?"

"I'll give you a complete rundown on all I know, if you answer me a question afterwards, as well." Darien looked at him. "Deal?"

"Deal." Lucas nodded.

"Very well. So where to start?" Darien cleared his throat. "There is a saying: The number of vices are constant in all humans. And knowing you as well as I do by now, with you not drinking, not smoking and not doing drugs, I am always wondering a little bit where you have hidden yours. Having said that, I can see a dark core in your energy patterns that has only rarely surfaced so far, and unfortunately in the only one situation I do know about where that seemed to have been the case, I was not present. So in a nutshell: I know that you also have something in you, just like we all do, and I am not at all afraid of it. All the contrary, I am really looking forward to seeing you break those chains."

"Why would you say that?" Lucas was surprised.

"Honestly? Because right now from a strictly energetic viewpoint it looks as if you are running with your parking brakes on… And even in this mode you are by far the most advanced and most powerful in our group."

"Wow…" Lucas was amazed. "Thank you for that."

"My pleasure." Darien grinned. "My turn: Why is this so important to you right now?"

"Honestly?" Lucas laughed. "Because my dark side has started haunting me."

"Explain." Darien looked at him.

"It started with a training session a while back, when I was trying to block Whirlwind." Lucas started. "After that I became aware of the power that comes with this darker side. And I also remembered the one occasion where it had come out. Now, when Professor Tatarski brought me into this contest I was confronted with it again, and then just yesterday I had a discussion with Psycho that among other things hit a topic from Buxton, bringing it up even more. And of course the Airmid discussion we had not too long ago also factors into that."

"Interesting." Darien nodded.

"How so?" Lucas didn't follow.

"Well, let's just say that I would have expected that something else would bring the issue to the surface. But never mind." Darien grinned.

"It begs one question for me, if you don't mind," Lucas said.

"By all means." Darien grinned.

"Should I go ahead and work on that dark side?"

"Of course you should." Darien nodded. "But why wouldn't you?"

"Because, honestly, I am afraid of the consequences," Lucas sighed.

"Newton said that for every action there is an equal and opposite reaction, so I can understand your concern," Darien laughed. "But that being said, you have been the knight in shining armor all the time I've known you now. You have more than earned a shot at being a little evil."

"Let's just hope that it ends at a little." Lucas sighed again. "For me this still feels a little like Pandora's box."

"And so it should." Darien smiled at him. "And as long as it does, I am not at all afraid. That feeling will keep you grounded."

"Thanks for the words of wisdom, Professor." Lucas smiled now, too. "I highly appreciate your help."

"Always my pleasure, mate." Darien patted his shoulder.

The boys walked back toward Darien's classroom.

"Oh, please don't forget to bring that flask on Monday," Darien said when they reached the entrance.

"Seems I caught you in a bad moment there." Lucas laughed. "I gave that to you days ago. Tossed it into your backpack, as you were too busy to look at it right away."

"Really?" Darien laughed. "Seems I completely missed that, sorry."

"Happens," Lucas grinned. "Have fun with it."

With that he walked away toward his own classroom, now feeling much more relaxed than before.

CHAPTER 9

Clarity

Much to Lucas' delight, one of his teachers had reported in sick, ending his day an hour earlier than expected. He was already on his way home when he spontaneously decided to visit Stephanie and have the planned chat with her about the party. He didn't even bother calling her first and just rode there, hoping that she would be in. He almost felt cheerful when he approached the door, which was a surprising change compared to the thoughts he had had only a day back, and once again emphasized the power that Jasmin had when it came to feelings. After ringing the bell he waited for a while and was about to leave again when he heard footsteps approaching. It was Stephanie herself that opened the door for him.

"Hi Guardian!" She smiled at him. "I did not expect to see you here."

"Hi Airmid." Lucas smiled back. "Do you have a minute?"

"Sure." She nodded. "Please come in."

Lucas stepped in and took off his coat and shoes.

"Is something wrong?" Stephanie asked.

"I hope not," Lucas grinned and followed her into the living room, where she offered him a chair.

"So what brings you here, then?"

"It's about that Christmas party of yours…" Lucas started slowly.

"Yes?" Stephanie looked a little insecure.

"Well, your mother approached me a few days ago, asking me if I would accompany you there."

"I know, she more or less forced me into consenting to that." Stephanie nodded.

"And that's exactly what I wanted to talk to you about." Lucas looked at her.

"Why? What did you tell her?" Stephanie was getting uneasy.

"Well, first I told her that I don't like the thought of being forced onto you in this matter," Lucas said.

"You didn't say no, did you?" Stephanie's eyes had filled with tears.

"No, I didn't." Lucas was stunned by her reaction.

"Thank you." The relief was clearly visible on her face. "I am sorry to cause you this inconvenience."

"I think we got at this on the wrong foot." Lucas almost had to laugh now.

"What do you mean?"

"It's no inconvenience for me to go to that party with you; I am happy to do that," Lucas said. "But this notion of being forced onto you was feeling a little strange. And that was what I wanted to talk to you about."

"Yeah, my mum was pretty strict about that." Stephanie had relaxed somewhat by now.

"Seems so," Lucas laughed. "Now, I still don't know exactly what she is expecting me to do there, so I wanted to hear your side of that, too, and make sure that we don't have different thoughts on it."

"Well, I guess she wants you to make sure that I behave." Stephanie smiled. "And I, of course, will try my best to do that. The last thing I want is to cause you trouble."

"Well, I guess you are right that she wants that…" Lucas grinned. "See, the only problem with that is… That's not what I want, and definitely also not what I will do."

"What do you mean?" Stephanie was curious now.

"Well, if your mother wanted a watchdog, she has hired the wrong guy. I will go there with you and be there for you, but what I will first and foremost do is stay out of your way as much as I can, and that's a promise."

"Don't you think that sort of defeats the purpose my mother had in mind?" Stephanie had to laugh now, too.

"That might very well be." Lucas smiled. "But the only person I feel responsible to in this matter is you. And if that's not good enough for her then I guess that's her problem."

"Please don't tell her that. If she finds out, she might prohibit me from going there after all," Stephanie begged.

"Well, actually, I did already tell her. And she accepted it."

"Really?" Stephanie almost couldn't believe that.

"I still have to ask you the question: How do you feel about me being there with you?"

"I feel fine," Stephanie replied. "And after having heard that, I have to say that I feel even better knowing that you are there, rather than being there without you."

"I am glad to hear that." Lucas smiled. "And I am looking forward to accompanying you." He had stood up again.

"Thank you for doing this for me." Stephanie walked over and gave him a hug.

"Anytime." Lucas hugged her back. "Now I will leave you alone again. I have kept you long enough." He smiled after she let go of him.

She gave him another intense hug after he had dressed up and then he walked out, whistling a happy tune on his way home. Somehow he now was unsure why he had imagined such a drama around this in the first place. But in the end he was just happy that it had turned out ok.

Lucas had arrived back home and gone straight to his room. He still felt relief after his chat with Stephanie and was also still wondering why he was so stupid in the first place. After walking up and down for a few minutes, he sighed and let himself fall onto his bed. He had just grabbed Professor Tatarski's book and started to read the next chapter when his cell phone rang. Lucas pulled it out of his pocket and looked at the display. It was Darien calling.

"Hi Professor," Lucas greeted him after picking up.

"Guardian, we need to talk." Darien sounded out of breath.

"Calm down, mate." Lucas was a little overwhelmed by this unexpected show of emotions. "What's happened?"

"I found something." Darien was not getting any calmer. "And you won't believe this."

"Then spit it out, mate, before your head bursts."

"I would rather tell you in person, if you don't mind."

"Sure thing. But you could have done this tomorrow in school, you know?"

"This can't wait until tomorrow." Darien was clearly eager to share his findings.

"OK, so where do you want to meet?"

"Are you home?"

"Yes, I am."

"Then I will come by, if you don't mind."

"OK." Now Lucas was getting a little uneasy. He thought about inquiring for further details, but before he even had a chance to do so, Darien had already hung up.

Less than ten minutes later the bell sounded. Lucas ran down the stairs, but his father was there already before he made it.

"Good afternoon, Darien," he greeted the visitor. "You look out of breath. Can I get you something to drink?"

"Hallo Mr. Trent," Darien replied. "No thanks, I am just here to see Lucas."

"By all means." Mr. Trent smiled. "Please come in."

Darien stepped in and quickly tossed off his shoes and coat.

"You act is if the world was coming to an end soon." Mr. Trent patted his shoulder while walking by him. "Is anything wrong?"

"Nothing to worry about, sir." Darien tried to grin. "I am just eager to share something with your son."

"Very well, I'll leave you to it then." He nodded and went away when he saw Lucas coming down the stairs.

"Sorry to jump in on you like this." Darien was still out of breath when he addressed Lucas.

"No worries," Lucas said with a straight face. "Come, let's go to my room. We have privacy there."

The two boys walked up to the first floor and into Lucas' room, Lucas locking the door behind them. He offered Darien his office chair and sat down on the bed himself.

"Now, what is important enough to make you compete with Cougar in a sports event?" Lucas asked.

"Sports event?" Darien seemed confused, his mind obviously far away.

"You just made it here in less than ten minutes. That was either backed by a competition or a death threat." Lucas had to laugh. As Darien's face still told him that he couldn't follow, Lucas continued a few moments later. "OK, forget it. Just tell me what's on your mind."

"You won't believe this…," Darien said and started rummaging around in his bag.

"I already don't." Lucas had to laugh. He had never seen Darien so very beside himself.

"Here it is." Darien pulled out something and tossed it to Lucas, who only just reacted in time to catch it. It was a flask like the one he had taken from the thieves.

"This is the one you got from that gang of crooks," Darien explained.

"So?" Lucas was getting curious.

"Guess what's in it." Darien looked triumphant.

"Some kind of chemical compound that Brix & Burton produces, I would think." Lucas turned the flask around in his hand.

"Wrong," Darien replied. "This is the same liquid that Cypher gave you in Buxton. Well, at least almost."

"Come again?" Lucas didn't believe what he had just heard.

"You heard me," Darien replied. "And I told you that you wouldn't believe it."

"So what are you saying? That Brix & Burton is supplying our bad guys with their magic enhancer? That would imply that somebody there knows about magic."

"I am not saying anything. I am merely presenting facts." Darien slowly calmed down.

"Yeah, but facts that point in that direction. At least from where I stand."

"Then show me a different direction."

Lucas had to think for a while. "Maybe the thieves mixed the crates in with the other stuff from the chemical plant."

"And why would they do that?" Darien asked.

"I don't know. Maybe for pure stacking reasons?" Lucas suggested.

Darien laughed out loud. "You can't be serious."

"I am just speculating. And honestly, I like every speculation more than the thought that this substance is getting mass-produced."

"And why's that?" Darien inquired.

"Are you kidding me?" Lucas was astonished. "Not even half a year ago we had to fight a ghost because of that shit. And unless you and Ghosthunter want to open up a business, I would really like to not do that again."

"Ghosthunter the Ghostbuster. I like that thought." Darien laughed. "But seriously, I agree that something bad happened with this stuff, but you have to admit that it has a huge potential for doing good as well."

"So does dynamite. And we all know how that one turned out." Lucas winked.

"Touché." Darien nodded.

"So what do you suggest we do now?" Lucas asked.

"I would like to find out more about it. And also about Plague's circle. Not only to make sense of what they are doing, but also to see if something dangerous is cooking somewhere in our vicinity."

"Do you have reason to believe that?" Lucas was curious.

"Well, you were the one that just reminded me what bad things already did happen with this substance…"

"Yes…" Lucas was waiting tensely.

"… and as far as we saw back then, it was one of the flasks that was needed for it…" Darien continued.

"Yes…" Lucas was getting even tenser.

"… and according to Cougar you dropped one crate that had about hundred flasks in it, and you said that there were several more of them around. Now add it up… If one flask brings that much trouble… How much trouble can several hundred of them bring?"

"Unfortunately, you are right." Lucas nodded and started thinking. "But thinking about it…" he started a few moments later. "… this whole thing looks way too big for us. We need to report this."

"And to whom do you suggest we report it?" Darien laughed. "Police? They'll pronounce you crazy where you stand, lock you up and throw away the key."

"I was thinking more along the lines of Angel and her circle. Or maybe someone even higher up."

"Well, then good luck finding her." Darien laughed again. "At least I haven't seen her for quite a while."

"Neither have I." Lucas nodded. "And I am open for better ideas if you have some."

"I don't." Darien shook his head. "That's why I want to find out more about all of this and see if we can make any sense of it. Maybe then we will have a good idea where to turn to for help."

"Ok, so what's the plan?"

"First, I will send an email again to my friend in Lions, hopefully he's had time already to look at this," Darien said. "Second, I would like to bring the topic up on Monday and see what everyone else has to say about it. Third… Well, I have not thought that far yet."

"Then let's stick to that plan," Lucas suggested. "We are after all generating the best ideas when the six of us are together."

"OK." Darien nodded. "I will head home now to send that email."

He jumped up and was already out of the room before Lucas even got on his feet. Racing down the stairs behind him, Lucas only just caught up with him again when he had already opened the door.

"See you soon." Darien didn't even wait for an answer before he pulled the door shut behind him.

"Yeah, see you soon," Lucas said silently, turned around and walked back up again. He had desperately wanted to get this whole topic over with, but now that Darien had told him about the contents of the flask, he was not so sure anymore. On the one hand he wanted to dive into this whole topic again and go as deep as it went to solve the puzzle once and for all. On the other hand it just wasn't right. The issue was much too big and complex for them and besides that he still had a life to deal with. A life that was full of schoolwork, an upcoming contest, a party that he now was looking forward to and a lot of other things that needed his attention as well. Additionally, after seeing Jasmin last time, he was quite sure that she also was hardly in the mood for adventure and to the contrary might even be in the mood for some help and cheering up herself. Lucas once again sighed and let himself fall onto the bed. He decided to let go of the topic for now, but head for Timestop bar next evening and see if he got lucky with Angel. He grabbed his book again and switched his focus back to computers.

Friday evening Lucas walked into the Timestop bar shortly after 7.30 p.m. He had still not gotten used to the atmosphere in the room, although he had been here lots of times in the past year and a half. All the clocks on the wall that were not ticking, the backrooms with the heavy curtains and the muttering in the room, with everyone trying to keep to themselves. He nodded a friendly hello to the barkeeper, ordered something to drink and then walked straight through one of the curtains. The room behind presented itself about halfway full, which was unusually empty for this time. Lucas took a quick look around, but there was no Angel. In fact, most of the people in the room he had never seen before. So he decided to pick up a newspaper and take a seat at an empty table.

"Another irregular visitor coming home, I see?" a friendly voice greeted him with a laugh.

"Whenever time permits, Drow," Lucas replied and looked up. "Unfortunately this is not all too often." He then stood up and offered his hand. "Nice to see you."

"Likewise." Drow shook the hand.

"Say, Drow, I missed you at the camping event in Buxton in the summer. I thought you would be there too?" Lucas asked.

"And I was. But obviously somewhere where you were not."

"Where did you stay?"

"C-3 was the sector. Together with all the other chatroom organizers."

"Interesting." Lucas was baffled. He had known Drow, the organizer of this meeting, for a while now; in fact, Drow had been the first person he had ever met in here, and so far Lucas had been convinced that he was at least as deep into magic as himself. And with this C-3 would not have made sense. The C-sectors at the camp were the camping locations for people that had no magical powers at all, which seemed extremely weird for a man like Drow.

"Not so much." Drow grinned. "But what brings you here tonight?"

"The same thing as most of the time: I am looking for someone," Lucas laughed.

"And who would that be?"

"Take a wild guess." Lucas was still laughing.

"Well, I am not so sure if you will have any luck with her, my friend. As far as I know she is on vacation."

"That's too bad." Lucas was disappointed. "But I will try my luck nonetheless, if you don't mind."

"Oh, I never mind." Drow patted his shoulder. "I am always happy to see you here."

"Thanks for the warm welcome." Lucas sat down as Drow turned around and walked to another new arriver to welcome him, as well.

Between reading articles in the newspaper, Lucas looked around the room occasionally. As always, the topics he could hear the others discuss were everything but magical, ranging from Christmas presents to holiday plans and the usual computer problems. It felt almost funny that a meeting like this had been the birthplace of his own circle. Looking at the people in here, someone would never have imagined that, but in the end that might even have been a good thing. After all, hiding in plain sight seemed to work out pretty well for Lucas and his friends so far.

It was around 9 when the first other person sat down at Lucas' table.

"Howdy," she greeted him without showing too much interest.

"Greetings." Lucas looked up from his paper. She was in her late twenties, smaller than him, sporty, with a long, blond ponytail. As she seemed to have no interest in him whatsoever, he quickly focused back on his articles, but not for too long. When Drow came by and started chatting with her, Lucas couldn't help the impression that he had heard the voice before, but he just couldn't make the connection.

"Excuse me," he addressed her after Drow was gone again. "Is it possible that we met before?"

"If this is your way of approaching girls, I would seriously suggest that you change your lines." Her face was extremely hostile when she looked over at him.

"Actually, this is my way of addressing anybody I think I have met before." Lucas remained completely calm. The situation felt somewhat funny for him. Not only was that girl more than a decade older than him, but also pretty much out of his league. Her suggesting that this was a blatant attempt to flirt was close to unbelievable.

"Your lines are not getting any better, fledgling. Why don't you stop it before I seriously hurt you?"

Lucas was a little stunned by the hostility, and even more the reasons for it, but somehow this kept him as calm as an ice block and made him eager to not back down. He thought for a moment about the best response for that, before he decided to start shooting back.

"You know, honey, if you want to challenge me then stop this game and bring it on. Otherwise maybe you could just back off and answer my original question?" his voice was still completely calm, almost cold.

"You don't give up easily, do you?" A grin had mixed into her hostile face, making her almost look a little mad right now, with her whispering voice adding to that impression. "But in this case you should. Before I let you anywhere near my pants, I will rip your head off."

"Oh, am I supposed to be afraid now?" Lucas had a hard time not laughing, but he did his best to look and sound as cool as possible. "Try to get something in your head, chick." Lucas almost couldn't believe that he had just used that word, but somehow it felt fitting. "You are a very beautiful girl, no discussion about that, but this does not mean that everyone is just after that hot body of yours. Now, if you want to try ripping my head off, fine, please feel free to do so. But don't expect me to stand idly by when you do. I've never so far hit a girl, but I will happily break this record and make an exception for you. Still, I would prefer if we could bury the hatchet and just try to figure out if we in fact did meet before."

The girl seemed impressed by Lucas' statement. She took a long while to think before saying anything else, and when she finally spoke again her face had lightened up significantly.

"You truly have balls, man, I have to grant you that," she said. "You are the first one ever to stand up to me."

"Sorry to have broken your sequence then." Lucas laughed now.

"Don't be, it is a very pleasant change, and you earned my respect for that." She smiled now. "Sorry for being so hostile, but unfortunately it's necessary most of the time."

"Don't be. In the end it's better to be safe than sorry."

"Appreciate your understanding." She extended her hand. "My name is Kung Fu. Pleasure to meet you."

"I knew that I had heard that voice before." Lucas grinned and shook her hand. They had met at the camp in Buxton briefly; she was part of Angel's circle. "I am Guardian."

"Oh boy, now I have embarrassed myself completely." The girl's face turned red. "And my circle as well."

"Why? Because you tried to be protective?" Lucas said. "From where I stand you did nothing embarrassing at all, so don't worry too much."

"I appreciate your understanding, but some things I said were very disrespectful. And for that I would still like to apologize."

"No apologies necessary, but of course gladly accepted if it makes you feel better." Lucas put his hand on her shoulder. "You are a really nice girl. It would be a shame if you would avoid me in the future just because of that bad start."

"Thank you," she smiled.

"So, what brings you here?" Lucas tried to change the topic.

"I am here from time to time, just looking for interesting new people, or maybe meeting old friends," she said. "And why are you here?"

"I was actually looking for Angel. But it seems I am out of luck."

"You are always looking for Angel when I see you." She laughed. "Well, this time you are out of luck for sure. She is not even in the country right now."

"Well, maybe next time I will look for you instead. But only if you promise not to rip my head off." Lucas winked at her.

"You are sweet." She grinned. "And somehow I would really like that."

"Well then, let's hope we do meet again." Lucas couldn't tell why, but somehow he really liked her, even after the run-in they just had, or maybe exactly because of it.

"Would you excuse me?" She had stood up. "There is an interesting group over there that I want to talk to."

Lucas nodded and watched her walk over to a table on the other end of the room. A group of seven had taken seats there and was chatting eagerly about something. Unfortunately he was too far away to listen in. When Kung Fu arrived there she pulled up a chair and joined the discussion. At first Lucas didn't think too much about it, but the more he watched the more he could feel the parallels between her approach over there and Angel's approach to him and the others a year back. Somehow it felt strange watching it from the sidelines, so strange in fact that after about ten minutes Lucas decided to leave. Angel wasn't coming anyway, Kung Fu was clearly busy, Drow did not seem to be a good person to talk to about his problems, and everyone else in the room was no good, either. It was somehow disappointing, but that had been to be expected after all.

Monday evening the group met again at the shack and once again the emotions seemed very mixed. Darien was impatiently waiting for his chance to share his findings, Marcus looked as if he was anticipating great breakthroughs, Stephanie just was happy, most likely because of the upcoming party, Jasmin looked sad and distracted and Cedric just seemed to be bored.

"I think I have never seen such a number of different emotions at the same time before in this room," Lucas stated after they had all sat down.

"It's Christmas time, what did you expect?" Cedric was laughing.

"Well, I did expect a lot from Christmas, but that's what makes all of this so interesting… Most of the emotions in here have nothing to do with Christmas in the first place."

The others just nodded in reply, all of them deep in their own thoughts, so Lucas continued after a while. "OK, let's do something before we all die by silence." He grinned. "The Professor approached me last week and told me something interesting about the flask we took from the thieves." Lucas put the flask in the middle of the table. "Professor, would you mind filling the others in?"

"Not at all." Darien seemed to have waited for this. He quickly brought the others up to speed with the same information that he had given Lucas, including the discussion the two of them had had afterwards. "And now we are eager to hear your opinion on this," he finally ended his explanations.

"I am with you, Professor, we should get to the bottom of this." Marcus was the first to jump in, obviously eager to get the thieves.

"I am with Guardian, this is too big for us." Stephanie was not quite as excited.

"I am with Guardian as well, but for a different reason: We have other things to do than this." Jasmin was next.

"I am with the Professor. I mean, what good was it to take out Wolfman if we now let Cypher and his friends roam freely with this strange shit?" Cedric finished the circle.

"Makes three on each side," Marcus commented.

"Not really." Lucas stepped in. "I have my doubts, but I am not exactly happy with those goons running around, either. And that is both the thieves and the black-robes."

"Well, unfortunately, that makes it three versus three again," Darien said. "I got a reply from my friend in Lions earlier today, and guess what: The smell is the same; it is the same substance. Which brings me to the point that this is definitely too big for us."

"So what do we do now?" Lucas asked.

The others looked at each other silently for several minutes. Lucas was about to say something again when he saw them nodding to each other. Stephanie was the one who finally commented.

"We do what we always do, and what has always turned out to be the best thing to do in the end," she said.

"And what would that be?" Lucas asked, but somehow he already knew that he wouldn't like the answer.

"Follow your lead, Guardian." Jasmin patted his shoulder while the others nodded in agreement.

"Could you idiots please stop this for a change? This is really getting ridiculous." Lucas was clearly unhappy.

"Ridiculous or not, you have to admit that it always turns out to be a wise path to follow." Darien patted his other shoulder.

"Not for me." Lucas was getting annoyed.

"Sometimes we have to learn to live with disappointments, Guardian." Cedric grinned at him.

"So hypothetically…" Lucas had realized that there was no changing their mind and therefore given up. "If we want to get to the bottom of this, what should we do?"

"Find out as much as we can about this substance," Cedric suggested.

"And about Cypher and his circle," Marcus added.

"So they are the main targets now? What about the thieves?" Lucas was surprised that Marcus had not jumped that direction immediately.

"I would still love to catch the thieves, but I am right now more curious why my dad's employer is producing magical potions," Marcus replied.

"I still think we should go after the thieves as well," Darien threw in.

"And why's that?" Lucas asked.

"Because they still have a few hundred flasks full of that stuff. And the thought of letting this fall into the wrong hands gives me goosebumps."

"Valid point." Lucas nodded. "So we would need to find out as much as possible about the substance, the circle that developed it and the thieves that stole it. That sounds like a hell of a lot of work."

"Much of it is Internet research to start with. So that's doable," Darien commented. "And maybe I can ship the substance to my friend at the university and let him take a look, but I doubt that it will do us much good."

"I could try to get hold of this police detective. Maybe I can hear something from him on the thieves," Marcus suggested.

"And maybe we should revisit the chapel and the house where we met Wolfman. Maybe there is still something going on there," Jasmin added.

"What about the pictures of the thieves? Did anyone already look at them?" Cedric asked.

"Yeah, I did." Darien nodded. "But there is not much we can use there. The license plates and VIN of the truck are the best part of it, and this is in the hands of the police now."

"Maybe we should all look at them together. Maybe we'll find something," Stephanie said. "Not that I don't trust your expertise, Professor," she quickly added.

"Good idea, twelve eyes always beat two." Darien nodded. "I will bring my laptop next week, then we can take a look."

"So that's a lot to do then…" Lucas sighed. "Are you all up to go that route?"

All of them nodded slowly but convincingly. Even Jasmin seemed to have forgotten about her other problems.

"OK, then let's do this." Lucas started thinking. "Professor, we leave the Internet and the university to you."

"Got it." Darien nodded.

"Cougar, see if you can get something from that policeman."

"Will do. Psycho, would you mind joining me? That could help," Marcus said.

"Sure thing." Jasmin nodded.

"When we go to the house and the chapel it should be at least Whirlwind, Cougar and me, and I would appreciate having you there too, Psycho, just in case. And of course, Airmid, we need you too, at least to be available."

"Works for me," Marcus grinned.

"I'll be there, too." Jasmin nodded again.

"Same." Cedric grinned.

"I will stay home and come to the rescue if necessary." Stephanie grinned too.

"And next Monday we all look at the pictures," Lucas finished the plan.

The others all nodded, with smiles on their faces.

"Why is it that my time hasn't been quiet and relaxing ever since I met you guys?" Lucas laughed.

"The choices you make." Marcus grinned and winked at him.

"Yeah, and somehow I wouldn't want it any other way anymore." Lucas smiled and all of them nodded silently. He then stretched out his fist to the middle of the table.

"Brother to brother, yours, to the end," they all said in unison.

CHAPTER 10

Fake

The next few days went by pretty uncomfortably for Lucas. He was still not convinced that going into this whole mess had been a good idea, and to increase his workload even further, many of his teachers had started coming up with suggestions and books for the contest. Those kept him so extremely busy that he hadn't had any time at all for preparations when he met up with the others that Friday afternoon. It was even luck that he had had time to fetch his robes after school. They had agreed to meet in a suburb of Luton, close to the house they had been in with Wolfman a while back.

"All set?" Lucas asked as he approached the others, him once again being last to arrive.

"Sure thing." Marcus nodded. "Do you think we should wear robes?"

"Not yet." Lucas shook his head. "And especially not here." They were walking along a very quiet alley. "Woodcock Road" the sign read, and seeing it gave Lucas a cold shiver. This had been the site of a very bad fight he had stumbled into. Not against dark mages, but against concerned citizens that mistakenly took him and Jasmin for Satanists. He was not exactly eager to provoke that mistake again.

When they finally came up to the house they were looking for, Lucas was amazed how much it had changed. The garden had been cleaned up, the canopy of the house fixed, including the stairs, the windows were all clean now and none of them were barred anymore, and even the door had gotten a new paint job, including one for the knocker, which now was shining brightly golden again.

"Quite a difference," Jasmin commented.

"Yeah, last time this was little more than a ramshackle hut." Lucas nodded.

"So how do we get in?" Marcus had started rattling the door, but it didn't move.

"I don't suppose that anyone of you has an 'Open Sesame' spell at hand?" Lucas looked around.

"That's more of the Professor's specialty, it seems," Marcus laughed. "And we will have a hard time cracking that lock; that's a state-of-the-art security piece."

"Let's walk around the house. Maybe there is an easier way in," Lucas suggested.

The others nodded in reply, so he walked off. Walking alongside the little villa, Lucas was amazed at how much it had changed. All windows were closed and had curtains on them, but through the curtains he could see offices, all of them looking quite similar and with nobody in them. He somehow had the feeling that something was wrong with what he saw, but he couldn't pinpoint it. When he turned around the first corner he was so shocked though, about what he saw that he just stopped, making Marcus run straight into him.

"Hey, what's up?" Marcus asked and tried to look past him.

"I think now it's time to put our robes on. Something is wrong here." Lucas had taken a step back so all of them could look through the small corridor in the hedge that had blocked their view so far. The area behind it was still looking like total wilderness. Untreated lawn, bushes and trees growing wildly, ivy hanging from the wall of the house, barred windows, opaque windows, all in all, looking at that angle, it much more resembled what it had been before.

"What the hell?" Marcus had taken a look around.

"Yeah, exactly." Lucas nodded. "Something is dead wrong here." He pulled out his robes and put them on, making sure his face was hidden deeply under the hood. After the others had followed his example he led them on down the side of the building, following the building's T-form all the way. They had almost reached the back end when he finally spotted a way in: A broken window on the ground floor seemed to be the perfect opportunity.

"There." He pointed it out to the others. Walking toward it, he examined it more closely. It seemed broken recently, as there was almost no snow inside the house. And when he looked around he quickly saw what had broken it: A tree had started leaning sideways and was now in reach of the window. A strong gust of wind would most likely have been enough to make one of the branches crash into it.

"Can we get in there?" Jasmin asked.

"Easily." Marcus nodded and stepped up to it. He quickly reached through the broken pane of glass and opened the lock allowing him to push the window open.

"Who wants to go first?" he grinned at the others.

Lucas took a quick look into the room. It seemed empty and judging from the dust on the floor, it looked as if nobody had been in there for quite a while.

"Looks safe," he said. "Cougar, you want to go first? Just in case?"

"My pleasure." Marcus bowed a little before holding on to the upper ledge of the window and jumping through it. Lucas watched him tiptoeing through the room and listening through the door.

"Seems clear," he then said and pointed a thumbs-up in their direction.

"You next, Psycho," Lucas said. "Whirlwind, you go third. I'll watch out, just in case."

"OK." Jasmin nodded and began climbing the window. Her move looked by far less elegant than Marcus' before; in the end Cedric had to help her to get in at all.

Cedric himself did little better after that, though. It might have looked easy when Marcus had jumped in, but it turned out to be quite a challenge.

Lucas had another quick look around before he finally tackled the window himself. He tried to copy Marcus' technique, but in the end Cedric had to catch him, too, or he would have fallen right back out onto the grass.

"How do you do that, Cougar?" Lucas asked after again having firm ground below his feet. "This looks so easy with you." Then he turned to Cedric. "Thanks for the help, by the way. That fall would most likely have needed Airmid's attention."

"Yeah, without enemy contact," Cedric grinned.

"OK, let's head on." Lucas walked up to the door. He listened carefully for any movement in the house, but he couldn't hear anything, so he started opening the door slowly. Unfortunately, the door seemed to be in as bad a shape as everything else in the room. Even with very cautious movement, it creaked quite loudly.

"I guess if somebody is here they will have heard us now." Marcus had taken position next to the door, pressing himself tightly against the wall.

"Then let's hope that there is nobody who could have heard that. But let's stay alert, just in case." Lucas had opened the door completely now, taking quick peeks around the corner. The corridor was as full of dust as the room they were in. There were several more doors along it on both sides, leading up to another one at the far end. The window on the back end, right next to the room they were standing in, was barred and only shimmers of light were reaching through it.

"Who wants to go first?" Jasmin asked from the very last position.

"I will, if you don't mind." Marcus had peeked around the corner, as well. "You stay here until I have checked out the other rooms in the corridor."

Lucas nodded and watched.

Marcus pulled out a flashlight, but much to Lucas' surprise, he didn't turn it on. He headed up to the next door, which was on the opposite side, just a few meters away, and took a position beside it, close to the wall. It looked a little like in an action movie, Marcus reaching for the handle, pushing it down slowly and then, with a sudden burst, tossing the door open. Everyone held their breaths. Marcus was primarily watching the rest of the corridor, especially the door at the far end. As nothing seemed to happen, he suddenly held his flashlight around the corner and turned it on, wheeling it around to light up as much as possible. It looked weird, though, as he was still pressed against the wall and had no chance to see what was going on. But again, nothing happened. After waiting for another few moments Marcus finally took a peek around the corner and started lighting the room again.

"Clear," he then whispered toward Lucas and gestured him to move over to that room.

Lucas nodded and the group cautiously walked over to the next room. It turned out to be a bedroom, but a quite old one and in very bad shape.

"Take a quick look around," Lucas asked Cedric and Jasmin. "I will watch Cougar."

Cedric and Jasmin nodded and started sweeping the room. Marcus had already moved on to the next door.

They continued this routine until they had swept through all rooms of that wing, but nothing changed. The rooms were all unoccupied and apparently had been for years. The windows were all either opaque or barred, and the only traces in the dust were from them.

When Marcus finally grabbed the handle of the last door, the one that would most likely lead to the main hallway, everyone was holding their breath again. Unlike the handles before, this one moved without making any noise whatsoever. Marcus seemed to have noticed that, too, as he stopped for a moment, listening at the door one more time, but apparently it was still quiet. Then he pushed against the door, but to everyone's surprise it didn't open.

"It's locked." Marcus whispered the obvious.

Lucas took a quick look from the doorframe of the closest room. The lock was a standard door lock, nothing fancy, but also nothing they could crack easily.

"Any ideas?" Lucas asked while stepping out toward it.

Cedric and Marcus had turned on their flashlights and were examining the lock.

"We could try to crack it," Cedric suggested.

"I have another idea," Jasmin said from behind. "But maybe it is crazy. I have no experience with such things."

"Neither have we," Marcus laughed. "So let's hear it."

"Couldn't we try pulling out the hinge bolts?" she suggested.

"That is ingenious." Marcus grinned and grabbed his pocket knife.

It took him about a minute to pull all three bolts out. The others were still standing close by, watching him.

"I will move the door out of the frame now, so take cover." He had grabbed the door on both sides. "Guardian, when I do this I will be exposed over here, so I count on you to shield me if somebody should be on the other side."

"Don't worry, I'll have your back." Lucas nodded and took a position from which he could see the doorframe but would not be spotted easily. Jasmin and Cedric had also taken cover in one of the rooms. Marcus quickly pulled the door out of the frame and leaned it against the wall before jumping to cover into the closest room.

The room outside was brighter than the corridor they were in, so Lucas needed a second to adjust his eyes. Lucky for them, it was empty.

"Amazing," Lucas said after stepping out into the open.

The main entrance hall that Lucas had just entered gave the impression that they had stepped into another world. Out here everything looked much nicer, cleaner and more frequently used. Even the door that Marcus had just pulled open was freshly painted on the outside.

"What the hell is that?" Marcus had joined Lucas in the hall.

"It's a front. A fake," Lucas commented and looked around. He already knew the place from his last visit here, but it had completely changed. Facing the main entrance was a big reception desk with a computer behind it and a large office phone that had some lights blinking. The staircase leading to the first floor had also been renovated. Lucas remembered that on his last visit there was an open hallway at the end of it, but when he looked now the view was blocked by a wall and a closed door with some sign on it that he couldn't read from down here. He also remembered that there were three open corridors earlier, but now all three had also been fitted with doors. Walking up to the one next to him he could see a sign on the door. "Restricted area. Authorized personnel only." A card reader was protecting it.

"Look at the sign," Jasmin suddenly said, pointing at a big company logo above the reception desk.

Lucas had been so busy looking around that he had missed it so far. But now that Jasmin had pointed it out, a cold shiver ran down his spine. "Jackson & Co – Import/Export" the logo read.

"Why is this Jackson guy always around when we get somewhere?" Lucas had pulled out his phone and started taking pictures of everything.

"Up here it says "Employees only"" Marcus said from upstairs. "And the door is locked."

"Same here." Cedric had pulled the dismounted door from the wall and looked at the backside.

"This one says 'Conference Center.'" Jasmin had walked up to the third corridor. "And the door is open."

Marcus and Cedric quickly ran over to her.

"Careful guys." Lucas tried to slow them down. "We still don't know who else is here."

The others slowed down instantly, Jasmin taking a step away from the door, Marcus and Cedric positioning themselves left and right of it. When Marcus pushed the door open, a quite nice corridor appeared behind it. The window at the far end was the only source of light, but it was by far enough to light up the short corridor. Only four doors were in there, two leading left, two right. Marcus stepped in first, Lucas following one step behind. "Conference Room 1" the first sign to the right read. They pushed the door open and discovered a nice room that could easily fit six or maybe even eight people.

"Take a closer look, please," Lucas said to Jasmin and Cedric.

He and Marcus continued on to the next door, this time on the left side. The sign read "Board meeting room" and the door was locked. Next on the right was "Conference Room 2", and it turned out to be a room that looked pretty much like the one next to it. The last door said "Video Conference" and once again, the door was locked.

"Why would somebody lock a Video Conference room?" Marcus asked.

"My guess would be because there isn't one," Lucas answered and stepped into Conference Room 2.

"What do you mean?" Marcus inquired further.

"All the rooms we have seen so far face the front side. The two locked meeting rooms would face out back, which would uncover the scam pretty quickly, given how the garden looks back there. So my guess is that all the other rooms don't even exist, just like the 'Employees only' area that we entered through."

"So what about the third wing? We saw offices there." Marcus had joined Lucas in searching the room.

"Which is interesting, given that this is the wing that said 'Restricted Area'," Lucas answered.

"Can we look in there?"

"One thing at a time, Cougar," Lucas laughed.

They took their time examining the conference rooms closely, but there was nothing useful in either of them. When they met back outside at the main entry room Lucas walked straight up to the reception desk. Something had not looked right when he examined it before, now he finally saw what it was that had caught his attention: The phone had a lot of lights blinking, which suggested that the people on those extensions were in calls right now. But as nobody seemed to be in the house, that just didn't make sense. And he was proven right pretty quickly.

"Even this phone is a scam." He laughed and held the device up for the others to see.

"Why?" Cedric approached him.

"Look. They didn't even bother plugging any cables in." Lucas grinned.

"This can't all be charade." Marcus had walked across the room. "I want to get into this restricted area. There must be something to this."

Lucas had set down the phone and joined Marcus at the door. It was a standard door, just like all the others, but the lock had been replaced with a card reader.

"Unfortunately, we can't pull the hinges on that one," Jasmin sighed from behind.

"I don't think we have to." Lucas had taken a closer look at the reader. "This is not exactly a high security device."

"What do you mean?" Marcus asked.

"Well, a normal card reader works like an electric door opener. Those sit on the frame, not the door. This one is just a replacement for the lock. When you insert the right card it will send a signal to the cylinder and let you turn the knob."

"And this helps us how?" Marcus didn't understand.

"That helps us because those signals are normally not highly sophisticated, coded signals," Lucas laughed. "May I borrow your knife please?"

Marcus handed over the knife and Lucas started dismantling the card reader.

"See here?" he pointed out two drilled wires to Marcus. They started out at a green circuit board and led into a hole in the door. "Those go to the locking cylinder. Now, the way this works is that the right card will just trigger the board to give those two power for a short amount of time, so you can open the door."

Lucas pulled the wires from the board and separated them.

"So if I hold them directly on the batteries like this..." He touched the contacts of the battery pack within the reader with both ends, and a silent humming sound became audible. "Then you should be able to open the door. Try it."

Marcus turned the knob, and to his surprise, the door swung open.

"Have you ever considered founding a burglar school?" Marcus smiled at him.

"No point in that. Every child can open a lock like this." Lucas laughed and reassembled the card reader.

"I couldn't." Jasmin looked impressed.

"Well, anyway... Shall we go in?" Lucas stepped out of the way, letting Marcus go first once again.

The corridor looked as old as the one they had come in through. But there was by far less dust. Marcus quickly approached the first door, leading to a rear-facing room. None of them was surprised anymore when it turned out that the room was not special at all. The window was barred, and the room was completely empty. Marcus then approached the next door, this time one that was facing up front.

"That one is an office. We saw this from the outside," he said before pushing the door open. But to everyone's surprise, the room was not an office at all. The window seemed opaque, and heavy duty metal stanchions had been installed behind it. The rest of the room was empty.

"What the hell?" Marcus couldn't believe his eyes.

"Fake again." Lucas had stepped in. "Look, the whole curtain and office room setup is just a picture glued to the window to keep the appearance. I knew there was something wrong. The offices looked too similar."

"This is getting ridiculous." Cedric looked frustrated. "What the hell is this house?"

"It's a front. Someone has gone to quite some length to make this business appear big and spectacular," Lucas said and followed Marcus down the corridor to the next room. By now they were pretty sure that nobody would be in here, so they didn't bother too much staying silent anymore.

"But why? And why here?" Jasmin had gotten curious, too.

"Why? I have no clue. Why here? Well, most likely because Jackson owned the house anyway and had no more use for it after we had dismantled his little circus group," Lucas commented.

"Two left." Marcus interrupted the discussion and pushed the last front-facing room open.

"That's a new one," he then said, sounding a little surprised, after he had walked in.

Lucas quickly followed him and took a look around. He had already been in here, half a year ago. The camping table was still standing there, including the black table cloth, the pentagram was still visible on the floor and even the chest was still here.

"This is where the Satanists held their mass." Lucas nodded.

"And it still gives me the creeps." Jasmin had walked in as well.

Lucas walked over and opened the chest. It was filled with the mass requisites, the cup, the plate, even a bottle of schnapps was in there.

"Didn't even bother to clean up." He laughed and showed the bottle to the others before putting it back in. "Let's see what the last room has to offer," he then suggested and walked out.

Marcus was again first in line. He pushed the door open and nearly stumbled. There was no room behind that door, just a staircase leading down.

"Now we know why this is restricted." Lucas grinned when he looked down. It was an old staircase, stone steps as a base, a cast-iron handrail, barely wide enough for one person, and very steep.

"Shall we?" Marcus asked and started walking down without waiting for an answer. When he reached the bottom he flipped what seemed to be the light switch, but nothing happened.

"Not even the lights work around here," Marcus complained and stepped aside into a room to let the others follow in. "Watch out, the room is not exactly high," he warned Lucas, but the warning came too late. Lucas had already bumped his head into the ceiling.

"Thanks for the warning," he laughed in agony.

Marcus started sweeping the room with his flashlight. It was a typical old-style basement with a few cupboards in it. Connecting corridors led away in two directions to adjacent rooms. Lucas had to walk in a ducked position to not hit his head again. He approached the cupboards and took a closer look. Most of them were covered in dust and spider webs; apparently nobody had been here for a while.

"Something is moving over there!" Cedric suddenly yelled, pointing to one of the corridors and taking cover close to the wall.

"Where?" Marcus had directed his flashlight to the spot, but the distance was too far for it to really be effective.

"There, I see it too." Jasmin pointed the direction as well.

Lucas tried hard, but so far he couldn't make out anything.

"Whoever you are, show yourself or face the consequences," Lucas yelled with a firm voice.

They all waited eagerly for about a minute, but nothing happened.

"Show yourself or face the consequences? Really?" Marcus whispered to Lucas.

"It was worth a try, don't you think?" Lucas whispered back.

Then suddenly Lucas saw it too. A movement, not much more than a shadow close to the floor. And a moment later he saw two tiny red dots where the movement had been.

"What the hell?" He tried to identify what that was, but Cedric didn't leave him much of a chance.

"TEMPESTAS," he suddenly yelled.

Lucas could see Marcus jumping toward Jasmin, pulling her down to the ground. He didn't understand what the purpose was, but followed the example and jumped down, too. A moment later he understood. Dust and shrapnel came flying through the air and even some of the cupboards broke and went ballistic. Lucas had to cough and choke so heavily that he almost didn't hear the screech in the other room.

"Are you mad?" Marcus yelled at Cedric after the dust had set a little bit. "You could have killed us all. What a loony idea was it to start a storm in a basement!"

"Sorry, but it did the trick, didn't it?" Cedric grinned with a little shame mixed in.

"Let's find out." Lucas was still coughing and trying to get the filth off his robes.

Marcus nodded and led the way to the next room carefully. The air was still filled with dust, which made it hard to see and even harder to breathe.

"Yeah, it did the trick," Marcus finally said after looking through the room.

"What was it? What did I hit?" Cedric was a few steps behind and still couldn't see it.

"Congratulations, Whirlwind. You have just killed a rat," Marcus laughed and took a step aside.

"That was quite an overkill for a rat, don't you think?" Jasmin was patting Cedric's shoulder.

"Yeah, right." Cedric looked a little contrite now.

"Let's get out of here. Nobody was in here for ages judging by the dust, and I don't want to die from asphyxiation down here if I can help it," Lucas suggested.

The others nodded and followed him back upstairs. Back in the light of the entrance hall they continued dusting down their robes.

"Mate, please take some CQB classes before trying something like that again, will you?" Marcus grinned at Cedric.

"What is CQB?" Jasmin asked.

"Closed Quarter Battle," Lucas laughed. "Military slang for fighting in houses. And I agree, Whirlwind, please tame your energy next time."

"So what do we do now?" Jasmin asked.

"I would say we leave. There is nothing of interest here." Lucas suggested. "Unless of course any of you have better ideas?"

"I would still like to know why Jackson secured this one wing different than the others. And what he is doing here in the first place." Marcus seemed unhappy.

"So would I, but the means of finding out are hardly in this house," Lucas replied.

"So how do we proceed with this?" Marcus asked.

"I would say we go about this two ways: For one, we still have a second location to look at. And for the other, I will feed the Professor the pictures of the hall, including the logo. Maybe he can come up with something that makes sense," Lucas said.

"Sounds good," Jasmin nodded. "Would you like to go to the church right away? Or shall we plan this for another time?"

"Well, we had planned on doing it right away, and I don't see any reason not to." Lucas shrugged his shoulders. "Unless any of you has different plans?"

The others just shook their heads in reply.

"So what way do we go out?" Jasmin asked.

"Interesting question." Lucas thought a little. "I would say we try to leave everything as undisturbed as possible and head back out the way we came in."

The others nodded and quickly wandered off. Marcus went down the restricted area, closing all the doors, Jasmin did the same in the conference area and Cedric headed back to the wing they came in.

"Hey Guardian, we might have a little problem." Marcus called Lucas.

"What's that?" Lucas was just in the middle of restoring the reception desk to its original state, but interrupted his work and walked over to him.

"I can't lock the door. This stupid knob doesn't move." Marcus pointed at the locking mechanism.

"Well, that is a little problem after all. It just means that I have to dismantle the card reader once again." Lucas laughed and signaled Marcus to give him the knife again.

The boys quickly went through the routine again and firmly locked the door, leaving no traces of it having ever been opened. Lucas then returned to the front desk, finishing up there.

"All set?" he asked the others when he was done.

"Yep," Cedric said while Jasmin and Marcus nodded.

"Then let's get the hell out of here." Lucas walked back toward the broken window. He could hear Marcus and Cedric closing the door again and reattaching the hinge bolts before following him.

"Seems the only thing we can't fix here is the window," Marcus grinned.

"Yeah, but we also didn't break it, so no worries," Lucas laughed.

"My little worry is only that if somebody discovers the broken window they will also discover our footsteps in there." Marcus pointed at the dust on the floor.

"Valid point." Lucas nodded after climbing out into the garden.

"Well, I guess there is a way to fix this, too." Cedric was grinning.

"What do you have in mind?" Lucas was curious.

"I'll show you." Cedric was still grinning. "Cougar, please close the window, will you?"

After all of them had jumped back out, Marcus restored the window to its original position. Lucas took a quick look around, and right now it really looked as if the footprints, both inside the room and out here in the snow, were the only thing that could give them away.

"TEMPESTAS," Cedric said firmly with his arm stretched out through the broken glass. The storm that followed had all the dust in the room flying through the air.

"Now, once this settles there will be no footprints left." He winked at Lucas. "Maybe I am better in Stealth operations than I am in CQB."

"Nice one," Lucas laughed. "Can you do the same thing with our footprints out here too?"

"That might be a little harder." Cedric shook his head.

"Don't worry, the forecast predicted snow for the next few days anyway, so Mother Nature will take care of that for us," Marcus said.

"Ok then, let's get out of our robes and then out of here," Lucas said. "Next stop: the Chapel."

The group headed out of the suburb and began a thirty minute ride to the chapel. There, they went through everything with the same precision they used in the house, but the result was even more disappointing. From what Lucas could tell, nobody had been in that chapel since their run-in with the Satanists in summer. The place looked exactly the same as it had before, and even the destroyed torches were still lying around the playground, right where they had left them. In the end, no matter how frustrating that was for all of them, all they could do was to leave and call it a day. On the way back to Luton, Jasmin threw in the idea of visiting Wolfman's apartment as well, but the suggestion was short-lived. It was getting late, the chances of finding anything in that apartment were slim at best, and in the end they all agreed that the risk of getting caught breaking and entering was by far higher in the middle of an apartment block in Luton than it had been in the abandoned house out on Woodcock Road. Ultimately they had to face the fact that, thanks to them, the Satanist group was gone, and the black-robe mages they were looking for would hardly use the same locations again. That angle was undoubtedly dead; Lucas just hoped that the other roads would bring more success.

CHAPTER 11

Clues

Lucas had tried to find time over the weekend to follow up on the logo they had found, as well as do his own research about Mr. Jackson. Unfortunately, other things once again were more important, this time revolving mostly around home and family, like clearing the entranceway from snow. So when Monday came and he was cycling out to the shack, he once again came completely unprepared. He did try to use the travel time to clear his thoughts, but in the cold this was not exactly easy. In the end he was just grateful that this time most of the attention would rest on Darien's shoulders.

Arriving at O'Brien Mansion he was second this time; only Stephanie had been earlier. He stowed his bike and walked in, greeting her in their usual way.

"I am happy that you are here." She looked frustrated. "I have been trying for half an hour now to get the fire going, but it just doesn't work. I don't know what I am doing wrong here."

"Let me have a look," Lucas offered. "I am no good at this either, but maybe together we can figure it out."

They started fumbling around with it, rearranging the wood, trying time and again, but it was no good. Even together they just couldn't get it going.

"What the heck are you two doing?" Marcus had entered without them noticing.

"Trying to be you," Lucas laughed. "But to no end."

"You both seem to have no clue whatsoever when it comes to this." Marcus laughed. "This looks pitiful."

"Well, then consider this being my official cry for help." Lucas winked.

"And I will gladly answer that call," Marcus smiled. "Look here, the small pieces you used down here are wet. They can't catch fire, unless you blast them with a flamethrower."

"Well, then we are in trouble," Stephanie sighed. "There are no dry pieces left to use, at least not in that size."

"That is trouble that can be fixed easily," Marcus laughed. "Do you have an axe around somewhere?"

"Sure, outside in the closet next to the firewood." Stephanie nodded.

"I'll go and get it." Lucas had jumped up and was walking to fetch the tool. Arriving back inside, he saw that Marcus had removed all the wet wood from the fireplace and also had removed two dry pieces from it, having all of those piled up right next to him.

"Ah good," he said and took the axe from Lucas. "Now see… This piece is as dry as it could possibly be, so it is perfect to be used. It is far too big now to use as a shaving, but that can easily be changed."

Marcus started carefully chopping down one wooden piece, creating multiple small ones. To protect everything else he used the second large piece as a chopping block.

"Nice one," Lucas complimented. It had taken Marcus only a minute to create enough dry wood chips to start the fire. Shoving a piece of paper below the chips and piling up larger chunks of wood on top, he quickly had the fire going. Lucas watched with fascination how the burning paper set the wood chips ablaze and those in turn ignited the larger pieces.

"We are lucky to have a boy scout in the group." Stephanie patted Marcus' shoulder.

"Just contributing my part to the whole." Marcus grinned and jumped up. "I'll take the axe back out. We should maybe keep the small branches in here, so they can dry up until next week."

Lucas took off his coat and sat down on a chair. Stephanie followed his lead, taking a place at the bench.

"Are you still OK with this Friday?" Stephanie asked.

"The day is marked red in my calendar." Lucas nodded. "I will be there."

"Thank you." Stephanie smiled. "I am really looking forward to this."

"Ditto." Lucas grinned. "We will for sure have a good time."

Finally the others arrived one by one, Jasmin and Darien being quite late, which was not really unusual for Jasmin, but quite unusual for Darien.

"Sorry for making you wait," he said, completely out of breath when he came running in. "I was so focused on the research that I completely lost the time."

"Well, let's hope it paid off at least," Lucas laughed.

"It quite did, but maybe you want to share your findings first? Mine will take a while, most likely."

"Very well, so let's start with our little field trip last week," Lucas said and started filling Stephanie and Darien in on what they had found out.

"Disappointing, but interesting," Darien commented after he had finished.

"Agreed with disappointing. Not so much with interesting." Lucas grinned. "Cougar, what about you?"

"Well, we did manage to find the right police station, which is not that easy in London," Marcus started. "We even managed to get through to this Detective Murphy, but all he said is that they are still looking and can't comment on a case that is currently under investigation."

"That's disappointing as well," Stephanie said.

"Well, hold your horses, Airmid," Marcus continued. "We did chat with a few others on the way out and one of them was more willing to talk, although he also did not tell me too much I have to admit." Marcus cleared his throat before continuing.

"What he did tell us was that the license plates were stolen."

"Figures," Cedric interrupted him.

"Yeah. More interesting, though, was that the vehicle itself was also stolen," Marcus continued.

"Come again? Someone mounted stolen plates on a stolen vehicle? What sense does that make?" Lucas was surprised.

"That's what they are wondering as well. They know who the thief of the truck was; apparently there was a dispute about the ownership that started all this, but this guy doesn't have it anymore, either, he reported it stolen as well."

"A thief that gets robbed, I like the sound of that." Lucas laughed.

"They are still trying to find the truck. So far they have no lead on it," Marcus said. "And that goes for our thieves too. No ideas, no luck. But the guys said that this Murphy is driving them incredibly hard to figure it out, so it at least seems to be in good hands there."

"Not exactly good news, but at least news." Lucas nodded. "Thank you, Cougar. And the same to you, Psycho."

"My pleasure." Marcus bowed a little.

"OK, Professor, the show is all yours." Lucas smiled at him.

"Well, where to start? I have quite a lot of information." Darien thought for a moment. "Let's start with the thieves. I checked the logo on the side of the truck. It was fake. There is no company like this; it just doesn't exist."

"Bad news to start with. We seem to have run out of luck." Marcus sighed.

"Not fully." Darien smiled. "I started looking around in discussion boards. And interestingly I found quite a few people that were talking about thefts like ours. The discussions were pretty scattered, so it took me a while to find the common ground: All the companies that got robbed have a high tech security system for their storage rooms. And those systems are all either built or at least deployed by a company called PowerSec Security Services."

"So that's how they stay undetected. They know the security systems." Marcus was impressed by the detective work.

"Yeah, well, that's kind of the problem," Darien said. "One of the things that PowerSec is proud of is that they have very highly skilled and trained experts on their team. With each system they deploy they do a test run, letting all their experts loose on it simultaneously, trying to push it to the limits. And from what I read about that group they are real professionals. Most customers deem the system unbreakable; even the military has some of them. So not even an insider would have a chance to break those."

"And what about their spooks? If they are so extremely professional, wouldn't it be a valid assumption that one or more of them has gone rogue?" Lucas asked.

"I thought along those lines as well, but I don't see how or why." Darien shook his head. "For one, if any of their guys can break the system at the test it immediately gets redesigned to fix the weakness. And for the other, those guys get paid incredibly well, so going rogue would most likely have more risks than profits attached."

"Interesting." Lucas nodded. "I am guessing that the military will be getting concerned by now, too. If somebody has figured out a systemic weakness in the PowerSec installations then they have the risk of being exposed as well."

"I agree. That's why was thinking about a military contractor being the thief, sort of trying the systems out without touching military equipment in the process. But this would be highly illegal, so I somewhat doubt that as well."

Darien waited for a moment to see if anybody else wanted to step into the discussion, but as they all were just looking at him with prying eyes he finally continued.

"Ok, next topic," he started. "My friend at the university got back to me. He took a look at our mystery substance. It turns out that the basic binding component is actually quite similar to what is used in fertilizer. The rest of it made no sense to him whatsoever. He described it as 'random components that don't have any reactive properties'."

"Did the stuff dilute already? I mean, we saw the power of this, so it can't be non-reactive," Marcus asked.

"No, it didn't. He sent the rest back to me and it still has most of its power. My guess would be that magical energy just cannot be found in a lab." Darien shook his head.

"So it means we are back to relying on your skills then, Professor," Lucas said.

"Mostly yes, unfortunately." Darien nodded. "But there is one thing that did come out of this analysis: The fertilizer base component is not only a binding agent for the potion itself. My friend said that the only reason to use something like this would be so the substance can easily bind to the soil and transfer its active ingredients into it quickly."

"To the soil? What good would that do for a magical ritual?" Marcus looked perplexed.

"Might be that mages in the end draw their energy from the soil; I don't know. But whatever the reason, this stuff works best if it is used in nature." Darien said.

"That might be why Wolfman had it in the shaft of the torches instead of in the burn chamber." Lucas nodded. "At last something finally starts making sense."

"But they also had the torches in the house, where there was no soil nearby. And don't forget that the guys in Buxton did burn it in the candles," Jasmin reminded him.

"Good point." Lucas nodded and started thinking. "And once again all the sense it made is gone."

"Could it be that this thing has more than one use?" Stephanie asked.

"Possibly." Darien nodded. "But knowing from you how hard it is to actually brew a potion that does one thing I somehow doubt it. Making a potion that does multiple things must be far more complex. And why bother? If you need two things done, use two potions."

"Interesting theory, though." Lucas looked first at her, then at Darien. "You yourself said once that this substance has multiple parts to it."

"I know." Darien nodded. "Right now it doesn't make too much sense."

"Well, let's return to this topic later. What else?" Lucas asked.

"I did research the company logo you sent me from the house, and afterwards took the liberty of researching our strange Mr. Jackson, as well. Jackson & Company is a small and quite dubious firm. It has clients all over the UK and Europe, but mostly they deal with either UK targets or a company in France. I tried to trace some of their shipments, which was quite easy, given that they don't have a fleet, or cars, or anything--they just hire other shipping companies to do the work."

"Why would somebody do that?" Jasmin seemed confused.

"I honestly have no clue." Darien shrugged his shoulders. "All I can tell you is that they are bogus, front to back. And they do charge horrendous amounts of money for very small shipments that they then just send via a normal parcel service."

"Sounds like money laundering to me," Lucas commented.

"Might be. But given what else Jackson is into, I even doubt that. This import-export fraud of his is not even important enough for him to open his petty cash supply. The amounts in there are so small compared to everything else, they just don't matter."

"What else is he into?" Lucas was curious.

"Well, you do know about JDC Inc. and Harlington Research already. He also has his foot in a lot of other biochemistry facilities, environmental corporations, real estate agencies and most importantly, a lot of investment companies that are gathering money like crazy but are currently holding back on investing. We are for the whole construct literally talking tens of millions of pounds. Oh, and I almost forgot to mention: There is always a companion in those companies, and together with him Jackson always has a majority."

"So what does a money-heavy investor like this do with a gang of Satanists?" Jasmin asked.

"Interesting question. And unfortunately I have no answer," Darien replied.

"My guess would be that he is just following orders." Lucas said. "So the real question is: What does his companion do with those Satanists? Or with this whole construct to begin with?"

"For me the interesting question would be: Who is that companion?" Marcus added.

"Yeah, that's a good one too." Darien nodded. "I tried hard to find out, but so far I only hit closed doors."

"OK, another end with more questions than answers." Lucas sighed. "Anything else?"

"Yep, I got one more." Darien nodded once again. "I looked for more information about Plague, Cypher and their strange gang. It turns out that they are leaking massive amounts of strange spells and ritual manuals, like the one we saw in Buxton. But interestingly they don't do it themselves. They always have their minions do it."

"What's so interesting about this? That's called delegation," Cedric asked.

"It's interesting because they always punish the guy that published it and then try to remove it from the net again."

"So? They are stupid and have a lot of leaks. What's your point, Professor?" Marcus said.

"There seems to be more to it than that," Darien continued. "I can't really put my finger on it, but I am quite sure that those 'punishments' are staged, and so is the whole removal thing. I think that they are deliberately leaking this out, but do it that way so they have plausible deniability."

"Which still is a little ridiculous," Marcus said. "Leaking something that only magic users believe in in the first place and then denying doing it makes no sense. The magical community wouldn't care about them leaking anything now, would they?"

"You have a valid point, Cougar," Darien said. "And there is no explanation for it, at least none that I could give you."

"So nothing concrete there either," Lucas sighed.

"There is one more thing about them," Darien interrupted. "By tracking the leaks I came up with a grid, and it's strangely wide."

"What do you mean?" Lucas' curiosity was sparked once again.

"If all my assumptions are right, then those guys have circles pretty much all over the UK. Which is awkward as it means that they would have to travel a lot for doing the mentoring."

"Not so much in fact," Marcus threw in. "At least not if you consider how many visits we got from Angel. That's easily doable."

"But you have to agree that it is also quite an effort. I would expect that a mentor has his circle close by, so he can keep an eye on things. Sitting in London and having a circle in Edinburgh is just stupid from where I stand," Darien said.

"Unfortunately, we are not getting anywhere with this," Lucas said. "Did you find any connection between the mages and Brix & Burton?"

"Unfortunately not." Darien shook his head. "And that is about all information I have."

"Very well, thank you for the effort." Lucas smiled at him.

"What do we do now?" Stephanie asked. "It seems to me that we exhausted pretty much all our options."

"I would not go that far, but you are more or less right that we don't have much to go on right now." Lucas nodded. "Any suggestions?"

"I will keep on the topics; maybe I can dig up something more," Darien said.

"Is any other circle close by? Maybe we can draw them out by taking another one apart?" Marcus threw in.

"I will check for that, too." Darien nodded.

"And what about the pictures?" Cedric asked.

"That will be next, I guess." Lucas nodded. "If the Professor has brought them."

"I sure have." Darien nodded again and pulled a laptop out of his backpack.

"The one thing I could think of would be to talk to that security company. Maybe they can shed some light," Jasmin added.

"I don't think they will welcome us with open arms," Lucas said. "Especially not if it is about a flaw in their system."

"They might not want to talk to us, but I think I know somebody they will have to talk to." Cedric grinned.

"And who would that be?" Lucas asked.

"My father. After all, he is a customer."

"And you think he will do that?" Lucas asked.

"Oh, if I tell him about Cougar's first run-in with them and that the security system is most likely the key, he for sure will." Cedric laughed.

"Good idea. And at least worth a try." Lucas smiled. "Thanks, Whirlwind."

"Shall we have a look at the pictures now?" Darien asked and pulled the first one up on the screen.

The others gathered around him, so everybody could have a good look at the screen. The first picture was the one from the tire. It was pretty dark, but it was easy to recognize that the truck used steel rims and was obviously not cleaned too often, at least not around the tires.

"Can you blow up that section here?" Marcus asked and pointed out a part of the tire.

"Sure thing." Darien made a few clicks to zoom into the outlined area. "What are you looking for?"

"I was hoping to read the make and model of the tire, but the picture is too dark." Marcus was piqued about not having used his flash when taking the pictures.

"I can fix that for you." Darien said and started clicking around in his photo editor until the contrast was high enough to read the imprints. "Unfortunately, the tires are a pretty common model, so unless you know something I don't, we won't get anywhere with those."

"Damn," Marcus cursed.

Darien switched to the next picture. It showed the back of the vehicle. They looked at it carefully from every possible angle, including zooming on every spot they deemed suspicious, but nothing stuck. Switching to the next picture, Darien showed the logo on the driver's door. It was a green tree in a circle with the company name 'Garden Ninjas – tree and lawn treatment' written around it.

"They have to be paranoid. A vehicle they stole from a thief, stolen plates and a logo that doesn't even exist," Stephanie said, looking at the picture.

"Yeah, so this one also does us no good." Darien had already switched to the next picture when Marcus interrupted him.

"Hold on a second--can you switch back, please?" he said.

"Sure." Darien nodded and brought the picture back up.

"What is this?" Marcus pointed at something between the tree and the circle.

When Darien zoomed in on the section, Lucas also took a close look. It looked like a shadow, but it was hard to tell.

"Can you do your contrast-thing again?" Marcus asked.

"Yeah, of course." Darien had already been working on this, having the same thought.

After a few minutes of clicking around, the shadow finally began to take shape.

"What is that?" Jasmin asked.

"Looks like another logo." Lucas had brought his head close to the screen. "So that's why the painted the new one on it. To get rid of the old one."

"I still can't make out what it says." Marcus had his head close to Lucas'.

Darien continued working the picture with all his skills, but the only thing that he could generate were a few outlines.

"I'll have to continue this at home where I have better screens and tools for this," Darien said after a while. "It was a good catch, though, Cougar. I totally missed that."

"Twelve eyes…" Marcus grinned.

"Let's go to the next then," Lucas said.

Darien brought up the picture of the upper front. It showed the VIN tag and a good look into the drivers' cabin.

"What is all that stuff in there?" Stephanie asked.

"The things I could identify are a map over here, some kind of duffle bag here and a coffee mug here," Darien pointed out.

"What about the map? Is there anything on it that could lead us to the thieves?" Marcus pointed at it.

"I am not sure." Darien said. "The picture has a quite good quality, but I still can't make out too much. Take a look. I did try to enhance it already." Darien pulled up another picture that showed only the map. Lucas looked at it carefully, but the quality was by far not good enough to read any names on it.

"Even good quality has its limitations," he said.

"From the scale down here it looks like a 1:250.000 hiking map." Marcus had turned his head almost upside down to look at the lines in question.

"Why are you breaking your neck for this?" Darien laughed. "I can flip the picture over if you like."

"That might actually help." Marcus grinned.

Darien made a few more clicks and rotated the picture by 180 degrees.

"Yeah, this is definitely a hiking map." Marcus studied it carefully. "But unfortunately there are hundreds of places that would fit this general layout. Without a reference point, there is no way we can pinpoint this."

"And even if we could find out where the map belongs to, it would still not help. The map shows an area of over hundred square kilometers; we can hardly search all of it," Lucas threw in.

"It would help a little at least," Darien objected. "And we could again run some analysis based on the location of the last camp and the fact that they will for sure want a quiet area again."

"Based on the topography, I would still like to try finding the actual map," Marcus said. "If you don't mind."

"Sure thing." Lucas nodded. "But this will most likely be like the needle in the haystack."

"Very likely. But that has never stopped us from trying so far, so why should it now?" Marcus laughed.

"Fair enough." Lucas laughed. "And we don't have too much else to go on, anyway."

"What about that bag?" Jasmin asked. "Is this any good?"

"I don't think so." Darien opened the previous picture again and zoomed in on the duffle bag. "There are no markings on it, no tags or logos, nothing to go on. And the same also goes for the coffee mug."

Darien switched over to last picture in the collection, the one showing the front license plate. They all looked at it carefully, but once again there was nothing useful to see.

"So what do we do now?" Jasmin asked after Darien had turned off his notebook.

"We don't have much to go on right now, unfortunately," Lucas sighed. "The Professor has most of the tasks again, with Jackson, the other circles and now the repainted logo on the van, and Cougar wanted to follow up on the map."

"For that it would help if you could send me your enhanced pictures, Professor," Marcus said.

"Sure thing." Darien nodded.

"Could you please send all the pictures to the rest of us, too?" Cedric asked. "I would like to look at them one more time if I find a quiet moment."

Darien nodded in reply.

"And then of course there is Whirlwind's approach to the security company. Maybe this will give us more insight. Have I missed anything?" Lucas looked from one to the next, but nobody said anything.

"Well, then I would appreciate if we could call it a night," he continued. "It currently is a stressful time for me, and I would like to get some sleep."

The others nodded and started packing up. When they stepped out of the hut it was quite refreshing for him, feeling the cold breeze on his face. Jasmin bid farewell quickly and jumped into her car. The others cycled to Luton together, through the cold winter evening. It was a quiet ride, none of them too eager to talk about anything. Lucas was under the impression that it had been a good idea to call the meeting short. The others also seemed tired and eager to get back home, which was a strange feeling in the middle of the so-called quiet time of the year, shortly before Christmas.

When they all said goodbye and parted their ways, it was only 8 p.m., far earlier than normal. Lucas arrived home ten minutes later and was very much looking forward to a hot shower and his bed by now. To his surprise, the house was deserted when he entered. It took him a moment to remember that his parents had been invited to a Christmas party at his father's employer and were not due to return until very late in the night. He wasn't used to being home alone at night, but it didn't matter too much, either. He leisurely walked up to his room and started preparing for the shower. The one advantage being home alone had was that he didn't have to look for his bathrobe, which would most likely have taken a while, given that his room was not quite tidy right now. He could just walk over to the bathroom naked. He took a long time, relaxing under the hot water and brushing his teeth afterwards, before he came back to his room. He had just put on his boxer shorts and a t-shirt he normally wore at night when the bell rang downstairs.

"Are you kidding me?" he mumbled and looked at his watch. It was 8:45 now. He quickly put on his jeans and hastened down. After taking a quick look through the peephole, he opened the door.

"I heard that you left no stone unturned in Luton trying to find me?" the woman outside greeted him with a smile.

"You have a hell of a timing, Angel." Lucas shook his head. "Please come in." He stepped aside and let her walk past before shutting the door. She was, as always, wearing her red robes and had the hood pulled deep over her face.

"Why did you ring this time and not just enter like you did last time you visited me?" he asked and led her into the living room, after she had taken off her boots and taken down the hood.

"Because I wanted to give you time to dress this time." She smiled at him. "So, what is it that is so utterly important that even Kung Fu feels obliged to tell me on my first day back from vacation?"

"I am sorry she did," Lucas said and sat down at the couch. "I did want to talk to you about something, but it could have waited a while longer. I guess Kung Fu just felt the need to push it."

"At some point you have to tell me how you managed to get that feeling into her body," Angel laughed. "But let's stop stalling, shall we?"

"Very well." Lucas nodded. "We have a little problem, and I was hoping for your advice on it."

Angel sat quietly and waited for him to continue, so after a few moments he did.

"A while back we found this strange potion while dealing with the Satanist group," he started. "We were confronted with it again in Buxton, where it seemed to have been part of this ghost encounter we had. And now we have stumbled upon it again, but this time not in small quantities as before, but in larger amounts."

Lucas stopped and waited for Angel to say something about it. But a very short "And?" was the only comment she made.

"And now we are not sure what to do about it anymore. We classify this substance as highly dangerous, as has been proven by those guys in Buxton already, but the sheer quantity that we have discovered now is too big for us to handle. Now I was hoping that you could give us some advice."

"Well, as your mentor I can't anymore," Angel started.

"Why is that?" Lucas interrupted.

"Because you are a Magus now; you don't have a mentor anymore. And although some of the others in your circle have not made this transition yet I still have to stay out of it and leave it to you."

"So does this mean that you are no longer available for us?" Lucas asked.

"I am still available for your circle, and it will stay that way until all of you have made the step up. But there are things that I am not supposed to interfere in anymore, as those are the responsibility of the Mages in your group now, which right now means that they are the responsibility of you, Psycho and Airmid."

Lucas looked contrite and didn't know what to say. So after a minute of silence Angel continued.

"Having said all this I hope that you understand that I can't give you advice as your mentor anymore. But as a friend I can still offer friendly advice."

"And what would that be?" Lucas was immediately all ears.

"Be very careful," she said. "What you have stumbled into is big, but not too big for you. In the end, the six of you have to make the decision all by yourselves, but I am quite certain that you can handle even something that size. And remember: You are never alone out here. There are always others to help if you are in dire need."

"Thanks for the pep talk, Angel, but I still don't know how to tackle something as large as this. Plague and his circle obviously have a wide net of supporters on their side, and we don't."

"Are you sure that you don't? That you are the only one looking at this right now?"

"No, I am not. But I can also not be sure of the opposite. And I have no way of sharing information with those others, even if I knew that they were there. It's frustrating."

"Well, Guardian, that is the way magic works. You always stand in the shadows and have to work from out there. But rest assured, at some point you will learn to detect the others that are in those shadows with you."

"I hope this happens rather sooner than later," Lucas sighed. "And I sincerely hope that I will then find out that you and your friends are in the same shadows as well."

"Is there anything else I can do for you?" Angel asked after a moment of silence.

"Actually there are two things…" Lucas started. "First, I am wondering why the others have still not advanced to the level of Magus. I know that I have been a little slack with this--maybe it was my responsibility to act at some point."

"It wasn't." Angel shook her head. "The others have not made the transition yet."

"But why?" Lucas was a little confused.

"Well, let's see… The Professor has a lot of insight, but he has never woven the fabric of magic intentionally… Cougar is lacking some training lately; he is still stuck with two spells and hasn't done a new one yet. Whirlwind is close. Once he starts understanding what he is actually doing, he will advance. And just for the sake of completeness: Airmid only made the step because of a technicality. While her potion brewing gave her the leap up, her spellcasting is still not at that level at all."

"Interesting. Thank you for the insight." Lucas nodded.

"Sure. And again, this is not your responsibility, unless you want to take it. Until they step up they are still under my wing."

"Understood, thank you." Lucas nodded again.

"So, and what was the second thing?" Angel smiled.

"Tell Kung Fu that I said hi," he grinned.

"I see a nightmare approaching fast," she laughed. "But I will do it."

"Maybe you could share her phone number with me? Then I wouldn't have to tell you." Lucas winked.

"What am I? A dating agency?" Angel laughed again. "You two and your games are going to kill me at some point. Can't you just grow up?"

"Hey, I am the younger one. I have the right to be childish," Lucas defended himself with a grin.

"What have I gotten myself into here?" Angel shook her head with a grin and stood up.

"The normal nightmare of life I guess," Lucas said. "After all, you were the one that just transitioned yourself from a mentor to a friend. Now I can ask you for such things."

"You know the only thing I hate more than nosy children?" Angel looked at him.

"No…" Lucas said.

"Nosy children with a valid argument," she grinned. "Now I better get out of here, before you bring up another great idea of yours. Have a good night."

She had put her boots on already and was pulling her hood back up before walking out into the night. Lucas watched her walk away for a while, being a little unsure what had the upper hand, the friendly feeling from the conversation about Kung Fu, or the bad feeling of being on his own with the thieves and the black-robes.

CHAPTER 12

Priorities

During the remainder of the week Lucas caught a lucky break, as everyone in school was already in Christmas mood, keeping the workload to a minimum. So he was well rested when he rode his bike over to Stephanie's place for the party. At first he had been unsure of what to wear, as he never had been at a party before, so in the end he decided to stay true to himself, wearing jeans and a more or less elegant shirt.

Mr. O'Brien opened the door and led him in.

"Nice to see you, Lucas." He smiled and patted his shoulder. "Please come in; you are quite early."

"Thank you, sir." Lucas nodded and stepped in. "Better early than late."

He put his coat on a hanger and his boots on a plastic mat beside it and then followed Mr. O'Brien into the living room.

"Stephanie is not ready yet, so you are stuck with me for now," he said with a grin.

"I hope I am not keeping you from something?" Lucas asked.

"Ah, nonsense," he grinned. "Can I offer you something to drink?"

"Tea would be nice; it's quite cold outside."

"Sure thing." O'Brien nodded and went into the kitchen to boil some water.

"Your wife said that I could stay in your guest room after the party. Does that offer still stand?" Lucas had walked with him to the kitchen.

"Of course it does." He nodded. "Agatha has already prepared the bed for you. Come on, I'll show you; the water will take a few minutes anyway."

Mr. O'Brien led the way back to the foyer and to a door at the back of it.

"Here it is." He opened the door and stepped in.

Lucas followed him into the room and had a quick look around. It was a rather small room, one bed couch in the corner that, in its current expanded state, filled up half of the room, a small desk and chair beside it and a mirror right next to the door.

"Lovely." Lucas smiled. "Thank you."

"And the bathroom is just next door. It's not much, but I guess it will do for one night." O'Brien smiled.

"It's in fact more than enough, thank you." Lucas put his backpack into the guest room and then stepped out, closing the door behind him.

They walked back to the kitchen, where the water was already boiling.

"Any special wishes?" Mr. O'Brien opened a cabinet and stepped aside.

Lucas had to gasp when he took a look into it. The whole cabinet was filled with different sorts of tea--Lucas estimated far more than hundred.

"Jesus…" he said. "I have never seen such a variety of teas."

"My wife is a big fan of tea," O'Brien laughed. "She would fill the whole house with them if she could. So, what would you like to have?"

"I think I will stay with classic Earl Gray if you have it. Even if I only read the nametags, the water will long be cold before I'm halfway through." Lucas was overwhelmed.

"You are almost certainly right." O'Brien laughed and grabbed two boxes from the very top shelf. "We don't make Earl Gray that often. Do you prefer a pre-packaged one or an open one?" He showed both to Lucas.

"I'll go with whatever is less work to make." Lucas was still a little beside himself.

"Next time you should ask for beer." O'Brien laughed and started preparing the open Earl Gray for both of them. "There we don't have as many choices."

"Would be a good plan. But I don't drink alcohol, so it is unfortunately a little flawed." Lucas laughed too.

They sat down in the living room and chatted a little about day–to-day topics just to make the time go by.

"How is your friend, by the way?" O'Brien asked at one point.

"Which one?"

"The one that got shot--Marcus was his name, right?"

"He is fine, thanks for asking. Hasn't Stephanie told you that?" Lucas was a little cautious with this topic.

"No. And she wouldn't talk about it at all. We wouldn't even know about the incident if his mother hadn't called us the day after."

"Well, we are all happy that he came out of it without major injuries, and we try not to think about it too much."

"Sounds a little like denial to me, if you don't mind me saying. And that's not good." O'Brien looked a little worried.

"Believe me, it's not. We were all in the hospital right after he had been brought there, we saw the wounds and we have all dealt with it on our own terms. In the end if we keep this image alive it will keep us from doing our best, because it will keep us afraid," Lucas replied calmly.

"Fear makes you cautious, so it can be helpful," O'Brien suggested.

"It can also paralyze you and stop you from helping those that need your help. Sometimes taking a calculated risk is necessary, and I think all of us understand that by now. What Cougar's injury did show us, though, is that sometimes risk and foolishness are quite close together. We understand that now, too."

"Wise words from a young man." O'Brien seemed impressed. "In the end I think it's best to try staying out of fights as much as possible."

"I couldn't agree more." Lucas nodded. "But I think you should stay out of those by conscious decision, not by fear. Our German teacher once taught us a saying that is all too true. There is unfortunately no good English translation for it, but what it more or less says is that if you are frightened to death you still wind up dead. And that's the worst choice you can make."

"And again wise words." O'Brien laughed. "I am glad for your friend, and I hope that you don't face something like this again."

"Don't worry," Lucas laughed. "I intend to grow quite old."

"So I heard that one of the bullets hit Marcus in the leg. How long will it take him to get his full mobility back?"

"Unfortunately, I can't judge the peak mobility he had, but so far it didn't look as if there were any restrictions for him. He is quite agile and jumping around already, actually has been ever since they let him out of the hospital."

"So he was lucky enough that both bullets missed any vital parts? The kid truly does have a guardian angel."

"And the favor of the goddess of healing, yes." Lucas nodded with a grin.

"It seems we have to cut our conversation short." Mr. O'Brien suddenly grinned and pointed toward the staircase.

Lucas turned around and took a look. Mrs. O'Brien was just coming down. Judging from her face, she was not exactly happy.

"That child is driving me crazy," she said to her husband. "I would never, ever have worn such an outfit."

"That might be a good sign." Mr. O'Brien laughed. "After all, the outfits you like to wear are more than twenty years old. If she would wear one of those she would be the laughingstock of the party."

"Better laughingstock than party slut." She seemed seriously offended. "The way she is dressed, every boy will jump at her right away and she is still too young for that."

"May I inquire at what age you had your first boyfriend, or at least more intense contact with a boy?" Lucas was not sure if it was wise to ask that question, but somehow he couldn't stop himself.

He was already close to taking cover behind the sofa, given that Mrs. O'Brien's face turned somewhere between darkish red and purple, when he heard Mr. O'Brien laughing so loudly that he was afraid of hearing him fall from the couch next.

Nobody spoke until Mr. O'Brien finally had calmed down enough to talk again.

"She had her first experience at fourteen," he said. "Face it, honey, Lucas has just caught you with your pants down."

Mrs. O'Brien seemed to be caught completely on the wrong foot. She didn't move, didn't say anything; she was just standing there with her purple-red face.

"Come on, honey. I'll make you some tea. That will get your thoughts straight again." Her husband was laughing again. He had stood up, taken her hand and was now pulling her into the kitchen. They had not even closed the kitchen door yet when Stephanie peeked around the corner.

"Is it safe to come down now?" she asked shyly.

"Why wouldn't it be?" Lucas smiled at her.

"Well, my mummy was quite outraged when she left my room before. And I am a little afraid that my daddy will be as well." She finally walked down into the room.

When Lucas looked at her he had to gasp. Stephanie was wearing tight black jeans, a semi-transparent white blouse with a tight white top underneath and a red woolen vest.

"Holy crap," he said after he had caught his breath again.

"Is something wrong?" she asked.

"Depends on your definition of wrong." He laughed. "You look overwhelmingly gorgeous in that outfit."

"So you also think that it is too extreme?" Stephanie looked a little unsure again.

"Depends on what you want to achieve with it, I would say," Lucas said calmly. "And I am not really a good judge of this. I don't know how people are dressed at parties."

"Well, what I want is at least a little attention, preferably from some boys."

"I can guarantee you that you will have that," Lucas laughed.

"Are you OK with me going there like this?" she asked.

"Steph, I am good with you going there however you like to go. If you are good with it, go for it." He smiled at her.

Stephanie's parents came walking back into the room. Her mother had obviously calmed down; her father was still cheerful.

"You know, honey, maybe you should take an example from your daughter and try this outfit for a change." Mr. O'Brien seemed impressed when he saw Stephanie.

Lucas could almost feel the blood rushing back into Mrs. O'Brien's head, so he decided to go for a quick retreat.

"I think it's time for us to leave," he said.

"You two have fun. And stay safe," Mr. O'Brien replied.

"Thank you, sir. We will." Lucas nodded and walked to the foyer with Stephanie.

"I told you to call me Stan," He heard Mr. O'Brien say from behind, but ignored it.

They quickly stepped into their boots, put on their coats and walked out. Stephanie led the way, with Lucas walking next to her. The night was clear and very cold. They had to walk carefully so as not to slip on the icy ground but in their good mood this was hardly a problem, and it was not too far, either. After about ten minutes of walking they arrived at their destination. The house was extensively decorated and it seemed as if every single light was on inside. When the door was opened they could see that the party was already in full swing, although they were still pretty early.

"Hi Stephanie. Welcome to the best Christmas party in town," the girl that had opened the door said. She was about Stephanie's age and looked pretty much like her, except for her long white-blonde hair. Her outfit suggested that Stephanie had not been far off. Tight pants and a red tummy top were all she was wearing.

"I didn't know that you had a boyfriend," she said after letting them in. "And a cute one too," she added with a flirtatious grin.

"Rebecca, meet Lucas." Stephanie did the introductions. "And he is not my boyfriend, just a friend."

"Don't say that too loudly or I will take him from you." She grinned and somehow Lucas had the feeling that she was checking him out quite intensely when they walked into the living room. A quick look around reminded him why he never liked parties, even though he only knew them from stories. The room they had just entered had some tables with chairs in it and a bar on one side. He couldn't tell what the people were drinking, but from the smell alone he was sure that there was a lot of alcohol involved. The next room was lit by a color organ and loud music was audible. He counted about twenty people in both rooms, about half girls and half boys, all of them younger than himself. It was hard to get precise numbers, though, the strobes and color organ in the dance room made it almost impossible to see anyone.

"Our resident barkeeper is Charly." Rebecca introduced them to a man in his early twenties who was standing behind the bar. "He will mix you whatever you want, but I would encourage you to test his specialties. They are really good."

With that she left to answer the door again.

"What can I get you two?" Charly asked.

"What are those specialties that Rebecca was talking about?" Stephanie asked.

"They are called the Blue Goo, the Pink Drink and the Black Powerpack," he answered.

"Sounds dangerous," Lucas laughed.

"Blue is good to keep you up all night, pink is helpful to get emotional and black will give you enough juice so you can dance all evening without getting exhausted."

"I would really like to try one of those." Stephanie had turned to Lucas. "Do you mind?"

"Stop asking me that." Lucas had to laugh again. "Do whatever you like to do. Don't even take notice of me."

She smiled and turned back to Charly.

"Then let me have this Black Powerpack for starters," she said.

"Sure thing. And what can I get for you?" he asked Lucas.

"Coke would be nice if you have it." Lucas was a little unsure, but that seemed the easiest way to go for now.

"Sure thing. What do you want in it?"

"Excuse me?"

"What do you want in it? Rum? Schnapps? Vodka?"

"Nothing." Lucas shook his head. "Just plain Coke."

"That's a new one," Charly laughed and started mixing things together. Lucas watched him with fascination. The speed with which he found all the right bottles, and the way he mixed it together, which looked like precision work, even though it was all done without any scales, made this guy look like an experienced professional.

"You do this a lot, don't you?" Lucas asked.

"Yes." Charly nodded and started shaking the drink. "Almost every day for more than three years now. Best job I ever had."

In the meantime others had joined them on the bar and Charly took their orders as well, just nodding, not even taking notes. When he turned back to them he just put two big glasses in front of them.

"One Black Powerpack and one regular Coke, just plain. Enjoy," he said with a smile before turning back again to serve the others.

Lucas looked at the drinks. At first glance it was hard to distinguish them. The Black Powerpack proved true to its name, pitch black, even darker than the Coke, bubbling heavily and smelling quite intensely.

"You are sure that you want to drink that?" Lucas laughed.

"Why? Is it a problem?" Stephanie looked unsure.

"Not for me. It just looks a little like tar, and I, personally, would not drink something that looks like that." He grinned.

"I am sure that it will not kill me." She grinned back. "And it smells quite good too."

"Well then... Cheers!" Lucas lifted his glass in her direction and took a sip. He then watched Stephanie drink the first gulp of hers, but quite to his surprise it seemed to be not too bad--or at least if it was, Stephanie did a good job not letting him see it.

"I would like to dance a little," she said. "Do you want to join me?"

"I think I'll stay back and find a place somewhere over here. If you want to meet some guys here, it is better if I am not too close by. I might scare them off."

"OK." Stephanie smiled. "Have fun."

With that she walked off onto the dance floor and out of his sight. Lucas took his glass and walked to the corner table, closest to the exit and farthest away from the dance floor. It was empty, and judging from where the others had taken their places this would be the last one anyone would like to have anyway. Sitting down on the comfortable corner bench he started scanning the room. People were coming in regularly and the rooms were filling up quite quickly. And even though the new arrivers normally came in groups of either girls or boys only at a time, the balance remained pretty much intact. And they still looked all about Stephanie's age at most. The most interesting part for him was watching the bar. The longer he watched, the more he was convinced that he was in fact the only one in the room not drinking alcohol. He was curious if this was even legal for people younger than him, but somehow this seemed to be the least of the concerns anyone had in the house. It also raised the question in his mind how a girl that age would finance a spectacle like that, but again he seemed to be the only one that was wondering about it.

An hour later the party was at its peak. Lucas estimated sixty people in the rooms, maybe even more; all tables were filled now; the dance floor was also packed to an extent that it seemed incredible that people were still able to move there; and Charly was working to the breaking point to resupply everyone. Lucas had so far been alone at his corner table. A lot of people had looked at him and then whispered to others, which felt a little annoying, but he was not unhappy about the situation.

Another hour later, suddenly a girl approached Lucas' table. She was almost as tall as he, short red hair, quite slim and wearing a tight shirt and a skirt that looked all too short, especially for a girl her size.

"Hey there, lone stranger," she said in a voice that gave away her blood alcohol level. "Is that place taken?"

"No, please be my guest," Lucas said and made room for her.

She grinned and sat down right next to him, almost on his lap and put her glass on the table.

"Is that the Blue Goo?" Lucas asked, looking at the dark blue drink. In his mind this stuff looked even worse than the concoction Stephanie had ordered.

"Yep. And it's working wonders," the girl laughed.

Now that she was sitting right next to him, the smell of alcohol was even more present. Lucas almost worried that he might get drunk just from her breath.

"I am Jessica, by the way." She offered him her hand.

"Lucas. Nice to meet you," he replied and took her hand, which she immediately used to pull him close and give him a short kiss.

"Nice to meet you too," she said. "It is a shame that you are here all alone. It's a waste."

"And why do you figure that?" Lucas laughed.

"Hey, back off, chick. I saw him first." Without warning Rebecca had shown up, pulled Jessica from the bench and sat down herself. She looked even more hammered than Jessica.

"You saw him first, but I was here first," Jessica replied and tried to regain her seat. And before Lucas had a chance to react, the girls were in the middle of a brawl. For about a minute he backed off and watched, but it soon became clear that this fight was going nowhere fast, so he finally jumped in the middle.

"Jesus, girls. Stop this." He shouted and pushed them apart. "What's the matter with you?"

"I saw you first," Rebecca replied defiantly.

"But I was here first," Jessica said with the same tone in her voice.

"And I asked neither of you to be here," Lucas said with an annoyed tone in his voice. "The table is large enough for three, so either you two start getting along or I suggest you both get lost."

"I don't share my men with other girls." Jessica had a sparkle in her look.

"Neither do I." Rebecca returned the look with hostility in her face.

"And I am not your property, so get over it." Lucas was still standing between them.

He looked around, hoping for help from anyone nearby, but that hope was futile. Most of the others were either dancing, drinking or too drunk to even notice the fight. Only Stephanie seemed to have noticed. She was standing at the bar right now, waiting for a drink and giggling her lungs out. When Lucas spotted her, it made him even more annoyed, and this intensified when she took a glass with bright glowing pink liquid in it, waved and walked off, leaving him alone again.

"And who do we have here?" Suddenly a third girl had approached Lucas as well. She was holding a glass of the same pink stuff that Stephanie had just walked away with, smelled far less of alcohol than the other two, but had sort of a mad look on her face. For Lucas the situation was getting pesky. Caught in the middle of three beautiful young women who were fighting over him was not exactly what he had imagined as a party.

"What the hell is wrong with you girls?" Lucas took one step back, letting go of the other two.

"Shortness of men." The answer was from the new arriver.

"Come again?" Lucas didn't believe his ears. "There are at least two dozen men in here; why are you bothering me?"

The new arrival started laughing madly, which almost frightened him for a moment.

"Look around you," she then said. "Those idiots are so drunk, they wouldn't even notice us if we slapped them in the face. They are no good."

"Well, in this case you should maybe not give them so much to drink," Lucas suggested.

"Stay out of this, Maxim," Jessica interrupted. "I was here first."

Another fight started, this time between Jessica and Maxim.

"I had it with you girls." Lucas was getting really angry now. He walked over to the bar, addressing Charly. "Could I borrow the soda dispenser for a minute?" He pointed at a two liter glass bottle filled with soda water that had a pressure dispenser on top. Charly nodded and handed him the bottle. He walked back, took position in front of the still fighting girls and started spraying both of their faces with the soda water.

"Hey, what's wrong with you?" Jessica complained after stopping the fight.

"You are. Now get the hell lost before I forget my manners."

Jessica and Maxim started cursing but finally walked away. Lucas sighed in relief when he heard a giggling behind him.

"Nicely done. Now we are finally alone." Rebecca said.

"You get lost, too. Or do you prefer getting a shower as well?" He pointed the soda bottle at her.

"Your loss." Rebecca was visibly angry but finally walked off to bother someone else.

Lucas walked back to the bar, returning the soda bottle to its original place.

"You know, when you started drinking Coke I was sure that you were different, but right now you completely lost me," Charly said.

"And why's that?"

"Not drinking is one thing, I can understand that. Not dancing is another thing, I somewhat get that as well, but scaring away three hot chicks and not even keeping one… I don't get that. Or are you gay?"

"No, I am not gay," Lucas laughed. "And you are right, those three were hot, all of them. But this felt just wrong; I can't help it."

"Well, suit yourself, but let me tell you, there is no easier way to get a hot teeny girl than a party like this one." Charly shook his head and walked off to prepare another drink.

Lucas went back to his table and sat down, taking a few deep breaths. He would have liked to have one of the girls around, but this was one of the situations where his dark side threatened to break free, and he still was not comfortable allowing this. He tried his best to calm down, but his heart was still pounding, his blood packed to the limit with hormones. Even in as deep a meditation as he could get to in this room, it took him nearly an hour to calm down completely. And he hadn't even come out of it fully when the next issue caught his attention: Stephanie had returned from the dance floor and from the way she moved, it was all too clear that she also had had too much to drink. This by itself wasn't too worrying for him, as it was to be expected, after all, but when she stepped onto a bench and started dancing there Lucas started growing worried. He didn't want to interrupt her, as she was not really in danger right now, but he kept a close eye and had his focus ready just in case he needed a shield charm to keep her from falling.

It only took a short while before her dancing started drawing the attention of a group of guys who were drinking at a nearby table. They started jeering and clapping, which caused Stephanie to step onto their table and continue the dance there. At this time Lucas was still mainly worried that she might trip and fall, but his worries quickly changed directions when her movements became more erotic in nature and the guys started groping her. Lucas was for a moment unsure what to do, as Stephanie still seemed to have no problem with the situation, but when she started unbuttoning her blouse, he j lost his temper. He jumped up, walked over, pushed one of the guys aside and without further warning, grabbed her and carried her out of the room. At first she floundered and tried to fend him off, but when he put her back down in the foyer she just stopped.

"I think it's time to go home now," he said in a firm voice and pointed at her shoes.

She took a breath to say something, but when he raised his finger in a warning manner, she stopped and put on her shoes. Lucas quickly did the same thing and after both had taken their jackets, he pushed her out the front door.

During the walk home he had to support her, which made walking the icy roads a real challenge this time and prolonged the walk significantly. To fuel his annoyance further, Stephanie hummed some kind of song all the way and was clinging to him a bit too closely for his comfort sometimes. She even grabbed his ass a few times, but he was unsure if this was intentional or just happening when she stumbled. Arriving back at her home, Lucas had a hard time supporting her while at the same time searching her coat pockets for the key. When he finally managed to open the door, he felt relieved.

"Are you home already?" he heard a voice from the living room. It was Mr. O'Brien.

"Yeah, we are," Lucas replied. "It seemed to be a wise choice."

He had just helped Stephanie out of her coat and shoes when her father entered the foyer.

"What happened to her?" he asked when he spotted his daughter, looking alarmed at first, but nearly having to laugh a moment later.

"She has overdone it a little it seems," Lucas grinned. "We should get her to bed."

Mr. O'Brien nodded and together they walked her up the stairs. Up on top Mrs. O'Brien had come walking out of what seemed to be the bedroom.

"Oh my God, what happened to my sweet darling?" she said and ran toward her daughter.

"Nothing happened, Mummy, I am having the best time of my life," Stephanie slurred.

"She just had a little too much. She will be fine by tomorrow," her father smiled.

Together they laid her down in her bed.

"Sleep well," Lucas said and headed for the door.

"Where are you going?" Before either of them had left the room, she was already back out of bed, leaning on it and pointing at him.

"Only downstairs to my room," Lucas said. "I will be here when you wake up tomorrow, I promise."

"Don't leave me now." She was staggering toward him. "I want you with me in here tonight." She pointed at her bed.

"But honey, that would be inappropriate…" her mother started.

"Why?" she interrupted. "I want to have a boyfriend, too. Everyone else had one, why not me? He must stay here and be my boyfriend. After all, he carried me away from the others; he owes me."

"But honey, please come to your senses." Her mother tried again.

"No, no, no." She started jumping up and down, getting more and more unstable with every jump. "I want him now. Period."

Lucas walked toward her and took her in his arms. "Relax, Steph, relax. If you want me with you, then of course I will be with you." He stroked her hair and brought her back to her bed. "Is it OK if I go and get some stuff from downstairs? I promise I will be right back."

"Yes." She nodded, sitting on her bed. "But hurry, and don't play fools' games with me."

"I won't. Promise." Lucas stepped out of the room and pulled her parents with him. After closing the door, Mrs. O'Brien moved close to him.

"You are not seriously considering taking advantage of that situation, are you?" she whispered.

"Do you trust me?" Lucas looked at her with a very calm face.

"I wouldn't have asked you to go with her if I hadn't trusted you," she whispered back.

"I didn't ask if you trusted me two weeks ago. I am asking you: Do you trust me tonight?" Lucas was still totally calm.

"Yes," she said after thinking for a moment.

Lucas looked at Mr. O'Brien, who just nodded silently.

"Then trust me," he said and ran downstairs, returning a minute later with a blanket and a pillow. "Trust me," he whispered again and walked back into Stephanie's room, closing the door behind him.

There he had to take a few deep breaths. He knew that the situation he had maneuvered himself into right now was way out of his expertise, and also way out of his comfort zone. He once again felt his dark side creeping up to the surface and had to fight hard to keep it down.

"Ah you are back." Stephanie's voice sounded firmer than before, but still not quite like her.

"Sure I am. I did promise you, didn't I?" Lucas put the blanket and pillow down on a rug that was at the far end of Stephanie's bed. He then walked over to her and sat down next to her on the bed.

"So what now?" he asked.

"Now we have some fun." She suddenly grabbed him from behind, knocked him over and sat down on his chest.

"Interesting definition of fun you have here," Lucas laughed, although deep inside he didn't feel at all like laughing. This was not the Stephanie he knew. And this was not heading in a direction he liked at all.

"Yes, and I am sure you will like it." She started giggling and before he had a chance to react, she had thrown her blouse away.

"Somehow I doubt that," he said, trying to think of a way to end this whole mess quickly, but there was no exit strategy this time. When she started pulling up her top he got so uncomfortable that he did the only thing he could think of: Try to get out from underneath her. But even that proved to be difficult. He was still only lying on the bed halfway, his feet still placed on the floor, which gave him very few options, and as Stephanie was an experienced horseman, she had a quite good position and knew how to hold it. First he tried to just push her aside. When this showed no effect, he tried to wriggle out from underneath her and finally he even tried pushing her off the bed completely, but it was no good. Stephanie just sat there in what looked to be an easy balancing game for her and giggled her lungs out at his futile attempts.

"I knew you would like it." Stephanie was still giggling. "And I love wild horses. This is fun." She had pulled her top off and was swinging it above her head like a lasso.

Lucas was getting desperate. He knew that there was no easy way out of this position, let alone out of the whole situation, and to make things worse he felt that he had started to like it. In the weak moonlight he couldn't see much more than silhouettes of her body, but even those had enough effect that parts of him just begged for him to play along. He had to pull all his concentration together and constantly remind himself of who this beautiful girl was, and why it was him that was in here to resist the temptation. When Stephanie tossed away her top and started stroking his breast, he knew that it was now or never to get out of this.

"Don't you want to touch me too?" he heard her asking, but his focus right now was completely elsewhere. He knew there was only one way out of this, and he was desperate enough to use it now.

"EFFERUS!" he said in a deep, hissing voice and suddenly Stephanie was lifted up, floating away from him and then landing slowly back on the bed beside him. She seemed stunned for a second, just long enough for him to jump up.

"Oh that was mean." He could see the sparks in her eyes. "Don't you start pulling magic on me." She had jumped up too, standing between him and the door. The moonlight was shining on her fully now, giving him an ever harder time focusing.

"What are you so afraid off?" she asked. "I know you want this as badly as I do." When she started pulling down her jeans, Lucas had to turn away to resist, even though she was still wearing her panties. His hand was shaking wildly and he could feel sweat on his forehead. He started cursing himself for being a good guy and for once really envied Cedric, who for sure would have just gone for it from the beginning.

"Am I so ugly that you can't stand looking at me?" she said perkily.

"Not at all." He replied.

"Then don't turn your back on me, coward," she hissed.

Lucas could hear the mounting anger in her voice, and was quite sure that she would start some kind of offensive soon, so he pulled all his strength together and decided to drop the velvet gloves and push back. He had no real plan yet, but it didn't matter anymore; after all, he had done nothing but improvise so far, anyway.

With a quick move he turned around on his heels and looked her straight in the eyes. His heart felt like exploding, but right now he didn't care at all. He approached her and took her in his arms, trying to have as little body contact as possible and keeping his hands only on her upper back. She seemed stunned at first, but then her reaction was quite the contrary to his, pushing as close to him as she could and touching whatever she could reach. He gave her a long kiss on the cheek and let her proceed for a few moments, until he figured that she had calmed down enough. Then he made a step back, picked her up gently, tossed her into the bed and sat down on top of her for a change, locking her hands down beside her head.

"Finally I cracked your hard shell." She grinned at him with a face that was both sweet and mad. "Why don't you release my hands, so I can help you out of your shirt, too?"

"Not so fast, honey." Lucas tried to put on a horny grin, but it was just a charade. "You've teased me long enough, now it's my turn."

"Yeah, I love being teased," she replied. "Raises the anticipation and will for sure be good in the end."

"So then let's play a little game. If you are up for it?" he locked both hands above her head now, using only one of his, so he had the other one free to gently move one finger along her neck.

"I am up for anything, as long as you are up for a game of mine afterwards," she said with an evil grin.

"Deal. Once we are through with mine, I am all yours." Lucas put on the same evil grin.

"Deal. Bring it on." She nodded.

"So here it is: I will tie you to your bed right now and will just stay here and do nothing, until you fall asleep. Then I will release you and do whatever comes to my mind. Once you wake up from that, I'm all yours." He still had his evil grin on, but he had to fight hard to keep it convincing.

"I had never taken you for that type." Stephanie's face now showed a mixture of delight and the still visible pure madness. "But beware, I am a light sleeper, so you won't have fun for long." With that she started giggling evilly.

"That's fine." He grinned. "So are you going to behave by yourself until you fall asleep, or do I really have to tie you up?"

"You would have a hard time tying me up here." Stephanie giggled. "Ropes don't stick well to my bedposts."

"Believe me, MY rope sticks everywhere I want it to stick." Lucas tried to look even more evil now.

"You might be right about that." Stephanie's face cleared for a moment before it became mad again. "But don't bother, I will honor the game, if you do the same."

"Be sure I will." He nodded. "So hurry to sleep now; I don't want to wait all night."

Lucas let go of her and jumped out of the bed, sitting down on his pillow on the far side. Stephanie rolled under her blanket and whispered a "Good night" with a wink in his direction.

"Good night," he said, again putting on his evil grin.

When she turned on her side, Lucas dropped the grin and took a few deep but quiet breaths. His heart was still pumping, his body still screaming for him to take the chance he had here, but finally his mind won the battle; it was over.

About an hour later, when he heard Stephanie breathing deeply and regularly, he picked up his blanket and pillow and silently walked out of the room. When he came down the stairs, he saw her parents both sitting in the living room.

"What happened?" Mrs. O'Brien asked.

"Nothing happened," he replied. "She is sleeping now. And we all should do the same. It is quite late."

He walked to the guest room, hearing Mrs. O'Brien sigh in relief behind him. He had just put down the pillow and rolled out the blanket when he recognized Mr. O'Brien standing in the doorframe.

"Do you mind me asking you a question?" he asked.

"That was already one." Lucas was tired, but still smiling. "But sure, anytime."

"And will you give me an honest answer?"

"Always." He nodded.

"Why?" Mr. O'Brien asked.

"Because I know that this wasn't what she really wanted. And that is all that matters," he replied.

"Thank you." O'Brien nodded. "We are really grateful to have you here."

Lucas smiled and watched him walk away. He then took a long, cold shower to relax his still rebelling body before getting into bed. Finally arriving there, he had not even pulled his blanket straight before he was already fading into sleep.

CHAPTER 13

Perspectives

It was around 10 a.m. when Lucas woke up next morning. It took him a moment to realize where he was and when he finally did he had to sigh, remembering last night. He quickly made the bed, took a shower and got dressed, trying to leave the room as undisturbed as possible. Then he walked over to the living room, where Mr. and Mrs. O'Brien had already set up the breakfast table.

"Good morning." He smiled at them. "Is Stephanie up already?"

"Morning," Mr. O'Brien replied and stuck his head out of the kitchen. "Haven't seen her yet. I am guessing she is trying to sleep off her hangover."

"Why did you allow her to get so drunk in the first place?" Mrs. O'Brien had put down the newspaper she was reading. Lucas was unsure if it was pure curiosity in her voice or a little hostility.

"Honestly?" Lucas laughed.

"Agatha, drop it," Mr. O'Brien shouted from the kitchen. "You can't blame him for that now."

"No, it's OK," Lucas said to him before turning to her. "There are two reasons you should maybe consider for this," he started in a firm, cool voice. "One, I told you from the get-go that all I would do is keep her safe, nothing more. You accepted that. And two, have you ever thought about the alternative?"

"What alternative?" she asked.

"If I had stepped in and stopped her from drinking yesterday, what would have happened?" he asked, but the question was rhetorical.

"She would have been better off, at least," she replied, but Lucas didn't even listen and continued.

"First, she would have been angry at me for patronizing her, which I don't want. Second, she would have felt as if she had just missed out on something important and fun and would have despised both of us for it. And third, ultimately she would have drunk anyway, but this time somewhere where neither of us would have been around to watch out for her, and that would have been just one thing: plainly stupid," he said.

"Sometimes I wonder if you are really only sixteen years old." Mr. O'Brien was laughing when he came out of the kitchen.

"I hadn't thought about it that way," Mrs. O'Brien said.

"This boy knows more about nurturing than the both of us together, Agatha." Mr. O'Brien patted Lucas' shoulder. "You should give him more credit for that."

She nodded in reply. "Sorry for coming at you like that before. I know that you only have the best intentions," she said to Lucas.

"Don't overestimate me," Lucas laughed. "I am not a saint. And don't worry, I can understand your feelings."

"Earl Gray?" Mr. O'Brien asked Lucas on his way back to the kitchen.

"That would be lovely, thank you." Lucas nodded.

"Do you hear that?" he asked when he handed Lucas the cup.

They all fell silent and listened.

"I guess our darling is awake now," Mrs. O'Brien said and jumped up. "And I better go take a look."

Lucas was last to recognize the sniffling from upstairs that sounded like Stephanie was crying heavily.

"I guess the night is not over yet," he sighed.

"The night is, now comes the hangover," her father laughed. "Don't worry, she will get over it."

"I still can't understand why somebody would put himself through this voluntarily." Lucas shook his head.

"Nobody can, but still almost everybody does." Mr. O'Brien laughed again.

They sat down and silently drank their tea, waiting for the girls to come down. Lucas could hear that Stephanie was arguing loudly with her mother about something, but couldn't make out what was going on. About twenty minutes later, Mrs. O'Brien finally came back down.

"Hangover?" her husband asked.

"That too." She nodded. "But primarily she is embarrassed by her behavior last night. She said that she wouldn't leave her room until you are gone, Lucas. She is afraid that you are mad at her."

"Well, you better tell her that she should start growing vegetables in her room then, because I am not going anywhere until I had a chat with her." Lucas grinned.

"Feel free to tell her that yourself," she laughed. "I am not going into that lion's den again until she has gotten rid of her bad mood."

"Can I go up?" he asked.

"Nobody will stop you." She smiled at him and made an inviting gesture.

"The question was more along the line of is she properly dressed for me to go in?" Lucas rephrased.

"By now I think everything is proper for you," she grinned.

Lucas sighed and walked upstairs. As Stephanie's only answer to his knocking was, "Go away," he decided to just go in.

She was lying on her bed, her face buried in her pillow, and she was still crying. Lucas was happy to see that she at least had put on a t-shirt. He closed the door behind himself and sat down on the bed next to her.

"Go on, say it. I am the most stupid idiot on this planet," she nearly yelled at him when she pushed her face out of the pillow, looking at him. She then immediately started crying loudly again and hammering her head into the bed.

Lucas just sat there silently and started stroking her back gently.

"Why don't you say something?" she again yelled at him.

"Because there is nothing to say," he said in a friendly, soft voice. "Come here." He then pulled her up and took her in his arms, pushing her head firmly against his body.

"Why are you still so nice to me?" she asked through her tears. "After all I have done?"

"You haven't done anything," Lucas replied calmly, still stroking her back.

"Aren't you mad at me?" she sniffled.

"No."

"I don't understand you." She finally started easing up a little bit and pulled herself out of his arms so she could look at him. "I put you through the party that you clearly didn't like, then forced you to carry me out of there in front of everybody else and in the end harassed you like a mad man. How can you still not be mad at me?"

"Well, I have to admit that I was a little mad when you left me alone with those three chicks at the party. That was not nice." He laughed. "The rest was not you. That was just the effect of too much alcohol, and there is no point being mad because of that now, is there?"

"Not even for what happened in here last night?" she asked shyly.

"Nothing happened in here last night. So why should I bear a grudge for that?" he smiled. "And besides that, I have to admit that it is not exactly punishment to be harassed by you." He grinned.

"If that is so, why didn't you give in to it then?" She seemed curious now.

"Because you didn't really want that. So it would have been the wrong thing to do."

"But nobody could have blamed you if you did," she said.

"I would have blamed myself." He laughed. "In the end your wellbeing is more important to me than my own. So that was the only right choice to make."

"So we are still friends?" She sounded shy again.

"Of course we are. Nothing has changed." He gave her a hug again. "And what do you say, shall we go down now and have breakfast?"

"I'd like that." She nodded. "But I should get freshened up and dressed before that."

"Sounds like a plan. Can I leave you to that?" he asked.

"Sure, don't worry. I'll be right down." She nodded.

Lucas stood up and walked out. Just when he was about to close the door, Stephanie addressed him from behind.

"You know, Psycho once told me that the only way you could recognize love was if the other one would put your life before his own."

"She told me the same thing once," Lucas laughed.

"So that would mean that you do love me, then, wouldn't it?"

"Isn't that a rather philosophical question?" He had stuck his head back into the room.

"Well, it has a practical one below, but I am somehow afraid to ask," she sighed.

"If you don't ask, you will hardly get an answer," he laughed. "So what is it?"

"The real question is: If you do love me, why aren't you my boyfriend?"

"The truth is that following Psycho's definition, I would love a lot of people. And besides the fact that our relationship is complicated enough already without involving relationship problems, the real question would be: Do you love me too? Because in the end a one-sided feeling hardly ever helps." With that he closed the door behind him and walked down to the living room.

"Stephanie will be right down, she is just freshening up," he said to her parents before sitting down and grabbing his tea. He could clearly see that they both were relieved and impressed by the result. He was just feeling happy to have left the topic behind, at least for the moment, and was looking forward to the breakfast.

Monday afternoon Lucas arrived a little late for their weekly meeting. When he entered the shack Jasmin, Stephanie and Darien were already there, the fire was burning with high flames and the room had already gotten quite warm.

"I see you remembered the lesson from last week?" he grinned at Stephanie, who immediately jumped up to give him a hug. When she finally let go of him, he continued his rounds and greeted the others.

"And I see you brought your laptop again?" he pointed at the table while talking to Darien. "Did you find something with the logo?"

"I did, but I could have told you that without the notebook. Whirlwind asked me to bring it--didn't tell me why though."

"How are you doing?" he then asked Jasmin, who looked a little happier than last week.

"Well, my boyfriend seems to be no more and I am slowly getting used to that." She sighed. "Will be quite a change, but I am sure I will manage."

"I am certain that you will." Lucas smiled. "When you need something just call."

She nodded and smiled. He then walked over to the bench and sat down. Only five minutes later Marcus arrived, followed shortly by Cedric.

"Who wants to start?" Lucas asked after they had all sat down.

"Why don't you start by telling us how the party went?" Marcus asked nosily.

"It was interesting," Lucas replied shortly. "But how the hell do you even know about that?"

"It seems our parents talk quite a lot lately." He grinned. "Your mum told my mum who told me. And now stop holding back, we want to hear details."

"First, I think you are the only one who wants to hear details." Lucas laughed. "And second, the story is not mine to tell, so if you want to hear details you have to ask Airmid."

"I want to hear them, too," Jasmin jumped in.

"And so do I." Cedric had raised his hand.

"But I don't really want to talk about it." Stephanie made an unhappy face. "My head still hurts from that, and for the rest I might need a shrink."

"Physical pain normally is your expertise, so maybe you should try casting your spells on yourself for a change?" Jasmin suggested. "And if you need a friend more than a shrink, I am always happy to be there for you."

"I might take you up on that offer at some point, Psycho, thank you." Stephanie smiled. "But for now I would appreciate if we could shelve the topic."

"Ok, so let's get back to our other issues, shall we?" Lucas said.

"I will start if you don't mind," Darien said. "I only have a small detail to report, although it is an interesting one."

"Don't make us wait." Lucas grinned.

"I managed to reconstruct the shape of the repainted logo at least partially, and guess what--I found it. It is the logo of PowerSec."

"That's an interesting detail indeed." Lucas nodded. "So companies that deploy PowerSec security systems get robbed by thieves that are driving a van that has been stolen from PowerSec. Either this company has a hidden agenda, or that's a hell of a coincidence."

"I would consider a third option," Darien suggested. "Maybe you were right after all and they do have a rogue expert. Cougar said that the stolen van was part of an ownership dispute. I dug into this and found the court ruling for it."

"How can you find this?" Marcus was curious.

"Court rulings are public, all of them. You just have to know where to look," Darien said. "The issue revolved around the fact that an employee made a down payment for the van and never got reimbursed by the company due to a technicality. For that he argued that he had a legal right to own the van because it had never been fully paid by PowerSec. They argued that he was allowed to use the van for personal travel as well, and that the down payment was an advance payment for that privilege. In the end PowerSec came out as winner."

"Why did the dispute start? When he could use it as he saw fit anyway, what was the problem?" Lucas was curious.

"The problem was that he left the company, and he didn't quite do this voluntarily," Darien replied.

"So we have a rogue spook out there." Lucas nodded. "That explains a lot, because in the end it means that the stolen goods are not really the target, it's all just about making PowerSec look bad."

"Do you know why the guy was let go?" Stephanie asked.

"No. He did say in one of his court statements that the company was on a destructive streak after parting ways with their lead expert. So maybe he was unhappy about that." Darien shrugged his shoulders.

"So who are the others, then?" Marcus was curious, too.

"Most likely just a gang he had picked up from somewhere. But I honestly have no clue." Darien shrugged his shoulders again.

"Ok, anything else?" Lucas asked after a moment of silence.

"No, not from my side." Darien shook his head.

"Anybody else?" Lucas looked around.

"Short thing from me as well." Marcus was next. "I tried to find a matching map, and narrowed it down to three that would fit the picture. Unfortunately, I can't do anything more; the image is just too blurred."

"Still a nice one," Lucas smiled. "What else?"

"I have two things," Cedric started. "First a quick thing: my father will meet the PowerSec CEO next week, so maybe I can tell you more then."

"Great, thanks." Lucas nodded.

"The second thing is a little trickier," Cedric continued. "I have looked at the pictures again, and I think I found something."

The others looked at him eagerly.

"Professor, can you bring up the picture of the drivers' cabin again?" Cedric walked over so he could look at the laptop. The others followed his example.

"Here it is. What did we miss?" Darien asked.

"There." Cedric pointed at an area of the picture. "Can you zoom in on that?"

"Certainly." Darien nodded. "But that's just a plain coffee mug."

"It's not the coffee mug that I am interested in," Cedric said and looked at the zoomed picture. "There. Bring this area up a little bigger."

Darien nodded and adjusted the zoom.

"What the hell is that?" Lucas tried to make out what he was looking at.

"It's a reflection in the mug," Cedric said. "I am not sure, but to me it looks like a GPS screen. What do you think?"

"Let's see if we can get a little more contrast into that." Darien started working his skills again. After a while the picture started to get clearer.

"Yeah, that is a GPS, all right." Marcus nodded. "And from the looks of it, you really hit the jackpot with this, Whirlwind."

"Why? What do you make of this?" Cedric asked.

"From the screen layout, those seem to be coordinates--my guess would be recent waypoints or favorites. It's unfortunate that it is still too blurred to read them."

"Wouldn't do much good, either, I would guess. It looks like only the last pair of numbers is visible on each line," Jasmin added.

"That would not be a problem," Marcus said. "In the end the last pair is what we need to pinpoint them. If you know the general area, which we do, those are the ones that matter most."

Darien was still working as hard as possible to make the numbers clearer.

"There are six lines," he said. "My guess is that those make three pairs of longitude and latitude. Those are fours." He pointed out some numbers. "The others are trickier. We have to group them into possibilities. 1 and 7 go together; 2, 5 and 7 are also easily confusable; so are 3, 6, 8, 9 and 0."

Stephanie had grabbed a piece of paper and a pencil and started writing all possible combinations down as Darien named them. Marcus had grabbed a map and was marking them one by one.

"I think the first one is easy," he said after only two marks. "This is approximately the place where we found them. We can skip the other combinations." He pointed out the right one on Stephanie's sheet.

The others cheered for a moment before continuing their effort. Unfortunately, with the other coordinates they were not so lucky.

"I marked the second set in green, the third set in blue," Marcus said and let the others look at the map after having marked all spots.

"Some of the pairs are in the middle of nowhere, others are quite central. Finding the right spot out of those will be a nightmare," Jasmin said.

"Maybe not." Lucas had spotted something. "Look at that blue dot here." He pointed one out. "Isn't that the industrial area south of Luton?"

"Yes it is." Marcus nodded. "What's your point?"

"Correct me if I'm wrong, but isn't Brix & Burton located there?" he asked.

"You are right." Marcus nodded. "How could I miss that?"

"So we figured out two. What about the third?" Stephanie asked after marking the correct set of numbers for the last line.

"Those were the two locations we knew about. The last one will be hard, I guess." Marcus sighed.

"Let's try something." Darien pulled over his laptop. "Cougar, you said that you narrowed the map down to three possible releases. Do you know which ones?"

"Sure, I have written it down somewhere, wait a sec." He started browsing through his coat pockets. "Here you go." He handed a piece of paper over to Darien.

"What's the plan?" Lucas asked.

"It's a long shot, but let's assume the thieves have a second hideout and that map is showing the location of the hideout," Darien explained.

"Good assumption. How does that help?" Jasmin asked.

"Let's further assume that Cougar was right with those three maps; then I can find out exactly what area they cover." Darien started pulling up specifications. "And with this I can mark this area on our map." He stood up and started drawing boxes on the big map. "And now we just need to see where we have green dots within my boxes." He grinned at the others.

"Farfetched, but ingenious," Lucas smiled.

"Leaves two possibilities." Marcus pointed out the two dots.

"Yes, but this one down here only just scratches the area of the map. It would be a bad idea from a navigation point of view to use that map if you want to go there," Darien pointed out.

"Then I guess we have a winner." Lucas put his finger on the point and Stephanie instantly marked the correct numbers on her sheet.

"That was great work, guys," Lucas complimented.

"If our assumptions are correct, that is." Darien slowed him down a little.

"So how do we go on from here?" Lucas looked around.

"We should give those coordinates to Inspector Murphy," Stephanie suggested.

"And tell him what exactly? That we think we might have figured out which map was in the drivers' cabin, and we think that we could enhance a blurred mirror image on a coffee mug enough to read numbers from it, based on which we think that we found GPS coordinates that seem to match one of the possible maps? That's a lot of assumptions. I doubt Murphy would take us seriously," Marcus said.

"So what do you suggest we do, then?" Stephanie asked him.

"I would suggest we go there and take a look. And once we know that we have the right place we call in the cavalry and let them finish off those bastards."

"You know, Cougar, I've heard that plan before. And last time it didn't turn out that well," Jasmin threw in.

"Yeah, but just because I was clumsy," Marcus replied.

"What other options do we have?" Lucas asked.

"I can't think of any." Marcus shook his head.

"Neither can I." Darien looked unhappy, but he had to agree.

"Whirlwind? Girls? Anything?" Lucas asked again, but nobody answered.

"Very well, then, here is what I would suggest we do then: We go there and see if it is the right place, but this time we go all together," Lucas started. "We just confirm the place, no pictures, no poking around, no confrontation--nothing. We stay out of sight all the time. Once we are certain of it, we call Murphy and tell him. Then we just wait for SO-19 to arrive. And again: NO INTERVENTION."

"I don't like that plan too much, but unfortunately I have nothing better to offer, either," Jasmin sighed.

"I think we should bring some extra muscle, just in case," Marcus said.

"What do you have in mind?" Lucas asked.

"I was thinking about crowfeet or something along that line. Something we can just throw from cover but that will give us a chance to stop their getaway if we have to."

"Sounds good. Can you get some of those?" Lucas smiled.

Marcus nodded in reply.

"I would also like to bring a flask of your healing potion, Airmid, but this would mean that we have to meet again the day before we go there to freshly brew it," Lucas added.

"That's not a problem. With Cougar's help, this should be done in no time." Stephanie nodded.

"So what about we meet on Thursday to brew the potion, just the three of us, and then meet again on Friday all together and make the trip," Lucas suggested. "We could start shortly after noon, if this is OK by you. Would give us plenty of time, and this time it's not a search; we can just move straight there."

"Looking forward to both meetings." Marcus nodded.

"I would like to accompany you for the brewing, as well, if you don't mind," Jasmin added. "And I am good with the dates, too."

"This will be interesting." Darien nodded. "Let's hope nothing bad happens. I am in, too."

"Tell me when and where, and I'll be there." Cedric nodded.

"Cougar, can you please also try to get a phone number for Inspector Murphy, so we can reach him quickly? That would be very helpful," Lucas added.

"That should not be a problem." Marcus nodded.

"Are we bringing robes?" Stephanie asked.

"Might be a good idea, although I doubt that we will need them," Lucas replied.

They quickly finalized the plans and started looking up the best travel routes for Friday. The area was not too far away, but as there was a quite good train connection available and weather forecasts predicted it to become even colder over the next few days, they decided to take the short hop by train and only go the last kilometer by bike. After everything was clear, they parted for the day, to meet again on Thursday.

When Lucas arrived back at the shack on Thursday he could already see smoke rising from the chimney from quite a distance. He had arrived early, but to his surprise Stephanie and Jasmin were already there. When he entered they were fiercely discussing something but immediately stopped when the door opened.

"I am sorry, did I interrupt something?" he asked.

"Actually, you did." Jasmin nodded. "But come in and get warmed up; we will continue this outside."

The girls took their coats and walked out. Lucas watched them gesticulating wildly and emotionally. When Marcus arrived a few minutes later, they decided to start preparing everything they would need for the potion. After the many trial runs they had already had, they knew the recipe pretty well by now.

"What is that all about?" Marcus asked Lucas, pointing at the door.

"Don't know." Lucas shrugged his shoulders. "But I do have a hunch."

"Party?" Marcus asked.

"Yep." Lucas nodded.

"You know, I am really curious what happened there. This seems to have made quite an impact on Airmid."

"Nothing happened, Cougar, nothing that was not to be expected," Lucas replied. "But I agree, it seems to bring up a lot of emotions in her."

"If nothing happened, then why are you so secretive about it?"

"Because it is not my story to tell. It was her party; whatever details she wants to share, it is her decision, and we all have to respect that."

"But you were also at that party. Didn't you have any experiences there for yourself?"

"I had a run-in with some drunk girls, but other than them getting a soda-water shower there is really nothing much to tell."

"And why would that be? Weren't they pretty enough for you?" Marcus asked smugly.

"They were pretty all right," Lucas laughed. "Actually, all three of them were."

"So what's the problem then?"

"The problem is that I am quite certain that they were all only prancing around me because they were hammered. And that is hardly a basis for anything."

"Jesus, mate. You were not supposed to marry them, just have a little fun for a change." Marcus laughed. "Lighten up a little."

"You know, Cougar, this type of fun might be something Whirlwind and you are very good at, but frankly, I am not. And sorry, but I have no intention of ever starting something with a girl that just knocks at my door because of drinking too much of this odd shiny pinkish whatever it was."

"They had the Pink Drink there? Was Charly at that party, too?" Marcus seemed surprised.

"You know Charly?" Lucas was surprised now, too.

"Not intimately, no. But I've met him at a few parties myself. He makes quite good drinks. And the Pink Drink is notorious." Marcus laughed. "Well, I still think you should lighten up a little in that matter, but I do of course respect your decision."

"That's very kind of you," Lucas replied with a touch of irony in his voice.

After finishing the prep work they sat down silently and waited for the girls to come back. Unexpectedly, it took far more than an hour before they finally showed up, both of them looking a little strained.

"Is everything all right?" Lucas asked.

"Everything all right--as good as could be expected." Jasmin tried to grin, but even Lucas noticed that it was not serious.

"Anything we can do to help?" he asked.

"Not right now. But maybe later," Jasmin said with a mild smile, and this time it seemed serious.

"Shall we start then?" Stephanie asked. "I see you have already prepared everything? Perfect."

The others nodded and after a little while of relaxation for Stephanie, they began the brewing. It took them a while to finish everything up and in the end it took Stephanie a lot of energy to prepare three flasks.

"I am sorry, but this is all I can do," she said, breathing heavily.

"This is more than enough; thank you for the effort, Airmid." Lucas smiled at her.

"Anytime." She tried to smile and handed the flasks to Jasmin, who put them on the desk.

The others started cleaning up the shack, Stephanie leaning against the wall next to the fireplace, looking into the fire.

"Are you all right?" Lucas asked her ten minutes later, as she was still standing there.

"Yeah, just a little weak, that's all." She nodded.

He laid his arm around her shoulder and pressed her against himself, which she answered by pushing herself close to him and giving him a hug. Lucas had hugged her before, but somehow this time it felt different; it felt closer. And although he was unsure about it, he didn't want to let go. So they just stood there like this until Jasmin and Marcus had finished the cleanup and were ready to go.

"Shall we leave the two of you out here?" Jasmin asked. "Or are you coming, too?"

"We are coming." Stephanie looked far more relaxed now than before. Lucas was amazed how much energy she seemed to have drawn in those few minutes. He didn't really understand it, but he just felt happy that it worked that way.

CHAPTER 14

Disparities

When Lucas and the others boarded the train next day, they all seemed happy and eager to get going. Whatever problem Jasmin and Stephanie had discussed the day before had obviously cleared from their minds by now. Marcus had organized a phone number for Inspector Murphy and they all had either noted it down or saved it in their phones. Additionally, Lucas had divided up the three flasks of healing potion they had made. Marcus was keeping one in his backpack, Darien kept the second, and Jasmin the last. Those three seemed to be the logical choice to him.

"Remember everyone: No intervention, no poking around, no risk this time. Our sole goal for the day is to find the thieves and make sure that police get there to apprehend them." Lucas gave his pep-talk.

The others nodded agreement, but Lucas was not particularly sure if Marcus and Cedric had gotten the message. Somehow he was under the impression that they were eager to make a statement this time and get one back for the thieves shooting Marcus in the first place. It was a joyless situation for him to be in, trapped between also wanting to set an example and wanting to keep all of them safe.

When the train arrived and they stepped out, a clear, sunny sky welcomed them. They unhurriedly rode their bikes up the narrow forest, weaving toward the apparent location. A few hundred meters before reaching the spot they hid their bikes between the trees and continued on foot.

"The coordinates are right over there where the trees get lighter," Marcus whispered after looking at his GPS.

"Let's continue very carefully then," Lucas suggested.

They slowly continued forward until reaching the edge of an opening. The site was pretty similar to the location where they had first encountered the thieves, only bigger. There were two pretty wide dirt roads leading up to the area. One obviously came from the nearby town, the other one led deeper into the forest.

"What kind of strange bushes are those?" Stephanie whispered and pointed at big, snowy blocks standing at the opposite edge of the clearing.

"Those are no bushes," Marcus laughed quietly. "Those are most likely huts."

"Huts? With leaves on them?" Stephanie looked unbelieving.

"Those are not leaves, either. Those are camo nets," Lucas explained. "Strange, though, that they are hiding the huts now under nettings," he then whispered to Marcus.

"We should have a look inside," Marcus suggested.

"The hell you will," Lucas quickly objected. "That is what gave us away last time."

"Let me at least look through a window. Just to check out if there is really something in there," he almost begged.

"OK, one window, and then you get straight back here." Lucas rolled his eyes.

Marcus didn't lose any time. He immediately sneaked over to the first hut and started looking for a window. Lucas and the others held their breath and watched the surroundings anxiously to ensure nobody was coming. When he finally came back, Lucas had to sigh in relief.

"So what did you see?" he asked.

"It's them, all right," Marcus whispered. "They still have the pallets from Brix & Burton in there. The setup is very strange, though."

"And why's that?" Lucas inquired.

"The doors of the huts open outwards," Marcus replied

"So?" Lucas didn't catch what he was getting at.

"So... with the nets pulled over the huts so tightly, the doors will not open at all. If you are inside one of those huts you are trapped," Marcus explained.

"So are you saying that they are not here?" Jasmin asked.

"I would guess not." Marcus nodded.

"Maybe they have just cut the nets open at one hut," Darien suggested.

"Valid idea." Marcus nodded again.

"Anything else we need to check?" Lucas asked.

"I would like to scout a little down the road, just to see if this would be a valid escape path for them," Marcus said.

"OK, but be careful." Lucas nodded. "Whirlwind, please go with him."

Cedric nodded and the two headed off, following the dirt road. Much to Lucas astonishment they were back not even five minutes later.

"That was quick," he said. "What happened?"

"Dead end," Marcus answered. "They are not going anywhere fast down this road."

"Where does it dead end?" Jasmin asked.

"At a river. I have no clue, though, why somebody would build a road like this just to end it at a river."

"Easy to explain, Cougar." Darien smiled. "The river will be part of the old canal network. In earlier times they would have used it to transport the wood or charcoal away from here."

"Makes sense." Marcus nodded.

"There is something else that would make sense," Lucas said. "And that is calling Murphy."

"But the thieves are not here," Marcus objected.

"The thieves are not; the goods are though," Lucas replied. "And if the police establish a watch here, they will sooner or later catch them."

"All right, I will make the call." Marcus nodded and pulled out his cell phone. He had to walk a few meters off, though, to get reception, so the others again waited and watched.

"I reached Murphy himself," Marcus said after returning. "He told me to get to safety and leave the rest to them. They are on their way now."

"We are not doing that, are we?" Cedric asked Lucas.

"Of course not." Lucas shook his head. "We will stay back here in cover and wait until it is over. If we can't be the ones to catch the thieves, I at least want to watch the police do it."

They settled down and waited eagerly.

"What is taking them so long this time?" Marcus grew impatient, as nothing had happened for almost half an hour now.

"It's strange, I agree." Lucas nodded. "Last time they arrived in less than twenty minutes."

"But this time it's a detective and his crew, not SO-19," Darien pointed out. "They are normally not on high alert."

They waited for another thirty minutes before they finally spotted something.

"Here they come," Stephanie whispered and pointed down the road.

Lucas needed to focus completely on the area to see the movement. It was people approaching on foot, trying to move stealthily, but not very successfully. He counted seven silhouettes, but it was hard to be sure, as he still could only make out shadows.

"They are more intelligent this time," Marcus whispered. "Not rushing in with horns blazing."

"Detective, not SO-19," Darien repeated.

"Wrong... Both of you...," Jasmin stuttered.

Lucas had his focus on the huts at that moment but immediately looked back at the arrivers. When he saw what Jasmin meant, his heart nearly stopped. It was not the police sneaking up the road, it was Plague and his circle, wearing their distinguishing black robes.

"What the hell are they doing here?" Marcus whispered.

"The more interesting question would be: How did they know where 'here' is?" Lucas whispered back. "Everyone, get your robes, just in case."

They watched the black-robes advance to the edge of the clearing and then stop.

"What are they doing?" Jasmin asked.

"Look!" Stephanie whispered and pointed at the hut.

Lucas looked over and immediately saw what Stephanie had spotted. A group of squirrels had started jumping around on the huts, climbing to the windows and onto the roof, jumping from one hut to the next and then after a while collectively running over to the other mages.

"What was that?" Marcus whispered.

"My guess would be that they have someone in their group that can talk to animals," Darien whispered back.

"And have them do their bidding?" Marcus looked at him. "What kind of magic is that?"

"Traditionally it is called Witchcraft, I would say. But also some Druid lore speaks of such things," Darien said.

"What do we do now?" Jasmin asked. "Those are not thieves, those are mages."

"For now I would say we wait and observe. There is no point in picking a fight at this time," Lucas replied.

The others nodded and continued watching. After a short while the black-robes suddenly walked out into the open.

"Are you sure the area is clear?" one of them, a man, asked another one.

"You know, Firebolt, sometimes I am not sure why I speak at all. You don't believe me anyway," the other one answered in a quite intimidating voice. It was a woman.

"Just checking," Firebolt replied, seemingly unimpressed by her hostility.

"Shut it. Both of you." A third one, a man, shouted at them. "If Cat says we are good, then we are good. Now let's move, we have work to do. Unless, of course, any of you would like to test my patience, or the patience of Lord Archeveque."

Nobody replied to that. The group just walked over to the huts.

"Cat? THE Cat?" Darien whispered.

"Obviously." Lucas nodded.

They had split up by now and were opening all four huts. Only their leader and a second one were staying back, watching the vicinity.

"Hey, Eagle, can you please have a look at this? I think we found something," one of them shouted out from a hut.

"What is it?" the man that had been standing outside with their leader replied and walked towards the hut.

"I know those voices," Marcus whispered. "I've heard both of them before."

"The one in the hut is Cypher." Lucas nodded. "The other one I don't know."

"Eagle, we also found something over here!" another man shouted from the second hut.

"I can't be in two places at once," Eagle replied. "At least not yet. Make sure that whatever you found doesn't walk away. I will be right with you."

"This one is packed with supplies and tools. Nothing of use for us," Firebolt said, walking out of the third hut with Cat.

"Hey Cleric, it seems we found it." Eagle walked out of the first hut again. "There are seven crates in stacks there."

"That's a start," the leader said. "See what Woodpecker found. Maybe he has the rest."

Eagle was already walking toward the second hut.

"Firebolt, help Cypher getting our crates, will you?" Cleric commanded.

"Sure thing, boss." Firebolt nodded and walked into the hut.

"Cat, could you spare a minute?" a man shouted from the last hut. "This will take forever to search by myself."

"I know that voice, too," Marcus whispered.

"So do I." Lucas nodded. "That's Plague."

"Are you sure?" Marcus had turned pale.

"I am positive." Lucas nodded. "What is it?"

"If that is Plague then we have a serious problem," Marcus replied. "Because that voice belongs to Detective Chief Inspector Murphy."

"So that's how they knew about this place," Lucas said. "Damn."

"And that's why he was so determined to crack the case in the first place," Darien added. "Personal interest."

"This might also be why the police are taking so long," Stephanie said. "They are not coming at all."

"Cougar, please fall back and call them again. But this time not Murphy, just call the local constabulary," Lucas said, and Marcus immediately took off.

"There's another six crates, which leaves only the one missing that Plague has found already." Eagle had one crate shouldered as he came out of the hut.

"Good, very good." Cleric nodded and watched them carry out the rest.

"There is nothing in there to identify those goons," Cat said as she and Plague walked out of the final hut. "They seem to be very careful."

"I don't care. We have what we came for, let those idiots roast in hell," Cleric said.

Marcus had returned to the others, reporting that the police were on the way now.

"What shall we do now?" Jasmin asked. "They have almost all their crates already out. They will be long gone before police arrives."

"I know." Lucas nodded. "But I am not sure if it is wise to attack them head on."

"Maybe we don't have to," Darien suddenly said. "Look over there."

Lucas turned his attention to the road, where a white van was just approaching the scene.

"Those are the thieves," Stephanie whispered.

"That will be interesting," Cedric grinned.

The thieves had stopped their car on the far end of the clearing, leaving a good view for Lucas and the others. When the doors opened, five guys with black suits jumped out, almost looking like a Ninja squad.

"We've got company," Cleric shouted and walked into the middle of the open space.

Quickly the others came out of the huts, too, and started taking positions.

"What is that? A bunch of clowns trying to rob us?" one of the thieves asked and drew a gun. "Bad idea."

"So is pointing a gun at me," Cleric replied calmly. "FULMINARE," he shouted and suddenly a stream of flame shot from his hand, knocking the man with the gun over.

"Big mistake," one of the other thieves said and took cover behind the van, the others following his example quickly, some jumping into the van or behind it, and one taking cover behind a pile of wood.

"What is the matter with you?" Cleric shouted to his people. "Don't stand around like statues; let's give those bastards what they deserve."

"With pleasure, master." Firebolt started laughing despicably. "INCENTUS," he shouted, and the pile of wood that one of the thieves had used as cover suddenly caught fire.

"That's a very one-sided show," Marcus whispered. "Shall we get involved?"

"No." Lucas shook his head. "Let them duke it out and let's hope the police arrive before it is over."

One of the thieves had grabbed a rifle from the van by now and had started shooting at the black-robes. Another had followed his example, using a pistol. The one Cleric had hit was still lying on the ground, and the last two were nowhere to be seen.

"TERGUM," Lucas heard Plague cry, and suddenly the pistol-swinger was tossed through the air.

The next thing he heard was a cry when a bullet from the rifle hit Cat. And another one shortly after, with Firebolt tumbling down.

"FULMINICTUS," Plague cried, and the bad guy with the rifle suddenly started shaking as if he had touched electric wires. After that Plague quickly jumped into cover as the shaking let the bad guy fire off his rifle erratically, spraying the whole area with lead.

"Nooooooo," Lucas heard Cleric cry. "FULMINARE," he shouted and tossed the rifle guy down with another stream of fire.

It took Lucas a moment to see what had upset Cleric so much, but then he spotted it: The rifle rounds had completely perforated the crates, and liquid was running out of them now, suggesting that most of the flasks had been broken.

"I will kill those guys!" Cleric shouted.

"Calm down, master." Plague walked up to him. "We have bigger problems than that. Two of us are wounded, and there are still two thieves out there somewhere."

"One more reason to kill those three, to show the others what happens to people who play chicken with us." Cleric was outraged, but he had not even finished his sentence when a cry of pain made him turn on his heel. It was Eagle, who had just been hit by a shuriken, which was now sticking out of his arm.

"Eagle!" Cleric shouted. "Plague, Cypher, get Eagle out of here; without him we are lost."

"Yes, master." Cypher nodded and grabbed Eagle, retreating toward the road.

"Woodpecker, can't you do anything? There must be a way to find those clowns," Cleric shouted.

"I can't attack something that I can't see," he replied. "Sorry, master."

"DAMN IT." Cleric was still outraged but was slowly recognizing the defeat. "We will finish this another time; let's get out of here."

He was picking up Cat, dragging her out. Woodpecker followed close behind, supporting Firebolt, who had been hit in the leg.

Lucas and the others watched the mages retreat.

"What do we do now?" Marcus whispered. "Shall we go after them?"

"To what end?" Lucas asked. "We should focus on the thieves."

"The one that was hit twice seems to be in a very bad shape. Judging from the massive burns he will be dead within 20 minutes unless we do something," Stephanie whispered.

"We should also alert the police to the two others that are still hiding, or they will get away," Jasmin added. "If they are not gone already."

"No, they are not. I can still see them." Darien shook his head.

"OK, here is the plan," Lucas said. "Airmid, you try to help that wounded guy, but only as much as necessary to keep him alive. Take the potion for it; save your strength." Lucas signaled Jasmin to hand her the flask before continuing, "Whirlwind, please accompany her and keep her safe. Cougar, now would be your best time to place the crowfeet under the wheels of the van. And while you are at it, you could also hang a sign up there, telling police that there are five bad guys around. Professor, you keep an eye on the remaining two. If they pose any threat to our people, you have to guide me so I can stop them. Psycho, watch out for other arrivers and alert us."

Everyone nodded and started with his assigned task. Lucas watched eagerly as Marcus, Cedric and Stephanie approached the van. He could see her examining the downed thief and judging from the way she acted, it didn't look too good. Then for a second he had to hold his breath. The thief suddenly stretched out his arm and grabbed Stephanie's leg. Lucas was about to jump to the rescue, but Cedric was already there. He just stepped on the thief's hand, freeing her from his grip. Lucas sighed in relief when he saw it, but the relief was short-lived. A second crook was approaching them from the other side of the van. He looked a little zombie-like, mostly covered in blood, and he was holding a gun.

"SEPERATIO," Lucas cast, just in time. A shot was fired, but the bullet just stopped at his barrier. Then things happened in an instant. Cedric extended his arm, which the thief with the gun shortly afterwards acknowledged with a loud cry that caused him to let go of his gun. Lucas could only guess that Cedric had just hit him with his Condolesco charm. He was just about to fire up his Repellum spell when suddenly Marcus appeared out of nowhere and ran the guy over, knocking him against the van door, leaving him lying there only half-conscious and crying in pain. He then joined Stephanie and Cedric, patrolling around them, covering their backs.

The cry of the one guy had not even died away when another thief started an even more painful one. It was the burnt one that Stephanie had just covered in the healing potion, which Lucas knew from past trials was a very painful experience.

"Police approaching," Jasmin suddenly whispered.

Lucas whistled just loud enough for the three guys at the van to notice, causing them to immediately retreat into the forest, joining him and the others a few moments later.

"Nice job," Lucas complimented all three.

They just nodded in reply and settled in to watch what would happen next.

"Armed police! Don't move!" Within an instant the whole SO-19 team had deployed at the clearing. They fanned out, some walking toward the huts, others approaching the van.

"Don't move. Armed police," the police officer in front shouted at the guy Stephanie had just healed when they spotted him.

"I just saw an angel," he said to the policemen, "and she healed me."

"You don't look very healed to me," the officer said. "Turn around, hands behind your back."

A second man quickly approached and put the man in handcuffs.

"Suspect apprehended," the first one then said into his radio. "Request medical assistance."

Then they moved on. The second guy was unconscious when they found him.

"Gun!" the front man suddenly shouted, leading two others to jump in, holding the thief down on the ground.

"He is unconscious, Sergeant," one of them said.

"Thank you, Constable. Cuff him, secure the firearm," the sergeant replied.

Moving on, they found the third thief and his rifle.

"This one is dead," the constable announced and took the rifle.

"Look, there is Inspector Corben," Marcus suddenly whispered to Lucas.

Lucas had spotted him at the same moment. Corben had jumped out of the command vehicle and was walking toward the van now.

"Van secured, three suspects, two detained, one deceased, Inspector," the sergeant reported.

"Very well, thank you." Corben nodded. "Sergeant Fisher has so far not encountered any suspects; it seems the scene is secure."

"Sir, we might have a problem." The constable came running, holding a piece of paper. "I found this on the passenger door of the van."

"What is it, Constable?" The inspector took the paper and read it. Then he grabbed his radio. "All units be advised, two more suspects expected to be on scene, I repeat, two more suspects expected to be on scene. The scene is NOT secure."

"Where are they, Professor?" Lucas whispered to Darien.

"Up there in the trees." Darien pointed out. "The police guys can look for hours and will still not find them."

"Can we help them somehow?" Lucas asked.

"We can show ourselves and guide them," Darien suggested.

"I would rather not do that." Lucas shook his head. "Can you help me aim, so I can throw one of them out of his tree?"

"It is quite a long distance. I am not sure if you can hit such a small target so far away just from my aim." Darien shook his head, too.

"Why don't we treat them like apples?" Cedric grinned.

"What do you mean?" Lucas was not sure what he was aiming at.

"Shake the tree, bring them down," Cedric laughed.

"Nice idea." Lucas nodded. "Try it."

"Tempestas," Cedric whispered.

Lucas was still fascinated by that spell. A storm arose just around the area that Cedric had targeted, violently shaking some trees, while all around the weather remained nice and calm.

"Aaaarrrrghhhh," they heard the thief cry before crashing into the ground with a loud thud.

"Armed police! Don't move!" The SO-19 officers were there in an instant.

"Where the hell did that wind come from?" the sergeant asked Corben.

"I have no clue." Corben almost laughed. "But it seems the suspect expected this as little as we did. That makes four down, one still on the loose."

"Take cover, take cover," Lucas suddenly heard the officers next to the hut yell.

"All units be advised, we are taking hostile fire. Proceed with caution," a voice said through the police radio.

"Professor, what is happening?" Lucas whispered.

"It looks as if the last guy doesn't like going down without a fight. He threw something at the officers."

"We need to take this bastard down." Lucas was determined. "Let me try something."

Lucas focused to build up a single energy stream, right out of the palm of his hand. He then stretched the hand out in the direction of the thief.

"What are you doing?" Darien asked.

"Can you see the energy beam?" Lucas asked.

"Yes. What are you doing?"

"Creating my version of a laser targeting system," Lucas laughed. "Point and shoot."

"That's a cool one," Darien laughed and started guiding Lucas' hand. "Ready when you are."

"REPELLUM," Lucas whispered.

A moment later, once again a cry was audible throughout the forest, followed by a bump that suggested the thief had crashed into another tree.

"Nice shooting," Lucas complimented Darien when they heard the police officers run toward the crook.

"Suspect apprehended. Scene secured," a voice then said through the radio.

"Is everyone all right, Sergeant?" Corben asked when the second team brought the last thief back.

"Constable Cartwright has been hit in the arm, but the wound seems negligible. Constable Choice is treating it now," the sergeant replied.

"Thank you, Sergeant Fisher." Corben nodded.

"I still don't get how those goons could both fall from the trees. If they hadn't we would have had a very hard time finding them," Fisher said.

"I don't get that either, Sergeant. Maybe we had help from higher up. Let's just be grateful that it happened the way it did." Corben smiled.

"Forensics on scene, sir. They are asking for permission to begin their sweep." A woman approached Corben.

"Send them in. We are done here." Corben nodded.

The forensics team walked in and started working the huts and the van.

"I think it's time to leave now," Lucas whispered. "We have done our part."

The others nodded and slowly fell back, trying to stay as silent as possible so they would not be spotted. They stowed their robes once they had reached their bikes, and made their way back.

"It's a shame that we couldn't just step out there and help the policemen," Jasmin said when they were sitting in the train.

"I agree. I would have loved to take these thieves head on." Marcus nodded. "Especially the last one."

"Well, Angel has warned us about this." Lucas sighed. "No knights in shining armor, just a life in the shadows. We did well, though; it was a full success."

"I prefer being in the shadows. Glamour is not good for the health," Darien grinned.

"What do you mean?" Marcus asked.

"How do they say? Big symbols make big targets." Darien laughed. "If we had helped SO-19 openly today, chances would have been that they would have asked us again."

"And what's your problem with that?" Marcus said.

"For one, that might be your dream, but it isn't mine. More seriously, it would not have taken the bad guys long to notice our value, and then we would have been the prime targets for everyone. And honestly, I don't want a bull's-eye painted on my forehead," Darien grinned.

"So what happens now with the other mages?" Stephanie asked.

"Nothing. It will take them a while to rebuild their supplies, especially now that their resident poison cook has been wounded. I don't think there is anything more we can do." Lucas smiled.

"Poison cook." Marcus hit his forehead with his open hand. "Now I know where I have heard Eagle's voice before. He works with my father at Brix & Burton."

"Which explains why the crates were in the stolen goods from there." Lucas nodded.

"Do you think his bosses know about this?" Jasmin asked.

"I don't know, but right now it hardly makes a difference. Let's just hope they stay quiet for a while. I could really use some time without bad guys." Lucas laughed.

When he was finally alone, on his last leg home, Lucas started thinking about the black-robe mages again. He was well aware of the fact that even now, with their stash destroyed, nothing had really changed. It might have slowed them down a little, but nothing would stop them from creating more of the substance, no matter what he and the others did. But this was not what bothered him most. The substance raised a lot of uncertainty, and it was after all dangerous, but only in the hands of magic users, and those were scarce compared to the total number of people around. And in the end he was not even sure if this would really be as problematic as they thought; after all, the group in Buxton didn't have any clue what they were doing. In the hands of experienced, or guided, mages this stuff might even be helpful. What bothered him much more was the way that those mages had dealt with the thieves. He had to admit that they were mostly acting in self-defense, and also for sure were under emotional stress, given that the thieves had stolen something important from them, but even that did not justify the use of that much force. After all, Firebolt had killed one of them, another one would be dead by now if it hadn't been for Airmid and her potion, and Cleric would for sure have given short shrift to the third one, if it hadn't been for the other one injuring Eagle. Looking at the situation made Lucas aware that they had left the play area now and with them getting closer to Cleric and his group, they had entered the grown-ups' table. And while with Wolfman and his lot it had all been about getting beaten up, now it was about getting killed. And this was a perspective he didn't like too much, although he was quite sure that sooner or later they would run out of options and be pushed into playing along with this game. He had to sigh when he realized that, and he cursed himself for letting them be drawn into this mess--a mess that he didn't even understand, didn't even have a clue where it would lead. It was another one of those stunning revelations. He once again had to realize that the world was not as easy as it looked, and that he now was consciously fighting for a good cause, but in the end didn't even know what that cause was, and what he was fighting against. It made him wonder about a lot of things--about his priorities, his motives and his decisions--and in the end, he realized that although it might be easy to think about and judge situations and decisions afterwards, it was all but easy when you were in the middle of them. It even made him think about those reports he always heard in the news, about company bosses and politicians making bad choices and being punished for it. Those people suddenly earned his respect, as he realized that they were in the same bad situation, the only difference being that they couldn't hide in the shadows like he could.

Arriving home, he tried to ease his mind and forget about thieves and chaos mages, at least for a short while, and try to get some rest.

CHAPTER 15

Darkness

Much to Lucas' relief, the time following the incident proved to be quiet. Except for their Monday training sessions, which finally turned back to real training, magic had almost vanished into the background again over the next month. It was mid-January on a Thursday afternoon. Lucas had just finished packing his backpack and was about to head back to school for his extracurricular course in cyber security when there was a knock on the door. When he opened it, Cedric was standing outside.

"Hey mate. What a pleasant surprise." Lucas smiled at him. "Please come in."

He had only a little time to spare if he wanted to stay on time for the course, but he also didn't want to turn his friend away.

"Are you heading out?" Cedric asked, pointing at his backpack.

"Have to be in class in an hour, yes. But this still gives us about 15 minutes or so." Lucas grinned. "What's brings you here?"

He led Cedric into the living room and offered him a seat on the couch.

"I had a chat with Angel yesterday, and it left me confused," Cedric started. "And somehow I was hoping you could shed some light."

"I doubt it." Lucas laughed. "But try me."

"I have heard the pep-talk about new responsibilities after becoming a Magus Minor before, but I never really got the point. What is different now?"

"The only thing that is different is the magnitude," Lucas said. "At least, that's the only thing I have found so far."

"What magnitude?"

"Prior to that step you had two or maybe three very specific spells at your disposal. This gave you an edge in some situations, but didn't help at all in most others. Now that you can create spells on the fly, you are way more flexible, but this also means that you will be tempted to use magic in way more situations. And that gives you more responsibility."

"So what shall I do now?" Cedric asked.

"The same thing you always do: Be careful. As long as you use your spells wisely and only in times of need, nothing will change."

"Have the others advanced already?"

"Airmid has, and so has Psycho. The others have not. So be careful what you tell them."

"That is strange," Cedric said. "So far I always was the last; now I am up front?"

"That's the way it seems to be. My guess would be that Cougar will join in, too, in a short while. Let's see how the Professor will do. It seems his head start is becoming a stumbling block for him now."

"Can't we do anything to help them?"

"No, they have to do this on their own. It's unfortunate, but that's the way it is." Lucas shook his head. "Sorry that I have to cut the conversation short, but I should get going," he continued after looking at his watch.

"Sure, sorry for keeping you." Cedric nodded and jumped up.

"No problem. I am always happy to see you." Lucas patted his shoulder and walked past him to the foyer.

After bidding Cedric farewell, Lucas cycled back to school, arriving ten minutes early for his class. It was the third time he had had it so far and he pretty much liked the content of the lecture. The teacher, a young professor from Oxford University named Shimmerman, showed him a lot of details revolving around security--everything from the concepts behind firewalls to the important things to consider to write secure code up to entry control systems to provide physical security for servers. And of course, they also touched topics like cryptography and the mathematics behind it, authentication mechanisms, and a lot more. For Lucas, who was used to rather easy topics in class, this was a major change. The lectures were going so deep down that he really had to focus to follow what the teacher told him.

When he entered the classroom he immediately noticed the difference from the last times. Professor Shimmerman had set up four notebooks and a network switch and was already waiting for him.

"Hello Professor. Sorry that I'm late," Lucas said and put down his backpack.

"You are actually a little early, Lucas." The teacher smiled. "So if you want to get something to drink there is still enough time."

"Thank you Professor, but I am fine." Lucas was not used to being allowed to drink during classes. Most of the teachers didn't tolerate this. But then there was a lot about Professor Shimmerman that he was not used to. With him he didn't feel as small as he normally did with the other teachers. He almost felt like a peer and not a student, and that for him was even more amazing, as Professor Shimmerman was way superior to all the teachers he had here in Luton.

"Well, then I guess we can start." The Professor smiled.

"Sure." Lucas had grabbed a notebook and a pen.

"You might want to fire up your laptop as well, Lucas. You will most likely need it."

"Yes, Professor." Lucas nodded and did as he was told.

"I have taught you a lot of theory so far; it is time we put it into practice. Those laptops resemble a simulated web application. Those two are yours, the two in the front are mine. The topology is simple: The first computer has a direct line to the simulated Internet and acts as the firewall. The second one runs the website and is only physically connected to the firewall. Our simulated Internet is just a direct connection between the two firewalls. My computers are set up exactly the same way yours are. I'll give you ten minutes to prepare and find out as much about the setup as you can, plus change any configuration you deem problematic up front. In the first eight minutes of this I will be here to answer any questions you have; after that I will take up my machines and start preparing as well. When the ten minutes are over, we try to break into each other's network, with the simple goal of bringing the web server down. Questions?"

"Two for starters: What are the admin passwords? And what are the IP addresses that are used?"

"Good questions." The Professor scribbled the data on the chalkboard. "I would suggest you change those passwords immediately."

"Will do." Lucas nodded.

"Oh, I almost forgot... Here is your USB stick." Shimmerman handed him the small device.

"What is that for?" Lucas asked.

"Your own laptop does not have access to the network and our test environments don't have access to the Internet. So if you need any tools you have to get them on your equipment and transfer them via USB key."

"So I am free to use the Internet?" Lucas was surprised.

"You are free to use whatever tool you deem necessary." The teacher nodded.

"One more question: Why aren't we doing this on virtual environments? That would have been less effort to set up I would suppose."

"Easy to answer." The teacher laughed. "Because on a virtual environment you could easily have attacked the underlying virtualization technology as well, and that is one layer of complexity I didn't want to add. Additionally, I wanted to give you the opportunity to pull a cable if you deemed it necessary."

Lucas nodded and took a seat close to his two notebooks.

"The time starts now," Shimmerman said and hit a button on his watch.

Lucas quickly tried to make sense of the environment. The firewall was a Linux installation, while the web server used Windows. Both systems he was very familiar with and had an easy time around. He quickly changed the passwords, disabled all accounts that were not in use and, following that pattern, went through all he had learned so far, trying to make his system as safe and foolproof as possible. He then started transferring some basic tools, like network scanners and sniffing tools, but quickly ran out of ideas regarding what else he would need.

"The time is up," the professor suddenly said. "Are you ready?"

"Ready as I'll ever be." Lucas nodded.

"Then let's bring it on."

Both started simultaneously typing and clicking, running command after command. Lucas had parallel monitoring tools open on all screens, to see if something was going wrong in his environment. He typed as quickly as he could, trying to find weak points in his teacher's defenses when suddenly, after only about five minutes, the screen of his firewall laptop went blank.

"That's one point for me," the teacher grinned.

Lucas tried hard to get the laptop back up, but the operating system would not boot anymore; whatever Professor Shimmerman had done, it had fried it. Lucas thought for a moment and then immediately started improvising. He built up a makeshift firewall on his web server, reset the network addresses and plugged the Internet line directly into it.

"Impressive move." The professor complimented and immediately started hitting his keyboard again.

Lucas tried really hard to rebound, but it was no good. After another five minutes in the defensive position, finally his web server crashed too.

"Damn it," Lucas cursed.

"Nice run." Shimmerman smiled.

"Nice for you, yes." Lucas laughed. "You flattened me."

"Well, that was to be expected after only two lessons, don't you think?" he laughed. "You know what your main problem is?"

"No. Please enlighten me, Professor." Lucas shook his head.

"You are too defensive. You try to play it safe. This means that while you are plugging one leak after the other and are always reacting to my moves I have time to think and plan my next attack. If you want to win in a challenge like that you need to be aggressive. You need to hit me hard and constant, so that I have no time left to breathe."

"I will try that next time." Lucas nodded.

"Then let's do this again."

"But my machines are toast..."

"Not for long; there are recovery partitions on the machines. They are reset in ten minutes," Shimmerman laughed and started working.

"Can you tell me what I missed? How you were able to kill both machines? Otherwise the next run will most likely even be shorter."

"The web server was easy--you left too many holes in your firewall configuration. You should always disable everything by default and only allow what you really need. On the firewall you forgot to apply a patch to one of the system daemons. This left the system vulnerable."

Lucas nodded and prepared the patches on his notebook, so he would not lose time when round two started. When time finally came, he worked as quickly as possible to secure his system and prepare some attacks of his own. First he started flooding the lines, trying to overload one of the machines, then he added small viruses to the game, and in the end even tried to trick the network card with malformed packages, but once again it only took about ten minutes before both his machines were down.

"You are still not aggressive enough," Shimmerman said. "The DDOS attack attempt was nice; it was the only good move you made, but futile. You can't DDOS with one computer. You just don't have the power for that."

"I was trying to find other attack angles, but I couldn't. Everything I could think of was airtight," Lucas sighed.

"That is because you still think like a sys admin. You have to start thinking like a pirate if you want to win. Think in directions that nobody else would. Be aggressive, be ruthless, don't hold back."

They did the run a few more times, and although Lucas managed to keep his system up longer and longer each time, the end result always stayed the same. When the two hours were over, he was exhausted and looking forward to getting home.

On his ride home the cold wind gave him some of his energy back. He was thinking about his options, about what he could have done better, and what had gone wrong all the time. In the end one thing stuck in his mind: "Be more aggressive, think like a pirate". The more he thought about this, the more he realized what a vulnerable spot the teacher had hit in him with this comment. Once again it came down to his dark side, and once again he had to realize that by burying that part of himself, he was not quite whole. But this time it was worse; for the first time he found himself in a situation that he could not win without it, where he would in fact fail miserably, just because he was standing on the side of the light.

He went to bed early that evening to shake the dilemma from his head, but even that didn't work. That entire Friday he was beside himself, he almost fumbled a test because of it, and on Saturday it was little better. By then he was so mad that he couldn't stand it anymore. It was no longer only about the contest. The discussion he had had with Marcus a while back, about how he had handled the girls at the party, had also resurfaced, and so had a lot of other situations where he had fought down his temptations or his anger, just to stay the way he was, being what he deemed "true to himself". Right now it was as if a little demon had awakened within his mind and was now gibing him up and down for all the things that could have gone so much better if he hadn't been so stubborn in the first place. And the voice got louder with every passing minute, making him second-guess many of his decisions and almost driving him crazy. Shortly after noon he just couldn't bear it anymore. He decided to pack his robe and cycle out to the woods, where he would be undisturbed. Out there he wanted to confront his dark side once and for all.

On his way there the cold wind got his emotions down a little again, making him now second-guess even his decision to do this. What would happen if he liked it? What would happen if he happened to a bad guy after all? He realized that he had to forcefully drive those ideas out of his head when the first thoughts of suicide emerged in his mind, something else he was not used to. But at least those thoughts brought an advantage: Now he had something to fight against, a real purpose in embracing his dark side, because in the end being a bad guy still beat being a dead guy.

Lucas arrived at a quiet clearing shortly after 2 p.m. He had not seen anybody during the last twenty minutes of his ride, so he was pretty sure that out here he would be undisturbed. He chained his bike to a tree and put his robes on. He thought a little about how he would proceed now, but couldn't really come up with a good plan. In the end he decided to start with things he already knew. He looked for a broken off branch in the nearby forest and carried it out to the clearing. It was big enough that he could hardly drag it along, which was exactly what he wanted. He then took position a few meters back and started letting his emotions free-flow. At first his routine kicked in, calming him down for a spell, but he fought it as hard as he could, siphoning as much rage and anger as he possibly could, picturing every bad situation he ever had in his mind.

"REPELLUM," he then cried with a power that he only had felt when Jasmin was hit by the baseball bat.

The branch took off and sailed a few meters through the air before crashing down to the ground. Lucas immediately felt better, freed, but he also felt that there was more to it. He closed his eyes for a moment and tried to listen to his inner voice. And amazingly, it was very easy to do that.

"Destroy it. Show no mercy," he heard his inner demon whisper.

So he walked up to the branch again and prepared for something new. He wanted to let his shield charm work like an axe, splitting the branch in two. He slowly built up all the fibers of energy, forming a wedge right on top of the branch.

"ASCIUS," he then shouted.

A loud creaking noise was audible and suddenly the branch just fell apart, having been split cleanly in the middle.

Lucas felt relief when he looked at the piece of wood. He was not really happy, but somehow it felt good to be destructive. But his inner demon was still far from satisfied.

"You idiot, stop fooling around!" it cried. "Let me out, I will show you how to do it right."

He started feeling even more uneasy about the situation. He really had no clue what else he could do, other than maybe hack the branch into even smaller pieces, but that for sure would not have satisfied his demons either. On the other hand, he was afraid of relinquishing control of himself to this voice, this dark side of his. And then, he also had no idea how to do that, anyway. After a few minutes of thinking, the situation had made him so extremely angry that he just went berserk and let his new Ascius charm hammer down multiple times on the branch. But even when he had exhausted all his energy, he didn't feel any better. He knew that he had still not achieved anything. His anger turned into frustration, which quickly turned into desperation. When his inner voice came back, mocking him again, he just fell to his knees and started crying. In his entire life he had never felt so lost, so alone as he was feeling right now. He couldn't stand life anymore and what was worse was that he couldn't stand himself anymore, and there was nobody to turn to. He laid there on the ground, crying and shaking, his robes wet from the tears. Every second felt like an hour, every thought that passed through his mind caused additional pain. After quite a while, he was even more exhausted, he had run out of tears, his voice was gravelly--he just didn't know what to do anymore. All had gone silent in his head, no more feelings in his body, he was just empty. He closed his eyes and started taking deep, slow breaths. Good, bad, reputation, self-esteem--none of that mattered anymore to him. And in the middle of his emptiness, he suddenly felt a warmth, a strength that was building up. It was a feeling he had never felt before, a different kind of power, a totally new form of energy. When he focused on his inner self and tried to find a picture for what he felt, the first thing to pop into his head looked somewhat like a DNA helix, but one that had three strands rather than two. He slowly stood up again and looked at the parts of the branch lying on the ground. Still no emotions had come into his body, he felt cool, almost relaxed.

"Are you ready for it now?" he heard his inner demon whisper.

"Yes," he said out loud, but calmly, and nodded.

Then he stretched out his arm toward the branches. He didn't think, didn't try to focus, was not doing anything he normally would when casting a spell. And then it happened. An immense feeling of rage and destructiveness razed through his body and into his arm, and before he really consciously knew what was happening, he heard himself yell in a deep, almost trembling voice, "INCENDIO."

In the same instant a jet of blue flame shot from his hand, setting the branches ablaze.

When he took his next deep breath, he was amazed. He felt no energy drainage from his body, even though the spell had been quite powerful. And even more surprisingly, the feelings had not taken hold of him; they just vanished into the background. For a while he watched the branches burn down, until only pieces of wood and charcoal were left. He was at first unsure what to do next, but then he decided to give it another go and see what else his darker side could do, and if after all he was in control of it. He took another deep breath and once again stretched his arm out toward the remnants of the branch. Then he relaxed his mind and made way for his emotions again. This time he completely focused on pure destructiveness. His face remained completely calm while the emotions were rising rapidly inside him. And then the same deep voice came back:

"DESINTEGRATUS," he yelled and quickly had to take one step back, because the effect almost frightened him. What had been left from the branches had just turned to fine dust and was immediately blown away by the wind.

Lucas once again took a few deep breaths and tried to grasp the situation. The powers he had just unleashed were far more potent than he had expected, and they were far more frightening. But somehow it didn't bother him, somehow those powers felt different now than they had before. They were no longer haunting him, no longer holding him back, but had also not taken over. They were not at all controlling him. It felt as if the two parts of him had just come together in peace and were now joining forces to make him whole.

On his way back home Lucas shifted his focus back to the school contest. Ideas kept popping up in his head at a rate far beyond what he had seen before, and it felt as if he had just unleashed his brain for the first time. And now he was really looking forward to the next session with Professor Shimmerman; he was almost certain that this time he would beat him.

When Lucas arrived home, a man was standing outside their garden. He was sure that he had seen him before, but he couldn't make the connection right away. After thinking for a moment what he should do, he decided to jump off his bike and find out what the man wanted.

"Hello Mr. Trent," he greeted him with a friendly voice.

"Hello Inspector Corben." When Lucas heard the voice he remembered. "Almost didn't recognize you without the uniform."

"Do you have a minute to talk?" Corben asked. "Unofficially, of course," he quickly added.

"Sure." Lucas nodded and started walking beside the inspector.

"That incident with the Ninja-Thieves last year…" Corben started. "It took me a while to make the connection." He pulled out a piece of paper and handed it to Lucas.

Lucas opened it. It was the paper Marcus had pinned to the van to warn SO-19 about the other two thieves.

"That was your doing, wasn't it?" Corben didn't look at him.

Lucas was unsure what to say. He thought for quite a while, and before he even started, Corben continued.

"I am not here to blame you, or anything else. I would just like to know."

"It is not my writing," Lucas finally said. "But it was my idea, yes."

"Then I have to thank you. Without that hint they would have gotten away, and most likely more people would have gotten hurt."

"Don't thank me," Lucas replied. "We were just doing what's right."

"Then I guess that 'angel' the one suspect mentioned was your work, too?"

"Again not my work, but to keep it simple, yes."

"But the dead guy was not you, was it?"

"No, and the other two injured were also not our doing."

"But you know whose it was." Corben now looked at him.

"Yes I do." Lucas nodded. "At least I know one of them, but unfortunately I can't prove it."

"You are aware that there was a reward on the capture of the thieves? And a quite big one, too."

"No, I was not. But I honestly don't really care."

"Why? All you have to do is come forward, and you will walk away rich." Corben winked.

"You know, Inspector, what we did was try to set something right. It never was about money, and we don't care about money, either. And more than that, we will not come forward. It would raise too many questions that I am not willing to answer."

"I have to admit that I don't know how you did what you did, and I would be very interested to learn more about it, but I respect your wish for privacy."

"I appreciate that." Lucas nodded.

"There is one more thing, and after that I will leave you alone." Corben had stopped.

"Shoot." Lucas looked at him and smiled.

"Have you ever thought about being a C.I.?"

"What exactly is that?"

"A confidential informant. Someone who tosses us information without ever getting named."

"And why would I want to get into this?"

"You said that you wanted to set things straight--well, this is one more way to do it. And of course there is money in it as well, but you don't care for that. For example, I am sure the homicide team would love to hear what you know about the dead thief. And as a C.I. you would not be named."

"See, Inspector, the problem is that I don't exactly trust the police with this."

"Why?"

"Because homicide is the wrong team in this case. You should have this looked into by Internal Affairs."

"Are you saying that there was a policeman involved in this incident?"

"I am not saying anything. I know how it is, and I have no proof whatsoever."

"So if you have that much distrust in the police service, why do you trust me enough to first help and now tell me this?"

"I don't necessarily distrust the whole police force, but I don't have high confidence in it, either. And I tell you because of all the policemen I know, you seem to be the one that is most trustworthy. But in the end, I am not even sure if you could help in this case. You have seen what they did with the thieves."

"Unfortunately, yes, and I don't understand that, either." Corben nodded. "But I am still certain that we could handle them if necessary."

"We will see." Lucas said and started walking back slowly.

"If you don't mind, I would like to deliver that information to the homicide detectives. Without naming you, of course."

"If you do, I insist that you tell them not to share that information with anybody else. The man that was involved in this could easily make the connection and trace it back to us. And although I am not really afraid of him, I would rather not have to get involved with him again, either."

"Understood." Corben nodded. "Your information is very valuable. Are you sure that you don't want to be a C.I.?"

"Very sure, yes," Lucas laughed.

"I have to accept that choice." Corben nodded again. "In this case, thank you one more time for your help."

"Nothing to thank me for. It was our pleasure."

"Here is my business card, with my personal cell phone number on the back. If you ever need assistance, no matter what, give me a call." Corben handed him the card and then walked away.

Lucas waited until he had disappeared around the next corner. It felt strange having a conversation like this with a policeman. He was not sure how much Corben knew or anticipated, but after the run-in with the doctor in Luton General Hospital not too long ago, Lucas was ready to accept anything as possible. On his way into the house he also thought about that C.I. proposal again. At first he had declined it because he wasn't too eager to share more with the police than he absolutely had to, but now he was not so sure anymore. After all, being able to confidentially call them and just drop a hint would be far easier than convincing some local constabulary that they had just "stumbled" upon something that needed immediate response by SO-19. He decided to bring the topic up with the others on their next meeting, where he had to tell them about Corben's visit anyway, and let it be for now.

When he arrived at his room the topic was already forgotten again. Too powerful were the thoughts about his private training session earlier, and the implications that would have. Too strong was the urge to reevaluate old decisions based on his new self. So he started to think about the situations where he had struggled with his dark side before, reliving them. He first thought about the situation with Jasmin and the baseball bat attack. He knew that at that moment he would have killed the guy if he had had the proper means to do so. Now that he thought about it again, the feeling was quite different. He had to admit that he still would have tried to hurt him a lot more than he actually did, but that he never really meant to do permanent damage. It was strange to see, and he could not really tell why it was that way. Right now it made no sense to him. So he jumped on to the next thing that popped into his mind, the three girls at the party. Interestingly when he ran this situation through his mind, the result changed only minimally, but the reasons did veer off very far. What he found in his mind now was that he maybe would have had a little fun with them--not more than would have been appropriate for a large audience--but that the reason for not pushing it any further was no longer insecurity, or the strange wish for honor, it was just plain annoyance and self-preservation that would be his reasons now. This discovery led him straight on to his little scene with Stephanie later on. And while this time he was very sure that the result would have been very different, given the amount of self-restraint it had taken him to not give in even in his old state of mind, surprisingly it wasn't. The only difference he could feel when reliving that situation was that he no longer felt the urge to turn away from her. And in that very moment he realized what it was that had really changed now. By allowing his dark side to participate, he had taken all the dammed-up energy away. Now he was listening to what that path had to offer and then making an educated choice, which all parts of his mind could easily accept. This finding was so stunning for him that he started laughing loudly and uncontrollably. For so long he had been afraid of this part of himself, only to find out that his fear was in fact the only thing frightening about it whatsoever.

When he had finally managed to stop laughing many minutes later he felt relieved and exhausted at the same time, and those feelings were so strong that he didn't even bother changing his clothes. He just let himself fall into his bed and slept away.

Chapter 16

Revelations

Over the remainder of the weekend Lucas was so extremely relaxed and self-confident that even his mother noticed the change. This feeling held even through the school day and was still present when he headed out to the shack. The only thing at that point that kept him from being totally happy was the question that was raging in his mind: Should he tell the others about his finding? Should he show them what he had learned? Up to his arrival there he was still unsure and so decided to keep it his secret for now, just to play it safe.

When he had stowed away his bike at the shack, he realized that he was almost half an hour early and was in fact the first to arrive. To help occupy himself while he waited, he decided to carry some firewood from the storage place to the door, so it would be readily available, and if he should have enough time left, maybe start making some wood chips to start the fire later on. He was just walking around the corner with his first stack of wood when he saw somebody standing near the forest line. When he took a closer look, he could see that the person was wearing a dark blue robe and as usual, had the hood pulled deeply over his face. Lucas put the wood down and took his robe out of his backpack, also pulling his hood deep over his face. He then walked over to the person, who started slowly walking back into the forest as Lucas drew closer.

"Greetings," Lucas said when he found him waiting a few steps in.

"Good afternoon, Guardian," the other one answered.

"I see that you have an advantage over me," Lucas said calmly. "You know who I am, which is something I can't say about you."

All he could tell so far was that he was dealing with a man, and he sounded older.

"Believe me, I don't know that much about you," the other one laughed. "I am called Gremlin. I am a mage as well, and I am here in peace and as a friend."

"It is my pleasure to meet you, Gremlin." Lucas bowed. "Please don't take it personally, but I don't trust easily these days."

"And you have no reason to trust me, I understand that." He nodded.

"So what does bring you to me?" Lucas asked.

"I am here on behalf of the Council of Magic Users. It is my duty and my pleasure to welcome you to a rather small group within the community," Gremlin smiled.

"And what group is that?" Lucas was curious.

"The group that advances above the crowd," Gremlin said. "The ones that call themselves Magus Major."

"Well, thank you, then." Lucas bowed again. "Maybe you can enlighten me as to why I am in this group now."

"I think you know that answer already, but to give you the short version: Because you managed to unify your personality and with it managed to break out of your magic specialization. That is what defines a Magus Major."

"I have to say that it is pretty strange being named Magus Major at my age. How long does it normally take for somebody to make that step?" Lucas was a little proud now, but still didn't fully trust the guy.

"Well, strange is not the right word; impressive would be the one that I would use. And to answer your question: a long time. A majority of all magic users never make it to that level."

"That's odd. I mean, it took me a while to get here too, but it was not that big a challenge after all. I would expect everyone to make it in due time." Lucas was intrigued.

"Easy for those who made it, impossible for many others, as you will learn over time," Gremlin laughed.

"So, I am curious… Why isn't Angel bringing me this news? She was always the one to tell me so far."

"Very simply, she is not a Magus Major yet. So she couldn't tell you even if she wanted to."

"You have to be kidding me." Lucas said in disbelief.

"You will soon find out that I am not. There are not that many of us around."

"OK, what will happen now? I guess you didn't just come here to bring your best wishes, now did you?"

"No, I didn't. One of my duties is to invite you to our irregular meeting that we normally hold in London on Friday evenings."

"Irregular?" Lucas asked.

"Yes, we only convene the meeting if something is up that needs discussion, which normally is about every other month."

"And I am expected to be there?"

"Not expected, just invited. If you can make it, we all appreciate your inputs; if you can't or don't want to, nobody will bear a grudge."

"Sounds OK. And where is this meeting held?"

"It is in a pub called the Duke of Summerset in the middle of London," Gremlin said. "And it is a casual meeting. No robes."

"Just out of curiosity... If it is irregular, how do I know about it beforehand?"

"Ahhh, very good question, Guardian." Gremlin smiled. "For that reason I am bearing a gift for you."

Lucas waited patiently while Gremlin searched through a bag he was carrying under his robes.

"Ah, here it is." He handed Lucas a small wooden box.

"Thank you." Lucas carefully opened it. It contained a really beautiful, golden digital watch. "Wow. This is quite a gift. Thank you."

"I am glad you like it. I did not have much to go on, other than knowing that you are into computers, so I chose a quite sophisticated digital minicomputer as a front." Gremlin seemed to be very happy.

"You made this?" Lucas was highly impressed.

"Yes, the whole thing is handmade, just for you." Gremlin bowed.

"I am not sure that I deserve something like this."

"But I am. So please, try it, so we can adjust the wristband if necessary."

Lucas took off his own watch and put the new one on his wrist. It was a little heavier than he was used to, but he just loved it. And it fit almost perfectly on the first try.

"Ah, almost. We should tighten the band by just one nudge," Gremlin said and pulled out a small screwdriver. Lucas handed him the watch and observed as the older man put on his watchmaker's magnifying glass and with skillful hands readjusted the band.

"Now it should fit." He handed the watch back.

"Perfect." Lucas smiled after putting it on. It really was a flawless fit now. "But how does this help me to know when the meeting will be?"

"When you look at it, you will see that the watch has a calendar integrated into it. When a meeting is scheduled you will see it in there. And it will flash up on the main display the first time you look at it after it is confirmed."

"Cool feature. I would love to see the technology behind this." Lucas was impressed.

"Oh, it's not technology, it's magic," Gremlin grinned.

"I am really impressed, Gremlin. Really," Lucas said truthfully.

"Then you are too easily impressed, I would say," Gremlin laughed. "There is more."

He grabbed his arm to show him. "You see the divider between those two buttons here?" He pointed to the side of the watch, where two big control buttons were located. "This divider is actually a button, too. Try it."

Lucas pressed the button down and the watch sprang open. He looked into the underlying compartment and was impressed again. It looked like a locket, with a place for a picture on the bottom and a beautifully shimmering surface on the top part, which seemed to be mounted at the back of the digital clockwork.

"That is really nice." Lucas again was impressed. "What is that material there?"

"I am glad you like it." Gremlin smiled again. "The material is nacre. And this is what I wanted to show you. Press your thumb on it briefly."

Lucas did as asked and the nacre surface instantly turned purple.

"What is that?" he asked.

"It is a means of identification. If anyone other than a Magus Major or Magus Superior touches this, nothing will happen. Only for us will it turn purple," Gremlin explained.

"Very nice," Lucas smiled.

"One more thing: If you ever need to call a meeting, all you have to do is press the nacre surface constantly for half a minute. It will turn green then and you will get the message once it is scheduled."

"Wow. That is quite a potent tool you have given me," Lucas said. "Why do I deserve to get this?"

"Every Magus Major has something like it," Gremlin said. "It's our way of communicating with each other."

"So what do you expect from me now?" Lucas asked.

"Nothing," Gremlin laughed. "Neither my appearance nor my gift come with any duties attached."

"Well, then once again: Thank you." Lucas smiled. "One more question, if I may: You said before that you are here on behalf of the Council of Magic Users. What exactly do you do for them? And what exactly does this Council do?"

"Those are two questions," Gremlin laughed. "First, I took the task of welcoming every new Magus Major into the group and supplying them with these communication devices. Regarding the Council itself, the question is not so easy to answer, as I honestly don't know. All I can tell you is that they have a watchful eye on things that happen on a global scale. But you can of course address this question to Lady Gaia when you meet her at the Duke of Summerset."

"And who is Lady Gaia?" Lucas asked.

"She is a member of the Council. And she lives in the UK, so she sometimes attends our meetings."

"I will ask her then; thank you, Gremlin."

"Once again, my pleasure. But now you have duties to attend to, and so have I. Godspeed, Guardian, until our travels lead us to each other again."

"Godspeed, Gremlin." Lucas bowed and watched him walk away.

When Lucas finally lost sight of the older man, he started walking back to the shack. By now the others had arrived, too. The firewood was gone, smoke was coming from the chimney and his backpack was no longer there, either. When he stepped into the room, the others were eagerly waiting.

"Guardian, finally," Stephanie smiled and sighed in relief. "We were worried."

"No need to be," Lucas said. "But thank you for it."

He took off his robe and joined them at the table.

"Why did you wear your robe?" Darien asked.

"We had a visitor, and it seemed fitting to meet in robes." Lucas tried to evade as best he could.

"And who was that?" Marcus asked.

"I am unfortunately not at liberty to tell," Lucas said. "Sorry."

"Anything we can help with?" Darien now asked.

"No, everything is fine. You know by now, too, how these things go," Lucas smiled. "There is another topic I wanted to discuss with you, though."

He quickly summed up the conversation with Inspector Corben.

"Nice one." Marcus grinned. "Why didn't you take the offer?"

"Should I?" Lucas asked and looked at each of them.

"Hell yeah." Marcus nodded.

"I would not do anything official, no," Darien said.

"Neither would I. I don't trust uniforms." Cedric was next.

"I would not do it, either. It raises too many questions," Jasmin threw in.

"I think the decision is solely yours. And whatever you decide is fine with me," Stephanie smiled.

"I think the best way is to not do something officially, but give him a call now and then and feed him information if something does come up," Lucas suggested. "What do you say?"

A lengthy discussion started, revolving around the topic, but in the end they decided to stick to Lucas' plan and keep the information flow to a minimum. After that they engaged in a training session, focusing on Jasmin's area this time. When they were on their way back home afterwards, Darien addressed Lucas.

"Forgot to tell you earlier: I am sorry, but I will not be able to accompany you at the contest," he said.

"Pity to hear. What are you doing that day?" Lucas asked.

"I've got an offer from Harlington Research for an internship. One whole month in various research projects."

"Wow, congratulations. So Mr. Dexter kept his word?" Lucas said.

"More than that, I would say. He didn't even wait for my call but approached me. And he did it personally."

"Nice." Lucas smiled. "Seems you made your career already."

"Yeah. I am really looking forward to that." Darien nodded.

"What did the principal say to this?"

"He was very supportive, cleared the whole road for me."

"Cool. I am looking forward to hearing details, then," Lucas grinned. "Will you also need to skip our meetings?"

"Don't think so. After all, they also have normal working hours there."

Lucas felt really happy for Darien. He knew how eager he was to join HRC later in his career, and that internship seemed the perfect jumpstart for that. It was just a little sad that it would stop Darien from being at the contest. He had really hoped to get moral support from him. But by now he was confident enough, anyway, so the happiness clearly came out on top.

It was mid-February and Lucas had just gotten home from school when his phone rang.

"Hi Guardian, it's me," Darien greeted him. "Turn on your computer; you have to see this."

Lucas could hear the sense of urgency in Darien's voice, so he ran up to his room.

"See what?" he asked after his computer had booted up.

"I sent you a link via mail. The video is on YouTube by now. It was sent to our government earlier today."

"OK, I'll watch it right away and call you back." Lucas hung up and opened his emails. He quickly picked out Darien's text and opened the link. "Nature is coming to an end" was the title of the video, and Lucas froze when he saw the first picture. It was a man in a black robe, with a pointy black face mask and hat that was speaking which made him almost look like a member of the Ku Klux clan. He was standing somewhere in a forest. Lucas at first thought that it might be one of the student circles around Plague, but in the end he was not so sure anymore.

"Children of Earth, listen to me carefully," he said. "For a long time now we have ruthlessly exploited our planet and because of this, we have brought our whole race to the brink of extinction. The demons of fossil fuel have eaten up our natural resources on both ends, not only depleting their own energy source, but also causing catastrophic effects to our holy planet. For a long time we have kept the gods appeased, as you promised us to stop this carelessness, but now the gods are angry. They have started showing their wrath clearly, by emphasizing what you have done to their beloved Earth. Take a good look what the future will bring." The speaker at that point stepped aside and the camera showed an area of dead trees that was dotted with dead animals, as well. "This is what our planet will look like shortly. This is what the end of our race will look like. We are no longer willing to watch this heresy and wait for the gods to kill us. If you don't take immediate decisive action against this, we will."

After the video finished, Lucas quickly called Darien back.

"Hi Professor," he said. "I just watched the video."

"And what do you say?" Darien asked.

"What shall I say? There are tons of videos like this out there, although I have to grant you that the area he showed was quite dead. I have seldom seen something like this."

"Look again. Look at the area." Darien seemed overly excited.

"What am I looking for?" Lucas asked.

"The background. Look at the background."

"Hold on a sec." Lucas had finally spotted what Darien was pointing at. "Are those the huts where the thieves got caught?"

"I am almost certain they are," Darien said. "And get this: HRC has been tasked to find the spot and get to the bottom of this. Someone seems to be really worried by the message."

"I can understand that, even though it will most likely be a fake. Or at best a side effect of some spilled chemicals from the Brix & Burton heist and not something done by fossil fuels."

"So what do we do?" Darien asked.

"What do you mean? I don't see a reason to do anything."

"Well, should I at least give HRC a hint where this spot is?"

"Feel free. I don't think there is much to it. Just don't tell them why you know."

"Of course not," Darien said.

"Anyway, I don't see a reason for us to get involved," Lucas said. "Other than what you might get involved in through your internship, of course," he quickly added.

After Darien had hung up, Lucas watched the video again. The message was somewhat strange. It sounded far more aggressive than most similar videos he had seen in the past. And it was based on a very local phenomenon, so Lucas didn't get how this could generate enough punch to make some politician nervous at all. Additionally, what struck him as strange was how these guys had found the area in the first place. After all, it was very remote, and no one other than their adversaries in the black robes, the thieves and the police knew about it. He was sure that the thieves couldn't have had anything to do with this, as they certainly were breathing sifted air by now, so either this strange eco-freak was actually part of Cleric and his bunch or there was someone else within the Police service that was playing a double game. Or of course it could also just be a coincidence, but Lucas didn't believe in those anymore. Another thing that did cause him major discomfort was the pure destruction he saw on the screen. The only explanation he had was that maybe some canisters from Brix & Burton had spilled, but even that struck him as odd, as when they had examined the crates earlier at the first location he hadn't seen any warning signs on them, and he was quite sure that a renowned chemical plant like Brix & Burton would not easily dismiss safety protocol. Unfortunately, the only other explanation he had was that this was a fake, but that didn't make sense, as a fake would hardly cause anybody to jump, let alone pay for an investigation. All in all the situation made little sense, so he was more than ever curious what Harlington Research would find out.

When next Monday came and Lucas was heading for the shack he was still curious about the video.

"So, do you have any results yet?" Lucas asked Darien as he sat down.

"Results on what?" Stephanie asked.

"Didn't you tell them?" Lucas was surprised.

"No, as you said that this is none of our concern, I didn't bother. But I did bring the video, so you can see for yourself." Darien shook his head and grabbed his laptop.

The others watched the video eagerly.

"Is that the thieves' hideout?" Marcus had spotted the huts immediately.

"Yep, it is." Darien nodded. "Good eyes."

"What happened there?" Stephanie seemed shocked by the pictures.

"Well, that's the interesting part," Darien started. "HRC did analyze the soil very thoroughly."

"And?" Marcus looked tense.

"And the report states that this was caused by a fungal infection of the trees, which spread to the bushes and in turn to the soil itself."

"Come again?" Lucas asked. "What about the chemicals?"

"That is exactly the interesting part. The samples showed no unusual traces of chemicals whatsoever," Darien replied. "According to HRC's scientists this was a purely natural cause."

"And what happened to the animals, then?" Jasmin asked.

"That's where it gets a little bit fuzzy. Some of the researchers speculated that they died from food poisoning, due to the dead trees, others said that it was the fungal spores themselves that caused some sort of asphyxiation."

"But wouldn't they stay away from a dead area by natural instinct?" Jasmin asked.

"That's exactly what bothers the scientists, too. And they have no explanation for it."

"So what do they say about the fact that this is only limited to a small area?" Lucas had gotten even more curious by now.

"In their opinion it is pure luck that the violent outbreak of the fungus did not spread further. They think that the heavy winter sun on the clearing was what made it thrive only there."

"Have they given a reason for the fungus being there in the first place? I mean… if this thing can cause that much damage it has to be new, or it would have caused major havoc before somewhere else."

"Well, they do have a simple explanation for that, and I don't like it too much."

"Why, what is it?" Marcus asked.

"Basically what they are saying is that the guy in the video was right, that this actually was a result of climate change," Darien sighed.

"I don't believe that." Lucas shook his head. "If we are that close to disaster with global warming, then there should have been signs somewhere else too."

"There are signs all over the planet," Darien replied with an unhappy look on his face. "It just seems that we have drawn the lucky card to be the first ones that get hit with full force. At least this is what the scientists say."

"Do you have reason to doubt their findings?" Jasmin had spotted uncertainty in Darien's face.

"Honestly, yes, I do." Darien nodded. "The answer is far too convenient. There must be something more to it."

"Especially at this time of year," he added after thinking for a moment. "Fungi don't normally thrive in winter."

"So what do you think it is?" Stephanie asked.

"I really don't know. And it is causing me headaches," Darien had to admit.

"Why don't we go out there and have a look for ourselves?" Lucas suggested.

"To what end? Do you honestly think we can find something the great minds of HRC can't?" Darien asked.

"Wouldn't be the first time," Lucas grinned. "And after all, they might have a whole lot of experience and a bunch of sweet tools, but they do lack the very best tool."

"And what would that be?" Darien inquired.

"Your eyes, Professor. They see more than any microscope could."

"All right, if you think so." Darien nodded. "But we should bring masks and rubber gloves, just to be safe."

The others nodded, agreeing. So Lucas devised a plan to drive there the next day and take a quick look. They decided on all the details and then shelved the topic to get to their training. Unfortunately, though, with the video still on everybody's mind, none of them could really focus too well, so after only an hour of trying they had to cut the evening short, because of rising frustration levels.

Lucas was still thinking about the video on his way home, and even throughout the next day in school. The one idea that wouldn't go out of his head was that somebody had faked the report. Knowing HRCs new owner, Marcel Jackson, this sounded more and more plausible every time he ran the thought again. The only thing that he couldn't figure out was the motive. Why would Jackson want to have a fake report about an environmental problem? When Lucas headed for the meeting with the others he was determined to find out, but decided to keep to idea to himself for now.

Both the train ride and the last kilometer on the bikes were very quiet. Everybody was deep in his thoughts, and nobody was eager to share. Marcus was the first to break the silence when they were near the clearing.

"I think it is time to put our masks on now," he said, pointing at a dead tree nearby.

"Agreed," Lucas nodded, and Darien started handing them out.

They got off their bikes and made the last meters on foot.

"This looks even worse than on the video." Stephanie was shocked.

"Yes, it seems to be spreading." Lucas nodded.

"Not anymore." Darien was standing in the middle of the clearing, and although only few parts of his face were visible under the cap and the mask, Lucas could tell that he was pale.

"What is it, Professor?" he asked and approached him.

"This was not a fungus." Darien's voice was shaking. "At least not solely. The fungus is there all right, but it could not have done something like this."

"What is it then?" Lucas was looking around now, too.

"I am still checking, but I do have a hunch." Darien had walked a few steps up and down the clearing. "The place where you stand now, Guardian, seems to be the epicenter of the outbreak."

"Right here?" Lucas had taken a step aside.

"Yes, exactly." Darien nodded.

"Wasn't that the place where…" Lucas started.

"Yes, exactly," Darien interrupted him, obviously thinking along the same lines.

"Oh my God." Lucas was getting pale now too.

"The place where… What?" Stephanie had joined them. "What is it?"

"The place where Cleric and his guys had stacked the crates with the magical substance," Marcus finished Lucas' sentence.

"Oh my God." Jasmin was getting pale now too.

"Are you saying that this strange magic enhancer has side effects?" Stephanie asked. "Side effects of that scale?"

"It would seem so." Darien nodded. "The whole area is flooded with magical energy. But I need to take a closer look to be sure."

"Isn't that dangerous for you, too?" Stephanie seemed concerned.

"Not really." Darien shook his head. "The spreading has stopped by now."

He knelt down, put his rubber gloves on, and then put one hand firmly on the ground. "INTUERE MAGICA," he cast with a firm voice.

The others watched him eagerly as he focused on the soil.

"The whole area is so flooded with energy that I can't make out anything concrete," Darien sighed.

"Can't you try to break the energy up somehow?" Lucas asked.

"I have been trying to do something like this before, but I never got it to work," Darien said. "After all, spell magic is not exactly my strong suit."

"Take a sample and try to align with its energy," Lucas said. "We have always been best when under pressure, and I guess that this is as much pressure to you as an attack is to some of us."

"Very well, I will try." Darien nodded.

"Don't try. Just do it," Lucas said firmly.

Darien knelt there for a while, focusing on the ground. Lucas could see his stress levels rising.

"I can't align. I can't connect to the energy." Darien shook his head.

"Take your glove off," Lucas said calmly. "Feel the soil, feel the energy, then flow into it."

Darien nodded and tried it again. He took a while longer, and Lucas could once again see his face getting red from the strain. It almost looked as if he was about to give up when he finally shouted.

"EXPLORARE MAGICA."

Then his body started shaking violently and his eyelids were flickering at extreme speed.

"Professor!" Stephanie was about to jump to him, but Lucas held her back.

"Let him finish this," he said.

"But he looks in pain," Stephanie insisted.

"He looks stressed. But so do you when you cast your healing magic. So let it be for a moment; you can help him a little later," Lucas said in a firm, almost strict, voice.

A moment later Darien collapsed to the ground. Lucas immediately let go of Stephanie, who ran over to him.

"I am fine, I am fine," Darien said and waved a little. "Don't worry."

Slowly he stood up and patted the snow from his clothes.

"What was that?" Marcus asked.

"That was amazing," Darien grinned. "I am still not used to spellcasting, but the results are worth it. Thanks for the guidance, Guardian."

"Anytime, Professor. Returning the favor was long overdue, anyway," he grinned.

"So what did you find out?" Stephanie was curious.

"This is not a side effect of the substance." Darien was still a little out of breath.

"Are you saying that this was not the work of the potion after all?" Marcus asked in disbelief.

"No, I am not saying that at all. This was the work of the substance all right, but this is not a side effect. This is what this stuff is actually intended to do," Darien said.

"Come again? What about the magic enhancement that we saw?" Lucas had a hard time following.

"My impression is that they built this energy battery into the potion to make it look like a useful substance and hide its true nature. But the main component in it definitely is this."

"But why would they want to kill patches of forest?" Stephanie asked.

"I am thinking that killing it like this was never intended," Darien speculated. "I think that it was intended as a slowly spreading, disease-like thing."

"And why did this happen then?" Stephanie looked around.

"Overdose…," Lucas replied with shock in his voice. He was walking around now, taking a closer look at the effect.

"Correct." Darien nodded. "Remember that the one thief repeatedly shot the crates, making most of the flasks burst? This stuff was never meant to be used in such quantities."

"So what do we do now?" Jasmin asked.

"I don't think there is much we can do. Nobody would believe this anyway," Darien sighed. "And I doubt that we can easily brew an antidote for that."

"Then we have to stop the supplies," Lucas said with a firm voice.

"And how do we do that?" Darien laughed in agony.

"The thieves already caused them a setback, destroying their stash. If we take out Cleric's circle, or at least this Eagle guy, the supply should run dry quickly. After all, he seems to be the one that actually creates it."

"You don't really want to confront them head-on, do you?" Stephanie sounded afraid.

"I have no plan yet," Lucas sighed. "But first we need to find them, then we can think about how to stop them."

"I don't like this," Jasmin said. "This sounds like a fight we can't win."

"Unfortunately I agree." Lucas nodded. "But it is still a fight that needs fighting."

The others nodded slowly and silently.

"Relax guys. We will find a way to do it. But for now let's head home; there is nothing more we can achieve here," Lucas said and walked to his bike.

The others followed him silently, and it stayed that way for the entire trip back.

CHAPTER 17

Unfair Approaches

The next two weeks proved to be nerve-wracking for Lucas and the others. They spent a lot of time looking for ways to find Cleric and his circle and at the same time devise a plan to deal with them once they found them, but nothing they did seemed to stick, not even a little. And besides that, the end of the semester was approaching fast with last exams agonizing all of them. Even Darien, who was free from the exam stress, had his head full, already being buried to his neck in work at HRC. Lucas, on top of that, was also training hard for the contest that was also coming up quickly. By now he had learned almost everything there was to learn--at least it felt so--and using his newfound unity, he was now able to beat his professor eight out of ten times in the challenges he built for him.

"This is annoying," Stephanie sighed when they were once again sitting together in the shack. "How are we supposed to stop them when we can't even find them?"

"There has to be a way." Marcus was angry too.

"We have exhausted all the ways we could easily use. I searched for everything I could think of on the 'Net, we have tracked down all the leads we had, and nothing helped," Darien said. "I can think of only one more thing to do, but this would be time-consuming."

"And what would that be?" Lucas asked.

"Shadow one of them. Maybe he will lead us to their meeting place."

"How do you want to shadow someone you can't find in the first place?" Stephanie laughed in agony.

"There are two people in that circle that we could find quite easily: Eagle and Plague. After all, we know where they work."

"Interesting idea." Lucas nodded. "But as you said: Very time-consuming."

"Couldn't we use your tracer socks again?" Marcus suggested.

"And how do you suppose we get them to wear those?" Lucas laughed.

"Not them. I am thinking more along the lines of their cars," Marcus said. "If we can hide them somewhere in the cars of both Plague and Eagle, maybe we can see where their routes intersect."

"That's actually a fabulous idea," Darien smiled. "Let's just hope they use cars. After all, Plague works in London."

"I am quite sure that Eagle has a car. Brix & Burton is not easily reachable with public transportation," Marcus replied.

"It's a bit risky, but it sounds like a plan." Lucas nodded. "Professor, can you find out where Plague lives? It will for sure be easier to slip a tracer into the car at home than at a police station."

"I will try." Darien nodded. "Cougar, can you take care of Eagle?"

"Sure thing. It is time that I visit my dad again," Marcus grinned.

"And I will take care of Plague if you can get me the address, Professor. I am in and out of London regularly anyway these days," Cedric offered.

Lucas nodded silently. He was happy that they at least had another plan to find the black-robes but even more that it was one that would not involve him right away. Even if Marcus and Cedric managed to plant the socks instantly it would take a week or two until they would be able to find the pattern and plan the next steps. Long enough for him to finish the semester and compete in the contest.

Two weeks later Lucas had finally completed the last exams for the semester and was now in full motion for the contest. His friends had managed to put the sock-plan into action, but right now he didn't care too much; his mind was focused on the upcoming challenge. It was Thursday morning and after a long drive, he had finally arrived at Oxford University, where the event would be hosted. Some of his teachers had chosen to accompany him, foremost Professor Tatarski. Principal Snyders had also announced that he would be there, and even his parents had made time to come and watch. They entered the building, Lucas and Tatarski leading the crowd. When they stepped through the large wooden doors, Lucas was amazed. It was an old, awe-inspiring building with thick stone walls and high rooms. And yet the area had a modern touch, with all the computers and state of the art furniture inside. To add to the impression, the main hallway had been decorated festively, with a big green banner hanging across the hallway reading, "Welcome to the first national security contest, hosted by the Universities of Oxford and Cambridge,"

"How would you like spending some years in these sacred halls, Mr. Trent?" Tatarski laughed.

"I am not quite sure, sir," Lucas responded. "But honestly, I have other things on my mind right now."

"Understandable." Tatarski nodded and smiled at him.

They walked along the hallway until they reached an open double door with a desk next to it. "Registration," the sign there read.

"Are you sponsors or spectators?" the lady behind the desk asked.

"Most of us are spectators. This young gentleman is a contestant." Tatarski quickly took the lead.

"Spectators please enter the auditorium, your seats are to the left." She pointed at a box that had ID cards with the text "Visitor" in it. "Please wear those. For the contestant..." She then turned to Lucas. "What is your name?"

"Trent, ma'am. Lucas Trent," he answered.

"You are from Luton IT-College, correct?"

"Yes, ma'am," Lucas nodded.

"Fine, fine." She took a green marker and put a line over his name. "Please step into the room over there." She pointed at a door behind her.

"I guess I see you later then." Lucas smiled at the others and walked away.

The room seemed to be some sort of classroom. In the front there were three rows of tables with chairs, in the back the remaining rows had been removed and the tables stacked near the wall and folding screens had been placed there, forming small cabins. The first two rows were already filled with other teens around his age, eagerly hacking into their laptops. To Lucas' surprise they all were wearing the same green T-shirt. Up front a team of older people, apparently teachers, was standing and chatting.

"Here comes the next one. Seems we are almost ready," one of them said when he spotted Lucas. The chatting immediately stopped and all of them turned around.

"Ah, Lucas," Professor Shimmerman smiled at him. "Gentleman, may I introduce you to Lucas Trent, our contestant from Luton."

"Nice to meet you," another one said, and all of them shook his hand.

"Here, please put this on. We do have a dress code here." Shimmerman handed him a green shirt and pointed to the cabins in the back.

Lucas walked into a cabin and took a look at the shirt before putting it on. It was a high quality short sleeve piece with stitching on both sides, as well as on the sleeves. On the front it said "IT Security Contest" next to some sort of logo; the left arm read "University of Oxford"; the right one "University of Cambridge." What really amazed him, though, was the stitching on the back. "Lucas Trent – Luton," it said in big letters. He quickly exchanged his shirt for the green one. When he looked into the mirror afterwards, he couldn't help but feel a little proud.

On his way back he looked at the shirts of the others. He found that many of the contestants seemed to be from the greater London area, reading names like Heathrow, Wimbledon or London City on the shirts. But he also saw Glasgow, Nottingham and Edinburgh stitched on others.

"Hi everyone," he said and pulled up an empty chair. The others barely noticed him, eagerly staring at their computers. For a moment he thought about getting his laptop, too, but then decided against it and just leaned back to relax. Observing the others, he almost had to laugh. They were all so dogged that he was afraid some of them could eat their computers, just to be closer to them. And funnily, the few girls that were in the group looked even grimmer than their male counterparts.

Over the next ten minutes the room filled up. All new arrivers except one showed the same behavior as the others. Only that guy was, like Lucas, just watching. Lucas stood up and walked over to him.

"Hi there," he smiled.

"Howdy. The first one that has not lost his voice in here," the other one laughed.

"Makes two." Lucas laughed as well. "I am Lucas Trent from Luton."

"Kevin Donaldson, Canterbury," the other one replied and shook his hand. "Nice to meet you."

"Ditto," Lucas replied. "Seems we will have a fun day."

"Definitely will." Donaldson nodded. "Although I don't think those eggheads will be much of a challenge," he then whispered and grinned.

Lucas had to laugh. "Don't you underestimate them."

"Ladies, gentleman, welcome," one of the professors interrupted the conversation abruptly. Lucas hurried back to his chair and sat down. "Let me quickly make you familiar with the rules: There are 24 contestants in the tournament. Your first challenge will be a one-on-

one, drawn randomly. The twelve winners will advance, losers will fight in three-way challenges for the remaining four spots of the finals. The finals are one-on-one again, winner advances, loser is out. The challenges themselves are easy. Each challenge brings different systems, but all contestants always have the same systems. The setup sheet you will get will tell you what the systems are and what your key thing is to protect. You have ten minutes to prepare; after that, the contestant that first penetrates the protected resource of his rival is the winner. Each one of you will be given two students as advisors on a rotating basis. They are not allowed to touch anything, other than lending you a hand for physical things, of course, and they will only give advice when asked. The only rule of the challenge: Do not connect any devices to the lab network. You will have Internet access for your notebooks, an Internet enabled PC if you prefer to use that, and a USB key to transfer data in and out of your systems. Other than that, you are free to use whatever technique you deem helpful to achieve your goal. For the spectators and sponsors, a system status will be displayed at all time, and an expert panel will comment on your efforts. You will not hear that, though, as you will be separated. Any questions?"

Silence prevailed for a few moments until Donaldson broke it.

"Seems we are all eager to prove ourselves, sir."

"Yee-hah," Lucas yelled with a laugh.

"And so you shall." The professor nodded. "Good luck, gentleman."

Another teacher quickly started drawing names from a bag. Lucas' first opponent was a guy from Edinburgh. He looked a little younger than him and wore big, round glasses.

"Good luck," Lucas said to him when they walked out to the contest, but once again the other one didn't even respond.

When they came close to the entrance Lucas could hear someone commenting from inside, almost sounding like a sports event.

"And here come the next contestants," the speaker announced. "Ladies and gentlemen, please give a warm welcome to Mr. Shaun Chadley from Edinburgh." The crowd cheered as he walked in first. "And now his opponent. Please welcome Mr. Lucas Trent from Luton." Lucas took a look around and smiled as he walked down the aisle. The auditorium was filled over capacity; people were standing behind the last row. To his left there was a lot of cheering and people holding banners, to the right most of the people were wearing suits and looked way more serious. When he finally came down to the stage, he started feeling a little bit like a lab rat. Four big rooms made of Perspex had been placed there. They each held a computer rack, a table with multiple screens, keyboards and other devices on it, and two guys in suits standing in front of them. The teacher that had brought them over showed each of them to their cabin, right next to each other.

"I am Mike, this is Luke; we are your advisors for this round," one of the suits welcomed him.

"I'm Lucas. Thanks in advance for the help; let us not waste any time."

Lucas stepped in, the others followed, and Luke closed the door behind them. Suddenly all he could hear was the humming of the servers; all the outside noise was gone. He quickly looked at the factsheet provided and had to grin. The setup looked almost identical to one that Shimmerman had trained with him time and again. He was just through with the sheet when a teacher entered.

"Don't notice me please, I am just here to make sure that no rules are violated," he said.

Lucas was already looking at the server monitor and in parallel booting up his notebook. He started closing down some security holes that he knew from his training before turning to his advisors. He then quickly outlined his strategy to them.

"What do you think about the plan?" Lucas asked.

"Sounds solid to me." Mike nodded. "A little aggressive maybe. You should watch your back a little, just in case you missed something in your security config."

Lucas nodded and continued his prep work. He prepared a honey pot as a distraction and then focused on his attack vector. When he had finished everything to his satisfaction, he looked up. The countdown still showed three more minutes before the contest would start.

"Have I missed something terribly important?" he asked his advisors.

"You might maybe want to switch the encryption algorithm on that trap you laid. The one you have now looks a little too obvious," Mike suggested.

Lucas nodded and followed the advice. When the countdown finally reached zero and a green light started flashing Lucas immediately released a full-focused attack. And it didn't even take him a minute until he had found a leak in his opponent's defenses. And only half a minute later the lights in the other cabin turned red and his own cabin suddenly was all green when he had finally reached his target.

"That was the most awesome hack that I have seen so far," Luke complimented and shook his hand. "Nice job."

"Thank you," Lucas smiled. "Professor? Was everything within the rules?"

"Of course." The teacher smiled and opened the door, where a cheering crowd welcomed Lucas back. He grinned for a moment before following the professor back to the contestants' room. In there a teacher had set up a twin-screen PC, showing the match status on one screen with a video feed of the cabins, and the tournament tree on the other. Lucas could see his name in the middle of the tree, and four others also already listed.

"The tree is sorted by the score you achieved," Professor Shimmerman explained. "Currently you hold high score, so you are in the number one spot."

Lucas nodded silently and watched the two contestants duke it out, and only two minutes later his name switched from first to second place, with the name "Donaldson" now showing up first. Lucas watched most of the time, trying to get a feeling for everyone else, but it was almost impossible to see much on the small video feed. The list filled up quickly and after the relegation matches had completed the tree was all set. Lucas took a quick look. Out of the six girls that had started only two were still in the game, and one of them had come through relegation, now facing Kevin Donaldson in the first round.

"Seems we will have the honor of bashing our systems against each other in the finals," Donaldson, who had been standing next to Lucas most of the time, said.

"Let's hope so." Lucas smiled. "It would be fun."

"To fun." Donaldson offered him his hand and Lucas shook it.

"To fun." He grinned.

Lucas made it through the next two rounds with ease, bringing him up to the semi-finals. Remaining with him were a girl named Julia Montgomery from Nottingham, a boy named Curtis Klein from London City and Kevin Donaldson. They were sitting in the contestants' room waiting for their next matches, Lucas and Kevin joking, the others still tense, when a teacher came in.

"Lady, gentlemen, you now have a one hour break. We need to rearrange the stage for the big finals," he said.

"Oh perfect, I am hungry," Donaldson said. "Is there a cafeteria somewhere on campus?"

"How can you two be so cheerful all the time and still come out with top scores?" the girl asked.

"If you stop fighting it's easier to win," Lucas laughed. "And in the end I am primarily here to have fun. There is nothing to lose."

"Ditto." Donaldson grinned. "So, what about the food?"

"I would like to join you if you don't mind," Lucas said. "But I need to browse through my emails first."

The boys walked to the cafeteria, which was far bigger than what Lucas was used to from Luton. A lot of the spectators and some of the sponsors had also made use of the break and were sitting at the tables, eating and drinking. Lucas ordered a sandwich and something to drink before he pulled out his cell phone to check his mails. But the first thing that caught his attention was not an email, it was a text message from Darien, asking for his callback. So he excused himself and called him.

"Hi Professor. What is so important?" Lucas asked.

"Sorry to disturb you; I know you are at the contest," Darien said. "We think we found the meeting place of Cleric's circle, Cougar checked it out earlier today. And we think we have an opportunity to get them there."

"And when would that be?" Lucas was not exactly happy about this distraction right now.

"That's the problem," Darien said. "It's tomorrow evening."

"So this would mean that we need to sit together tomorrow at noon latest to come up with a plan. That's a hell of a timeline, mate."

"I know, that's why I wanted to talk to you right away."

"Damn it," Lucas sighed. "OK, well, count me in."

"Oh and Professor..." Lucas quickly added, "if this goes down tomorrow, we should brew some healing potion again. Can you take care of that?"

"Sure. And thanks. Oh, and good luck at the contest," Darien said and hung up.

Lucas walked back to the table, but somehow the black-robe mages wouldn't get out of his head now.

"Are you all right?" Kevin asked him.

"Yeah, sure." Lucas nodded. "Little trouble back home, but never mind."

The boys took their time finishing lunch and returned to the contestants' room five minutes before the hour was through. The other two were still sitting there, eagerly staring into their laptops. When they saw that, Lucas and Kevin looked at each other and just shook their heads.

"OK, people, break is over." Professor Shimmerman entered the room. "Julia, Lucas, you are up first. Good luck."

As they walked down the corridor, Lucas could see that the girl was overly nervous. He would have really liked to cheer her up, but he was quite certain that there was no point in that, so he disregarded the thought. Entering the auditorium, they were once again announced and cheered. Lucas immediately looked at the stage to see what had changed and noticed that there were now only two cabins left, and each of those had two server racks in it now.

"Oh boy, that will be fun," he mumbled and laughed.

Once again Mike and Luke were his advisors and joined him at the door. Lucas quickly read through the scenario, and what he saw struck him as odd. His main server, the one that he was supposed to protect, had only one job: Send out a file every five minutes. Everything else in the network was not considered important according to the sheet. He quickly discussed this finding with his advisors, who confirmed his opinion.

"Professor." Lucas turned to the watching teacher. "Can I task one of my advisors to pull a cable for me on command and plug it back in when I say so, or would this be considered interference?"

"If you tell him exactly what cable, and exactly what to do at what time and all he does is follow that simple command that is fine." The teacher nodded.

"Very well." Lucas nodded and jumped up, running to the backside of his racks. "Mike, sorry for demoting you to the job of a trained monkey, but I need you here."

"Anything you need," Mike grinned and walked back to him.

"This cable." Lucas pointed out a green network line. "Pull it out here when I tell you and plug it back in when I tell you. We might need to do this a couple of times."

"Was that specific enough, Professor? Or do I have to explain to him how to plug a network cable without tearing it apart?" Lucas asked.

"No, that's fine," The teacher laughed.

When the green light started flashing Lucas immediately went offensive again. In contrast to earlier contests, though, his desktop PC showed nothing but a stopwatch, running in full screen mode.

"Now Mike, pull the cable," Lucas shouted thirty seconds into the contest.

"What are you doing?" Luke asked.

"The server is only needed once every five minutes. There is no reason to leave it connected and vulnerable during the remainder of the time," Lucas answered without looking up from his monitor.

"Oh, that is mean," Luke laughed. "That's almost unfair."

"I think that's the point of the contest, isn't it? Being unfair." Lucas grinned.

Over the next twenty minutes Lucas had Mike plug the server back in only for the short window in time that it was needed and then unplug it again. Then finally he managed to break through Julia's defenses and capture his target. And immediately the lights went red in her cabin and green in his.

"Mike, please plug the server in again; I guess it's over," Lucas laughed.

He walked back to the waiting area without taking too much notice of the surrounding people. During the competition he had been able to keep his head clear, but now the mages were back, and he just couldn't help it. He pulled up a chair in the far corner of the room, trying to relax and get his game together for the toughest challenge of the day. The thoughts about the magic substance and the challenge they had to face tomorrow were so strong in his mind that he didn't even notice Julia crying in the front row. When he was finally back in his chamber for the grand finale, his mind had cleared a little, but he knew that whatever he would do now would be half-hearted at best. He noticed that he needed a lot more advice this time than he had throughout the entire competition, and if it hadn't been for the two advisors he would have missed a lot of configuration issues on his systems. When the challenge started Lucas was everything but ready. He found himself completely defensive from the very beginning, and even though he rebounded a few times and fought with all his skills for nearly an hour, in the end he did not have the focus anymore to make it. When the red light in his cabin signaled his defeat, he was exhausted. He knew that he had just thrown the contest away because of his problems back home, and he knew that there was nobody to blame but himself, and that made him feel really bad when he stepped out of the chamber.

"Nice fight." Kevin approached him for a handshake right outside. "You almost got me."

"Almost." Lucas laughed, although he didn't really feel like it. "In here this might be good enough; out there in the world there are no points for second place. In the end I just have to bow before you; you are the better man."

"You know, I somehow have the feeling that you let me win," Donaldson said when they were walking back to the waiting room. "I've watched you in your matches before; you left me more loopholes in the finale than you did in the entire competition all together."

"I guess I am just exhausted," Lucas said. "Maybe we will have time for a rematch at some point. Then we will find out."

Throughout the awards ceremony Lucas was still beside himself. At that point he was happy to have come out second, as this meant that most of the attention went to Kevin instead of him. On the bus back home the situation was different, though. Everybody came to congratulate him, everybody wanted to hear details, and he was left with little other choice than to answer their questions and try to smile through it. Finally back at home, he just went silently up to his room and locked the door. The thoughts just weren't going away, he had no plan, not even a remote idea how to handle a group as violent as Cleric and his lot, and time was running short. At some point frustration seamlessly changed into fatigue and he fell asleep.

CHAPTER 18

Enemies & Allies

The next day Lucas was still exhausted when he woke up. His head had cleared a little bit, but the night had not brought any regeneration at all. His parents had prepared him a huge breakfast with a Congratulations card before they had left for work. He deeply enjoyed it, and it even pushed his energy up a little. For him his second place yesterday felt like defeat, so seeing that his parents had a different view on that almost made him smile. When he got to school later on, he couldn't believe his eyes. A banner with his picture was hanging from the ceiling in the middle of the entrance hall, with the slogan "Lucas Trent – School Hero" written next to it. The news seemed to have traveled fast, as everyone he met at the corridor cheered at him or came shaking hands in congratulations. And this didn't end until he left at noon. The whole school was celebrating, and one teacher even suggested naming the new computer room that the school had gotten as a prize for his second place after him. When he was riding his bike out to the shack and the sun was shining on his face, he was almost cheerful again, and suddenly very certain that they would find a solution for the upcoming challenge, as well.

At the shack Darien, Marcus and Stephanie were already waiting. Pictures were laid out on the table, and they were studying them when he came in.

"Congratulations mate," Darien said when he saw him. "I heard you gave them a hell of a fight and came up pretty close to the top."

"Thanks. And yes, pretty close, but not on top, unfortunately," Lucas smiled.

"Don't bother too much," Darien said. "Given the competition you had, it is an amazing achievement to reach second place."

"Thanks." Lucas nodded. "What do you have here?" He was eager to change the topic.

"Surveillance," Marcus grinned. "I went to their hideout yesterday and took a few pictures."

"Few is an understatement." Lucas laughed when he saw the amount of paper on the table.

"Yeah, and those are only the ones I printed," Darien laughed.

"So what are we looking at?" he asked.

"An abandoned subway station, or maintenance terminal or something like that." Darien explained. "Built underground with only two ways in and out, and the surrounding area does not look very helpful. Most of the buildings are either abandoned, as well, or are occupied by people that I would prefer not to meet if I don't have to."

"So what is the occasion? And why do we need to move so fast?" Lucas asked further.

"It seems to be a weekly meeting, and we have to move fast because we lost one tracker already, so we can't cross-reference anymore, which means that if they change the schedule we are done."

Jasmin and Cedric had arrived by now, as well, and they were all studying the pictures now.

"How are we going about this?" Marcus asked. "A frontal assault doesn't seem like a good idea."

"And it would not be helpful, either." Lucas shook his head.

"What is our main objective?" Jasmin asked.

"Stop them from brewing more of that substance," Lucas replied. "But achieving that will be a challenge."

"The only way to ensure this would be to kill Eagle," Cedric said dryly.

"I hope you are not seriously considering this option?" Jasmin looked at him.

"What are the alternatives?" Lucas asked.

"Are you kidding me? You are thinking along this line as well?" Jasmin was outraged.

"No, I am not." Lucas tried to calm her down. "This was a serious question. What are our options? Whirlwind gave us one, most of us don't like that one, so we have to come up with something better."

"Burst the circle wide open, like we did with Wolfman," Marcus suggested.

"I don't think that this would stop them. They are way too determined." Darien shook his head.

"We could try to make the effect of the substance public. Or at least known to Brix & Burton. Maybe they can stop him then?" Stephanie suggested.

"And how do you want to prove this, if not even Harlington Research can come to that conclusion?" Darien sighed.

"Proof. That's it, that's the solution." Lucas stamped his foot.

"Yeah, but we don't have any," Darien reminded him.

"No, not for the environmental thing. For murder." Lucas was excited.

"Which murder?" Stephanie asked.

"Have you already forgotten? They killed one of the thieves. We just need proof so the police can lock them up." Lucas smiled.

"Nice plan. And how do we get that proof?" Marcus seemed not so convinced.

"The way Cleric behaves, I would say we go in, confront them with the facts, hope they confirm it and record the whole conversation to give it to the authorities," Lucas suggested.

"And then hope we get out before they kill us, too," Jasmin said.

"The plan has a flaw," Darien said. "What good is the recording if you don't know their names?"

"You are right, unfortunately." Lucas nodded and thought for a moment. "We need to keep them there long enough after the confession for Corben and SO-19 to arrive and take them into custody."

"That sounds dangerous," Darien said.

"Agreed." Lucas nodded again. "And I am up for better ideas."

They continued discussing for a little while longer, but they couldn't come up with any better plans.

"Ok, so let's do this," Lucas started. "Professor, we need equipment to make a good quality recording. Any ideas?"

"Sure, that's easy. I'll handle it." Darien nodded.

"Good. Then you will stay one step behind and record. And once we have them confess to the murder, you fall back and call Corben." Lucas quickly shared the phone number with Darien and asked the others to note it as well. "Don't tell him your name, just that I sent you. There is no need for him to know all of us."

Darien nodded.

"How do we get there?" Lucas asked. "Any ideas on that?"

"There is a train station not far away, so it is easy by public transportation," Marcus replied.

"Good. Airmid, there seems to be a good hiding place back here, close to us but well protected. You should stay there until we need you. Give one potion to Psycho and keep the others yourself. I am quite certain that this will not end without a fight."

"Will do." Stephanie nodded.

"Cougar, Whirlwind, the three of us will go in front. I will stay in the middle, you cover my flanks. And we improvise from there." He continued, "Psycho, stay one step behind us and assist wherever you can. But your first priority is to stay safe."

"Roger." Jasmin saluted.

"Anything else?" Lucas asked.

The others instantly stretched their fists out into the middle of the table.

"Brother to brother, yours, to the end," they said.

They met again only a few hours later, heading for the abandoned station. Lucas watched them on the train ride, but once again none of them showed obvious signs of stress or insecurity. They all seemed very confident going into this. When they arrived at their destination, they all slipped into their robes and looked each other in the eyes one more time.

"Let's do this," Lucas finally said and started descending into the station.

They slowly walked down the staircase and into the first hall. From there Lucas could see Cleric stand in the next hall, his back to them. They approached carefully along a sidewall to remain unseen as long as possible. When they reached the passageway to the next hall, Stephanie ducked down in the cover position they had seen in the pictures. Then Lucas looked at Darien, who just nodded in reply, letting him know that he was recording. Walking around the corner, Lucas quickly checked out the room. It was a wide open hall, the ceiling about four meters high, five pillars in a line on each side supporting it, a big stone altar in the middle of the room where Cleric was standing, a fireplace, laid out with stones like a campfire, to the right of the altar and an old escape route to the left. Then he spotted the others and for a moment stopped, unsure what to do. Besides the people he had expected, that being Cleric's circle, there were also six other persons in the room, all wearing plain, black robes. He cursed the situation, but then quickly decided to go through with the plan anyway and walked into the room, taking a position that let him oversee everything and at the same time gave cover for the others, having a pillar shield them from most of the bad guys.

"Good evening, Cleric," Lucas addressed him firmly, making him turn on his heels. "Finally we meet."

"Who are you?" Cleric hissed in a mixture of surprise and anger. "And why are you invading my turf?"

"They call me Guardian," he said calmly. "And I am here to set things right that you have done wrong."

"And what would that be?" Cleric laughed and gave the others a sign to close in.

"Remember the band of thieves that stole your precious potion?" Lucas' voice remained cool. "Five came in, but less came out."

Cedric, who had walked in on Lucas' left side, had moved over to the right now, together with Marcus, shielding him from the others.

"They stole from us; we had the right to get our property back," Cleric yelled angrily.

"And burn them in the process? Or electrocute them?" Lucas was carefully picking his words.

"If they steal from us, they get punished. And if they die from it, so be it." Cleric was getting even angrier with every sentence.

"So you show no remorse for taking a life?" Lucas asked.

"Remorse?" Firebolt was laughing despicably. "Roasted to a crisp is the best an outsider can be."

"The only thing I regret is that I didn't have time to kill them all," Cleric said.

"But maybe it is time now to kill you." Plague was standing on the side, halfway between Cleric and Lucas. "I remember you. Last time you escaped, but this time you won't. I hope you made your will."

"And all of you goons are good with that? Not a single one of you is willing to confess and ask for forgiveness?" Lucas addressed the crowd.

They all started laughing despicably.

"I don't know what stupid god you pray to, but you can stop praying; you will meet him soon." Eagle said.

"Well, if this is your last word…" Lucas signaled Darien to leave.

"Yes it is. And that was your last word." Cleric grinned. "FULMINARE." A jet of fire was aimed at Lucas.

"SEPERATIO," Lucas said calmly and waved his hand. "Not so much, I would say," he smiled.

"You mind me starting this off?" Cedric asked Lucas.

"Not at all, be my guest," Lucas smiled.

"TEMPESTAS," Cedric cried, tossing the other black-robe group down to the ground with one focused storm.

"Those idiots are nerve-wracking." Plague jumped in. "TERGUM."

Lucas, from the corner of his eyes, saw Marcus being tossed through the air.

"LEVIPES," he heard him cast and before crashing into the wall, he managed to turn around, hit the wall feet first and just run down to the ground.

"Are you all right?" Lucas asked.

"Sure. Takes more than that to get me down," Marcus laughed.

"Your petty magic is pathetic." Woodpecker addressed Plague. "I'll show you how this is done. INCENDIO," he then shouted and pointed at Cedric.

"ONITO." Cedric reacted instantly, and the flame that Woodpecker sent toward him was met halfway by a tornado that appeared out of Cedric's fingertip.

"I had about enough of this," Lucas said. "REPELLUM," he shouted at Eagle and made him fly through the air and hit a wall.

"COLLIDO" was the next thing that Lucas heard, and it was one of the unknowns throwing that at Jasmin, who tumbled back and fell down.

A fierce battle started, with spells flying all around and in between people trying to get into hand combat with each other.

"They are too many, Guardian. We can maybe stall them, but there is no way that we can overpower them." Cedric shouted in one of the few calm moments, after he had made one step back and was waiting for the next attack.

"Unfortunately, I agree. I hope the cavalry arrives soon." Lucas nodded and tossed his next spell at an attacking opponent before tumbling back, being hit by something.

At that moment the emergency exit on the left wall burst open.

"Did somebody call for an exterminator?" A woman in yellow robes entered, followed by someone in dark gray, then another one in green, one in red and a second one in green.

Lucas instantly recognized the voice. It was Kung Fu.

"We were actually doing fine, but now that you are here, you could maybe help us clean up a little?" He smiled at her, leveraging the one quiet moment he had while the black-robe group was dealing with the surprise.

"Who are you? And what are you doing in my lair?" Cleric regrouped first and was outraged now.

"I already told Plague to stop harassing my kids. But he seems to have a hearing problem," Angel said.

"Guardian, this is your show. Call the shots," one of the green-robes said. Lucas recognized his voice as JJ, the leader of Angel's circle.

"Highly appreciated." Lucas nodded while ducking out of the way of an attack. "If you could keep those clowns over there down it would help." He pointed at the ones he didn't know.

JJ and the others of Angel's circle quickly joined up with Lucas and his friends, Kung Fu taking a position right next to him, the rest focusing on the left flank. Then things suddenly started to get chaotic again. The group that Lucas didn't know started charging and throwing spells at whomever they could find, tossing some of the friendlies down, while at the same time also taking hit after hit. Woodpecker fired at Cedric once more, who countered and now jumped into a duel with him; Marcus started duking it out with Firebolt; and the remaining four had rallied in the middle, now facing Lucas and Kung Fu.

First to raise his arm was Plague. "TERGUM," he yelled in Lucas' direction.

"SPECULUS," Lucas yelled back, raised his arm and watched Plague fly back under the power of his own spell. He then lowered his arm again and waited for the next one to do something.

Plague was quick to jump up and throw another spell, and Cleric also tossed one at Lucas, keeping him so busy that he almost didn't hear Cat hissing something. When a group of spiders, rats, worms and other resident animals formed around her and then slowly came creeping toward Lucas, he finally recognized the threat.

"Are you sure you want to do that?" he asked Cat, who just laughed despicably and started to sing.

"Fine," Lucas then said. "INCENDIO," he yelled in his dark, low voice and set the whole armada of insects ablaze. For a moment the effect almost stunned him. It was the first time he had used his new powers for real, and he was even more amazed now how powerful they were and how much they had brought him forward. He took a deep breath and smiled.

"That's a new one," he heard Marcus laugh from the side.

"Would you mind taking care of that chick for me? I normally don't punch girls," Lucas said to Kung Fu.

"Luckily I don't have that limitation in my codex," Kung Fu winked. "COLLIDO," she then yelled, and Cat tumbled back. "See you later, sweetheart," she then said to Lucas and walked toward her opponent.

"What's it gonna be, Cleric?" Lucas now made a step toward him.

"You are annoying," Cleric answered and drew a knife. "How about this?"

"GUARDIO," Lucas yelled as he saw the knife flying in his direction. "Is that all you have?"

Much to Lucas' surprise the knife didn't just fall down after hitting his shield. It stayed in the air. When he looked at Cleric, he could see that he was moving his hand around, which the knife acknowledged by making the same motions, trying to stab Lucas over and over again.

"Nice toy you have there." Lucas laughed. "Correction… Nice toy you HAD there. DESINTEGRATUS." The knife immediately turned into dust and scattered.

"What have you done to my artifact?" Cleric was outraged. He started throwing spell after spell at Lucas, who constantly had to reenergize his guarding spell to resist. After about a minute Lucas felt the drain this took on him, but at the same moment spotted Cleric getting drained as well.

"Learn it, Cleric. It doesn't work," Lucas said firmly. "REPELLUM." He then cast, but much to his surprise, Cleric only tumbled back a little; he didn't fly off like expected.

"You should learn that this is still my turf." Cleric had recovered quickly. "FULMINARE."

Again a jet of flame appeared in Lucas' direction. Lucas briefly thought about a shield again, but his emotional side reacted more quickly than he could.

"FRIGUM," he cried and stretched his arm out, blasting a stream of ice crystals at Cleric.

The two spells met in the middle and annihilated each other. Cleric was trying to push harder to gain ground; Lucas didn't push at all. It was mockery that he felt right now and that pure feeling was giving him all the energy he needed. And slowly but steadily his ice crystals crawled closer to Cleric, until they finally hit his arm, spiking through it, making the bad guy cry in pain. Lucas could see blood dripping down from his opponent's hand when he finally stopped the spell.

"That's a new one, too." Marcus had joined him. "TARDESCO," then he suddenly shouted at one of Cleric's companions who was just about to sneak to the emergency exit. "Excuse me, I have to get this idiot back."

Lucas took a quick look around. Kung Fu was still fighting with Cat, Cedric had knocked Woodpecker unconscious and was now fighting with Plague, Eagle was still lying in the corner where he had tossed him in the beginning, Firebolt was down, too, and bleeding from his nose, and the other black-robes were all contained in a corner in what looked to be one of Jasmin's banning circles. Behind him he could see one of Angel's people, one of the two wearing green robes, lying on the ground and the other one with the green robe kneeling next to him.

"JJ, are you all right?" Lucas asked without knowing who of the two was who.

"I am," The kneeling one answered. "Hopper is not. He got hit by a flame jet, and it's not looking too good."

"Airmid!" Lucas yelled. "Please help JJ and Hopper."

Stephanie immediately came running around the corner and approached them.

"Cougar, if you have a hand, please be so kind as to guard Airmid and JJ." Lucas turned to Marcus who was just dragging the escapee by him.

"Sure thing," Marcus nodded.

Lucas then turned back around and just saw Cleric trying to head for the exit now as well.

"Not so fast," he shouted. "LIGAME." He watched Cleric trip due to the magical rope that he had just wound around his whole body. "EFFERUS," he then cast and let him float back to the middle of the room. Only at that point did it occur to Lucas that something else had just changed. He was now casting two spells at once, holding Cleric tied up in his Ligame charm while at the same time floating him in. He had never been able to do that before.

Cleric started yelling and cursing, and suddenly something hit Lucas like a punch in the face. He had no idea where it had come from, but from Clerics despicable laugh he was sure he could guess.

"LEVIATUS," he cried and lifted Cleric about three meters up. "Now you don't move up there, or I will just let you drop, you got me?" Lucas said in an angry tone.

A quick look around showed that everything was under control. Cedric was still fighting with Plague, and Angel was now challenging Eagle, but both looked all right, so Lucas turned to Hopper.

"What's the verdict, Airmid?" he asked.

"The burns look bad, very bad. We should give him some of our potion," she said with an uneasy face.

"Do whatever you need to do." Lucas nodded. "You are the expert at this."

Stephanie nodded and pulled out a flask. "Hold him down for me please," she said to Lucas and JJ before turning to Hopper. "This will hurt, a lot. But it will help."

Hopper seemed more unconscious than conscious at that time, so she just started pouring the liquid over his face. Only seconds later a cry was audible that was almost deafening. Lucas and JJ had to use all their strength to keep Hopper lying still. The minute that followed was about the longest Lucas had ever felt before. He could see the flesh and skin regenerate under Stephanie's potion, which was nice to watch, but seeing Hopper writhing in pain and crying because he couldn't bear it was heartbreaking.

"We have to do something, Guardian," Airmid suddenly said. "I am afraid that he will die from the pain."

"Psycho, help," Lucas yelled, and Jasmin immediately came running over. "Can you do something to ease his pain?"

"I will do my best." She nodded. "Let go, I'll take over."

Lucas moved away and let Jasmin work her magic. Looking around again, he saw that Angel had brought down Eagle by now but Cedric was still fighting Plague. He decided to walk over and help.

"You mind if I interfere?" he asked when he reached Cedric.

"Not at all," Cedric replied, sounding a little out of breath. "I am running out of ideas anyway."

"Then how about this one?" Lucas smiled at Plague. "DOLORUS." And suddenly Plague started crying loudly. Then he fell to the ground, rolled in a ball and started shivering, while still crying loudly.

"What the hell is that?" Cedric laughed.

"Pain spell. I took an example from you," Lucas laughed.

"Guardian!" Lucas heard Darien cry from behind. "The cavalry is approaching. They will be here any moment now."

"Who is the cavalry?" Angel asked.

"SO-19." Lucas replied and ran back to her. "Police. We figured that we don't need to kill them when we can have them arrested instead."

"Good thought," Angel smiled. "So what do we do now?"

"You move out through the emergency exit. I will meet up with them and do the handover." He ran out into the adjacent hall, meeting up with Darien.

"Here is the recording. I made a copy, just in case." He handed Lucas a USB key.

"Thanks." Lucas nodded. "Take my robes and leave with the others. I'll meet you at the train station."

Lucas took position outside the passageway so he couldn't be seen from inside anymore and only peeked into the room. When all friendlies had left the hall, he cast his Seperatio charm over the emergency exit so nobody else could get out and then slowly brought Cleric down to the ground. He had just released all his magic when he heard the voices behind him.

"Armed police. Don't move," they shouted.

Lucas raised his hands and turned around slowly. "I am one of the good guys, please don't kill me," he said with a smile on his face.

"He is with me, leave him alone." He heard Corben's voice from behind. "Please point out who else is with you." Corben then seemed to address him.

"No more friendlies in here," Lucas replied. "Everyone in the next room belongs to the other side."

"You heard him," Corben said to his men.

Lucas watched SO-19 walk by him into the next room, Corben staying behind.

"So what do we have here?" he asked. "Your companion just said that you have all I would need."

"Decide for yourself," Lucas said and handed him the USB key. "This is a recording of a conversation from earlier between me and the people you will find in the next room. Part of it is the confession of the murder of the thief a few months back. I don't know what you can make of the rest, but you will for sure find something."

"That's really an impressive feat of work," Corben smiled. "Homicide will be very grateful."

"I will be grateful if I have seen the last of those guys," Lucas smiled in return. "And be careful, there is a police officer in the room with them. When you look through the police call logs from the evening of the murder you will find out that this particular officer got a call with a hint leading to the thieves' whereabouts shortly before that. And he seems not to have reported it, as you only arrived after our second call."

"Do you know who this officer is?" Corben was curious.

"You will find out yourself shortly. It is Detective Chief Inspector Murphy," Lucas said. "Last I saw him he was lying in there, wearing a black robe."

"Murphy? He was in charge of the investigation. That explains a lot," Corben said. "Including why you were so cautious."

Lucas just nodded in reply.

"You did a great job with this," Corben said. "How can we reward you for it?"

"This time our call and the outcome were in both our interests, and once again we didn't do this for a reward. I hope that I will not need to disturb you anymore, but if I do, I would appreciate if you would come to our rescue again," Lucas said and started walking toward the staircase.

"Rest assured that I will," Corben yelled behind him.

"Godspeed, Inspector. Until our paths cross next time," Lucas said before walking out of sight, leaving the station.

When he arrived back up on street level he took a deep breath and smiled. Once again they had made it through a tough situation without too many problems. And now he knew for sure that he was not alone anymore.

Chapter 19

News

A month later, Lucas and the others were again at their weekly meeting in the shack.

"Finally there is some light on all of this." Darien had been reading a newspaper, waiting for the others to get settled in.

"Light on what?" Lucas asked.

"The thieves. Here, look at the news article."

Lucas took the paper out of Darien's hand, quickly browsing through it.

"What is it?" Stephanie asked.

"It basically says that two security experts that formerly worked for PowerSec were leading the crew and were in fact the brains behind it all," Lucas summarized.

"Those would have been the two guys that hid at the trees in the end," Darien added.

"According to the article, the other three were just regular crooks that they picked up for additional muscle. One had a prior conviction for petty theft, and the other two for armed robbery," Lucas said.

"That explains their quite different behavior during our two encounters," Marcus nodded.

"And take a look at this." Lucas handed the paper back to Darien.

"Highly decorated police officer implicated in murder-case," Darien read the headline out.

"I guess that was the last we'll see of Plague," Marcus grinned.

"I would guess that this was the last we see of any of them," Darien added after reading the article and passing it on to Cedric. "They are all gone for a long time. Murder, accessory to murder, assault, grand theft and embezzlement. We won't see them around anymore during our lifetime."

"The only unfortunate thing is that they will have quite some time to hone their skills while they are in prison," Lucas said. "But I guess that's the problem of the guards now."

"Let's just hope they don't start a riot and break free," Marcus said.

"Maybe somebody should tell our government that this was all a hoax." Stephanie was holding the paper now.

"Why?" Darien asked.

"Look here." She showed him the article. "They are still blaming fossil fuels for the dead forest and are planning on investing vastly into research for alternative energy sources now."

"Yeah, and they are planning to tax the petrol and coal industry heavily to finance that," Darien added. "This will be bad for their stock prices."

"No matter if it was a hoax or not, it seems that something good came out of it after all," Lucas nodded. "And once again, it wouldn't have if we hadn't fumbled the first encounter with the thieves."

"What are you saying? That we should have let them continue?" Jasmin asked.

"All I am saying is that all of this is not so easy. They did do a lot of bad things, but it seems that some good also has come from that. The world is not black and white, not even when it comes to those guys," Lucas sighed.

"It is weird how we keep ending up with that conclusion time and again." Darien sighed too. "It is getting a little drab by now."

"Maybe just because we still have not gotten the message?" Jasmin laughed.

"I just hope that it stops at some point," Darien said.

"At least for this topic I am quite certain that it is over now." Lucas looked at them. "We can all be proud, we have finally done it."

"Let's just hope it stays quiet now," Stephanie said.

"Forget it, Airmid," Lucas laughed. "When you guys are around, it never is quiet."

"And none of us would have it any other way," Marcus replied.

Lucas smiled at him, happy to be there amongst his friends, and happy that this episode of his life was finally over.

Somewhere far away in a secret chamber, a man in gray robes was sitting behind a desk when a woman in green robes entered the room.

"Hello Lady Gaia. What can I do for you?" he asked her.

"I am sorry to disturb you, Lord Archangel," she replied with a little bow. "It is about Guardian and his group."

"What about them?" Archangel looked up at her.

"They have dealt a fatal blow to Cleric and his circle," she said.

"I know," was his short answer.

"How will this interfere with the greater plan? Will this not force the other side to move earlier than planned?"

"Might be."

"And how shall we deal with this, milord?" Gaia asked.

"Is there any indication that he is aware of our plan?"

"No. Not that I could tell at least." She shook her head.

"Then I see no reason to do anything."

"But Guardian will hardly be able to handle this on his own if it unfolds right now."

"I hope that at some point somebody explains to me why everyone keeps underestimating that kid so tremendously," Archangel laughed. "Relax, Gaia. He has dealt with everything so far. He will deal with this, too."

"So what shall I tell him about all this when he asks me?"

"The truth, Gaia, the truth. He is a Magus Major now; he has earned the right to be treated like one."

"As you wish." She bowed a little and left him alone.

Archangel sat there alone, looking at a picture of 16-year-old Lucas Trent, who had changed a great deal since his faith-twisting visit to Timestop bar less than two years ago.

www.ingramcontent.com/pod-product-compliance
Lightning Source LLC
Chambersburg PA
CBHW022005010726
47494CB00003B/896